## SIMON & SCHUSTER CHILDREN'S PUBLISHING
### ADVANCE REVIEWER COPY

TITLE: Other Side of the Tracks

AUTHOR: Charity Alyse

IMPRINT: Simon & Schuster Books for Young Readers

ON-SALE DATE: 11/22/22

ISBN: 978-1-5344-9771-9

FORMAT: hardcover

PRICE: $19.99/$23.99 CAN

AGES: 12 up

PAGES: 448

Please send a URL for any online coverage related to this book to:
childrenspublicity@simonandschuster.com.
Please send two copies of any review or mention of this book to:
Simon & Schuster Children's Publicity Department
1230 Avenue of the Americas, 4th Floor
New York, NY 10020
212/698-2808

Aladdin • Atheneum Books for Young Readers
Beach Lane Books • Beyond Words • Denene Millner Books
Libros para niños • Little Simon • Margaret K. McElderry Books
Paula Wiseman Books • Salaam Reads
Simon & Schuster Books for Young Readers
Simon Pulse • Simon Spotlight

# OTHER SIDE OF THE TRACKS

## CHARITY ALYSE

A Denene Millner Book

SIMON & SCHUSTER BFYR

NEW YORK LONDON TORONTO SYDNEY NEW DELHI

## SIMON & SCHUSTER BFYR

An imprint of Simon & Schuster Children's Publishing Division
1230 Avenue of the Americas, New York, New York 10020

Text © 2022 by Charity Herndon
Jacket illustration © 2022 by Alexis Franklin
Jacket design by Lizzy Bromley © 2022 by Simon & Schuster, Inc.

SIMON & SCHUSTER BOOKS FOR YOUNG READERS
and related marks are trademarks of Simon & Schuster, Inc.
For information about special discounts for bulk purchases, please contact Simon & Schuster
Special Sales at 1-866-506-1949 or business@simonandschuster.com.
The Simon & Schuster Speakers Bureau can bring authors to your live event.
For more information or to book an event, contact the Simon & Schuster Speakers Bureau at
1-866-248-3049 or visit our website at www.simonspeakers.com.
Interior design by Hilary Zarycky.
The text for this book was set in New Caledonia.
Manufactured in the United States of America
First Edition
2 4 6 8 10 9 7 5 3 1
Library of Congress Cataloging-in-Publication Data
Names: Alyse, Charity, author.
Title: Other side of the tracks / Charity Alyse.
Description: First edition. | New York : Simon & Schuster Books for Young Readers, 2022.
| "A Denene Millner Book." | Audience: Ages 12 and up. | Audience: Grades 7–9.
| Summary: When Zach, a white boy from Philly moves to a racially divided town, he
befriends Black siblings Capri and Justin, but when the police murder one of their friends,
the town erupts into an all-out war, with Capri, Justin, and Zach caught in the middle.
Identifiers: LCCN 2021050742 (print) | LCCN 2021050743 (ebook)
| ISBN 9781534497719 (hardcover) | ISBN 9781534497733 (ebook)
Subjects: CYAC: Race relations—Fiction. | Police brutality—Fiction. |
African Americans—Fiction. | LCGFT: Fiction.
Classification: LCC PZ7.1.A4926 Ot 2022 (print)
| LCC PZ7.1.A4926 (ebook) | DDC [Fic]—dc23
LC record available at https://lccn.loc.gov/2021050742
LC ebook record available at https://lccn.loc.gov/2021050743

*Dedication TK*

# OTHER SIDE
# OF
# THE TRACKS

# Preface

ONCE UPON A TIME, THOUGH NOT <u>TOO</u> LONG AGO, AFTER
the close of the Civil War, formerly enslaved African Americans
and their families left the hardships of the South behind to experience the liberty of the North. Some hightailed it to the city, others dreamed of settling for a simpler life. They wanted to keep
the positive aspects of nature that were found in the South. They
wanted to gaze upon the stars that reminded them how vast the
world was, when it felt as limited as the moldy cabins where they
once lived. They wanted to keep the rivers that serenaded them
after the drums of their forefathers were crushed. They wanted to
look upon nature's easel, painted with the wildflowers that grew
with no gardener. These people sought refuge in a town located on
the outskirts of New York City, called Bayside. But the pure white
descendants of Puritan people who built this town had an idea they
thought was better. They'd separate Bayside so the Blacks could
have their own place to live.

The land that was given to them sat across train tracks that led
to only two places: New York City and back to the South. See, to
Bayside, this town was still a generous gift and *some* gift it was. They
named it Hamilton, after a Black man named Micah Hamilton, who
left his comfortable abode in New York City to become the first
schoolteacher they would have—someone to teach them Chaucer,
Shelley, and Equiano. Bayside also provided Hamilton with lumber

and stone to build, schoolbooks with which to learn, and seeds to start growing their own food. In the beginning, Bayside wasn't off limits. Well, not entirely, as anyone Black could cross the tracks for supplies from a grocery shop or hardware store when it was needed. But once Hamilton could work as a town on its own, both it and Bayside grew further apart. The newly liberated enslaved were more than grateful and went right to work to make this land a place they could call their home.

But the sun didn't shine on Hamilton like it did Bayside. It was almost as if it avoided it completely, except for a few days in the summer when it felt generous enough to share its light. Gray clouds overshadowed it, threatening to rain and spit hail, but never did. The sky was not the only thing that remained dark in this town; all the people did too. No one who lived in Hamilton was white. The only white that ever speckled the town were the flakes of snow that got shoveled aside—just as the Blacks were when Bayside was split and the town was separated. On the other hand, the sun shone bright in Bayside each morning and the moon shone almost equally bright at night. There were hardly, if ever, any moments where Hamilton's dark clouds stretched across the tracks that separated it from Bayside.

Barely anyone dared to leave these towns that their ancestors built with their own hands. For those in Bayside, well, they experienced too much comfort in their little bubble to move. Those in Hamilton were afraid of moving away. The outside world was an unfamiliar place. Moving out of Hamilton would mean they'd have to build something else from the ground up.

Though it was now the twenty-first century, one could say that Bayside and Hamilton still stayed within the confines of a postbellum world. They had their separate law enforcement, schools, even community colleges. Older brother Bayside always kept a watch on its darker brother Hamilton, providing his schools with used schoolbooks, football uniforms, and, if needed, extra money. Presently in the town of Bayside only a few Blacks lived—those who were blessed enough with the money and patience to bear an old and quiet town separated by a gray river that led to New York City.

Even after the train tracks stopped being ridden upon and the station was nothing but an abandoned wooden square, Bayside never offered to join the two towns together. A resident could be born in these towns, attend school, get married, raise children, and die in their respective graveyards, separated from one another and the outside world. In fact, almost everyone did, and for a long time nothing changed.

Until . . .

# Capri

IT'S FUNNY HOW A PERSON CAN LIVE IN NEW YORK THEIR whole lives and never travel to the city. I've only been there once, when I was eight years old.

The night sky was painted with dark oil and hid the glittering stars I usually saw shining in Hamilton. My grandmother, who we called Ma, held my hand tight, and Justin, my older brother, held the other. Our mama, who we called by her first name, Essie, was making her way quickly ahead of us in her white peacoat with a matching fur band wrapped around her cropped hair. She seemed to dance with the crowds, weaving in and out of them expertly, with a careless smile, making sure not to shove nobody, gracefully leaping and spinning around each person she passed. She was like a young child, giggling and laughing the whole way to the theatre.

"Come on, *slowpokes*, this is the city. You have to *move*," she called to us over her shoulder. Ma, hushing her, mumbled things under her breath that I couldn't hear over the noise of the traffic, but even she was smirking the whole while. Essie was a real beauty.

Careless.

I wanted to be just like her.

Essie had Justin when she was fifteen and me, just one year later. We all lived with Ma in Hamilton at first, but after Essie started her acting career, she was almost never home. Now, Essie was bringing us into her adopted home. Broadway didn't smell like magic and new opportunities as Essie described; it was more like hot pretzels and perfume wrapped in a cloud of stale cigarette smoke. She said New York's streets was paved with gold that glimmered brighter than the stones on the yellow brick road. I only found graying sidewalks with blackened gum and a few people wrapped in old blankets.

But the lights—the lights she didn't get wrong. They did outshine the fireflies we caught behind Ma's house in the summertime. Each theatre was playing, as Essie said, a different world for us to peek into; worlds of sadness turned happy, stories of love, music, and dancing. Essie said it was like visiting a magical library that opened its books for us to travel through, and it was. Each book lined the streets, illuminated with bright lights. *Something Rotten!, The King and I, Hamilton, and Wicked!*

Some of the names from the shows wasn't familiar; others I'd already watched Essie act out for me in her bedroom, putting on different hats for the characters, singing their songs and proclaiming their lines like she was born into them. Even though I never been on the streets of Broadway before, I felt like I knew just as much about theatre as anyone else, including the old women I overheard talking about the different versions of Essie's show they'd seen when Ma, Justin, and me sat in the theatre. They said they couldn't wait to judge and see if it was better than the one in London that they'd saw that summer. That night, I didn't need to see no show in London to compare to Essie's.

I knew hers would be the greatest of all.

Essie told us we had great seats, but she didn't tell us how great they actually were. We didn't have nobody sitting in front of us but the orchestra. Ma even smiled when she saw the three reserved seats with our names written on them. It made me feel real important, like a star on television or something.

The conductor of the orchestra winked at me and told me my dress was the most beautiful thing he ever saw. I did feel beautiful in the bright blue dress Ma got from the charity store downtown. It was used, but Essie said used dresses wasn't ever really old. My dress was new because it was the first time *I* wore it. She said it was my turn to create an adventure in the dress—that new adventures for an old dress was like retellings of old stories to ears that never heard them.

When the curtain lifted and the lights dimmed, Essie ran across the stage in tears, and I wanted to run up on stage and hug her. Ma could tell I was agitated and assured me Essie was only doing her job to entertain. Still, I believed everything Essie was saying under them bright lights. I believed her when she cried after burying her lover in the play, when she danced across the stage with the chorus, when she fell in love again, and when she died in the end. I believed it all and stood with the audience when they clapped. I agreed when the old ladies said this was the best version of the show they'd seen, even though I didn't see no other one.

*My* Essie truly was a star.

Only three months later, when I found out Essie's heart stopped onstage, I assured Ma that she was probably just acting. When her open casket sat in front of me at the church on Sixth Street later that week, I told Essie it wasn't funny anymore. I told her she had to wake up now. Her skin was blotchy and the blush they put on her was too bright. She always told me the right shade of blush for her complexion was hard for people to find. That's why she always did her own makeup before her performances.

They forced her eyes shut; no one was able to see the light that flew from them when she acted, sang, danced, or told her stories. Her lips were glued shut, hiding the smile that kept my heart believing in miracles. Her hands that once brushed my hair were frozen and stiffly folded over her thin body. I couldn't look away.

"The show is over. Wake up," I whispered, nudging her rock-hard shoulder.

"She's dead," Justin said, standing next to me. He was staring at her too, frozen just like me. "She not coming back, Capri."

I looked around the church. It was small and cold. The sweater Ma made me wear was tight around my shoulders and didn't shield my arms from the goose bumps that ran up and down them in waves. The pale gray paint on the walls was peeling, and the Black Jesus on the stained-glass windows turned ashy with dust. It smelled like mold. Flower spreads were scattered around with condolence messages on them, and everyone was wearing black, even Essie. This wasn't the way her shows were. The theatre always had beautiful gold lights above. The seats were burgundy and comfortable, not hard like the brown pews we sat on. I looked again at Essie. How could someone who had so much life look so . . . imprisoned?

Ma didn't think it was a good idea for Justin and me to ever go back to the city. It was because Essie was everywhere. The pictures from the shows she was in still littered the walls of almost all the theatres. A theatre in New York City decided to keep a billboard of Essie plastered to their side wall, in her memory. I only saw it that one time we went. Essie rushed us to look at what they'd done for her. In the picture, she was wearing a white dress with a crown of many colors, her legs stretched into a split leap. She was smiling wide, soaring across the sky like a rainbow.

Essie lived her life the way she wanted and died doing what she loved.

I always vowed somewhere inside of me, to do the same.

# Justin (Present)

WHEN MAMA DIED, I DON'T THINK I GOT A CHANCE TO feel it. Not like Capri did. Her death came out of nowhere like those sticky things that used to cling to my socks after running in the grass all day as a kid. I had to pull them off my ankles before the blood spotted my white socks and the pain distracted me from getting up and running again.

I was eleven years old when her heart stopped. Her sudden absence was the sticky pain that pricked me around the ankles, almost knocking me off my balance for good.

At Mama's homegoing, our whole world laid before us, lifeless. I watched Capri stare at the knockoff corpse faking like my mama lying in that casket. She touched its cheeks, its hands, and even whispered for it to wake up.

If I ever fell and couldn't get up outside, Ma was always there running toward me with a warm rag, a bandage, and an embrace that let me know she'd take care of everything. She didn't do any of those things that day. Just stood behind us, wailing on Pa's shoulder. Went through dozens of tissue boxes, eyes fixed on my bootleg mama under the spotlight that they clipped to the casket. I watched people after service run up to Capri before they did me. Hug her tight, tell her she looked just like Mama. Watched them give her flowers to carry and lay on the casket. I watched them cover her wounds with little bandages, slowly, carefully, one at a time. Told me I had to take care of Capri. That I had to be a man now. Never say "no," and help Ma and Pa more since they were old. Even told me that God gave me the shoulders to carry it all, like I was some kid bodybuilder. What they didn't know is all the while, I was there, lying on the ground, covered in the prickly needles of a dead dad I was too young to remember and a mama whose face I'd have to fight to never forget, needing help with ripping the prickly stickiness off, before my world was covered in crimson. But no one was running toward me with a warm rag, bandage, or hug. I didn't even get a chance to cry about it.

Sometimes I wish I could hit the replay on that day. Tell the funeral director that they did so bad on Mama that she didn't even *look* like herself, instead of telling them she looked good when they asked me. What if I wouldn't have read that poem on the back of her obituary about God picking another flower for his garden, and instead cursed the heavens so loud into that microphone that the rafters on the old church shook and the ground underneath me quaked? Until it pulled the old church mothers out their assigned pews to drench me with anointing oil meant to drive anger out my being and back to the lake of fire it swam out of.

Maybe if I did, I wouldn't have spent my whole life trying to walk a tightrope threaded with all their expectations. Hands tied tight behind my back, eyes forward, ignoring the dragging of the chains they wrapped around my ankles while they was watching to see what I'd do. No one in Hamilton would've saw me as *the* Justin Collins either. The responsible orphan boy who stepped up when the last of his irresponsibly, flighty, dream-chasing parents died off.

So, on that tightrope I walk slowly, carefully. One foot in front of the other, willing myself to never slip and fall where they can see me.

*Right foot.*

Remember to never move on the whim of emotion but think logically, study hard, and never say no to picking up somebody's groceries even when I'm tired.

*Left foot.*

Paint that neighbor's fence, or tutor on a Friday night instead of hanging out with friends.

*Right foot.*

Wake up at five in the morning and run before walking Capri to school, so I can bring my A game as captain of Hamilton High's basketball team to the courts.

*Left foot.*

*"You're a great example, Justin!"*

*"Keep it up, Collins!"*

But when the curtain closes, and the lights dim, I can be like my flighty irresponsible parents. I can use those early-morning runs as a cover to get by myself and lie on the dirt beneath the trees that surround this town. I can scream so loud that even the cicadas and crickets have a hard time singing over me. I can scream until I remember that I can be angry. I can laugh until I remember that I can be happy. I can cry until I remember that weeping still exists in my soul. But when the curtains come back up, I take my place on that tightrope again.

I'd like to say that's why I like literature so much. Heck, if I wasn't so good at playing basketball, I'd probably be a writer. I mean, look, Langston Hughes didn't care about looking soft when he wrote his poems. He wrote how he felt and now we get to read it and somehow understand emotions we didn't even know we had. You know Jo from *Little Women* or Francie from *A Tree Grows in*

*Brooklyn?* They knew that they had to leave where they grew up to grow. It's the same with me and Hamilton. Don't get me wrong, I love it. It's where my roots are; my ancestors built this town from practically nothing. I'm proud of it. My friends, my family, my little sister, they're all here.

But I'm sure of one thing: this town's not *it* for me. Hamilton wasn't *it* for my parents. If I'm gonna die young, I'll be buried here, just like them. But if I'm gonna live, I won't be.

So, I always tell myself, *I'll be golden boy Justin for another year, 'cause as soon as I get that scholarship, when I get out, I'll be whoever I want.*

# Capri (Present)

MY BUTT FELT NUMB. TINGLES SCURRIED ALL THROUGH my feet and up my legs. The pews never got softer. Gosh, they could have at least invested in cushions. The second Thursday of every February was Hamilton's annual Black History Revival Service and like every year it lasted four hours too long. Luckily when the musty smell began to rise from the dampened underarms of church mothers and deacons who shouted and danced up and down the aisles while the musicians got it in, it was my secret sign that things were about to end. Everybody had their workout and couldn't ignore the knocking of their stomachs to go home and eat, they said "amen" and "go on" less and less, which let our Reverend know when to stop preaching. The organist played "The Blood of Jesus" while they passed around the gold offering plates filled to the brim with communion cups. I watched John Watson in front of me grab two and stuff one in his pocket.

This boy always said he believed that over time the grape juice fermented and swore it got him drunk when he swallowed some of his stash after church. His ma, Sister Wynona, would kill him if she found out what he was doing. About everyone in Hamilton went to church or considered themselves *some* type of religious, but Sister Wynona even believed nail polish was the devil and bought her own stash of white gloves to church. She'd sit by the door passing them out to the "heathen" girls whose nails were, as she said, "dipped in Lust's spit."

Reverend Sails directed communion in his thundering voice behind the altar. "And He said drink, for this is the blood, the blood which was shed for you."

In unison, the congregation dipped their heads back and took down the shots of sour grape juice. My jaw tingled at its bitter taste. I stuck my tongue to the roof of my mouth to clean off the stale bread. Maybe they gave us the old grape juice cups and waited for the bread to get hard so we would actually feel like we was drinking Jesus' two-thousand-year-old blood and eating his torn-up body.

"Now, church," Reverend drawled on, flashing a faux, pearl-white smile, "we'll have a selection from my daughter, Rosamae Anne."

Rose stood up from her seat in the front row and walked up the two steps to where the mic sat. She removed it from the stand and bought it to her glossed lips.

*"Are you washed in the blood?*

*In the soul-cleansing blood of the Lamb?"*

Her voice and the organ seemed to dance together. It was always my favorite part of any service and made the long hours worth while, hearing Rose sing. Her voice was soft sounding but contained a strength unlike any I heard. She carried it almost effortlessly through valley and mountain notes, through riffs and rolls, and I was happy to take that journey with her. I clapped loudest when she finished.

I didn't believe my older brother Justin when he came home one night after school and told me he asked Rose out and she'd said yes. Rose wasn't just beautiful on the outside with her caramel skin and bone-straight licorice hair, but on the inside as well. She was the senior class president at Hamilton High and taught this class every Friday at the church that she named "Find Your Voice." It was a class where she gave free singing lessons to whoever was interested. It was honestly a privilege to have someone like her so close to us. I told Justin all the time he better not mess that up.

"Great job, Rose," I complimented after church when I caught up with her. She smiled, like she always did when someone complimented her voice, little dimples serving up the perfect accent to the amber blush powdered on her cheeks.

"Thanks, Capri. Are you coming by for dinner tonight?"

I shook my head.

"Nah, Ma would go off if me and Justin both missed dinner. She already had a fit when Justin missed on Sunday night." When I said this, she looked confused. One of her thin-but-well-sculpted eyebrows rose and the other stayed leveled.

"I thought Justin was eating dinner with y'all after church Sunday. That's what he told me. He said this week he'd be eating with y'all too."

I blinked.

"Right, that's what I meant to say, he *was* with us last week, I . . ."

She lifted her white glove–covered hand. "Didn't anyone tell you it's bad to lie in church? I'll be seeing you, Capri." Before I could say another word, she rambled away, on the prowl for Justin.

Oops.

While I watched Rose walk away, a large woman in an all-white suit dress took her place in front of me. It was Sister Geraldine Billings, the gossip of the church. She always waddled her big self down the aisles and positioned herself by large groups so she could ear-hustle talk about someone's family issue, pregnant daughter, rebellious son, or new car they couldn't afford to keep. Everyone knew whatever Sister Billings heard would be reported on the phone that night, like she was a newsboy on the street. But still we all kept her around—for her cooking.

Sister Billings could cook the mess out of anything, better than anyone on those cooking shows Essie always watched. I remember Essie sitting by the couch with a pencil in her hand, copying the TV cooks' instructions. Her duck would always come out overly seared and she'd always use carrots instead of celery because she didn't like eating green things, unless it was gelatin. But Sister Billings, she could burn.

Sister Billings smiled through that large gap of hers. "Will you tell your grandmother to call me, please? She's had my casserole dish for the past three weeks now and I need it back. Sis Sands wants me to make her my famous sweet potato casserole for the Black History celebration dinner." She folded her hands over her bulging chest. I couldn't help but feel sorry for the buttons she tried closing; they looked like they was gonna burst and pop an eye out. That's probably why her husband was half blind.

"I'm sure Ma will get it to you soon. She's been busy," I half lied. I really needed to work on this lying-in-church thing. I silently asked for forgiveness. Again.

Truth was, Ma hated Sister Billings ever since she spread a rumor about her being pregnant so she could go to prom with Vandor Hutchins, this guy apparently *evvveryone* went crazy over when they was teenagers. When Sister Billings randomly gave Ma a dish of her famous vegetarian lasagna not too long ago, Ma said Sister Billings was probably trying to poison her. She threw it away immediately, and made my grandpa take out the trash.

Sister Billings lowered her gaze and leaned real close. Her breath smelled like a mix of butterscotch candy and stale communion juice.

"Busy doing what? I saw her walking real quick downtown yesterday. Looked like she was in a hurry, wouldn't even stop to say hello to me. I waved and everything. I bet it's because its nearing that time of year . . . you know the month of February was when your mother died."

"I know," I responded quickly. "I actually have to go. I'll tell Ma you asked about her."

"But Capri—"

"Bye, Sister Billings." Before she could say another word, I pushed through the crowd and out the peeling green door in the back on the church.

Revival nights and Sunday afternoons were the only days I had the Sunlight all to myself. My friend Easy closed down the Sunlight Record Shop and Café on those days because he believed everybody in Hamilton should be at revival and no one should work on Sundays, 'cause of God's law and all. He gave me the key though—knew I'd want to sneak in and get some dancing in. He was about the only person in town that knew I still did it. Well, him, Justin, and my best friend, Perry.

Dancing is like breathing; it's something I have to do to survive. I love how it feels when my feet lift from the ground, like they're dancing on the orchestra's chords. How my hips move with the sound of the drum, and my body floats on the air when the song reaches its climax. Dancing peels the sticky emotions that cling to my heart and my soul and brings 'em out real slow. It sticks them to some wall far away, I'm sure—far enough away that if someone tried to clean it up and bring it back to me, they wouldn't be able to.

I grew up always watching Essie cut it up onstage at the theatre in Hamilton before it was turned into the Sunlight Record Store and Café. She'd push me in the white stroller with the blue lace that she got from Ty's Thrift downtown and would park me in front of the stage. They let her have the theatre to herself after closing for some extra practice time and I'd watch her perfect her routines. Essie was a star to everyone in Hamilton. They gave her so much support; anything she needed to shine, as long as she followed the rules by *staying* Hamilton's star only. But that never worked with my Essie. Pretty soon, she became the whole world's star too. They couldn't keep a lid on her. Someone would always spot Essie sneaking her way over to New York City for auditions and, the next day, coming back here to perform. Truth is, not everyone was happy with her leaving so much, but the people on the outside couldn't get enough of her.

At her homegoing, Reverend Sails said she turned the nativity story they held every year at the church into a ballet, directed and choreographed by herself. Justin played baby Jesus and I wasn't born yet. Ma has the tape and I watch it every Christmas Eve. Essie played the Virgin Mary, gracefully dancing across the little stage in the theatre for three hundred people, like she did on Broadway. She made me want to leap like she did, and spin, and stretch my arms above me as if my fingertips were grazing the stars. Now Essie's just a forgotten memory buried deep inside a grave next to my daddy's, behind the church whose walls were the last to hear anyone say her name. No one speaks about her anymore, unless it's used as one of the countless examples of why it's dangerous to leave Hamilton because everyone who does either dies or *almost* dies. They tell us that everything we need is here and that if we abandon this place, we abandon our history, only to rot away into nothingness. That this town and all who built it would fade away. But that's the thing. I don't believe our ancestors built this place with the intention for us to stay forever or wrap the shackles that fell from their bodies back around our ankles. They came here fearless of the unknown. With their dreams leading the way, they embraced the future they couldn't even see yet and made a new place their own. Why couldn't we do the same? Why was anyone else who ever dared to leave treated like they never mattered if they didn't solely exist under Hamilton's gray skies? My Essie's memory is still honored and respected on the outside. A few years after Essie passed, a famous award show even called, saying they were presenting a memorial to Essie. They told me they hired a body double to perform one of her famous jazz routines and everything. I passed the phone to Ma, making sure to keep it on speaker so I could hear all of what was being said, clapping and spinning around as Ma listened to the person talk. They asked Ma if we could come and accept the award, maybe say a few words about my Essie. Ma hung up on them before they could even finish saying that they'd fly us out for free and get us a place to stay for the night. She told me if I picked up the phone again, it would be my behind. The ringing that carried on the next few days felt like I was ignoring my own mama, back from the dead, calling out for me to remember her.

I don't remember much more about her than the little things, like how her favorite band was Ambient Light. She'd always play their records, even though they were available as CDs. She liked the light crackle she'd hear when the record spun on the player, and lead singer Granite Michael's voice rang out. Her favorite band became my own after she passed on. Listening to Ambient Light made me feel as if she were still here, singing along. To this day, in the Sunlight, that's the only music I'll dance to.

I remember Essie putting one of her crimson-colored skirts on me, and pulling it above my chest, like one of those strapless dresses. My little legs stretched out from the bottom and she smiled her huge grin, the one that could light the night.

*"Mm-mm sweet pea, you have the legs of a dancer."*

It made me believe that having dancer's legs was something I couldn't control. It was something I was born with, and that meant it was something I was meant to do. For my sixth birthday, Essie enrolled me in Pepper's Dancing Studio across from the grocery store. She signed me up for jazz, tap, and ballet. I needed the ballet part for the basics; it's always good to be trained classically, she said. Tap was for my rhythm, but jazz is my favorite.

Jazz can be improv; it affords me a chance to dance how I feel. I can stretch my joints to the music without anybody telling me I'm off the beat or my timing is bad. It's not rehearsed, the instruments tell their own story, and they don't care what nobody thinks about them. At my first recital, Essie gave me this bright pink dress to dance in. We all had costumes but somehow Essie talked my instructor into letting me wear the dress she bought for me. The song was short, but I'll never forget that performance. I felt so free, so beautiful. So much like Essie.

After she died, Ma took me out of dancing. She said "it wasn't good for nobody because dancing made people think they could survive off of they looks and body, not off they brains and book knowledge," the latter of which she insisted was more important. She said people like Essie lived in their dreams and plucked reality from their lives, then died because of them. She couldn't stand watching me follow in Essie's footsteps, especially since I was good at it.

It's funny, sometimes I watch Ma pull out a magazine with

Essie on the front and just stare with this proud smile on her face, but whenever I bring her up, she chides Essie. Saying dancing made Essie lose her mind, made her think she was a child, being carefree and leaving us six months at a time to tour. Said the longest Essie was with Justin and me was a year and a half after we were born. The rest of the time she spent in New York or some other place, except for monthly visits here and there. That's why I called Essie by her first name and Ma, Ma. She seemed to be more of a mother than Essie, but I'm not mad about that. Essie wasn't really a mother; in my mind she was a shooting star. Constantly moving, here one weekend, gone for months; meeting new people, seeing new places outside of Hamilton. It was a blessing to get a glimpse of her shining. I know Ma would be disappointed if I chose Essie's direction over the one she planned for me, especially after all she's done for me and Justin, with raising us and all. Ma wants me to graduate from Hamilton Community College as a nurse, and work at the clinic she's been a secretary at since before Essie was born. Maybe I won't dance professionally and will go to school to be a nurse like she wants. But Ma won't make my "feet stop tapping and my fingers stop snapping," as Essie would say.

You see, being alone in the Sunlight, standing under the single spotlight onstage surrounded by all the records that lined the walls and aisles—my only audience being pictures of those who *attained* their dreams—helped me feel something I couldn't feel being holed up in Hamilton all the time. Freedom. I let out a breath and closed my eyes, my hands stretched out above my head toward the stars, and let Granite's low, slick voice take me away.

# Justin

*I TUNED THE GUYS AROUND ME OUT AND TUCKED MYSELF* into Francie's world. Tried seeing it the way she saw it; innocent, like every day was one big adventure. This week's read was *A Tree Grows in Brooklyn*. Francie was pulling me into childhood through her prose. When I turned the pages of that book, I was running beside her. Learning from her. Not the least bit worried about the weights that tacked themselves to my life. I found myself taken by her gospel, baptized with faith that every corner of the world could be explored.

I read a lot of books like this lately because I believed that these classics contained a key. A key that would open some ancient door where a wise old man rocking in a creaky chair would invite me in, sit me at his feet, and tell me exactly what I need to do. Like these books would solve all my problems and give me the escape I needed. Set me free from all the thoughts swimming around my mind, drowning every other thing under its current.

*"So when you messin' wit me, you messin' wit my crew. That's not somethin' you be wantin' to do, Foo! Cuz, I'll mess wit ya girl and kiss ya mama too."* Jay spun on his heels and made a motion like he'd dropped the imaginary mic he was pretending to hold in his hand. The guys around him stopped making the beats they invented with their basketballs and knees and clapped and whoo'd like the freestyle he came up with was the best rhyme since J. Cole or something.

"Imma go down in rap history, y'all wait. As soon as I drop this single I'm working on, imma send it to one of those big producers in the city. They gonna go nuts over my rhymes. I told you I don't play." Jay, who was standing on the sidelines of the courts, surrounded by his worshippers, started doing this dance to celebrate what he thought was something special, but it came out looking like he was having some sort of standing seizure.

Laughter crept up on me, but I snorted to keep it down from my spot on the bleachers. Our team had been at it since school got out, even though we were supposed to be at church with the rest of the town for revival service. Told our families we had to practice in order to keep our winning streak going. The only thing up there with church in Hamilton is sports, so they let it slide. What we said was half true. Ever since word hit that college scouts were coming to our games, we worked to get the attention of the white guys with the clipboards and golden tickets. "Snow Fairies" we called them because they granted the wish almost everyone had, the option to go to college and get the heck out of Hamilton. Some people just wanted to brag that they got recruited; they knew they wouldn't follow through on the offer once the reality of leaving this place hit.

When a "Snow Fairy" from my dream university, Village U, contacted Coach Hill about a highlight video he saw of me, I knew everything my mama Essie said about dreams was true. If you believed in them long enough, you'd see them sparkle right before your eyes. All you had to do was reach out and grab them. The Snow Fairy told coach that if I kept up my game, grades, and behavior, I would be looking at a full ride offer come senior year. Room and board, classes, meals, books—all free. He sent a bunch of stuff in the mail too, pamphlets for the college and a gold and purple flag that I kept hidden in my desk drawer at home.

Coach warned me not to put all my stock in no verbal offer, not until I got a Letter of Intent, something solid from Village that I could sign to secure my spot on the team and the scholarship. He told me to look into the other colleges that contacted him about me, to keep my options open while I waited. But I didn't pay them no mind. None of their campuses were as beautiful as Village's. I didn't see their colors when I closed my eyes. Couldn't picture myself running up and down their courts, sporting their uniforms, no matter how hard I tried. Plus, none of them offered me a full ride. There was no way Ma was gonna help me with that part if it didn't go her way. All the money my mama left to Capri and me had one condition: It would only be released to us after we graduated college. It was like she was forcing us to get out of Hamilton, not that Ma noticed. She had the perfect plan for us: graduate from Hamilton community or not at all.

That's why I couldn't let Coach Hill discourage the offer from Village, even if it was only verbal. I could already see myself sitting at a fold-out table, wearing Village U swag, signing on that dotted line with Ma, Pa, and Capri standing beside me while the cameras flashed. I could see all the articles on the high school recruiting websites titled "Hamilton High basketball star Justin Collins, signs with D1 school, Village U, his first and only choice." I could hear Ma finally accepting the fact that I was leaving, letting go of her fears of what might happen if I did and blessing me. I could already feel her tight hug, smell her perfume, hear her whisper that she'd see me soon for Christmas break. I wouldn't have to whisper behind her back about my excitement with Pa and a couple of others around town anymore. I wouldn't have to tiptoe around how I felt. I could be loud about it.

Nothing worth having ever comes easy, that's what my mama used to say. The day after senior year started, the Snow Fairy contacted Coach Hill with some news. The verbal offer still stood, but there was only one spot left on their roster. The choice was between me and some other guy. He wanted to know more about the both of us to help them decide who was the right fit. Not just when it came to our game, but our personalities too. He sent a questionnaire in the mail last week that's due the end of this month, asking about accomplishments, awards, and future dreams. If it was just a few months ago, I would have been able to answer those in no time. The approaching deadline for what I always dreamt of loomed over my head like an apparition haunting me—buzzing from my email inbox at least once a day, reminding me that time was running out.

I always planned to submit for early decision to Village U. Planned to be the first application in their mailbox. Planned to be the first senior in my class accepted to a college outside of Hamilton. Planned to cash in on that golden one-way ticket out of here, if I got it. Had it all laid out for a while now. After going pro, I'd take the money I made from playing ball and use it for a good cause. In science class a few years ago, we watched this documentary on the Ebola virus. Nobody was paying no attention; they were just texting each other and scrolling through social media, but I couldn't take my eyes off the screen. Made a promise to myself that day that when I became a famous ballplayer, I'd donate all my money to help find cures for the diseases that plagued my brothers and sisters from another country. Now it seemed like that orange African sun melted away in the horizon, replacing itself with the crappy streetlight that buzzed and clicked on and off every few seconds on King Ave.

"Yo, you tryna be like them white hippies with the long beards or somethin' now? Why you wanna know how to grow trees in Brooklyn?" I looked up from the pages of *A Tree Grows in Brooklyn*. Jay's big head blocked the sun and cast a shadow over its worn pages.

Jason "Jay" Crenshaw thought he was the greatest guy to ever walk on the earth since Jesus Christ—like he was some sort of gold-skinned Greek god and everyone else was his lower and less-than subjects. "High and Mighty Crenshaw," as I liked to call him, stood at six foot six and 240 pounds. He played on the basketball team, but the only reason why he *really* made it was because of his size. Truth was, he sucked at ball. I mean, this dude couldn't get one into the net if someone placed his black behind right at the rim.

He was on this *becoming a famous rapper* thing since eighth grade when he spent the summer in New York with his dad's side of the family. He went to his first rap concert and the neon lights and booties mixed with all that weed smoke must have gotten to his neurons because, since then, he had the idea that he was gonna be some huge rap artist. Problem was, none of his rhymes made any sense and he only ever rapped a line or two before busting out in some dance from the nineties mixed with something from today. Imma be straightforward when I say this: I'm not a fan of Jay. He's gotten on my last nerve since we met back in elementary school. I looked back down at the pages of my book, trying my best to ignore him.

Before I knew it, his meaty hand scooped up my book. He turned it around in his palms, studying it, and then scratched the side of his massive bald head. I stood up and reached for the book, but Jay, taller and faster, threw my hand back.

"It's not no book about teaching people to plant no trees." I reached for it again, but Jay, again too fast, backed up.

"Then what's it about, Justin? Is it one of those books like what my mama be reading? About those strong cowboys and the chicks that need taming?" He used my book to smack his butt a bunch of times and in a high voice said, "*Ooh, daddy, I've been a bad girl.*"

I crossed my arms over my chest. "Jay, give me my book back. Now."

He stopped being obnoxious long enough to stare at me, as if I were some sort of science experiment. I stared back into his coal-colored eyes. If he wouldn't let up, I wouldn't either.

Finally he threw the book at my feet.

"I don't understand you," Jay said. "Why you on the court anyway? The past few weeks you just been sitting around reading them dumb behind books. You don't even play ball."

I leaned down to pick up my book and dusted it off. "I could say the same thing about you." I smirked when the guys started to *whoo*. Jay shook his head and smiled, even though he found my joke anything less than funny.

"Yo, I'm telling you, man, one of these days imma punch you dead in your face and you ain't gonna be cracking no jokes then."

"I'll let you clock me when you get a shot," I replied.

Jay rolled his eyes and gave his high-pitched siren squeal of a sarcastic laugh, the one he always did when someone busted on his playing skills.

"Oh, when I make a basket? But I already did, my friend. Ask Capri. I was scoring. All. Night. Long."

My heart rate sped and I stepped up, my worn sneakers only inches from his.

"Aight, now you're taking it too far, man. That's my little sister."

We formed a battle line, a little space that Jay closed with one step. He was only inches from my face. The cold February air made the breath coming out his nose visible. I was more than ready. If Crenshaw threw a punch, I wasn't gonna back down. Anyone from as far as a mile away could feel the heat coming from our heads, signaling we were ready to settle something deeper than a joke gone too far.

"Justin! Justin!" A shrill voice echoed through the worn court.

And that's when I saw her.

She ran across the field toward us, arm lifted above her head waving to get my attention. The setting sun cast its golden shadow over her honey-colored skin and reflected off the silver charm bracelet that I got her for her birthday last year. She wore a blush-colored sundress with a white sweater to shield her soft skin from the chilly winter air. My lips twisted into a grin. I couldn't stop myself from smiling whenever I saw Rose close up or from a distance. This girl had my heart, my soul; every little atom that shaped me was wrapped around her finger and I melted at the sight of her. But the closer she got, the more I saw the expression on her face was anything but welcoming.

My smile vanished as soon as it reached its peak.

"You in trouble," I heard Jay sing from beside me.

I rolled my eyes. "Mind yo business, Crenshaw. This got nothing to do with you."

"It might when you need a witness for your murder." He smirked and took some steps back. "Come on, y'all, let's leave Justy to his demise." With that he walked away, his posse at his heels.

"Hey, babe," I greeted. I tried to keep the even tone I practiced whenever I needed to dilute a situation, like keeping my head on my shoulders whenever I brought Ma's dry cleaning late, causing her to miss early-morning communion.

*Okay, Justin. Good. Just keep it even.*

"You lied to me, Justin." She crossed her arms over her chest. I stuffed my hands in the pockets of my letterman jacket, which covered the tank I wore to shield me from the blistering cold. I never felt it when I played ball. To be honest, I usually threw my jacket to the side after the first five minutes of playing, but suddenly, standing in front of my girl, it was beyond frigid.

"You keep putting off dinner," she said.

"I know but . . ."

"We have to tell them sometime." She lowered her hands and gestured to her stomach. I bit the corner of my lip, my heart beginning to race.

"I know, Rosey, it's just—"

Before I could finish my sentence, she cupped my cheek with her soft palms, her eyes misting over with tears. I looked closely at her, the little nose that sat above her lips, the way her eyes sat spaced far from one another, one slightly greener than the other, one almost brown. Her face glowed with this unexplainable innocence. She didn't look a day over sixteen. It amazed me how something was even floating around inside of her petite frame. Amazed me even more how she carried this assurance, this sincerity that somehow everything would be all right just like the characters in the classics I read. I wished I could believe like she did.

"Justin, I love you," she whispered. "I know you're scared and honestly, I am too. I'm so scared and I still don't know what to do, but we decided one thing together and that's that we're not throwin' it away. We can't keep it a secret from our families for long. I'm going to start showing soon."

I could still remember the night Rose told me she was pregnant. It amazed me how just four months ago could feel like an eternity. My mind drifted back to that day. . . .

The smell of fried chicken filled my nostrils. I made my way from the wooden desk, blanketed in college applications, and straight into the tiny kitchen of the only home I ever knew. This house, just like the rest of the town, was built by freed enslaved African Americans after the end of the Civil War. Not much had been done to it since then, other than the roof being replaced and obviously the piping, but the basic structure stayed the same.

Almost every house in Hamilton is shaped like a little rectangle; each with three rooms, two baths, and a basement. Small but comfortable. Never been in a house bigger than this one, but I didn't mind it. I liked how close it made everybody have to be; wasn't no space. There was barely a place to escape to for solitude like those rooms white kids on television ran to when their parents pissed them off. Can't stay pissed for long with someone in these houses. You gonna bump into them in the hallway or while brushing your teeth, which always forced us to talk things out. The small space also helped me find the food Ma hid quicker. Only so many places somebody could hide a pan of Ma's golden-brown fried chicken. So, like tradition, I closed my eyes and let my feet do the finding.

I could lead someone anyplace in that house with my eyes closed; even to the hiding spot, right in the cabinet where Ma kept the cereal. I moved the boxes of Corn Flakes and Fruit Circles aside and reached for the pan of chicken, when something hard swatted my back.

"Boy, how many times I gotta tell you to wait till dinner?" Ma was holding one of my little sister Capri's old white heels that she used to wear to church when she was a kid.

"Did you just hit me with a shoe?" I asked her, my mouth ajar, voice rising to a soprano at the surprise. She nodded proudly.

"Yes, I did. Your triflin' tail always tryna get a piece of meat before you supposed to. What the Lord say? Better to wait than to be quick to do. You always quick to do." She moved me out the way with a push of her wide hips and shut the cabinet. "Betta be happy I ain't hit you with nothing harder than this shoe. First thing I could find lying around," she mumbled. "Ain't you supposed to be applying for those schools? Last day you got before school starts again."

I couldn't help but laugh once Ma started talking, because it was almost impossible for her to stop.

"I *was* studying but then I smelled that fried chicken," I replied. "You been hiding it in the same spot since I was a kid. I used to use that chair right there to reach it." I gestured to the old metal folding chair leaning on the fridge next to the broom and dustpan. "You gotta think of better hiding spots, Ma. It seems like you *want* me to find where you hiding that good food of yours. Best cooking in Hamilton, I tell you. You need one of those shows on the cooking channel you always watching." I lifted my arms animatedly above my head and stretched them over Ma, imaginary words, golden and shining filling the ceiling above them. *"Ma's Fried Good Time.* That's what you should call it. I want all the proceeds when you get that show, since it *was* my idea."

She shook her head like she was mad but couldn't stop her lips from falling into a smirk. "Boy, you tryna flatter me into giving you some food early but that ain't gonna happen. You know what? Since you in here, you can help me peel those sweet potatoes in that pot."

"*Aw, Ma!*" I whined.

"Don't 'Aw, Ma' me. You talkin' about cooking, you can get some done. Don't be asking me for no sweet potato pie unless you help. I ain't that little hen doing all the cooking without anybody's help." She walked a few paces over to the stove and lifted the large pot that sat next to the sink. "Now the water's dumped out, but the potatoes is still hot, so make sure you rinse them before you start peeling."

I wanted to deny her request again, but I knew nobody could win a fight against Ma. It was like believing a roach could win a fight against an exterminator. Useless. Plus, I really wanted some of that pie. Ma made the best sweet potato pie.

Even though she was in her mid-sixties, she didn't look a day over forty. She ain't like when people tell her that though. Always says she don't look a day over twenty-five. Ma always kept herself up; her thick black hair in big curls, always wearing that red lipstick and a dress even when she wasn't going nowhere. Always telling Capri that a woman shouldn't go out the house without a dress on. Capri wasn't the type of girl to wear a dress. The last time she wore one was at Mama's funeral.

I burned myself a few times peeling the potatoes and every time I sucked in a breath and winced, Ma would say she told me so. Finally I tried to stop being tough and ran the potatoes under cold water. Midway through peeling, my phone vibrated in my pocket and a rap song rang out. I ignored it the first two times, but it persisted.

"Boy, if you don't answer that phone. I can't take hearing that noise y'all call music. Whatever happened to the normal ring instead of those songs?" Ma crushed some sweet potatoes in a bowl with a big black spoon. "If it's your sister tell her to bring home some heavy cream. Your grandfather always forgettin' stuff at the store. He should just pay attention to the list instead of staring at those little girls that work the front counter. I'd be surprised if they didn't work the *streets,* too, the way they be flouncing around that grocery market. . . ."

While Ma continued on, I pulled my ringing phone from my jean pocket. Rose's name flashed across the screen. Before I could answer, the voicemail picked it up, and almost immediately, four missed calls showed—all from Rose—and a text message.

**Meet me at Hamilton Park near the courts asap. It's important.**

"Be back before six and bring home some heavy cream!" Ma yelled after me as I rushed to my 1997 Lexus SC. The only thing I had left from my dad. It was his car at my age and every time I drove in it, I felt connected to him. His dog tag dangled on the rearview mirror. I adjusted it, beeped twice to warn the kids playing baseball in the street to move out the way, and backed out the driveway. The park was only a five-minute walk, but I didn't want to waste no time. Rose never called so many times in a row.

I could see her sitting on the bleachers at the courts, the sunset shining against the silver metal. I could still remember exactly what she was wearing, white sweatpants and one of the hoodies I got from one of the colleges I toured earlier that summer. My heart raced in my chest. I hoped to God she wasn't breaking up with me, especially after what happened between us.

"I walked here. My dad offered to take me, but I walked," she said to me when I jogged up to her. "I couldn't let him see this," she whispered. Her face looked tired, her eyes bloodshot. I could tell she'd been crying.

"See what? Rosey, what's wrong?" I demanded. That's when she reached in the front pocket of the sweatshirt and pulled out this white slender thing that looked like a thermometer. I slowly grabbed it from her shaking hand.

"What's this?" I asked clueless, then I realized. A single black plus sat on the small screen on the white stick. I looked back up at Rose, who burst into tears before saying, "Justin, I'm pregnant."

# Zach

"*THIS IS IT, SON! THIRTEEN THIRTY-TWO HILLSIDE* Lane. Isn't she somehow rustic, beautiful, and Victorian all at once? Just like I remember her!" Dad clapped his hands together like a little girl in Disney World and ran up the stairs of our new home. Our new home in this forgotten town of Bayside. Have you ever watched one of those old Western movies where the sheriff goes to one of those freshly abandoned towns and the tumbleweed rolls on by? Everything is outdated in those towns. That's exactly how it is here in Bayside. Outdated. Except I'm not talking about in a Western type of way. It's so much worse. I'm talking about one of those eighteenth-century British flicks where the chicks fall in love with the lord of some hard-to-pronounce kingdom and they laugh at jokes about buttered toast and croquet.

I dropped my suitcase on the ground and stared at the sight before my eyes. Reflecting itself proudly back at me was a three-story Victorian-style mansion, accented with one hundred black shuttered windows stretching all over the house, six bedrooms and baths, a freshly installed elevator, indoor swimming pool, tearoom, balcony, and a bright green lawn, manicured every Thursday by the local gardener. Exactly as described in the brochure Dad read to me a billion times this summer, and another million on the way here. The same overly detailed brochure included in my great-grandmother's will. The great-grandmother I haven't seen since I visited here one summer at six. The old fart died and left Dad, her favorite and only grandchild, her house. The lawyer read her will out loud to Dad and me, the last of the Whitmans, after her funeral. She wanted to leave the Whitmans' "great and historical" abode to us. Apparently, everyone in my family, generation after generation, lived here since like the eighteen hundreds.

The only other people that attended the funeral were a few of Dad's coworkers and some of my great-grandmother's old fart friends from Bayside. They all smelled like the overly priced perfume department in the store where I *used* to work. All before Dad decided to move from North Philly to Bayside. What was he thinking, you ask? Why, I often ask the same thing. Why would he pack up and move from the city where he worked as a lawyer, with paid vacations and business trips everywhere, to come to Bayside and work at a tiny local firm as the only lawyer in town? I'll tell you: because he didn't want to "break family tradition," apparently, plus he's been dreaming of living here since he was a kid.

Dad peeped his shiny head from behind the bright red door and cupped his hands over his mouth. "Come on, Zach! I want to show you where I used to read!"

I rolled my eyes, grabbed my suitcase, and walked inside.

A large chandelier dangled in the foyer, lit by lights shaped like candles. The floors were marble and expensive vases and lamps sat on small rugs that were embroidered with designs of a young woman doing various things like knitting, playing with kittens, and hugging weird old men.

"That's your great-grandmother," Dad whispered. "She was beautiful, huh?" The woman on the rugs had long blond hair and wore huge dresses. Just like the old chicks from those British movies.

"She was weird. Who knits themselves on carpet instead of taking a picture like a normal person would do? And with kittens? Really, Dad?"

"She sure did love all seven of those cats." Dad looked in the distance and shook his head, giving a moment of silence to his dead grandmother and her pets. Finally he looked back at me with a grin. "She wasn't a fan of taking pictures, but she did get oil-painted portraits of herself. She said they were much better than taking photos because you could become a true *masterpiece*." He said "masterpiece" as if my great-grandmother was the model of the *Mona Lisa* or a Picasso original. "That one was painted by the great Picasso." He pointed to a large painting on the wall of Great-Grandma rolling down a grassy hill with some kittens.

*And I stand corrected.*

"She loved your Great-Grandpa, too," Dad continued. "Too bad he died before you were born. He was a lot like you, Zachy, all filled with angst and stuff." Dad stuck his hand on my head, patting my scalp, looking at me as if I were the crazy one on the rug. "I still can't believe you shaved that beautiful hair of yours. That nice *blond* Whitman mane." I looked at Dad's thinning hair, still blond, but situated around a huge bald spot that sat in the middle of his shiny, pale head.

"I still can't believe you lost yours," I mumbled.

He talked so much about that Whitman *mane* like it was the thing that gave him life. Growing up, he never let me cut my hair other than a little trim here or there. I looked stupid like Dad did the whole time I was in elementary school, with long hair down past my elbows. When I got in middle school, I let this girl I went to school with cornrow it. Dad freaked out when I got home, but that's how I wore it until high school, mainly because it bothered him, to be honest. After that, the Whitman mane stayed tucked in a ponytail under a beanie until I turned seventeen. About three weeks ago, I went to this barber over in North Philly and told him to cut it. He asked if he could sell it to one of those beauty supply stores owned by Koreans that made wigs. He said it was the best hair he'd cut. I told him whatever, though it was creepy when I watched him stuffing it away in some black plastic bag.

Dad still thinks I'll grow it back out, after I grow out of this "teen angst" stage he swears I'm in, but I actually like the way my hair looks. My barber hooked me up with a fade and added a part on the right side of my head and to me, it looks pretty dope.

"Once you're out of that stage, you'll take those ridiculous earrings out too." He used a finger to flick one of my earlobes where a small diamond stud was. "Soon as you meet new friends in Bayside, you'll stop trying to be someone else."

Heat rose inside of me. "And who's that, Dad? Who am I *supposed* to be?"

Dad rolled his eyes, as he'd always done after insulting me; somehow, he always managed to stay calm after throwing darts and when I responded, he ignored me, no matter what I said.

"Before your mother packed up to leave with that light head of hers to explore the jungle and give medicine to *those* people, she wanted to move to Philadelphia. She wanted us to help the poor people in need and we did. I helped them in their child support cases. I helped them get their government assistance. Heck, I even helped little Jaylin find out his real daddy was Tyrone. But even after I made that sacrifice to raise my son in the *ghetto*, she left us— not just me, but you too, and she hasn't lifted a finger to contact us since then. Your great-grandmother has afforded us this beautiful house. Look around," he demanded.

"Dad . . ."

"Zachary. Look. Around." I breathed heavily and looked around me. Marbled floors. Tacky carpet. Overpriced art. A winding stair-case that stretched into a hallway lined with a huge banister. High archways leading into many rooms, top floor and bottom.

"Adhere to me," Dad instructed sternly. "We moved where we should've been the entire time." His eyes grew dark. "The. Entire. Time," he repeated. "Now it's my turn. It's my turn to raise you the way I planned. I only have you for another year and I will use this year to *show* you who you *really* are. Behind all of that." He pointed a finger at my chest, his blue eyes never looking away from mine. "You are a Whitman and you will be proud of it."

I bit down on my jaw and clenched my fist, preparing for another argument. A soft knock echoed through the foyer. We both looked toward the door, which was slightly ajar. A petite blond girl in a short floral dress inched in.

"I hope I'm not interrupting anything." Her heels echoed around the foyer as she made her way over to where Dad and I stood. She smiled and extended her hand to my father.

"Hi, I'm Virginia. I'm your neighbor. Right across the street in the identical house."

Dad shook it and did that annoying fake grin he always shot at people to pretend he actually meant well. "Dick Whitman."

"I wanted to say that I'm sorry about what happened to Ms. Elizabeth. She was a saint." She put her hand on her chest and shook her head. She then turned to me, fluttering her blond lashes over her blue eyes. She extended her hand, fingers covered in those fake nails painted pale pink. I raised an eyebrow.

"Zach," Dad said through clenched teeth. "Shake Virginia's hand."

"I would, Dad," I said with a smile, "but I don't want to ruin it. It's so . . . clean, and like you said, I'm—"

"You're going to be going to my school," Virginia said, cutting in with a laugh. "Bayside High. You're a senior, right? I can tell. You don't exactly have the freshman doe-eyed look going on." When I didn't respond, she cleared her throat and faced my father. "Anyways, my friends and I were going to grab a bite to eat at the diner. I wanted to know if maybe Zach would like to come along. I saw him from across the street and I know moving into a new place can be hard, so maybe if he meets a few of *my* friends he can feel a little more at home here in Bayside."

"How nice of you, Virginia!" Dad complimented.

"Please call me Virgie," she responded. *Virgie*, what an old British-sounding name. I wasn't surprised. Before I could deny Virgie's offer, Dad accepted for me.

"Zach would love to go with you." He smiled at me. "Right, Zach?"

"Actually, I . . ."

"Or," Dad said, reaching into his pocket. He pulled out a cigar and lit the end. "You could stay here with me and I could tell you stories about your grandmother and my childhood here in Bayside." Suddenly a diner with British-named strangers sounded better than being here.

"Actually, Virginia . . ."

"Virgie." She batted her lashes.

"Virgie, I would love to go."

She grabbed my arm and led me out the door. "I'll have him home by ten, Mr. Whitman."

When she shut the door behind us, she let out a breath and grinned. "Don't need to thank me, it was my *pleasure*," she sang.

"I wasn't going to, but thanks," I replied. She looked at her watch and back up at me.

"Okay, to the diner." I watched as she sauntered quickly across the street to a pink Volkswagen Bug parked outside of her house. "You *are* coming, aren't you?" she asked turning around, one hand on the door handle. I scratched my head and turned around to look back at my new house, standing tall right below the setting sun.

"Right behind you."

"You're going to love it in Bayside; there's always something to do. We usually hang out at the diner, the food there is amazing, BT dubs. You're gonna love the guys, too. They're on all of the sports teams; football, basketball, baseball, you name it and I hang around with the girls on the cheerleading squad, being the head cheerleader and all, you know? I mean, I guess you can say we're the ones that provide the school with its spirit. Did I mention the school's name? Its Bayside High. Which is so big the school is bigger than any school on the outskirts of New York and it was founded by our ancestors." The more Virgie spoke, the more her words seemed to all mesh together, creating one sound similar to that of long nails against a chalkboard. As we drove down the streets of Bayside, I threw in an earbud and turned up the music, nodding every few seconds so she couldn't tell I wasn't listening to anything she was saying.

The town was . . . quaint, I guess you could say. There wasn't much to it, just a bunch of houses. Every lawn was bright green, even though it was February, and each was cut precisely the same length as the house next to it. The homes ranged in size, some small, some big, but they all looked kept up to almost perfection. No house was free of a white picket fence surrounded by winter flowers, none of the paint on the exteriors was chipped, and no windows were boarded. If we drove by someone jogging outside, pushing a stroller, or treating their lawns, Virgie would give her horn a light tap and they would exchange a little wave, as if they were fanning a fluttering butterfly in the brisk wind from their perfect little faces. One house, though, stuck out to me. Right in the middle of two brick single-family homes was a ghost of an old home. Vines and branches grew within the deep cracks spun into its charred walls. Whoever's home it *was*, is now just an eerie shelter for wildlife and litter. It looked condemned. I was surprised that something like that was even allowed to be in a town like this; it was like one moldy growth on a piece of white bread or something.

"What's up with that house?" I asked. Virgie's car slowly came to a halt and I rolled down the window to get a better look. The grass around the lot was brown and yellow; it stretched high above the broken interior and clung to the inside walls as if it were a living, breathing thing with a mind of its own.

"Oh, that house?" She tsked and shook her head. "It belonged to the first Black family that moved from Hamilton to Bayside."

"Hamilton?"

"It's this town that's located across the old train tracks on Amberlien Road. Bayside used to be huge but our ancestors split it up so the ex-slaves could have a place to live after the Civil War. They put them on the other side of the tracks and helped them build a town of their own, not like they took good care of it or anything. I heard it looks just like the ghetto now. Anyways, some doctor saved up some money and bought this house in like 1950. A few weeks after they moved here, their house burned down. Guess they didn't know how to take care of it."

Goose bumps sprinted across my arms. "*Sheesh.*"

"Tell me about it. Heard they were sleeping when it happened. Only one that got out was the dad. Lost his wife, a newborn baby, and a sixth-grade girl."

"Did they find out how it happened?"

"Probably a chicken grease fire or something. Anyways it was a long time ago." Suddenly, the car gained motion again and Virgie drove away. "What was I saying again? Oh, I think you're gonna *love* Brad. He's hilarious!"

As we drove off, I couldn't ignore the sickening feeling that bubbled in my stomach. The shell of a home that sheltered a family as they slept soundly in their beds was now a ghost steeped in the stench of death, and it bothered me.

# Justin

*I LOVED HER EVEN THEN.*

She held gently on to my hand. I walked on the side closest to the street as I'd seen my pa do with Ma when they went on summer walks. Me and Capri always ran ahead of them in the dense summer air, blanketed with warmth, catching fireflies.

Just like Pa and Ma, we walked together, like an old couple who lived an entire life together, slowly approaching the one that would soon follow. I wore Pa's brown bow tie; she wore her mother's cherry blossom lipstick smeared across her lips all the way to her chubby cheeks. The plastic wheels rolled across the pavement, freshly oiled by the water I'd poured into my pa's bright red oil pail. They held up a blue carriage, with a chestnut-colored doll baby swaddled and tucked inside. Caterpillars skootched across emerald blades of grass and monarch butterflies lazily flew by us, mirroring the spring I felt in my heart whenever I walked with her. Even at seven years old, I loved spending my days with her, even if it was just playing house.

She was beautiful to me even then. I noticed all the little things about her. Like her thick ebony hair pulled into four big ponytails that stretched down her back, twisted until the ends were roped together with bright red ribbons, the same Ma brought for Capri at Hamilton's beauty supply store. She reminded me of the girl from my favorite book, with the ruby-red slippers who left her black-

and-white world. When I spent time with her, I could see life in a brighter color, singing Munchkins, talking lions, and an emerald land adorned with hope.

At ten thirty in the morning, every morning in the summer, we had a routine. I knew my part and I played it. I would grab Pa's brown bow tie and throw it over whatever I wore, then take the two-block walk to her house. She'd be sitting in the front yard, on a blue-and-white-checkered picnic blanket, one that matched the frilly blue Easter dress she begged her mother to wear every day. I'd grab the stroller from her porch and feel strong carrying it down the three stairs that led from her house's door to the pathway leading to an aluminum fence that kept her identical house set apart from the ones around her.

She'd always say the same thing when I walked up with the stroller: "Darling, grab the child and be gentle, she is sleeping." I always did exactly as I was told; I would grab the doll baby from the space next to the fake apples and the old and used empty paper plates scattered around her and would place it in the stroller, gently. Then I'd hold out my hand and help her stand. She'd brush off her bum with a light swipe of the palm, tighten her grip on my hand, and we'd each take our free hand to push our imaginary child on a walk down the sidewalk. Everybody was surprised by us. It was as if we'd lived a life much longer than seven years. Like in the pastoral poems Mama used to read to me and Pri before bed, she was the shepherdess that snatched my heart, and I was the little shepherd boy that let her. When we walked close to one another, the adults would stand on their porches and point their cameras at us, snapping photos of the youngest couple in Hamilton.

Rose Sails and Justin Collins.

I loved being seen with her, being in photos with her. She never said anything as we walked, just hummed the songs we learned in Sunday school, the perfect soundtrack to every overcast day this town had. I didn't need no bright sun. I had one in Rose. Until everything began to change.

It was a Friday morning and the weatherman said there would be very dark clouds hovering. Ma feared that I would get caught in a thunderstorm. She was cornrowing Pri's hair, and Pri was yelling the whole time like Ma was torturing her, even though I knew she was just throwing a tantrum because she wanted to go to Easy's and listen to music like she did every day in the summer. I begged Ma to let me go out anyway and begged God to keep the rain away. He did, but another storm was brewing, and it would rumble like thunder between Rose and me.

I'd just reached my tenth birthday and me and Rose were sitting in the park on the blue-and-white-checkered picnic blanket. She'd asked me to pass the baby's bottle, but I wasn't paying no attention. The voices of the boys running across the basketball court a few feet away seemed to lift me from my spot and carry me there. Well, not on the court *exactly*, just on the sidelines watching. But I ached to play. My fingers tingled in anticipation when the ball was passed around and shot. I'd seen Pa watching the game from his favorite leather armchair. Ma would yell because she said that Pa won't no coach; the players he ordered from behind the television couldn't hear him. But still, he yelled.

I was never interested in the way the game worked; I only saw tall men chasing each other for a single orange ball. But looking at it from another angle, I saw something I hadn't before: a chance.

Before that day, I never needed no friends except for Rose. I wasn't close to the boys in Hamilton. They always passed by me and Rose on our walks, like we were a large tree to walk around. They never paid attention to me, they just walked right on by, carrying that orange basketball.

"Justin."

I watched as they high-fived one another when shots were made.

"*Justin.*"

I watched as they called each other's names, flailing their arms open and above their heads in anticipation for the ball to land in their outstretched and sweaty palms.

"*Justin. Justin Collins.*" She snapped in my ear multiple times. I turned to face her, blinking, unable to remember what she asked me. So, I went through the motions and handed her one of the used plates, dyed with some kind of red sauce that was embedded in the Styrofoam. Rose rolled her eyes and reached over for the bottle I didn't pass her, dipped its nipple into the open mouth of our plastic child, and fed it from the liquid that never escaped it. I couldn't take my eyes away for long, kept watching them play.

Then the unthinkable happened. One of the boys started walking over, basketball under his arm, and I looked away quickly—embarrassed. I tried playing it off like I wasn't watching them. Grabbed the closest thing next to me, which happened to be a teacup. I pretended to sip the invisible liquid Rose poured inside.

"Yo." The boy who had walked over stood over me, blocking the only flicker of sunlight in the sky.

I lifted my head and nodded in response like I'd seen the Italian gangsters on Pa's television do. Out of nowhere the boy tossed the ball at me; I dropped the teacup and caught it in one fell swoop.

"We're short one dude for ma team," the boy said, like he wasn't questioning if I wanted to play or not. I looked over at Rose, who smiled, revealing one of her missing front teeth.

"I'll be cheering for you," she said. I stood up quickly, excitement sending electric currents through my body. With that orange ball in my hand, I followed the boy to the court.

"Found one more," the boy said once we reached the other eight boys standing in a circle in the center of the court. They were all dressed in tees and basketball shorts.

"What's up with the bow tie?" one asked, lifting his ankle in a standing stretch. I quickly took it off and stuffed it into the pocket of my shorts.

"Is that your girlfriend?" another asked. They all looked past me to where Rose sat on the grass. I turned around and she waved.

"No," I said quickly, my heart burning inside my chest. "That's just Rose."

They nodded like they understood, but I knew they didn't. I wasn't gonna try and make them understand either.

"Why you playin' tea party with her?" a chubby boy finally asked, verbalizing everyone's thoughts.

I cleared my throat, buying time to think of a lie. "I have to hang out with her. I get paid five dollars to do it." I hoped that sounded believable.

"I wouldn't do it for a million dollars. Tea parties are for girls," the chubby boy interjected with a look of disgust.

"Yeah, but you'd do it for a plate of chicken wings, mac and cheese, and cake," said the boy who'd invited me over. "Let's just get to playing the game." Everyone separated and ran to their positions. The boy patted my back.

"That's Carlos. Don't worry about him. He's straight-up crazy sometimes." He worked a tornado with his finger to the side of his head. "I'm Tyree by the way." He stretched out his hands. I threw the ball to him.

"I'm Justin," I responded, but Tyree had already walked away to play.

That's when it started. This addiction I didn't have until it was pumped like a drug straight to my veins. Every day, I walked with Rose to the park. I switched up my bow tie for a tee and basketball shorts. Stopped grabbing the stroller because it was slowing me down, so she grabbed it instead and brought it down the steps before I got there. When I walked Rose, my legs took longer strides. It really did start to look like I was paid five dollars to do it. She'd done her best to catch up, her dress getting caught in the tight wheels that skit down the pavement. If I didn't jog ahead of Rose and was late to the courts, I always got put on a team with Crazy Carlos, who ran too slow, and Deondre, who had to take a pump from his inhaler every time he ran for five minutes straight. They slowed me down just like Rose did. I wanted Tyree to pick me for his team. He was the best on the basketball court; not only was he the tallest, but he was also already chosen to be on the middle school basketball team before the school year even started. If I wanted to get better at this game, if I wanted a greater high from it, I had to learn from Tyree.

Rose sat and watched me play basketball as she held on to *her* plastic baby. She cheered for me when I'd make a basket, yelling, "Yay, Justin!" But when the summer came to an end, she told me she was tired of just sitting and watching. Said she didn't want to go to the park to play when I came to get her one morning because walking wasn't as fun as it used to be. People stopped coming outside to take pictures of us. Lemme be honest, I knew why Rose didn't want to walk anymore. I knew it was wrong to leave her alone on the grass while I played happily until sweat poured from my skin. But I enjoyed it too much to sacrifice it.

"How about we play here instead?" she'd asked. She gave my attire the once-over. I'd given the bow tie back to Pa and showed up in basketball shorts. I stood there for a moment, weighing out all my options. Rose was beautiful to me, even then. No one could tell me different. No one could tell me I didn't love her. But like I said, basketball became something more than a tool to make friends; it was easy for me. I deserved to do something real for once, instead of playing pretend with Rose, playing pretend at Mama's homegoing a year before, playing pretend Dad and Mama to Capri, playing the perfect grandson to Ma and Pa. Playing basketball was the only time I could be one hundred percent real even with everyone watching.

She could read it on my face. She told me she'd been feeling sick and for me to go ahead without her. I could feel her eyes watching me cross the street from her spot on the checkered picnic blanket spread out on the grass. When I almost reached the courts, so close that I could hear Tyree and the boys yelling for the ball, I knew it wouldn't be the same without Rose cheering me on from the sidelines. I turned around and ran back to tell her that I was sorry, that I wanted to work something out where we could *both* get what we wanted. That I didn't want basketball without her.

Except when I reached her doorstep, I could hear soft whimpers escaping through her open window and that's when I saw it: Rose's small frame under her floral bedcovers, crying. I squeezed my fist. I wasn't good with tears. I wasn't even good with the random spurts of Pri crying some nights about Mama. Because truth was, whenever I saw someone being free in that way, free enough to allow emotions from the inside to flow unrestrained on the outside, my body wanted to do the same. I couldn't let Rose see me cry. *I was the reason why she was crying to begin with.* I wasn't good with disappointing people. I'd been so careful to never do it before. To save face, I ran straight to the woods, and there, under the covering of the trees, I cried too.

When fifth grade started for us that fall, we maintained our friendship and I pretended I never saw her crying that day. Things started to feel normal. We ate lunch together and played together at recess. Until I got closer with one of the boys I played with during the summer, Deondre, who was in the same homeroom as me. At first, we all hung out, but Deondre kept calling Rose boring. He didn't like coloring at a table and playing picnic. Rose tried playing basketball with us, but she traveled with the ball, ran too slow, and cried every time he shoved her. He asked why she wouldn't play with the other girls in her homeroom class.

"Because I don't want to," Rose responded with all the attitude she could muster. She stood before Deondre, fearless, hands on her hips, staring straight into his eyes. He didn't back down either. I wanted to tell Deondre to shut up, to go easier on Rose, but I didn't. Even though it's tough to admit, I was getting a bit tired of picnic.

"Come on, Justin, let's play basketball," Deondre finally said. I not-so-hesitantly followed.

The next day after that, again, I followed.

As a matter of fact, I followed the rest of that year.

Mama used to say that love is a winding path that leads to every other emotion before it reaches the heart. I don't think I understood that until things changed between me and Rose. It seemed like every emotion we had stretched out of us before it pulled love with it. Jealousy, anger, fear.

After I abandoned Rose for basketball and frozen pizza lunches with the guys, she found her a posse: two best friends named Keonna and Berlin. Berlin was a germophobe. Used to put her jacket on everything before sitting down on it. Keonna was a gossip. She could make a rumor go viral around school faster than a post on social media. So, when Rose started a rumor about me, I knew it was only a matter of time before it hit the town and I was dateless.

It was just two weeks before Juneteenth. Freshman year would be starting that September and I was trying to get noticed by the varsity coach. He only invited a few of the younger boys to play on the team, and only if they could prove they had what it took. Rose started frequenting the courts with Keonna and Berlin almost every morning we were out there. The girls around Hamilton always sat on the sidelines watching us play ball, hoping to snag a boyfriend for the month. I usually ignored them, but I couldn't ignore Rose. I pretended like her sitting there, flipping through magazines and social media, didn't distract me while practicing, or pull me to the corner where she sat to get a "water break."

"Yo, you thirsty *again*? You catch dehydration or something?" Carlos asked after I took my fifth water break in twenty minutes.

"Don't worry about me," I replied. "Plus, you can't *catch* dehydration with yo big head. It's something that happens when you sweat too much."

Carlos shrugged. "Whatever, you can't be *that* thirsty. You downed like one hundred water bottles already, you ain't sweating, *and* my mom said she tired of buying water for the team."

"At least he's drinking them," Tyree cut in. "Plus, she has to; you the water boy, that's the only reason why we let you play with us." All the guys laughed, and Carlos started cracking on Tyree's ashy knees. I walked over to the sidelines, close to where Rose and her friends sat. I could hear their conversation from where I stood, rifling through the water cooler. My ears perked when I heard my name.

"*Mm-mm*, look at Justin Collins, he so cute, y'all," Keonna said, her smile covered with braces. "His forehead shrunk, and he switched out those glasses for contacts. He even shaped up all the hair that was growing all wild from his head."

"He okay," Rose replied nonchalantly.

I picked up a water bottle, making sure to flex the little bit of muscle that had started to develop.

Keonna licked her lips lustfully, watching me put the bottle up to my mouth. "I think imma go talk to him. Justa see what's gonna happen. I think he would be the perfect guy to give my first kiss."

Rose stood up, waving her arms frantically around her as if she wanted someone to pass her a basketball. She was jealous. I couldn't help but smirk.

"No," Rose quickly said. "Don't do that, I saw this thing on his lip and girl it's nasty."

Berlin's eyes grew wide. She looked up from the phone she was texting on.

"You mean like the herpes virus we learned about in health?"

"Ew, never mind about that one," Keonna had said to Rose. Then she sat back into her seat.

*Herpes?*

I should have been mad, but the smirk still clung to my lips. If this meant what I thought it did, Mama was right. Jealousy was rigging Rose's heart before love ran behind it. I just had to wait patiently for her to admit it. And I did, for what felt like an eternity, and I got nothing. No texts. No calls. No DMs. Not even an email. I realized that she probably didn't even like me. She probably wanted to get me back for being a rotten friend, which I deserved. When the annual Juneteenth fair came up and the town worked together to set up booths for games, food, and the Ferris wheel Easy paid to rent, almost everybody and their moms had a date, except me. I was all alone and knew exactly why.

That night, as couples old and young held hands, went on the Ferris wheel, and walked among the crowds sharing ice cream and cotton candy, I stood around with my hands in my pockets, walking from booth to booth. I finally settled on the basketball game. Each time I won a round, I stuck a stuffed animal to join the pile next to me. Emptied out my entire savings of thirty-five dollars from my Mario piggy bank into the hands of the vendor.

"Come on, kid, if you keep winning all my stuff, I won't have anything else, which means I'll have to close down early," the vendor, an old Russian man with a bushy mustache, said from behind the booth. But I ignored him, handed him another three dollars, and began shooting the little basketballs into the hoop eight feet ahead of me.

"Hey."

"Hey," I responded without turning around, until a soft hand touched my shoulder. I shot one last basket before turning to see Rose. I tried playing it off that I didn't notice everything about her when she stood before me, but I did. I noticed her black dress covered in tiny roses—even the glitter she'd sprinkled across her neck and arms.

"You won all those?" she asked, pointing to the pile of miniature teddy bears of every color on the ground behind me. I shrugged but before I could answer, the vendor did for me.

"Yes, and he's taking away everyone else's chances." His hard Russian accent seemed heavier, his face red with frustration. Rose and I stared at one another and covered our mouths over with our hands to keep from laughing.

"Wanna ride the Ferris wheel? We only got it for one night," she said. When I followed her, I couldn't help but notice the shape that popped from her behind.

When we reached the top, we could see almost all of Hamilton and Bayside. The sunset hung over the skies of Bayside and, of course, Hamilton just got the less favorable ends of the purpling sky.

"The sun don't shine as bright in Hamilton," I said, glancing into the direction of the town across from us.

"It don't," she agreed. "But it doesn't mean the people here are like the skies we got. They shine even if the sun don't." Her eyes met mine, how she truly shined to me. "I saw you playing the other day, you got really good."

I lifted an eyebrow and smirked. *"Got?"*

She laughed. "I meant what I said, boy. Don't get too cocky."

As the Ferris wheel went around a few times, a comfortable silence swallowed the air around us. I liked the way it was, just the two of us again; enjoying one another's company.

"So, where's Keonna and Berlin?" I asked after a while.

"With their dates," Rose responded. "Where's Deondre and Carlos?"

"With their dates."

I nodded nonchalantly, though I wanted to ask her the question that stood anxiously on the edge of my tongue, hovering over a deep pool of chances. I bit my lip, my foot tapping against the metal floor, and finally the question jumped out.

"*Where's your date?*" we asked at the same time.

"You first," I said.

"I came alone tonight."

"Me too."

"You too?"

"Yeah."

"It's because *someone* started this rumor about me having herpes."

When I said this, and Rose jumped and almost fell off the ride, I wanted to laugh. I glanced away toward Bayside to catch myself.

"It's not true, you know," I whispered.

"I know," Rose responded. "Maybe whoever did it had a good reason."

For a few more moments, the ride spun its creaky cart to the top, once, twice, again. When we reached the top for the last time, I knew the time travel we underwent, back to childhood for just a few moments, was coming to an end too. Down below was the present, waiting to envelop us and drown us in our own separate worlds again.

Rose took my eyes prisoner.

I couldn't look away from her.

Then there it was again, something else looming on the tip of my tongue, preparing for a dive into deep and unfamiliar waters. Desire hung there, tempted to close the polite distance our bodies kept from one another. Before she could ask what all the staring was about, I switched seats from where I sat across to sit next to her. As I invaded every inch of her space, heavy silence still hung, blanketing us with both awkwardness and awareness of what was to happen next. I wasn't going to wait on her to say anything anymore. It was my turn. With a shaky hand, I grazed her cheek, then leaned in close and kissed her.

That kiss had me kicking it on cloud one hundred for the next week. It was even better than all the herpes rumors subsiding and all the girls trying to talk to me. Better than hearing that I got drafted for varsity. All I could think about was Rose's lips and how perfectly they fit mine. I planned to ask her out before my first summer training practice. I would walk to her house and knock on her doorstep wearing the same bow tie I used to wear on our walks. I asked Pa to borrow it and held it tight in between my fingers the night before, imagining how quickly she'd say yes and how we'd walk to practice together like old times, maybe even kissing in between each street, while we waited for the crosswalk sign to click to WALK.

I went to sleep with a smile, but it dropped to my stomach when I woke up to the sound of the duct tape holding my conditioner to my window being cut with what looked like a pocket knife. Hamilton is the safest place. No breaking and entering. No crimes, no murder. And I wasn't about to be the first one. First, I tried pretending to be asleep; whatever they wanted they could have. I didn't wanna risk running out my room and knocking on Ma and Pa's door either. If they could both sleep over Pa's snoring, there was no way they'd hear me. Mama always said real men didn't need to cause a fuss, they needed to use their brains. If I was gonna keep Capri breathing and sleeping soundly in bed, I would pretend to be asleep instead of throwing hands.

I squinted my eyes real tight and watched as my conditioner

was carefully pulled out the window. Then I saw two long legs make their way inside.

*Please God*, I prayed. *Don't let them come at—*

"Justin Collins." The voice was deep, sounded familiar. I instantly knew it was one of the guys from the varsity team. "You're being inducted into Hamilton High's Varsity Lions. Come without screaming and you'll get your respect. Scream like that joker Carlos did, and you'll pay a heavy price. We got a party planned down at the tracks tonight. You'll take your first sip of celebratory beer, and we'll go over this season's plays. Got it?"

I grinned. I'd heard about this honor. Tonight, I was finally going to be a Lion. I went without a fight. Let him blindfold me, tie me up, slide me out the window, and throw me in the back of a pickup truck with a bunch of other guys.

When we reached the abandoned railroad station near the train tracks, we were pulled from the back and sat on the ground. Our blindfolds came off first, but we remained tied up. I caught a glimpse of Tyree, Deondre, and Carlos reflecting off the camping lanterns scattered around us. *Good. We all made it.* The varsity guys stripped us of our sneakers and threw them on the telephone wire hanging above.

"Come on, man! My mom just bought me those! They the new Jays!" Carlos cried, trying to worm his way out of the ropes tightly tied around his skinny frame.

"Shut up, Carlos!" one of the guys spat. "This is your *initiation*. We do the talking; you do the shuttin' up."

Carlos silently sobbed beside me. I didn't know why he was complaining. This was something we'd been working for all summer. When one of the guys was about to grab beer from the cooler behind the truck, sirens wailed down the road and red, white, and blue lights reflected off the trees. The varsity boys scrambled to get away, but the Hamilton police surrounded them. Each of the boys lifted their hands in surrender. When the flashing lights echoed off their faces, I heard the crunch of leaves. My eyes darted to my left, and Rose, who hid behind a nearby bush, waved.

*What is she doing here?*

Once the cops realized what was going on and things settled down, she ran up to me. I was seated on the trunk of one of the squad cars, my shoeless feet dangling below me.

"I'm so glad you're okay!" she exclaimed when she reached me.

"What are you doing here?" I asked.

"Saving you. I'm the one who called the police."

"It was you? *You* did this?" I leapt from my seat and stood, towering over Rose.

She nodded hesitantly. "My dad told me the news about you getting on the varsity team over dinner. I had to wait until my parents fell asleep before sneaking out to wish you good luck before practice tomorrow. Then I saw you get kidnapped. So, I followed you on my bike and called the police to save—"

"I did *not* need saving." I emphasized each word, adding dagger after dagger to the next. "They were *initiating* me into the team. Now, since you called the cops, the guys got in trouble. They calling Coach Hill, you know that, *Rose?*" Her name was soaked with hatred. "They might not be able to play next season. If they don't play, how we gonna win?"

"I . . ." Rose did not know what to say. Instead, she sat there frozen, staring, shaking, and very confused.

"All right, Justin, I called your ma. I'm gonna take you home," a police officer said before ushering me away. I took one last look at Rose in disgust and never looked back.

Kids carry grudges between each other, but they never last long. In fact, in my case, I only remained angry with Rose for thirty minutes. I didn't get in any trouble. Pa was initiated just like me and apparently my father was too. Even the cop congratulated me on making varsity. But catching us with beer didn't hit that well. Thankfully, none of us took any sips before Rose called the cops. If we did, we would've gotten in trouble like the varsity guys.

When I'd climbed in my bed to sleep that night, Rose's face remained engraved in my mind. Her misty eyes when I'd yelled at her, the way her lip curled inward when I'd glared at her before walking away. When I'd finally gone to sleep, I dreamed of our kiss on the Ferris wheel. I remembered how my heart leaped out of my chest when our lips met; I remembered all the convincing I'd had to give myself to gain the courage to do so. Most of all, I remembered how in love with her I really was. When the sun arose in the overcast sky the next morning, I was on Rose's porch at seven thirty on the dot.

"Good morning, Justin," Reverend Sails greeted when he'd answered the door. I looked past him into the house. I could see Rose's white sneakers lined up among the other shoes in the hallway. "Are you looking for Rose?"

I nodded, still trying to catch a glimpse of where Rose could be. I hoped I didn't hurt her too bad. I wanted to apologize. I *needed* to.

"She's not here, Justin."

When he'd said this, my breathing froze.

"I . . . what do you mean she's not here?"

"She went to summer camp. Didn't she tell you? She'll be in New Jersey until the last week of August." My heart dropped.

"She what?"

"She's left already. You just missed her, actually."

"Which way did she go?" I asked quickly.

"Excuse me?"

"Which way did Rose go?" I prodded.

"She went toward Fifth Street but—" Before Reverend Sails could finish, I took off down the sidewalk. Obviously, my feet couldn't carry me to Rose, even being fueled with adrenaline and desire. I reached Fifth Street twenty minutes later, and Rose was, without a doubt, already gone.

# Capri

SOME SUMMER NIGHTS ME AND ESSIE USED TO SKIP stones across the bay that overlooked New York City. One time I told her I wanted to be like one of those stones. She asked me why and I told her if I was one of them stones, I'd skip myself right along that river to someplace like Rome or Paris. I remember that, for some reason, when I said that, Essie broke down into tears and pulled me in real close.

Nothing's changed since then. I'm sure a lot of people wanna get out of Hamilton, but they do nothing to get the job done. You gotta really not care about being uncomfortable in order to leave Hamilton. I can take being uncomfortable.

One time, there was a water leak in my room and I had to share a bed with Ma while Pa slept on the couch. Ma's room always smelled like those mints Justin and I used to take by the handful at Jo's Diner. The first night I slept in the bed with Ma, I smelled the mints and asked her if I could have some. She laughed and told me it was just her foot cream. Never ate any of those mints at Jo's again. Sleeping in that room was one of the most uncomfortable things for me. Ma always slept with a bunch of blankets and turned on the loud rotating fan. She always snacked on ginger cookies and got the crumbs in the bed too, so they'd always get stuck to my legs at night if I rolled over too close to her side of the bed.

Listen, if I can take the hot nights, painful crumbs, and loud fan, I can pretty much handle anything.

Maybe even Camp Sharp.

I stared down at the unopened envelope I held in my hand. I tried convincing myself of why I was strong enough, brave enough, to pack up and leave Hamilton to dance with people who probably had years and years of lessons, even though I only had a few before Ma snatched me out after Essie died. Attending this camp was a dream; all the biggest actors, singers, and dancers went to Camp Sharp and studied under experienced staff that worked on Broadway and in movies. Not only that, talent agents and scouts from performing art schools like Juilliard flooded the end-of-summer showcase, giving away scholarships. I'd thought maybe Ma would take my dancing more serious if I showed her I could survive a summer there.

The bell over the door rang, signaling a costumer, and I quickly threw the envelope back inside the sleeve of the Billie Holiday record where I'd hidden it. When I saw that it was only Easy, the owner of the record shop, and not one of those nosy-behind people from around Hamilton who forgot we were closed today, I slid it back out. He was the one that talked me into applying to Camp Sharp over the summer in the first place. He'd always encouraged me to dance, but even more so after Essie died. After her homegoing, he told me that I needed to follow my dreams because *"your mom,"* he called her, "died doing what she always talked about." I only called Essie mom when Easy was around; he never let me call her by her first name.

"Still haven't opened it up yet, huh?" he asked. I'd gotten the letter over a month ago and he swore that whatever was inside would be good news. But *of course*, Easy had no problem believing this dream was possible; he left Hamilton to pursue his. When he was eighteen, Easy played clubs in New York as a saxophonist and toured with some of the biggest jazz bands to date. Pretty soon, he was playing sold-out shows as a single act. No band. No drums. No singers. Just Easy onstage lighting the spark that made his music come to life. Now, under Easy's bright eyes were bags of wrinkles; he limped around with a cane, his caramel skin betraying his fight with AIDS—a fight that caused both his career to end and his return to Hamilton.

After he contracted AIDS, he got real sick and almost died. When he was fighting for his life, Easy said he wasn't thinking about the sweat coming from his pores, or the food he could never keep down, or even the fact that he was so close to death he could "feel the flames of hell," as he put it. All he could think about, he said, was Hamilton and the culture here, the people he grew up with, and the environment of the town, and how close everyone was. All the friends he met in the music world threw him away like a wet rag, he said. They didn't even bother to see him when he was hospitalized. He was all the way in Kentucky, and he still got daily calls from his friends in Hamilton. When he got better, he moved back here and opened a record store and café in place of the old theatre where Essie used to perform her community plays. He said he still lives by his music, and he does. On some days, the sound of a single saxophone fills the air of Hamilton. It amazes me how he could have ever wanted to come back to this town after getting free.

Camp Sharp wanted to see the way a dancer could perform without a bunch of instruments to help them, or music cues to give "answers," as they stated in the application. They sent a CD with a single 808 drumbeat to each applicant, and instructed us to create a routine for it. I was terrified, but Easy told me not to think about anything or even make anything up; he said I should just dance to the beat as my body felt. And I did. I felt good about it after I watched it over and so did Easy, but now, staring at the envelope, I couldn't help but think my heart would explode and splatter all over Easy's glass counter.

"I don't know if I'm ready to open it," I said. "I feel like I'm disappointing Ma."

Easy took off his brimmed hat, as he did each time he was about to make a point. He fingered the scarlet red feather perched on the side, and then slowly lifted it.

"You know I found this feather in New York City almost twenty years ago. I like to believe it came from a red bird, even though I'm pretty sure it came from some lady's jacket. Feels fake." He grinned to himself and let the feather fall on the counter. "This feather sat right next to some hot dog vendor's cart on the nasty New York sidewalk, in mint condition. Let's just say it did really come from a bird. What's a red bird coming to New York for, flying over the streets when it can fly someplace comfortable? Whatever reason it may be, it was in New York City, and guess what? This feather that fell wasn't stepped on or nothing. Still maintained its shape, ain't not one piece of this feather was separated or torn.

"Capri, this bird wasn't in his comfort zone, just like you." He pointed at me. "It wasn't where everyone expected it to be, like some lush green forest, but it flew where it pleased. And look at that." He pointed to the perfectly shaped feather sitting on the glass desk. "People made way for it, they ain't walk all over it. They avoided stepping on it, why? Because it's different, it's beautiful, it deserves to be taken care of." And just like that, he gently placed the feather back into his hat and walked to his office behind the store. Easy's stories never made much sense to me, but this one, for some reason, collided with my understanding. I closed my eyes and tried imagining myself onstage, under some spotlight like Essie used to. She was out of place too, just like the feather, but the city made room for her. Maybe Camp Sharp could make room for me too.

# Zach

"SO, EVERYONE, I BOUGHT A SPECIAL VISITOR WITH ME today," Virgie announced to her friends who sat in one of the cherry red booths a few feet from where I stood. She made me stay at the entrance of the small nineteen twenties–themed diner. Thought it would be *fun* to surprise her friends before she walked in with me. As she made them guess who she'd brought and shooed away with laughter guesses of a puppy, a cake, and some boy bands, I sat on one of the barstools. The whole diner was filled with people my age, laughing and slurping down milkshakes just like in those old black-and-white television shows. Photos of old white performers clung to the white walls of the diner. I searched for the Black people that made music in that era but couldn't find any. This whole town seemed to be some big time warp into segregation. I pulled out my phone to take a photo; none of my boys in Philly would ever believe a place like this actually existed, but when I tried to upload it to social media, I had no connection. I shook my phone in frustration.

"You okay, man?" someone in front of me asked. Probably another one of those stuck-in-the-past kids with a weird-sounding name. I rolled my eyes.

"Nah, man, I'm not. My phone is busted. There's no connection in this town."

"Everybody knows there's no connection here in the diner," the person said, laughing. "If you want it, you gotta go to the other side of town. Are you new here?"

"Obviously." I looked up and, to my surprise, right there in front of me was someone slightly darker than the bleached-white counter. He was a light-skinned Black kid, his brown eyes squinting in amusement behind the large, black-framed glasses he wore. Ear-length black hair styled in tight coils stretched outside of a white fry boy paper hat. He grinned.

"Name's Thomas." He pointed to the name tag that clung to his white shirt. He stretched out his hand for me to shake.

I shook it.

"Zach. My fault for being like that. I just moved here and—"

"Don't worry about it. This town's a dead zone. It would give anyone a headache."

"Yeah." I sighed. "I don't think a whole bottle of Tylenol can rid me from the migraine this is giving me." I gestured to Virgie, who was still making her friends play Guess About the Visitor.

Thomas laughed. "How about a milkshake? On the house? It always clears my mind when things around here get crazy."

I nodded. "Sure, man, that sounds good."

Immediately Thomas went to work, grabbing one of the glasses that hung above the counter.

"So where are you from?" he asked, his back facing me. He leaned over an open freezer and scooped vanilla ice cream into the glass.

"Philly, which is real different from here." I leaned on the counter. "Probably more like Hamilton, huh?" While Virgie drove to the diner, I couldn't stop thinking about that house that was burned down. Obviously, things changed because Thomas was here, and obviously he was still alive, but the way Virgie described the family dying was so nonchalant, heartless. I wanted to know more about that family and Hamilton.

He poured some milk into the glass and mixed it in with chocolate syrup and cookie crumbs, then he walked it over to this machine that did the spinning.

"So, you heard a little bit of the town's history, huh?" he asked, pressing the button. My milkshake spun, the cookie crumbs disappearing in the chocolate syrup and ice cream.

I nodded. "Yeah, Virgie told me some of it. I saw that house that burned down."

"Home of the McKulleys. They all died, except the dad." He slid me my milkshake. It looked good but I was more interested in details about those people, that town.

"So, they're pretty famous around here? Is that why the house was never rebuilt? Is it like a memorial or something?"

He shook his head as if my question was the dumbest he'd ever heard.

"Nah, far from that, man. Being Black in Bayside was what condemned that house to never being built again. Nobody wants to stay in a house where Black people slept, pooped, ate, and lived. God forbid, the color wash off on them." For some reason, when he said that, my heart quickened its pace. I heard about racism and segregation and all that in my school, but I didn't think it was *still* this serious.

"There you are, Zachy." I felt a pair of doughy hands wrap around my shoulders.

*Zachy?*

Virgie pulled on my sleeve. "Come on, Zachy, come meet my friends."

"It's Zach," I corrected. "I'm kind of talking to Thomas right now. Can I catch up with you in a bit?" She walked around from behind my back to face me. Her blue eyes were squinting in confusion; she looked in front of me and then around me.

"Who?" she asked slowly.

I gestured in front of me but noticed that I'd only gestured to the air. I looked all around me, and noticed Thomas moved to the register to check out a customer who was paying his bill. The line behind him was long, filled with teenagers holding long sleeves of receipt paper. Thomas was busy. I'd catch up with him later.

"Everyone," she introduced, "meet Zachy."

Sitting in the large booth were two guys and two girls. The guys were square figured and blond, their biceps bulging against the fabric of their way-too-small light blue and white letterman jackets. They nodded at me and I served one back. Virgie sat next to the girls, and the guys attempted to make room. I squeezed in a space at the end of the booth, one butt cheek barely succeeding in sharing a space with their colossal legs.

"I'm Brad and this is Brock," one of the guys introduced. Now that I was sitting, I got a closer look at their meaty faces. They both had blue eyes, large pig noses, and paper-thin lips.

"Y'all twins?" I asked.

"No?" one of them replied as if I'd asked them if they were ballerinas or something.

"I'm Ginger." I turned to the girl sitting across from me. She had red hair. *Clever name, Mom and Dad.* She smiled widely, revealing an entire row of bright orange braces that covered the top and bottom of her teeth. You'd think I was lying if I said she wore a pumpkin orange sweater, but I'm not. I scratched my head.

"Nice to meet you, Ging."

"—er," she finished. "Ginger." She still smiled. Except this time, a flirty smile. She extended her breast toward me and fingered a lock of her amber hair, as if my shortening her name was making a pass or something.

"I'm Lila," the girl next to Ginger introduced. Her voice was as flat as the top of Brad and Brock's gelled hair. Purple highlights decorated her bright blue hair and rings of every kind scattered her face. Two sat under her lips, which were painted pitch black. "I like your shirt. I got one just like it from LA on sale for five hundred at Bobby's Boutique. Same place you got yours?"

I had forgotten I was wearing a bleached and ripped black tee. I didn't think I was doing anything except moving boxes all day, so I hadn't dressed up to hang out in Pleasantville with the Brady Bunch.

"Nah, it sort of got bleached in the wash and ripped over time. I had it since like seventh grade." Everyone stared at me in silence for a few seconds, as if I'd grown a third head in front of them or something. Virgie cleared her throat.

"So Zachy is my new neighbor. I offered to show him around so he could make some friends before starting school tomorrow."

"Tell us about yourself, what are you into?" Brad or Brock asked me. I somehow forgot which one was which.

I shrugged. "I like music."

Ginger clapped her hands. "Music is so cool."

"What music are you into?" Lila asked me.

"Um, I like rap mostly, but I'm into rock too. Mostly the ambient or post hardcore stuff; nothing too crazy. I'm really into vintage jazz, like John Coltrane and Duke Ellington. Anything from the Harlem Renaissance is key. I produce my own stuff too, which is like a mixture of everything."

Virgie nodded like she understood. "I like rap, it's fun to dance to at parties."

"It can be, I guess," I responded. "But I'm not really into that kind. I like the more conscious stuff. I grew up in Philly, so a lot of the rap I like is stuff about the streets—what it's really like for people who had to struggle to get where they are now, as opposed to having stuff handed to them." Again, the silence followed, except it lasted a bit longer, and from the looks in their eyes, I might as well have grown three heads.

"So, you're from Philly?" BradBrock asked. I decided I was just gonna call them that from now on.

"Born and raised."

"What part?" they asked.

"North Philly."

"You mean, like the hood? With all the Black people?"

"I guess."

Then the questions started.

"What was it like?"

"What do you mean?"

"Being with all those Black people? Were you the only white one in your school?"

"No, but there wasn't many."

"Do they really sell drugs?"

"Do the girls really get pregnant by like three different baby daddies?"

"So, you have all Black friends?"

"Were you ever arrested?"

Annoyance crept up my spine. I could understand being curious, but this was on another level of white ignorance. They questioned me like I'd just come back from Mars and kicked it with a bunch of aliens for seventeen years, instead of coming from the only home I'd ever known. The "Black people" they questioned me about were friends turned family, not stereotypes straight out of some after-school special or antidrug commercial. Just as I was about to ask them what Jim Crow time warp they crawled out of, Virgie cut in.

"*Guys!* Leave all the questions to yourselves, you're being obnoxious." Everyone quieted and a few half-hearted apologies were thrown my way. Soon the conversation switched to them trying to explain to me what school would be like and what clubs I was supposed to join to maintain my *cool* status. When Thomas came to take our orders, everything changed.

"Sorry for the wait, everyone, it's been pretty busy," Thomas said, smiling. I nodded at him, but he didn't acknowledge me. Then I realized that I'd forgotten my milkshake; it must have melted on the counter. I turned around and saw that I was right. Brown liquid sprinkled with cookies trailed down the side of my glass and around the counter. The place was swamped; people were waiting by the door to be seated, and a few tables needed bussing. I noticed two other waiters, but they were sitting in booths talking to their friends.

"Yo, my fault about not drinking my shake, man, I forgot it was—"

"Why are you sorry?" BradBrock cut in. "That's not your responsibility. It's Tom's, that's why he works here, right, *Tom*? He's got it." He said his name as if he were a servant, who needed to be reminded of his place.

"It's cool, man," Thomas assured, finally acknowledging me. He gave me a grin, but it seemed forced. "Don't sweat it. I'll get to it when I can."

I started to stand. "Nah, man, I see some napkins. I got it." BradBrock lifted an immensely heavy hand and plopped me back into the seat with a touch of my shoulder.

"He's got it," BradBrock seethed through gritted teeth. Thomas nodded in agreement with them. When it was time for our orders, he wrote everything down carefully, as if he were taking notes in a biology class. When he got to me, I said I wasn't hungry. BradBrock added an order before he walked away.

"I also want a large cheese fry with mustard, pickle juice, mushrooms, and anchovies." Thomas wrote it down without question. When he walked away Virgie shook her head, stifling laughter behind her hand.

"You guys are *horrible*. I can't believe you ordered that."

"Y'all really gonna eat all that?" I asked.

They smacked each other's hands and laughed. "You'll see, newbie."

Twenty minutes later, Thomas arrived with everyone's food. When he presented the smelly cheese fries, BradBrock spoke.

"I didn't order this," he said flatly.

"What?" Thomas asked.

"I didn't order this, *Tom*." He said this like Thomas was hard of hearing. Quickly Thomas fished out his notebook and spun through the pages.

"But, Brad, you did. I have it written right here." He turned the notebook around to face Brad, but he ignored it.

"Did I order this, you guys?" Brad asked. Everyone at the table shook their heads "no," trying to hide their smirks. Brock whispered in my ear. *"Dude, just wait and see what happens, you're gonna be dying."*

Thomas apologized and leaned across the table to grab the fries from Brock, but before he could, Brad picked them up.

"I got it, man, don't worry." He stretched a hand by me, the fetid-smelling fries making their way up my nose. *"Ah,* arm cramp!" Brad wailed.

Immediately he lifted the fries and threw them toward Thomas's face. Thomas yelled out, the hot cheese probably burning his skin, down his neck, and through the fabric of his white uniform. Everyone in the diner turned to the noise and when they'd seen Thomas covered in gook, they laughed in unison, Virgie, Ginger, and Lila included.

"Dude, what the heck?" I yelled, turning to Brad, but he just nudged me with his elbow, unable to contain his laughter. Thomas looked at me, his eyes brimming with tears. I stood up and faced him.

"Dude, let me help you clean up," I offered, but he stepped back.

"I don't need your help. *Get away* from me." He slipped and fell on cheese that found its way to the floor. I stretched out a hand to Thomas, but he stood up and ran to the kitchen.

"Zachy! Where are you going?" Virgie called, running after me into the parking lot. The stars shone so bright in Bayside, street-lights were barely needed. It was a shame that a town so bright could be so dark.

I whipped my head around. "What is y'all's problem?"

She wobbled in her high heels, attempting to run across the

asphalt parking lot, looking like a drunk woman. She whisked a fly-away hair from her eyes and stood a few inches in front of me.

"It was just a joke, Zachy. People play jokes on Tom *all* of the time." She said this nonchalantly, like throwing food on someone was the same as repeating a bad knock-knock joke.

"Do people play jokes like that on you, Lila, and Ginger? Or Butch and Brett?" I asked.

"*Brad* and *Brock*, and no." She sighed. "We don't. But Thomas is different. He just moved here with his family a few years ago. It's like initiation into Bayside."

"Initiations last a few years now?"

"Well, no ones moved here since him."

"So, you're saying I'll get jokes played on me like that now? Because I moved here?"

"Well, no. You're different."

My heartbeat began to race. "What do you mean *I'm* different?"

"Thomas, he's well—"

"Black?"

"Don't say it like that, Zachy."

"Like what, Virginia? Want me to say it like the people I heard calling him a *nigger* in there while I walked out?" A playful glimmer shined in her eyes, reflecting off the moonlight. She held back a smirk.

"They were only kidding. We were all just having fun."

"If this is your idea of fun, I don't want any part of it." Rage bubbled within me. I turned to leave but she pulled me back. Her eyes, trained on mine, read impatient, with a little bit of anger. Then she closed them and took a deep breath.

"Your father told me your problem when he visited your

grandmother's house, before you all moved in. He said you were having a hard time accepting who you are. I understand; when I was four, I thought I was a mermaid."

"What are you trying to *say*, Virginia?"

"I'm saying you're not *Black*, Zach, so you can stop trying to act like it. Come on, your haircut, the way you talk, your music choice? You're not in Philly anymore, you don't have to pretend to survive. We accept you as you are."

"As I *am*?" I let out a sarcastic laugh. Virgie nodded her head and tugged on the sides of my shirt. She looked into my eyes and smiled.

"These last few months before graduation that you spend in Bayside, whether good or bad, depends on you. You can hang out with me and my friends, be the coolest guy in Bayside, and ignore all the funny little comments about the *few* Black people who live here, or you can be miserable. It's up to you. But I'm telling you now . . ." She paused and licked her lips sensually. "The first choice comes with perks." Then she stood on her tiptoes and brushed my lips lightly with her own. Her sticky gloss momentarily glued our lips together before she pulled away. "What do you say?" she asked breathlessly. "It's your choice, Zach."

She looked like a Barbie doll. Her face was over-caked with makeup, her smile plastic, and her personality mirrored my father's exactly. How could he even tell her all that? Didn't he understand that where I grew up *is* a product of who I am, and I wasn't ashamed or mad about it? Philly taught me so much about different kinds of people, not just Black ones. It taught me about culture, acceptance, and the beauty in everyone. There wasn't nobody higher than anybody and it wasn't nobody's place to put themselves above anybody else. Virgie closed her eyes and leaned in to kiss me again. I wasn't ready to throw any part of who I was away so I could survive on the valley with her and her friends. I placed my hands on her shoulders and gently pushed her away. Her eyes grew wide.

"Screw you," I said, before walking away.

Virgie repeatedly screaming, "You'll regret this, Zach!" faded farther into the distance as I walked away from the diner. I wasn't gonna follow her back in there and listen to whatever excuses her friends came up with for why dumping hot cheese on someone's face was morally acceptable. What happened to Thomas was the kind of stuff I only ever saw in movies. I low-key waited for a camera crew to run out, but that obviously didn't happen. The fact that no one batted an eyelash to what happened to Thomas surprised me. That meant the twisted moral code in Bayside didn't change much after what happened to the McKulley family. If that was decades ago and things were this bad, I couldn't imagine how much worse life had been for families like the McKulleys on the daily. We were one of four white families living in the neighborhood where I was raised and I never had to fear losing my life because of it.

I found myself walking in the direction of the McKulley's home before my brain could register what I was doing. I needed a place to gather my thoughts that wasn't filled with my father or clones of him. Knowing the people in Bayside, I was positive I wouldn't find them here. The McKulley house was like a living ghost story. As I walked through the empty shell that once was, I couldn't dodge the sick feeling it gave me. I looked up into the sky where a roof that was built to provide shelter for that family would have been— shelter they probably felt would protect them from everything going on in their outside world.

I knew places could be bad; Philly wasn't the best. I knew if I were to have kids, I'd want to keep them safe. I understood why Dad might have moved us, thinking we would be better off here after Mom left. But we weren't. I sat on the dirt-covered ground, resting my back against the wall, and plugged in my earbuds.

*Where the heck did Dad have us move to?*

# Justin

THE WORDS ON THE PAGE BEFORE ME DANCED, WHIRLED, and intertwined with one another. Lines became like the waves that bobbed under the deck down by the waters overlooking the city where I liked to read during the summer. Today, just as the sun rose, I felt like it was a good idea to work on the recruitment questionnaire outside for once instead of being cramped inside surrounded by all the papers on my desk.

The winter air still smelled fresh, like the pine trees Big Al sold at the gas station on Fifth Street around Christmastime. Every year Al would choose ten boys to join him in "chopping" the trees. He said that was when boys became men. When I turned fourteen, I was finally invited to get the trees, and boy was I hype. Thought I was big and bad wrapped in one of Ma's old blankets, sitting in the back of Al's rusty Ford pickup, driving down long roads to chop trees. I'd be lying if I said I wasn't surprised there was no axes in the back of the truck, or inside of it. All Al brought was a wad of cash and told me when I asked that the ax was *inside of him.*

I was even more surprised when we arrived not at a forest, brimming with green life, but a lot where pine trees of all shapes and sizes were wrapped together with wire and placed in large boxes. Big Al made all us boys watch as he made the owner of the lot sell him the pine trees for cheaper than the asking price. That was his idea of chopping the trees down. After we loaded all the trees in the back of the truck that we'd resell in Hamilton, Big Al told us that true manhood wasn't found in the strength of our bodies, but in the weight of our wisdom. He gave us ten percent of the profit he made on those trees. The other guys spent their money on candy cigarettes and video games. I bought a book that held pictures of all these different college campuses around the world inside it. Me and Pri used to spend hours going through it while Ma and Pa were sleeping. They both wanted us to stay in Hamilton for college, but we made other plans together. She had Juilliard in mind for dance. I had Village U for basketball. We promised that we'd help each other out by studying together, and we did at first. Every night we'd stretch all our textbooks out in front of us and go through it until we knew it all.

The pit of my stomach burned with regret. Since Rose's pregnancy, Pri and I stopped being as close. Our late-night study sessions–turned-chats about where we wanted to go after leaving Hamilton became sporadic until they stopped completely. Mostly because Rose needed me to hold her hair back when she threw up or hold her while she cried when her parents were at the church for Night Watch Prayer, which was every night. I missed the way Pri's eyes sparkled when she talked about dancing, I missed watching her dance routines at the Sunlight. I missed her smile. Now we just nodded to each other while getting ready for school and whenever I passed her in the halls, I gave her a quick wave, but that was it. Distraction and anxiety seemed to take over her too; she walked around trapped in her own thoughts. I used to be good at being there for her all the time, knowing what was wrong without asking. Now I snuck away from both Rose and Pri to get by myself. Guilt swallowed me whole, because I knew that avoiding the most important women in my life wasn't good for them. I needed to be their foundation, but I couldn't be if I was shaky myself.

I still looked at that college book some nights picturing myself on Village U's green quad studying a black inventor, chef, or abolitionist that I never knew existed until a professor taught me. I didn't know if I'd ever have that chance now. I tried hard concentrating on the empty page in front of me, and I was, in a way. I read and reread the words on the page so much that I had them memorized. One sentence, seven words. A question. *One* question was all I had to answer.

Why was it so hard?

The answer was my ticket out of Hamilton.

*How have you changed the lives of those around you?*

I thought long and hard about it. I could talk about how I volunteered at the soup kitchen the church held once a month, explain how I tutored the middle school boys in science. I could even write about how I created a little lab in the church basement where I helped elementary boys with experiments and lab reports.

*But that isn't really changing anyone's life.*

This was the first application I'd opened when my guidance counselor sent me ten only weeks after school started. Miss Peggy, Hamilton High's guidance counselor, made all the seniors choose ten colleges they wanted to go to, fill out each application, and send them off before each school's deadline, which varied. Honestly, mostly everyone viewed it as a joke. They'd send for the big schools like Harvard and Yale, fill out the apps just for laughs, but go to the community college, get a trade, or work in one of the mom-and-pop shops until they died. A lot of the people I went to school with were just happy to get that high school diploma; strolling across the stage like they just got the keys to the country or something, not just some empty folder that proved they finished high school.

I wanted something more. Wanted to walk across the stage of one of those big white-people universities. I wanted to grab one of their empty folders. I always imagined that for some reason, it would feel hot, burn my fingertips with a fire that would spark in my heart to continue pursuing *my* dreams. The first one was to get out and do *something*. Something besides basketball, rap, and working in Hamilton. *You live and die in Hamilton* should have been the slogan of the town. That's what everyone did.

The early-morning darkness hovered over me for what seemed like minutes before the sun decided to spark a flame through the clouds, even though I'd been outside for two hours. The grass on the school's football field turned bright green in the new light. It would only be a few moments now until the campus would be filled with people busting on one another, laughter, cussing, and other pointless conversations and gossip. But for now, I needed this morning silence; maybe it would give me some type of inspiration.

I pondered, lifted my pencil, and began to write, my heart burning with each word I pressed onto that paper. My answer was true, truer than anything I placed on my other drafts, at least I could say that. I had in fact changed someone's life permanently, might have ruined it too. Matter of fact, I felt in that moment that it was selfish of me to think that I could go off to college and leave what I did behind. Stupid to think any school would consider me after they found out what I did.

*Typical Hamilton kid,* they'd say. *No self-control.*

I stared at my sentence. Well, if one could even call it a sentence. It was more like a fragment. In big letters covering the full

OTHER SIDE OF THE TRACKS

allotted space for my essay, I wrote: *Knocked Rose Up.*

I affected the life of someone, for good. Like me, Rose had dreams, but because of me, they would be unattainable. I remembered clearly the first day I'd talked to Rose again, after our argument the summer before freshman year. I'd been working up the courage to talk to her three years since she left for camp and finally did one day in class. I couldn't concentrate on the lesson my science teacher was spewing—something about neutrons, or the periodic table, I think. It had to be, it was science class. Or was it English? When I heard him mention Hamlet, I guessed it could also be the Drama in Literature elective I picked up for an easy A. It wasn't like I could focus on any of the classes I was taking junior year at school. For the first time, a similarity lay in every period.

Rose.

She sat in the same spot, three rows ahead of where I was. Had the straightest black hair I'd ever laid eyes on, trailing down her thin shoulders into big curls. She always wore the same fluffy sweater in different colors, pairing it with a pleated skirt that lay just above her legs. As much as I loved her beauty, I also loved the way she talked.

I liked how her voice was low, tinged with a rasp, like one of those jazz singers Mama used to play on the record player she said she'd gotten from a fan after a show—another one of those secret admirers that showered her with gifts just to gain her affection. I was like those admirers, except I wasn't swooning over a stranger who pranced upon some stage surrounded by lights and admiring fans. I'd known Rose since we were born. She was familiar, like the sunrise every morning, and equally untouchable.

When class ended and the screeching of chairs accompanied

the closing statements, I noticed a pale pink nail-polished hand arise straight from the sleeve of an equally pale pink sweater.

"Mr. Valor, I have an announcement for the class." Rose's voice rang above the rest. The bell sounded, but Mr. Valor commanded sternly that everyone wait to hear what Rose had to say.

"You sat through an entire literature lesson," he said. *Ah, Literature. That was the class.* "You can sit a few extra moments to hear what Rose has to say." He stretched a hand toward Rose. "Go on," he instructed.

She stood with a grin and faced our frustrated classmates, all ready to run to the door.

"Don't worry, I'll be very quick," she reassured.

Everyone ignored her, allowing their eyes to glare and pierce through her, as if they could punish her for making them miss the fried chicken that was being served in the cafeteria. It got hard after a few minutes, and no one wanted the thin legs that were served after everyone grabbed the thighs and breasts.

"The church that my daddy owns—"

"Hurry up, Rose, there's chicken today and it's probably getting cold," some guy yelled from the way back row. His flabby stomach stretched so long over his torso that he had to sit sideways just to fit in his desk. A few others shared their agreements and opinions in a far from silent manner.

I turned around to face the boy. "Aight, let her finish. Y'all didn't even give her a second before y'all started saying stuff." The boy rolled his eyes and banged his fist lightly against the desk, a mini tantrum, which caused it to shake.

"*Anyway*," Rose sang, completely unaffected by the boy *and* me standing up for her. "We are putting on a car wash and potluck cookout to raise some money for a summer camp here where kids can get some Word in them, instead of hanging out in the streets with y'all triflin' tails." A few people laughed. "We could really use some food. If y'all are down to donate some of your favorite dishes, we can sell some plates and make some real good money. If you can't cook and you're interested in helping out, we are happy to have some volunteers." Before she could get the word "volunteer" out, my hand shot up.

"I'll volunteer."

Rose grinned and said something in response, but I couldn't hear her. The chairs screeched again all around me and the room filled with shouts and voices. Like cattle, everyone quickly made their way out the doors before they were even dismissed. I walked through the aisles, squeezing in and out of the bodies, straight up to Rose, who was grabbing her notebook from her desk.

"I'll volunteer," I said again when I reached her. She turned around, her emerald eyes burning holes in my stomach, breaking it up into large knots, almost making it impossible for me to say anything else. "I . . . I . . . I'll—"

"Volunteer, I know," Rose responded softly, with a smile. "You got your phone?" I nodded and pulled it from my pocket. She grabbed it from me and began to type; after a few seconds she handed it back to me. "I put my number in there and texted myself, so I'll have yours. I'll send you all the info later tonight." Before I could grab the courage to say anything else, Rose had walked out with her friends and I stood alone in Mr. Valor's third period Drama in Literature Course, holding on to my phone, which burned evidence of promise into my palm. When I reached the fundraiser, the place was already packed with what looked like the entire town. I even recognized some people from my class who were probably forced to come by their parents. There were white picnic tables set up, covered with everything from cupcakes and soul food to clothes and pies. I spotted her blowing bubbles with the children playing on the lawn in front of the church's sign: *Hamilton Community Church est. 1868 "Keep Christ in Hamilton."*

They ran around the sign, some blowing bubbles, some popping them; everyone grinning from ear to ear. I couldn't help but notice how long her legs were in the blue jeans she wore, or the little sparkle of a diamond that shone from her belly button when she'd lifted her arms above her head to pop stray bubbles that stretched too far for the children to reach. She was in the midst of blowing a lime-green bubble gun when she caught my eye. My heart raced against my chest, as it did every time we made eye contact over the years. It was funny, I could keep my cool around other girls but when it came to Rose it was different; just a glance from her sent my adrenaline soaring.

I watched as she handed the bubble gun to a little boy nearby and waved; I responded, "Hi," but she was too far away to hear me, so I settled on waving back in response.

"I'm glad you could make it," she said when she reached me, her grin sending the dimples in her cheeks to the surface. She had more of them than she did when we were kids.

"You have two extra," I found myself saying before I could shut my mouth. She lifted an eyebrow, clearly confused.

"Two extra?" she repeated.

"Good! Mr. Justin Collins is here. I need you two adding my homemade whipped cream to the sweet potato pie slices I cut up in the kitchen," Sister Billings said, interrupting. Thankfully. She pushed us through the crowd of people browsing and selling behind the outside tables into the kitchen.

It was empty.

The voices of the crowd were muffled when we got inside. A bowl of whipped cream lay next to pie slices scattered around a table. Sister Billings handed us two ice cream scoopers. I heard everything she was saying—"add just a smoof of cream, no more no less"—but couldn't keep my eyes off Rose. She stood with her hands in her back pockets, her curled ponytail releasing fly-aways along her jaw and neck. My fingers tingled to tuck them behind her unpierced ears.

"Okay," Rose said, clapping her hands together. "Let's get started."

I looked around the room—hadn't even noticed that Sister Billings left. It was just me and Rose alone for the first time in years.

"You all right, Justin?" she asked.

Honestly, I wasn't, but I was pretty good at pretending to be. I rubbed my sweaty hands together.

"I'm Gucci, why? Do I look nervous or something?" I cursed myself silently for saying "nervous."

"A little," Rose admitted. "But Sister Billings make *everybody* nervous, even Jesus a little." She grinned at her lame joke, and I began to feel a bit more comfortable. I missed those jokes.

"How much did she say she wanted on each piece of pie?" she asked when we dressed our hands with the gloves that lay on the table, next to the not-so-subtle sign written by Sister Billings that demanded we use them.

"A smoof," I responded.

"A smoof," Rose repeated, seriously contemplating. "Tell me, how much is a smoof anyway?"

I couldn't help but burst into laughter. "Beats me. How about this much?" I dipped my scooper into the whipped cream and lay it on the top of the pie.

Rose sucked her tongue. "Nope. I think that's too much. You know, we gotta eat that one now. It's a reject." She smirked, reaching over to grab two plastic spoons when I caught a whiff of her perfume. It was the one I smelled when she walked past me in the hallways or sat in front of me in class. Like fresh-picked cherries and vanilla. I paused. Everything stood still. Even the oxygen around me quit its job of providing breath to my lungs. I could see how long her eyelashes were when I was this close—the little beauty mark that lay right above her thick lips. All I could focus on was her lips. The lips I only kissed once before. The ones I ached to kiss again.

"Justin," she whispered out of the lips I couldn't tear my eyes away from. The lips inching their way toward mine.

The sound of heavy feet making their way across the floor pulled us apart.

"And what are you doing?"

We both looked in the direction of the doorway to see Sister Billings, hands on her hips. The frown lines that already dug into her normal face stretched even lower. Rose grabbed the ice cream scooper she somehow let slip from her hands.

"I . . . well we were . . . I mean I—"

"You," Sister Billings spat walking up to us slowly, as if we were hiding something. "You," she repeated, glaring between Rose and me. "You do you not understand the meaning of a *smoof* of cream."

She gave the word "smoof" an emphasis as if it were an actual measurement. We tried our best not to crack up as she "smoofed" four or five pies in a row, making sure for each bit of cream she added, to give an audible *smoof* from her lips.

"You almost made me laugh straight in her face," Rose said when Sister Billings left for the second time.

I smirked. "Yeah, well, you kept mouthing 'smoof' each time she said it."

"Because it was hilarious," Rose said, laughing as she continued to decorate the pies. "What made me mad was her taking the reject for her and my dad to eat. I swear everyone treats him like he's some kind of king or something."

"He *is* the only reverend we got in Hamilton."

"I know but still. He's still a dad. He tells lame jokes in front of the cute guys I like."

I had been laughing before but paused when she'd said this.

"What's going on with you?" she asked.

I looked down. "What do you mean?"

"I don't know, it's just *every* time we're in the middle of talking it be all normal, but then you zone out on me." She dropped the scooper into the empty plastic bowl. "Look, Justin," she said, turning to face me, "I wanted to say that I'm sorry."

I was so surprised I almost dropped the pie I was working on.

"You're sorry?" I asked, surprised. "What for?"

She held her left hand over her right elbow and let her gaze fall to her pale pink ballet flats. "For almost ruining your chance on the basketball team that summer. I should have never stuck my nose in your business, it wasn't my place."

"I was mad, yeah. But only for like two hours. I went to your house the next morning to talk, but you already left for summer camp."

She lifted her wide eyes in surprise, then punched me on the arm.

"*Ow*."

"So, you mean I haven't been talking to you for *three* years because I thought you still hated me? You were my best friend!" She hit me again.

"*Ow!*"

"Ugh. I can't believe this!" She held her head in her hands. "Justin! What the heck?"

"Don't blame me!" I exclaimed, rubbing the feeling back into my arm. "I thought you hated me after what I did to you. Thought that's why you left for camp."

Rose crossed her arms. "I left because I was *forced* to go to summer camp. My parents thought it was a good idea to get me out of Hamilton. Idle kids in a city with nothing to do start acting real crazy—"

"And cutting a fool." I finished the rhyme for her. "Ma used to say the same thing."

Rose laughed to herself. "So, all this time we thought we hated each other and we was both thinking it was our fault."

I smiled. "Looks like it."

Rose allowed herself to fall into my arms. At first my breath caught, but after a few short moments, my heart began to beat in rhythm with hers.

"You smell like you," she whispered into my shirt. I wrapped my arms around her waist.

"I missed you too, Rose."

"Would you think I was weird if I sort of rigged the volunteer schedule to make us work together?" I grunted in question, so Rose continued. "We were separate originally. I was supposed to be on the clothing separation duty with Jordan and *you* were supposed to be in cleanup crew. But I traded our jobs with the two people originally working for Sister Billings. No one in their right mind wants to work with her."

I didn't care if I had to work for Genghis Khan. I was with Rose again, actually hugging her. I would have given anything in the world for this.

"I wasn't interested in volunteering for no other reason but being with you," I whispered. Rose pulled away slowly and looked into my eyes.

"Really?" she breathlessly asked.

There I was again, staring at her lips; I couldn't help it. She inched them closer to mine and I filled in the gap between them until we were close, so close, it felt as if the breath exiting her body was all I had to breathe with. When I kissed her that day, I knew without a shadow of a doubt that I loved Rose still just as much as I did on the Ferris wheel three years ago.

"What, we don't recycle anymore?" Rose's velvet voice sent my head spinning. I walked into the double doors leading to the inside of Hamilton High and threw away the Snow Fairy's questionnaire, snapping out of yet another memory bent on driving me crazy, back to the present.

I hadn't noticed she was behind me and before I could stop her, she was reaching inside of the freshly changed garbage bag to grab the only piece of paper hanging out at the bottom. I watched her aim it for the recycling bin next to the trash, but Village University's name showed through. Her face tensed. Her eyebrows grew so close together, they'd almost become one. She looked at me, and her eyes said it all; she was asking me why I threw it away. She looked slightly amused, almost as if it were a joke. When I didn't respond with laughter, a concern clouded her pupils. I didn't want to explain. She began to unwrap the paper in her hand, but thankfully, someone interrupted. It was Carlos. He grabbed my shoulders from behind with his bony hands.

"Arooo!" Carlos wailed loudly.

Then the locker banging began. "*Arooo!*" the crowd responded all around us. The cheerleaders made their way out of the groups where they chatted and gossiped to the middle of the hallway and began their routine of hip shaking.

"*The lions roar aroo! Ah-Ah-Aroo! We ain't afraid of you, what-what you do. We will win, we will fight, and claim the courts with all our might!. Hear. Our. Battle cry. Aroo!*"

The cheer continued to repeat itself over and over again, each time reaching farther to the back of the halls.

"*Later,*" Rose mouthed, stuffing the balled paper into the pocket of her oversized cardigan. She'd been wearing a lot of those lately. Before I could object, she disappeared in the crowds.

"Jay-man!" Carlos exclaimed. "We play Harvest Creek Saturday night! One more game closer to the finals. How's the team captain feeling?" His fingers dug into my shoulders as he worked rough circles into them.

I shrugged him off. "I'm feeling like you need to up your defense or HC's gonna get a lot of baskets."

Carlos rolled his eyes. Together we walked to Calculus.

"Aye, c'mon, man. Lighten up! You know we can beat Harvest Creek with blindfolds and no hands."

"Still," I continued. "They got that one kid on their team now that's six-foot-seven. We need to watch out for him."

"So what?" Carlos scoffed. "If you kick a giraffe at the ankles, it'll fall."

I narrowed my eyes at my five-foot-five friend. "And where'd you hear that from?"

Carlos shrugged. "I don't know, but that don't matter, man."

I couldn't help but chuckle.

"You know we gonna win," Carlos continued. "We got you on the team." He gave my back a playful smack. "And after we *do* win, we gonna turn up at my house. My parents are visiting my mom's great-aunt in the boonies for her birthday, so I'll have the house all to myself. Deondre is bringing the booze, Jay is bringing the chicks, yo, this is gonna be a celebration party for the books." They made their way through the halls, past some nerd kid buying some pills from some other dude. Carlos smacked hands with the dude making the deal.

I shook my head. "You really think I didn't see that?"

Carlos rolled his eyes. "You the only one that ain't stressed about senior year. I'm freaking out. Some of us need some stuff to calm us down. That's why my folks left me home while they visit family. They wanted me to stay back and study. If I stay back again, my mom's gonna have my butt or, worse, my pops is gonna make me get my GED and work for him changing oil forever." He shuddered at the thought. "Man, I've been saving up to get to Hamilton Community College so when I graduate, I can open my own garage here and put my pops out of business." He held up a hand for me to high-five. I left him hanging.

"You got big dreams, Carlos, but when Coach Hill does drug tests you gonna be screwed." I opened the door to the classroom and took my normal seat all the way in the back.

"Or I'll buy piss from some kid and pass the test like we always do."

"Like *you* do," I corrected. Carlos fell into his seat, a whiff of strong cologne filling the air around us.

"See, that's why you never get laid. You smell like somebody's grandpa," Deondre, who was already seated next to Carlos, said from behind his desk.

I laughed. "He ain't lying, man. You stink."

Carlos shrugged them off. "No, y'all wrong. I smell like *Une femme folle de femmes*." Me and Deondre met him with blank stares. "A Manly Field of Women," he translated. "It's my dad's cologne. Y'all wouldn't know nothing about it with y'all dumb tails. It's French."

"*It's Fwench*," Deondre mocked. "And you a virgin." He cackled loudly. I couldn't help but chuckle. My friends were nuts.

"Whatever, man. I told you I slept with that one chick."

"Cows don't count," Deondre said in between laughs. Carlos shrunk in his seat and crossed his arms.

I tried avoiding Rose for the entire first half of the school day. I wasn't in the mood to explain anything to her about why I threw away that recruitment questionnaire. It was easy avoiding her in the halls, but as soon as lunch shot by, it was a lost cause. I sat with the team in hopes that Rose would maybe see I wanted to focus on the game, but she squeezed her body in between Jay and Tyree.

"Hey, guys!" she greeted, grinning. I sighed and she glared at me.

"Wassup, Ma," Jay returned with his slick grin. "You look nice today."

Rose winked at him. "Thanks." Then she went back to glaring at me. I could honestly care less. If she was mad at me, maybe it would give me a few days to myself so I could really think. I ignored her for a few moments as I went over plays with the guys at the table. Even though Tyree was on the football team, he always sat with us before a game, offering ideas on what we could do to win.

"So, the dude is six-eight, right?" Tyree asked, after taking a sip of his chocolate milk.

"Six-seven," Carlos corrected.

"Aight, six-seven, which is even better. I mean he got some height on all y'all but that shouldn't scare you. I'm sure with the right defense, y'all can run out the clock before he has a chance to shoot *or* make him throw to one of his other teammates who you know suck. They so bad, y'all can beat them blindfolded and without hands."

"That's what I was telling Justin!" Carlos exclaimed. "But whose gonna guard him?"

"Me," Jay volunteered. "I'm the biggest dude on the team. I can guard him."

Tyree shook his head. "Nah, if you guard him the way you usually guard in practice, he's gonna get fouls out of you and then you gonna eventually get kicked out the game. Besides, we need you in offense."

"How about Justin?" Everyone stared at Rose. She let her yogurt spoon drop from her mouth to the table, her face flushed. "I don't know much about basketball, but Justin's good at being gentle."

A few guys laughed and my face heated. Tyree lifted a hand and they quieted.

"Apart from that sounding highly suggestive, she might have a point. Justin never fouls anybody and still maintains a good line of defense that will run out the clock. He might even steal."

"I told you I got it," Jay reassured, but Tyree ignored him. He bore his bright brown eyes straight into mine.

"What do you say?"

I shrugged. "I think I can do it."

Tyree nodded. "Aight, then y'all gonna win." He gently shouldered Rose. "Nice suggestion."

"I *am* always right," Rose said sounding more smart-mouth then she did sincere. I rolled my eyes and pretended not to hear her. "That's why Justin should come to me when he's going through his *stuff*. Like attempting to quit something he always wanted to do because a trial opposes him."

The boys picked up on the heat radiating between the two of us.

"Ah-ah!" Jay exclaimed, breaking out into one of his whack rhymes. *"Trouble on the island of commitment? The girl mad at the dude, and he don't know what to do-foo!"* Everyone rolled their eyes.

"Look, everyone." Tyree glanced at his watch. "We got twenty minutes of the lunch period left, I think we can squeeze in some practice time before we practice again after school." A few of the boys whined, upset that their Friday night plans were gonna get destroyed, but Tyree ignored them. "Jus, you stay here, man, you need some time to yourself to get into the zone." He winked at me when everyone followed him away from the table.

I wasn't thankful for the alone time; I wanted to go with them.

When the table was fully clear, Rose removed the crumpled paper from her pocket and pushed it over to me. When I didn't grab at it or say anything, she cleared her throat just staring, not turning away for one second.

"What do you want from me, woman?" I finally asked in a hushed whisper. "You're *pregnant*. What am I supposed to do?"

"I don't know, go to *college*? It's always been your dream to get out of here and go to a university someplace far away. Don't let me stop you from doing that."

"Rose, you don't understand, aight? Let's face it, this dream of going to college is complicated now. This freaking questionnaire asked me what I did to change someone's life. I couldn't think of anything else than getting you pregnant. What would it look like if I went to school and left you and the . . . I can't go to school and leave you here by yourself."

"You won't! Wherever you go, that's where I'll be, okay? We can rent an apartment off campus."

"How, Rose? No one's going to support us when they find out I got you pregnant. Not your dad or my ma."

"I'll get a job, you'll get a job, we'll make it work, Justin." Silence. "Justin." Silence. "Justin Edward Collins, look at me." Then I did. Which was a mistake. One look in her eyes made me feel like I could trust her with everything. Like every single word that fell from her lips was completely true, as if they were already happening. "We can make this work," she reassured. "We ain't letting go of our dreams and if you need to live out yours until I can live out mine, I'm cool with that. You know why? Because I love you. I love you so much and so does our child. So, stop trying to carry this alone 'cause it ain't about you anymore." Her voice fell into a gentle whisper, and she placed her hand on her stomach. "It's about *all three of us.*"

I closed my eyes and took a deep breath. "You think I still got a chance?"

Rose grinned, nodding in sincerity.

"I know you do. You'll get your answer to that question. I'll help. You gon' get that scholarship and become a famous basketball player just like you always dreamt. I'm not letting you give up on your dreams. We in this together."

I let my hand lie over the crumpled questionnaire in front of me and looked at Rose. Then at her stomach. Half of my heart said it wasn't possible, but the other half believed everything she said could be.

"We need to start looking at apartments," I finally said, dragging the paper back toward me. She clapped her hands together and leaned across the table, planting a light kiss on my lips. I pulled her in deeper. Kissing Rose made me feel as if nothing could ever go wrong; when I kissed her, I never wanted to pull away.

"We gon' be okay," she whispered when we pulled apart for air. "We gon' make it. I promise." Then she gently pressed her lips back onto me.

# Capri

HAMILTON HIGH WAS LIKE THE ANIMAL KINGDOM. AT THE top were the carnivores, which are the athletes. These people walked around wearing discolored letterman jackets given to our school from Bayside. They always gave us their old stuff, like hand-me-downs from an older sibling. *We should be grateful for the donations.* Well, that's what our principal said since we didn't get a lot of funding from the government because we're such a small town. We got their used, ripped, and highlighted-in schoolbooks when they moved to electronic tablets and laptops, all their chalk when they got rid of their puke-green chalkboards for smart boards, and their sports gear. Trust me, you could tell the lettermans they gave us were old. The once-bleached white sleeves are now discolored to a dark beige and the Bayside Tigers logo was tackily made over to look like a lion, since that was our mascot. But the one thing I liked about the carnivores is that they didn't let it bother them.

They wore their letterman jackets all proud and called the tiger stripes on the lion's face war paint—the paint that fueled them to win against all the teams they played, including Bayside. Girls walked around with their boyfriends' jackets on, like they were brand-new or something, even though they weren't. The Bayside Tigers didn't let us forget that either when we played them, but it was no skin off our backs. We showed them who is really the best.

The carnivores got the first pick in *everything*; the hot food at lunch, the seats in the back of the class where it's impossible to catch them texting each other, and the automatic in to all the parties. Which is why I hated the fact that Justin was one of them. He played basketball for Hamilton since middle school and he was the best on the team. He played effortlessly, gliding across the courts as if he was on skates or something. He used to go to the parties and come home all late, and when I asked where they were, he never gave me no address; told me he didn't want me around that crowd. He stopped going to them in junior year after he and Rose got together. Justin wasn't *Justin* anymore. When he and Rose first started dating, he still made time for me. We'd joke around, go out to dinner sometimes, and look through this book he brought with our dream colleges in it. He'd even come to the Sunlight sometimes to watch me dance, sitting among the audience of record covers, cheering me on, promising that he'd always be my biggest fan. Now it was different. He walked around like a zombie, completely void of the life that used to shine in his eyes. He still carried around his books like always but read them like their pages are the only source of water in a volcano. On top of all that, he always whispered on the phone with Rose late at night or rushed to her place after school and on the weekends when he wasn't at practice. I couldn't tell you how many times he's missed dinner.

I didn't even remember the last time we shared more than three sentences with each other. Even though the carnivores at school never paid me no mind, they stopped me in the halls asking me what was going on with my brother. My response was always the same: "Why don't you just ask him?" Even though I knew that was easier said than done. I mean, I hadn't even asked him what's been going on. I had too much to worry about with myself, like Camp Sharp and dealing with Ma being disappointed if she found out I applied. Plus, it wasn't like he'd tell me anyways. Justin treated me like a little kid in need of a chaperone. He'd just stopped coming to my room to make sure I said my prayers before bed, even though I kind of missed it. I missed any form of communication with him. As much as I don't care about the carnivores, I miss seeing Justin with them. Grazing the halls with light shining bright in his eyes, with his friend group, right next to their king, Tyree Thompson.

He's the first-string quarterback. Tyree was one of the few around Hamilton who's vocal about wanting to get out. He stopped playing basketball after Justin joined the team, because he said Justin was too good to be on the same team with. Tyree thought he was better off getting a scholarship for an out-of-state college if he did what he was the best at, instead of trying to compete with Justin, who was too nice to play around with. One time, in freshman year, I accidentally bumped into him in the hallway. We both dropped our books. He helped me pick up mine first. When he handed them to me, he smiled. His smile wasn't perfect. His teeth were big, and the front ones overlapped one another slightly, but when he smiled his light brown eyes seemed to smile too. They squinted until they almost vanished. No one smiles that hard, that sincerely.

One thing I always liked about Tyree is that he never took his place on the Hamilton High hierarchy seriously. He treated everyone nice, never stuck no dudes up against lockers for their sneakers or fought. Never walked around the halls, spinning lacy panties around his finger like the other dudes on the teams did, and he never treated nobody who was lower than him like they didn't belong. In fact, he was kind of one of them in a way too.

Lemme explain: The bottom of the food chain is the herbivores who basically eat whatever is lying on the ground. They're the deer and the rabbits of the school, the ones who run down the halls and duck behind trash cans at the first sight of a carnivore walking by. They're the math and spelling geeks who get to go to Philadelphia and New York City to compete in the Math Olympics and spelling bees twice a year. People pick on them and throw them against lockers and stuff, but at least they get out of Hamilton sometimes. One of them even left for good: Kenan McPherson, class of 1989. He went to medical school in NYC before dying in a freak bus accident the day of his graduation. He's another one of the many examples given as to why it's dangerous to leave. But even that's never scared Tyree. He said he wanted to be a brain surgeon when our guidance counselor called all the upperclassmen in the auditorium and started talking about how all our dreams were possible.

I thought about my dancing when she said that. But I remembered how it wasn't as easy as she tried to make it. She said it like family didn't play a role into what you wanted to do. Like their words and negativity didn't start a war in your mind against what you wanted for yourself. She acted like we lived in a world where everyone was okay with us following our dreams, where we didn't have to listen to the opinions of the people who sacrificed their lives to raise their grandchildren instead of enjoying their old age. Like we didn't owe them something. When Tyree rose his hand high and volunteered to tell everyone how he was gonna accomplish his dreams, I couldn't breathe. The way he talked about his desires was how I remembered Essie talking about what dancing in New York did to her. When he approached the mic, the whole auditorium got quiet. Their king was talking, and everyone wanted to hear what he was about to say.

"I wanted to be a surgeon since I could remember." His voice echoed around the auditorium when he spoke through the mic. "When I was six, my mama used to drop me off at the library with a bagged lunch and make me stay there all day while she worked. I started reading the little kids' books at first, but after that, I got bored. I wanted more than just choo-choo trains and talking rabbits. I watched this older kid reading this book with a skeleton on it. After he put it down and walked out, I picked it right up. Ah, y'all wouldn't believe how nice this book was." His eyes glimmered with this hope, this faith in something that we had no idea about.

"It told me how the body worked. Like, I mean, it had *everything*. I didn't know we had so many systems working together that keep us breathing, y'know? So, I kept reading books like that; I went from reading fourth grade science books to fifth, then sixth, then eighth, then tenth. I learned about why my heart beat so quick when I ran; what was happening when I played sports. Everything is so connected, like when I move my arms." He lifted his arms and stretched his hands above his head. "My brain knows I'm about to do it like seconds before my limbs react." He laughed at this like it newly amazed him, even though he'd known it already. "I want to connect my knowledge of the body to help people. I want to operate on men, women, and children and help them feel better and I'm gonna do it. I'm gonna get out of here and go all around the world and operate on people. I won't forget about y'all, though, I'll send postcards." Even though he laughed at this, everyone was quiet.

The carnivores were confused and herbivores awestruck. Tyree walked away from the mic and straight to his seat in the carnivore section with that huge smile on his face. He was unbothered that he may have tarnished his rep. He sat with his hands folded behind his head for the rest of the assembly and when it closed, was still right at the top of the food chain, where he belonged. Whenever I saw someone so sure of themselves, I envied it. If only I could be so open about my dream of dancing for a living with Ma. I could stand with my head high, my shoulders back, feet planted, close-fisted, wide-eyed, and voice booming: "Ma, I don't want to go to no college for nursing. I wanna be just like Essie, I wanna dance onstage and there's nothing you can do to stop me."

If only I had the drive of a carnivore.

See, I'm an omnivore, which means I'm one of the average people. I'm the girl who got the average face with the average body that don't get hit on while she walks down the hallway. I'm usually hidden in my oversized flannels and squeaky Converse that I've worn since seventh grade, but that's cool. It's not a *bad* thing. I'm not bullied because I'm no outright nerd, but at the same time, I'm not the center of attention either.

Around here, no one pauses to look *at* me, they just see *through* me, but I'm used to it. When I was ten and the church's annual Hamilton Sweetie Pie Pageant came around, I didn't receive a personal invitation to compete. Ma went off when she found out. She dragged me with her to Sister Phyllis's home to tell her off because she was head of the committee. Sister Phyllis apologized to Ma, said she forgot about me. Yes, you got it. The daughter of one of the most famous Broadway performers, the one who was born in Hamilton and attended church every Sunday with her since she was born, was invisible. Ma signed me up for the pageant right there without asking if I wanted to, and not surprisingly, when everyone who didn't place was given their ribbons for participation, they were exactly one ribbon one short. Guess who they forgot?

Nothing's changed to this day. Most people still call me "little girl" instead of Capri, and I'm not asked to sing every Sunday in front of everyone like Rose or expected to win every basketball game like Justin. When they walk by me, I get a small smile, someone asks me how Justin's doing, or they want me to pass a message to Ma or Pa for them. It's never, "What's new, Capri?" or "Why are you walking around with tights and ballet slippers when it's dead winter, Capri?" To everyone in Hamilton, I'm just the youngest Collins kid—the quiet one who never surprises anyone. But that's the best thing about being invisible in Hamilton; I can have a secret life that belongs just to me. I get to decide who I let into it too.

No one follows me to the Sunlight when I sneak away after church. I don't even have to worry about no one trying to hook me up with their sons like my best friend, Perry, has to. I've always known who Paris Kilmann, or Perry as everyone calls her, was all along; growing up, her mama always put her in the prettiest dresses at church and everyone liked taking her photos because she's light skin with green eyes. She won the pageant the year Ma made me join, and when she saw that I got no ribbon, she walked right up to me, and placed her crown on my head. That's the only time I got a bunch of pictures taken of me, and it was only because she was by my side. After the pageant, she told me I could keep it because the diamonds on it were fake. I still have it on my nightstand at home. We've been inseparable since. After we graduated from middle school, we ended up on different levels of the hierarchy. It's because Perry's got the perfect-shaped body: double Ds and a popping butt. She doesn't need to be a cheerleader to get in with the carnivores; her looks and confidence do it for her.

Even though her eyes are naturally green, she's always wearing different colored contacts. One day she has blue eyes, the next pink, the next gray. I think she got tired of people asking her where her green eyes came from since her parents' eyes are both dark brown. I mean, how is she supposed to know? Anyways, now no one barely says anything about them because she always covers them up. Her place on the hierarchy didn't change things for us. We're still just as close. I can literally tell her everything. She's the only one besides Justin and Easy that I let into my secret world. She knows how I love dancing and she's the only other person I can really talk to about Essie and my real feelings. We both already got our futures planned too; if I make it big in the dance world after Ma okays it, she's gonna be my manager. We're both gonna get out of Hamilton and light up the world like the sky in Bayside.

I just had to stay focused on graduating from Hamilton High. Until then, I'd have another year and a half of hiding my omnivore self away in the musty smelling library where I stayed between classes, counting down the hours until the bell rang. It was the perfect place to get away from all the noise going on in the halls, except when certain people decided to grace me with their presence.

"Hey, Pri!" Perry practically yelled, sauntering up to me in knee-length bright red boots, skinnies, and an extra-low-cut sweater. I shushed her.

"Per, calm down, we're in the library."

She sat in the seat in front of me and smirked. "Pri, no one ever really silent in no library. It's a place to make out with ya man." She pointed behind her to a carnivore couple in full lip lock against bookshelves piled high with Bayside's used, ripped, and outdated books. Their letterman jackets were thrown a few inches away from them, and it looked like her pants would be too if they kept it up.

"That's just nasty," I said.

Per just grinned at me. "You just mad cuz you don't got no man."

I rolled my eyes. "Yeah, sorry, I'm not like you and got one every other month."

"Keeping them in rotation like clockwork." Perry got lost in doing her body rolls, but thankfully, she stopped. "Look, I be telling you, all you gotta do is ditch the big clothes and straighten that tight behind 'fro of yours and you would have a man. You got the dancer's body already, all you need is—"

I wasn't in the mood for the *Capri needs a makeover* talk from Perry that I've been getting since freshman year. I wasn't worried about my looks; I mean, I was pretty much fine the way I was. I had my mother's wild hair; tight curls too tough to maintain. I mean, even *she* cut it really short to control it. But I just brushed mine back in a ponytail every day. Who was I tryna impress? The dudes that walked around with brushes in their pockets, carried lip balm everywhere, and had like ten girls fighting over their attention, just to knock one up and ruin her life? I had a future to get to, and I wasn't trying to get sidetracked. Plus, I had nothing in common with the Hamilton guys. I mean, dating someone she grew up with never worked out for Essie. Why would it for me?

I don't remember what my daddy looks like. I mean, I got one picture of him. In the picture, Essie, me, and Justin are hugged up at a summer barbecue. I'm wearing a yellow dress and Justin a yellow bow tie with a gray suit and chauffeur's hat. I can only see the back of my father's head. He's wearing a white T-shirt, blue jeans, and muddy work boots. His shirt got some oil stains on it from fixing Pa's truck with him all day. I know that 'cause Pa told me that whenever my daddy came over, they always tried getting his '39 pickup to run again. It's still parked in the worn-down garage next to the house. Sometimes, I go inside and just run my hands across the truck's hood just 'cause he touched it once. It's like, in some way I'm holding his hand or something. I know he had locs in his hair, real long ones because they are toppled on his head in the picture. I can't see his face 'cause he's reaching down inside of some food pan. Funny, when I look at the picture, I can see the mac and cheese in the pan but I can't see my own daddy.

Ma said he was a wino.

He died from alcohol poisoning apparently a little bit after his twenty-first birthday. That's what Pa told me and Justin when he was thirteen and I was twelve. Pa said he got mama pregnant with Justin in her sophomore year of high school and with me just one year later in her junior year. He was in and out of our lives and unstable just like Essie was, but toward the end he tried to do right and joined the Air Force after graduating Hamilton High. Pa said despite all his faults, he was a good man, but I already knew that.

I think Essie knew that too.

See, when we was cleaning out me and Essie's room after she passed, I found something under a loose floorboard: a small box filled with a bunch of letters. I hid it from everybody in the room. I just put it back and sat in that spot until everything else of Essie's was dumped away by Ma. That night, as I lay under Essie's quilt, I read the letters my father wrote to Essie from his Air Force base. Essie talked about how easy things were when they met, how she missed him living in Hamilton, how she wished they could have married before he went off and then be together. She wished he could see her shows; she was getting so famous in New York. He told her about perception. I'll never forget that letter. It's been what keeps me sane here in this overcast town.

*My Dearest Essie,*

*Darling, I know that you long for us to all be together; but what would that do to your free soul? If I were to come to Hamilton and we were to move to New York with Pri and Justin, I would long for the sky. If you and the children lived on an Air Force base with me, you would only long for the stage. (Trust me, there are no stages here.) We are doing what is best for one another right now. I love you too much to make you stay here with me.*

*Darling, your perception is what matters most. Do not look at our lives as a mere separation; look at the sky and let that remind you of why we wanted to go. Do you see the gray clouds that hover over Hamilton? That sky has pushed us to grow wings.*

*We got tired of looking at the clouds, we wanted to experience the brightness of what lay above them. We both have. You are danc- ing, acting, and singing over an audience who adores you almost as much as I. You are causing the world to fall in love with you more and more with every passing day. You have become their bright sun. I am exploring the corners of the world as I always dreamt. Darling, I am physically able to see the sky above the clouds we were born under and honey, it is bright!*

*Every time you look at the sky remember that.*

*I will keep my promise to you. After I complete my time, I will be the father to our children that I never had. I will teach Justin all about planes and how they work and Capri about the rainforests of Africa. I will be your personal pilot and fly you wherever your talent takes you and our children will come along too. They won't have to live in Hamilton under the gray skies. They will be able to know what lies above the clouds and our dreams will give them wings. Until that day, remember to never give up. Hardships are soil, bad days are the sun, and sweat and tears give nourishing water to a seed that will birth a beautiful field where you can reap those dreams a hundred times over.*

*Forever,*

*Justin Jacob Collins*

Justin never talks about Dad, maybe because he doesn't remember him, doesn't want to remember him, or just doesn't care. After Ma and Pa told us all about him, Justin just said, "Is that all?" and then got up and went to play basketball with his friends. As much as I've wanted him to see Dad's letters, I keep them for myself. I don't need another person talking negative about something I cherish. Justin doesn't need to appreciate him either; he's already got his blood soaring through his veins, just like I got Essie's. We can't do nothing about that. Our parents saw the world from above the clouds and that's how we both see it. It's just so hard to do that sometimes.

"Capri? Girl, you even listening to what I'm saying?" Perry snapped her fingers in front of my face. I blinked away my thoughts and ventured back into reality. Books. Shelves. Carnivores making out. All right, I'm in the library.

"Yeah, I am," I lied. "I was listening to what you were saying."

Perry shook her head. "Look, Imma let you go; I'm supposed to be meeting Kalif in science section in like three minutes to hook up. But I came here to ask you"—she lowered her voice—"if you opened . . ."

"No, I didn't open it yet," I said, referring to the letter from Camp Sharp. She huffed exaggeratingly. "Hold ya breath, Perry, you gonna need that for that make-out session you about to have with Kalif."

"Seriously, Pri? Stop trying to distract me with your sorry sense of humor. You made me and Easy insane convincing you to send your audition tape in. What do you mean you didn't open it?"

"I did not make y'all *insane*. I just don't wanna look at it yet."

Her phone, which was sitting on the table, buzzed and a text from Kalif read, I'm in the library now. Omw to the science section. But she wasn't paying any attention, she was staring straight at me.

"You been carrying that letter around with you everywhere, haven't you? It's in your backpack right now, ain't it?"

Before I could snatch at the backpack next to me, she grabbed it. I screamed loud before I realized it. "No, no. *You can't open it!*" I grabbed at my backpack, but Perry was already working on the zipper.

"Yes, I can, Pri; if I don't who will?" she yelled back.

The carnivores, mid make-out, had the nerve to shush us. We both rolled our eyes at them simultaneously. While Perry was still glaring at them, I snatched my backpack from her and tucked it under the table on my lap.

"I'll open it at the right time. Right now is not it."

Perry looked away from the couple.

"Don't you wanna see if you made it to the next level?" Her voice echoed around the building. I shushed her and she gestured to a guy behind us who was watching a rap video with the volume on full blast, without headphones.

"Yes," I admitted. "I do. But I don't want to be disappointed."

Her phone vibrated again, then again, then two times more, but she ignored it. She stretched out her hand, staring right into my eyes. I sighed and dug into my backpack. I pulled out the envelope. The very thin and small envelope.

"It's so thin, Perry," I whispered. "Acceptance letters aren't that thin."

I felt it. I'd felt it too many times. I wasn't ready for rejection. She didn't respond; only kept holding out her hand. I finally handed it to her.

"Don't tell me," I said, covering my eyes.

I heard the tearing of paper and then silence.

"Pri," she finally whispered.

"I know," I said, my eyes still covered. "I'm not as good a dancer as the other people there."

"Pri."

"I know, Perry. I ain't as good as Essie either. She would've made it in a flash."

"Pri."

"I'm just gonna be a nurse like Ma wants."

"Pri, if you'd open ya eyes you'd see what I'm calling ya name for."

Slowly I took a hand down from one eye, and then the other. And in little letters, the littlest letters that would be the biggest news I'd ever read, stated right at the top of the page:

*Capri Collins, welcome to part two of the audition process for Camp Sharp.*

# Zach

**WHEN I WALKED BY THE MCKULLEYS' HOUSE TO SCHOOL** the next morning, I couldn't shake the weird pull I had to the town next door. It was almost like keeping quiet about Hamilton was this unspoken rule that everyone in Bayside abided by. I tried asking my father over breakfast about Hamilton and he almost spit out his milk—tried changing the subject casually to sports or some crap. The mystery of Hamilton crept upon me, connecting to my shadow, pleading with me to learn more about it. I was super curious, so like any normal twenty-first centurion, I googled it.

*And I found a lot.*

But it was mostly stuff about the past, like how the town was established, and this Micah Hamilton guy that the town was named after. When I found out who lived in the town from its website's "About Me" section, well, that's what sparked my curiosity and also when everything began to change. The section read:

> We in Hamilton would like to personally thank you for visiting our town's website! To some, Hamilton is just a little town on a big map. But to us, Hamilton is a jewel in a vast ocean; a culture filled with music, art, and a group of citizens who dwell together in harmony. Hamilton was named after Micah Hamilton in the year 1868. Along with a group of two thousand

six hundred ex-enslaved, Hamilton helped to build the town we inhabit today with his own hands. Over time, the town of Hamilton has grown to the population of four thousand citizens who share one heart for the longevity of our town. Don't hesitate to pay a visit to Hamilton while in the New York area for great historical and notable attractions, like these:

Henrietta's Homemade Chocolates and Other Sweets

Darlene's Antiques, est. 1900

Gray's Soul Food Diner

Easy MaeCollins's Sunlight Record Shop and Café

The Museum of African History

*Easy MaeCollins lives in Hamilton?*

I laughed to myself. "You're *kidding* me."

"Mr. Whitman? Do you have something you'd like to share with the class?"

Mr. Brown, the computer science teacher, walked away from the white smart board where he was lecturing to where I was sitting. Before he reached me, I quickly clicked the exit bar on the corner of the screen. By the time he got to my desk, the Intro to Computer Science lecture PowerPoint showed in its place.

"Um." I cleared my throat and spat out the first fact I saw on one of the posters hanging on the bleached-white walls. "I was just surprised that there are three main components of CPUs. *Crazy stuff.*"

Mr. Brown smiled proudly and eyed the poster I was referring to. He stuck his hands in his pockets and whistled in amazement. "Yes, Mr. Whitman. It amazes me each day that technology is advancing the way it is. I *am* glad to see that our newest student is so invested in computer science and computer processors. Everyone give Mr. Whitman a hand." A few people in the class broke out in half-hearted applause. My face grew warm and Mr. Brown's smile turned into a pointed glare. "If you're going to search the internet and *pretend* to pay attention in my class, please remember that I get alerts when websites are surfed that shouldn't be. This is not a geography class, Mr. Whitman. Please be sure to pay attention. You too, Mr. *Brock Ganton*. Body-building forums can wait." Brock, who was sitting a few seats in front of me, sunk in his seat.

I gave Mr. Brown a tight-lipped smile and salute and he thankfully went back to the lecture.

*So much for finding out more about Hamilton.*

That morning, Virginia called trying to pick me up in her little Barbie car to give me a ride to school. She showed up on my doorstep, wearing this super-short white skirt and pale pink crop top. When I walked by her as if she were invisible, she followed after me, the sound of her overly high heels smashing the poor ants on the sidewalk.

"Zachy," she said in her nasally voice. "We need to talk."

"We don't." I kept walking. I didn't even know how to get to the school, but I wanted to get as far away from her as I could. I walked in long strides, so for every step I took, she had to take three.

"Yes. We. Do." She reached out and dug her nails into my arm.

"Zach, Virgie, is everything all right?" my dad called out to us from the porch. I saw him, staring innocently, as if I didn't know he planned to turn me into himself.

"Everything is fine, Mr. Whitman!" Virginia assured with a grin.

I waved at him, as if everything were all right, and he shut the front door.

"What do you want, Virginia?" I asked, clearly annoyed. Her glossy lips stretched into a grin and she batted her spidery lashes.

"I think we got off on the wrong foot yesterday."

"You think?"

"I *think* you misunderstood me," she whined. "I didn't mean to come off like—"

"A racist jerk?"

She took in a breath, clearly frustrated that I wouldn't let her finish her sentences.

"If you would just kindly get into my car so that I can explain to you what I meant, I would appreciate it. These heels are *murdering* my pedicure." I had no intention of moving. She blew out a defeated breath and let her head drop, her blond bangs falling in waves around her face and eyes.

"Fine, we can talk out here." She sucked in her bottom lip. "I wanted to apologize for the way my friends and I acted last night. I know you grew up around people like Thomas, and so I can see why you're just as sensitive as *they* are when it comes to playing friendly jokes."

"You laughed after those guys dumped hot cheese on his face. What are you trying to say?"

"I'm trying to *say*"—she paused—"that I think you deserve another chance."

"*I* deserve another chance?" *What, is she crazy?* "I deserve another chance," I repeated to myself with a laugh. I couldn't listen to this girl any longer. "Excuse me, Virginia." Her heels clicked across the sidewalk when I started walking away from her again.

"Zach, stop walking. Now."

Her voice contained an authority I didn't even know could roar out of a four-foot-something girl. I stopped walking and turned around.

"You need me," was what she said, sauntering the few short feet it took to get back to her vehicle. "If you want to make it in this school, you *need* me," she called out, settling into the driver's seat. "You can either have the best year of your life here or the worst. It's all up to you. If you're not seen entering the school with me today, no one will talk to you."

I paused and thought about the offer she'd just presented me.

She was saying if I didn't get into her car, I wouldn't have to bear listening to her speak in that nasally voice or put up with the surprise visits to my house? I wouldn't have to hang around her friends and would finally get a sense of peace? She stared me down with a sinister grin as if she'd won. As if I'd bow down to her rule as the rest of her friends did. But instead, I did the exact opposite. I stood in front of her throne polished in strawberry-scented lotion and miniskirts, flashed a peace sign, and walked down the street. She met me with another sign from her longest manicured finger when she screeched down the street almost running me off the sidewalk.

I was late but I eventually found the school, sleep-deprived and suffering from a thundering headache. Chalk that up to my new room, where I just couldn't get a good rest. The whole way to our new house, Dad kept talking about this room he used to sleep in when he'd visit his grandmother and how he'd wanted me to have it. Let's just say it wasn't a room built for comfort. It was where Dad's grandmother collected glass dolls, and the bed was covered with them, so I slept under a blanket on the plush, hot pink carpet that smelled like old lady perfume and corn chips.

Dad was right about one thing: he said the room always had the best view of the New York City skyline. After I'd gotten home from escaping Virgie and her merry men, I sat on the window seat and looked at the city lights. It was always a dream of mine to perform my music in New York. It was that soil that birthed so many of the rappers, producers, and bands that I gained inspiration from. It was those city sidewalks that they sold their demos on and street performed. The lights shined in the city the entire night and never once went dark; the moon in Bayside didn't even shine as bright as the city that never slept, booming with music in its veins.

I planned to go this weekend.

If Dad stayed busy catching up with all his childhood friends, he wouldn't even notice that I would be gone for a few hours. Heck, I might get away with snatching some bills out of his wallet and staying overnight. I needed the polluted air of the city again. Bayside was even more suffocating than I imagined. When I got to school, the secretary at the office presented me with a gym uniform and told me to head to the field. She said she needed my dad to sign some papers. I grabbed them myself and promised her I'd give them to him to sign. I'd probably just forge them myself, like I did all the other field trip forms and teacher's notes since elementary school. I knew how to write cursive before any kid in my class. My parents always told me to "make it work" when I needed signatures.

Mom and Dad dropped me off to a kindergarten classroom inside a Philadelphia row home the first day of school, but after that day, I walked by myself. Dad was always busy at his office working for the city he hated more than anything, and Mom was always at her clinic, day and night. I'd catch the bus there after school and on the weekends and watch Mom work. I never liked bothering her with my teacher's notes about how well I was reading or how good my piano lessons were; it seemed like her life was too big for that stuff. She was always worried about getting a certain number of vaccines in on time or getting funding from the government for her clinic. She'd sit me in the breakroom, and I'd watch the telenovelas the women that worked there watched in slow times and on breaks. Over time, I started to understand the Spanish the actors were speaking.

One time, I was in the room when Mom was working on a patient who only spoke Spanish. He was trying to explain his symptoms to her, but Mom didn't understand. She went to grab someone who could speak the language to help her out and translate what he was saying, but I already knew.

"He's saying he keeps fainting after working for a few hours. He's worried because he has a family to take care of," I said. Mom looked between me and the man who was nodding profusely with this huge smile on his face. After Mom finished his examination and he left, she smiled at me and told me that I was a lifesaver.

Mom's smile could always make a person feel important. It wasn't those pretend smiles that people like my dad always flashed, it was genuine. Like she was happy to see everyone she came across because she cared about them so much. I never saw many of those smiles at home. I don't blame her for that. Living with my dad's complaining about his days at work could be annoying and that's probably why she spent all her time at that clinic. Last year, she asked my father if he wanted to go with her to Africa to offer medical and legal help to the people there. I remember it clearly because it was the day that everything really began to change. I was coming home from this gig me and my friends were playing and I could hear the yelling from outside of my house. Not like it wasn't a normal thing in Philly. Somebody always had their door or window open to let in the cool night air and the smell of burning incense out on the streets. Because of this, you could always hear somebody's conversation or argument or baby crying or television set and music blasting. It was what I was used to; what everybody was used to. What I *wasn't* used to was my parents letting their argument echo off the streets so the entire community could hear.

They had an image to uphold. Our house was the one the community went to when they needed help. Mom was always signing checks for late light bills, passing out groceries, handing out nonaddictive pain medication, and even watching kids on her weekends off. Dad always stood by, flashing his award-winning smile, secretly wishing his wife would shut the door to the people and never open it again, but he did a good job hiding it. When they argued, they usually made sure to do it in hushed tones, or with the windows and doors shut.

This time, it was loud, and I mean so loud, I was in my best friend Dee's truck and could hear it. I closed my eyes and took in a breath, squeezing the edges of the small piano I held on my lap. We'd just had a good show. The crowd swayed like waves to our music, as if they were one with it. For the first time, we played our original stuff instead of covers and I was surprised the songs I wrote actually affected the crowd.

But the screaming coming from my house wiped the happiness straight out of me.

*"I don't care about what you feel you're called to do. You dragged us to this crap hole!"*

I subconsciously winced and Dee reached over and grabbed my hand; she squeezed it and my grip on the piano tensed. She was always there for me.

When we were in fifth grade, she punched this dude named

Hampton straight in his face because he came at me when I tried to join his freestyle circle on the courts. At first, he let me spit something. After I did and he realized I was actually good and not some joke like he'd imagined, he said I was a wannabe and I would never be Black so I needed to stop trying to act like it. He pantsed me in front of everybody.

Dee was real quiet and never really talked to anybody. Nobody really messed with her either, because they thought she looked crazy. Her hair was always undone and not braided or straightened like all the other girls. Instead, she wore it in this big poofy Afro. She always wore oversized boy clothes: shirts that hung past her knees, and jeans that always fell around her waist. I wasn't surprised when she walked straight up to Hampton and decked him right on his mouth.

"Ya jokes aren't funny," was all she said before walking away. He spat out two teeth and started crying. Everyone, including me, laughed so hard that we all forgot my pants were still around my ankles. When I went to thank her that day, she said she didn't do it for me. She did it for herself. Later I found out Hampton was giving her problems about her clothes. Besides the teasing, me and Dee were more alike than we realized. We were both lonely at school and had no one to talk to, so I kind of hung around her. God bless her, she put up with me following her around. We never talked when we hung around each other, but I'm sure she liked the company just as much as I did. Plus, when she found out I was good in school, she started asking for my help. Protection from bullies for tutoring was an easy swap.

Over time, the quiet Dee I followed around became this talkative and silly girl. Sure, she dressed different, wasn't that good at school, and had trouble relaying words out loud from books, but she understood music. She banged on the drums like no one I'd ever heard, like playing was allowing shut-up emotions to escape outside of her into the world around her. *That* was what we had in common. In ninth grade, we started our nameless band with Sunny, this kid who killed the bass and this other kid we called Gerald, who murdered on the electric guitar. We were pretty big for a local cover group since our sophomore year, when we won this talent search. After that, we played in local clubs and began to get a name for ourselves.

*"You don't care about anyone but yourself, Marie! Zach's not even happy!"*

*"He seems pretty happy to me!"*

Mom didn't really have a problem with the band; it kept me busy and out of trouble, which was what she cared about. Dad thought my playing in the band, like everything else I was passionate about, was a stage I'd grow out of. After all, he *"had a cover band in high school too."* The difference was our songs weren't normal cover songs and didn't sound like some cheap karaoke knockoff. We remixed them to fit our sound, and if you ask the people around these streets, our sound was unlike anything they'd ever heard.

*"Really? How can Zach be happy? There is no one like him that lives here! He sticks out like a sore thumb!"*

*"You got to be kidding me, Dick, there are a lot of white people in Philly!"*

*"None like where I grew up that know what it means to be a purebred! He doesn't even know who he is, Marie! He walks around with those hoodlums making music as if he's one of them!"*

"We should probably be going, Dee," Sunny said from the back seat under the broken-down drum set we scattered around him.

"*We don't live in your fantasy town; this is the twenty-first century, Dick! As long as Zach's not in prison, I feel like we're doing a good job!*"

"Hello? Dee, you hear anything I said?" Sunny repeated over my parents' voices.

"Not. Until. Zach. Tells. Me. He's. Good. To. Go. In. There." Dee looked at me when she said this as if Sunny weren't even in the back seat. Her eyes glimmered with sincerity. "You know I can sneak you in my room tonight if you want someplace to crash."

I can't count on my fingers how many times I snuck into her room and crashed on her floor when my parents hissed angrily at each other until the early hours of the morning. She lived with us for a few months when we were in seventh grade after she came to school with bruises from her stepfather beating her. At first, she didn't want me saying nothing, but I couldn't keep it a secret. I told my mom. It was the first time she shut down the clinic early. We went to Dee's house to pick her up before her stepdad got home from work. Dee packed all her stuff and Mom took her shopping for clothes. They arrested her stepdad and moved her from our house into a group home where she's stayed since. I know what you're thinking and it's not the bad kind. She gets three hot meals a day. They even hooked her up with a receptionist job in the home and they let us use the basement to have band practice.

Dee said she'd met some of her closest friends in the home and she looked a lot healthier than what she did when she lived with her stepdad; she wasn't stick thin anymore. As a matter of fact, she looked really good. She wore her hair in locs of every color, so long they snaked down her waist. You would never find Dee wearing anything but black. Black jeans, black T-shirts, black boots, heck, even during the summer, when all the other girls wore neon colors, Dee wore black bathing suits. Even though her life was going a lot better than it used to be, she had this heavy up-and-down relationship with depression. Her arms were covered in tattoos that covered the scars she got from cutting when her depression got the best of her, but she never let that stop her from smiling that smile I'll never forget—the one that made me feel like she was always gonna be there and I would always be able to rely on her.

Dad couldn't see the beauty in any of this. He would force me to go with him on milk runs to the corner store, purposefully taking the route past the boarded-up homes, littered with *No Trespassing* signs where the drug-addicted and homeless posted up. He'd lean down real close and whisper one of his many lessons, all of them sounding the same way: *We aren't like Black people. We are better. No matter how much they got help, they'd always find their way back to drug-ridden cities because that's how they're wired.*

He'd specifically avoid the neighborhoods where white drug addicts tripped out on the curbs during our walk back, but I knew about them regardless because things like drugs, crime, and homelessness don't have a color. These disparities weren't selective about who they affected. I witnessed my mom hand checks and medications to white hands too. While my dad chose to ignore the faces of those with outstretched hands, I saw beauty.

Rainbows aren't all white, nor are they all black. They are filled with colors that dwell together in unity. Nature shows no prejudice to color; blue skies shine against snow-white mountains. Sunsets are filled with oranges, blues, purples, and pinks. Nature understands that beauty can only be truly found in integration, but my dad never got that. So, we never got each other. I watched Mom work, but we never connected deeply. If it wasn't for Dee saving me that day on the playground, I might have been like my dad, starting to judge people based on what lay on the outside. My relationship with Dee taught me the importance of never judging a person based on their skin or the stereotypes that chained themselves to them. People avoided the both of us because we were different, but through Dee, I learned to embrace that. She made me believe that family wasn't just the people who share your blood, but those who shared your burdens. There wasn't ever a time when she was too tired to sneak me in if I'd knock on her window in the early hours of the morning and I was never too busy to talk when things got real dark for her.

"Zach?" Dee had repeated still staring at me, her eyes searching for a reason to drive away and take me with her.

I opened the car door. "I'll catch you guys later."

"Good luck," Sunny said.

Dee didn't pull away from the street until I shut the door behind me.

My house smelled like the apple cider and cinnamon candles Mom always lit in every room—like home. It looked like home too—all Dad's art that he painted hung on the walls. I never understood how he could hate the city he always painted. Framed skylines at sunset, in the dark, and covered in snow hung around the low-lit row home where I'd lived since birth. They stood there, in the kitchen. Spilled Chinese food was scattered on the ground and our cat was munching on the dusty chicken. They didn't notice me come in, they didn't notice that dinner spilled; they just shot each other glares.

"What do you want me to *do*, Dick?" Mom asked desperately. "This is an opportunity I've been trying to get at for years. They need my help."

"You've been helping those people for years!" Dad exclaimed. "But that's *always* it, isn't it, Marie? It's not about your family; it's about them."

The upstairs hall light flickered as it always did, a dim buzzing sound coming from the plate that blocked the bright light from messing with Mom's low-lit ambience. I walked toward it; the third step creaked.

"Zach's home," Mom whispered as if I couldn't hear them yelling from outside. I could hear her footsteps as she approached the archway leading to the stairs. "Zachary, honey. We need to talk."

I followed her into the kitchen. Dad kicked the cat out of the way and gestured for me to sit at the table. I was still holding my piano, still gripping its edges, my knuckles white.

"Your mother has something to tell you," was all he said before walking out.

Mom crouched in front of me like I was eight years old again, like she was telling me that she was working late at the clinic and she needed me to walk the few blocks home by myself, heat up a TV dinner, and be in bed by nine.

"Zachary." She placed a hand over her mouth as if she were trying to block what she'd been trying to say from coming out. "I'm moving to Africa."

"*What?*"

She took in a breath and began to explain. "There's an option to run a clinic in Zimbabwe that needs a medical doctor. I wanted to know if you would like to come with me."

My heart quickened. "What about my life here, my band? We're doing *really* good."

"I know," she replied. "But you can make a new band in Africa, with new friends." She lifted a hand and touched the side of my face. Her thumb spun soft small circles on my cheek.

"Zachary—"

"Choose," was all I said.

She looked confused.

"Choose," I repeated. "Me or Africa, because I'm not going."

"Zachary, I—"

"You don't care about anyone but yourself. For the first time, Dad's right. I have a *life* here, Mom." I gently took her hand and removed it from my face. "You can't do this; you can't move this whole family away from all I know. They need you here."

She sighed and stood.

"You hear that, Marie? You are *ruining* this family," Dad spat, making his way back into the kitchen. I ignored him, and just looked at my mother, her eyes brimming with tears. Maybe if she looked at me, really looked at me, she'd change her mind. I was her son, after all.

"Mom," I said. "One more year. Give me one more year here in Philly. I graduate in one year. After that, go wherever you want. You just can't do this now."

She chewed on her bottom lip, thinking. What was there to think about? It should be a no-brainer: your family or your job.

"It's not that easy," she whispered.

That night, while Dad slept in the guest room, and Mom in their room, I snuck out and walked straight to the group home where Dee lived. One look at my face made clear to her I wasn't in the mood to talk about it, so we didn't. I just used my jacket as a pillow and lay on the floor. A few moments later, I felt her bring her blanket and lie down next to me. Our breathing and the radiator were the only noises. For the first time in a long time, it was quiet.

"You don't know how good you have it here," I whispered to her before we drifted to sleep.

That weekend, after I came home from playing a show, Dad was sitting at the table. The top buttons of his shirt were unbuttoned, and he drank rum straight from the bottle. When I'd walked into the kitchen, he slid a note across the table. It was from my mother. I only read the first sentence before crumbling it up and throwing it out.

*Zach, I'm sorry but I had to go.*

Mom left in April. Dee left me too. She died by suicide that summer. I don't blame Dee for what happened; she fought for years, and now she's finally free. But at the same time, I'm mad at her and mad at my mom too. They made me realize a hard truth too soon: holding on to anyone is a lost cause. Nobody that says they love you sticks around for you. The only reason why Dad never left is so he could look like the "good parent," who stayed around after the other straight-up left. The only one I have to look out for me is me. Family is *just* a word, friend is a weightless term, and blood carries no real connections.

My music is the only thing that stays true in my life; the only thing that never changes; never tried to change me, understood my emotions, and didn't pack up and leave me because it had some job offer in Africa. It's gonna take me where I want to be—a place where I don't need to think about anyone and can live for myself.

# Capri

I READ, REREAD, AND READ THE LETTER I'D GOTTEN from Camp Sharp until I had it memorized.

*"Dear Capri Collins,*

*"We at Camp Sharp would like to thank you for submitting your application. We would like to inform you that you have been accepted into the second audition process for the chance at a full scholarship into our Summer Program. Camp Sharp offers a dynamic summer experience to any dancer hoping to pursue a serious career in ballet, jazz, lyrical, contemporary, hip-hop, and tap. If you are accepted, you will be trained by the top performers on Broadway and the ballet stages across the world. At the end of your training, you will participate in a showcase performance on the Camp Sharp stage before the scholarship boards of many arts-focused universities, seeking to add more soon-to-be-famous alumni to their lists.*

*"For your second audition, you will need to wear appropriate dance attire. (No ripped jeans or baggy clothing.) Signatures on the attached release form from the applicant and applicant's guardian are required. Please be prepared to bring your proper health-related items (i.e., inhaler, water bottle, blood pressure pump etc.). We will be dancing, after all. Please also note that this audition process will be an all-day commitment; you will be given a number to participate in a choreographed dance routine.*

*Over the course of this audition the routine will be made more difficult. The five dancers who remain will be given a chance for the scholarship by competing against one another for the last and final audition before a panel of judges and a full New York–based crowd. . . ."*

"It's a waste of time," I whispered to them. "Who am I kidding?"

"If you don't shut up with all that negative talk imma fire you. Now we just gotta all pause and take in the situation. We'll figure it out." Easy stood in front of the counter with Perry, both of them in deep thought. After I read the letter for the third time and almost hyperventilated in the middle of the library at school, Perry took me to the bathroom, splashed water on my face, and told me to calm down. She told me to forget about the letter until after school when we'd show Easy and see what he thought. That was impossible. It was like asking a drowning person not to think about air.

*"The location is 3133 Broadway at the Little Light Theatre. The date for the second audition is Saturday, February twelfth at twelve p.m. sharp."*

How could she expect me to concentrate on school when the letter said I had to be in New York City for a group audition this Saturday? We suggested that Easy take me, but he said Saturday was the Sunlight's busiest day and that if he were going to cover for me, someone needed to be there. Essie always said that nothing worth having ever came easy; I imagined she meant giving birth or something. I never understood fully what she meant until now. Yes, I made it to the second part of my audition and yes, I was super excited about it. I mean, I was *one* step closer to accomplishing my dreams. But there was absolutely no way I could go. Saturday mornings was Ma's off day, which meant she wanted to clean the house from the mess we made of it during the week, and she needed my help. Justin was usually at basketball practice and Pa always went fishing and didn't come back until after six or so. How did I expect to sneak off when Ma would be home all day?

Easy drummed his fingers on the glass cashier's desk. I let the back of my head repeatedly bang against the corkboard filled with flyers and business cards on the wall behind me. The saxophone softly sang from the speaker above us. Besides that, it was so quiet, I could hear the broken clock ticking away. *Tick. Tock. Tick. Tock. Tock. Tock. Tock.*

Perry exhaled. "*Capri.* If you don't stop banging ya head against that wall to the sound of that broken-behind clock, and if Easy don't stop making that noise with his fingers, I'm gonna do something real crazy to the both of you!" Everything—my head banging, Easy's finger drumming, even the clock. She sighed. "Look, I'm sorry, it's just, I'm tryna focus. If you don't get into that camp, we're both screwed. You're my ticket out of here."

I gave her a faint smile. "It's all right."

The light bulb in Easy's mind finally went on. "I got it. Everybody name all ideas that come to y'all's heads and we'll debate them. When we come up with one that's undebatable then we have a plan."

Sounded easy enough.

"Okay, me first," Perry volunteered. She thought about it for a moment before stating her suggestion. "Aight, what if Capri pretends to be sick and when Ma goes out for medicine, Capri sneaks to New York City?"

I shook my head immediately. "The drugstore is up the street from my house. What happens when she comes back to actually *give* me the medicine and sees me gone for the whole day?"

After a few more moments of silence, Easy piped in.

"What about if you tell her you'll be working here on Saturday? Tell her you're picking up some overtime hours."

Hmph, that could work. But Saturdays were for cleaning.

"How am I gonna get out of cleaning?" I asked.

Perry piped in, carrying a smile. "Wake up at six a.m. and start cleaning. That way you'll be done around seven thirty or so. Your audition isn't until twelve. Get dressed and put your dance clothes under your outfit. Be at Easy's about eight and tell her your shift at Easy's isn't over until seven."

"Almost a twelve-hour shift?" I asked. "What will I do with all that extra time in New York City?"

"Come home early," Perry suggested.

"No! Enjoy that extra time," Easy piped in. "You haven't been to the city since you was a child. Sightsee, give yourself an experience you'll never forget."

"How will I get her signature?" I asked, waving around the letter. "It says here that I have to have a guardian's signature."

Perry smiled menacingly, grabbing a pen from the front desk. "Call me Ma." With a swipe of the hand, she signed my grandmother's first and last name on the letter. It wasn't at all shaky like mine would have been.

"Okay, and what if Ma comes to visit and drop me off lunch or something?" I countered.

"They don't call me *Easy* for nothing. Don't worry about it. Spend as much time in the city that you need after the audition. Perry and I will cover for you."

Perry's eyes widened and she looked straight at Easy. "Perry gonna cover for who?"

Easy pointed at me. "Your best friend, the one that needs that audition so she can make it, so you in turn can make it? Wasn't that what you just said, Miss *Perry*?" She sighed and Easy continued. "You'll tell your ma that you'll be restocking and organizing the new shipments from the back stockroom, which means that Perry will cover the register while I work on the sales floor. Once the night shift starts, Perry will handle the drinks in the café and I'll MC the open mic like always. Once the Sunlight is filled with half the whole community, your ma won't be able to spot you through the crowds. When she gets home from open mic, you'll already be in bed."

Perry pursed her lips. "I'm fine with working during the day, but Perry has a date Saturday night." Easy shooed her away with his hand.

"Invite him to the Sunlight. He can help you work." Then he stared straight into my eyes. He smiled widely, his eyes disappearing in the wrinkles around his face. "What do you say, Capri?"

My heartbeat quickened. "I don't know."

Perry sighed and threw her hands in the air. "Oh, gosh."

"But," I continued, "I'll think about it."

"What is there to *think* about? This is your dream! You got an audition at freaking Camp Sharp. That has been your dream since you were like twelve. . . ." Perry went on to continue her rant, but Easy shushed her.

"Perry, shut up." He grabbed my hands. "Capri, you take all the time you need to think about this. I know it's hard not having support from your ma and pa. I know it's hard having to do this on your own. But I do ask that you to think about it long and hard. This might be your only opportunity to chase those dreams of yours."

"Besides," Perry added, "Justin can help you."

"I don't know if he'd be up to sneaking to New York City when he has a basketball game," I replied. "Plus, I don't know if I can really trust him at this point in my life. He's been acting weird lately and has been avoiding *everyone*."

"Except Rose," Perry piped in. "I saw them in full lip lock in the cafeteria and girl your brother looks like he can *kiss*. I been wanting to hook up with him since freshman year."

"I think we lost her," I said to Easy as Perry fell into an unknown land filled with visions of things that would never happen.

Easy smiled softly. "Capri, the first time your mother went to New York City, she traveled alone." He laughed at the memory. "She went to the audition in her Sunday's best; wore a bright yellow floral dress. When she walked by the record shop, it was almost like the sun had left the sky to stroll on by. That's probably why she *got* the part in the first place. She dressed like the bright star she would one day become." He gave my hand a squeeze. "She was just like you, honey. She wouldn't let me make no calls for her, didn't wanna use none of the connections I had. She wanted to make it on her own, just like you. You can do this, Capri. You are a beautiful and talented dancer. Anybody that can't see that is a fool and you won't really be alone, will you? Your mother is with you wherever you go."

Essie always said that sometimes certain once-in-a-lifetime chances flew above us, and it was up to us to grab ahold of them before they flew away. Camp Sharp was a wonderful opportunity, I knew that. But Ma, she'd always been there. She lost her daughter because of the very thing I was trying to do behind her back.

"I still need to think about it," I said.

Perry sighed but Easy smiled patiently and with a gentle nod said, "Trust yourself, Pri. In you lies the answers for your path."

# Zach

**_I WANNA THINK OUT LOUD_**

*Would their ears be wounded if they heard, my bloodcurdling*
*cries?*

> *I wanna cry out loud*
> *The world is silent here*
> *Party of one.*

I let *My Anthem*, the third album by my favorite band, Ambient Light, carry me the entire school day. Thank God for wireless earbuds.

> *So let the words fall from my mind*
> *Into the crowd around me*
> *And let them sink into their bones like rain*
> *Or drown me out.*

I loved the band because they were different from anything that usually played on mainstream radio stations. They were underground but not because they sucked or had low-class production. They were offered signing deals with major record corporations but declined them all. They wanted to stay the independent, self-produced band that they were. Ambient Light is one of the reasons why I decided to pursue music to begin with. Anybody can be good at playing the guitar, piano, drums, and bass if they practice enough, but not everybody's capable of creating something that moves somebody. Like, actually digs into their soul and pulls out answers to things that they'd been searching for their whole lives but never uncovered.

That's why it took me months to write the songs my band finally released at that club we played in Philly. Up until then, I was hesitant about letting people in, mainly because my music was so different, but the response from the crowd was out of this world and I was stoked.

After Dee died, all the songs got buried inside again.

Music for me is alive; it grows within my soul like a tree. Its branches sprout songs that people can take a bite out of and *feel*. But they could also pick it apart like it's some sort of experiment, taking the beauty and meaning right out of it.

*Sprout up from the trees,*
*Gain wings to fly,*
*She walks on the ground,*
*But still feels alive.*
*Could we all touch the soil,*
*And the clouds together?*
*Have wings and be still,*
*Will we drown if we leap,*
*Together?*

They ran around the field, their perfect hair shining against the sunlight, all in their matching red-and-white uniforms. When the guys jumped, their short shorts hiked a little too far up, giving a view no one wanted to see. That's why I "accidentally" left my gym clothes at "home." I sat on the front row of the bleachers, hands behind my head, earbuds blasted as high as they could go. The brightness of the sun, though it wasn't hot, reminded me of the summer days when we'd have block parties back home.

The city block parties in Philly were different from any suburbia cul-de-sac summer "shindig." Every kind of person you could think of was there; it was never just your neighbors and their kids that you grew up with, people from all over the city came. It would be blazing hot, but the Polish Water Ice guy would bike around with his freezer and scoop you some ice out of the only two flavors he had: blue and red, which both tasted like vanilla. And the food, it was amazing. There were people grilling steaks, burgers, dogs, cheesesteaks. Mexican food, African, Jamaican, Israeli, Greek, Italian. Me and Dee would sit on the curb and play music with my guitar case open in front of us. People would drop bills or join in. We didn't need nobody playing music from their trunks or open car doors, we were the music all together; the laughing kids who chased each other with water guns and balloons, the sizzling of the food, the longtime friends making small talk and reliving old memories, the sound of nearby traffic; together *we* were the music. I closed my eyes and for one moment, allowed myself to go there again. I could almost taste the Polish Ice until someone nudged my knee. I took out my earbuds.

"You sittin' out too, huh?"

One eye opened at a time. Thomas sat next to me, mocking the position I sat in, except when he tried to put his hands behind his head, he almost fell in between the bleachers. I reached out and steadied him.

"I thought no one was allowed to talk to me," I said with a smirk. He rolled his eyes behind his large-framed glasses. Virgie was right: since deciding not to be her friend, everyone avoided me like the plague.

"Yeah," he agreed. "Virginia sent out a mass text saying not to talk to the new kid. She said you just got out of a group home, juvie-type facility."

"Did she say what I did to get into the group home juvie-type facility?"

He nodded. "Murder."

I let out a laugh. "I got off for murder and my place of escape is Bayside?"

"You got away with it because there was no proof."

I shook my head. "Looks like I had a good lawyer."

Thomas smirked. "Looks like it."

We watched as everyone played capture the flag on the field. Virgie and her girlfriends from the diner sat on the sidelines, bathing in the sun, and no one seemed to bother them about joining the game; not even the two gym teachers in the middle of the field acting as referees.

"So," I said. "Why aren't you in gym and why are you talking to me? Don't you already have enough problems for them to have a reason to hate you even more?" I nodded over in Virgie's direction. She noticed me, rolled her eyes, and flipped her hair.

"They'll hate me regardless. Asthma."

"What?" I questioned, confused.

"I have asthma. That's why I can't participate. It's severe so I take a health class, but for some reason, I still have to watch gym."

"That's not fair."

He chuckled and rested his hands behind his head, this time succeeding in leaning against the bleacher behind him. "Is anything really fair?" he asked.

"Can I ask you something, man?" He grunted in response. "Why do you put up with the way they treat you?" I closed my eyes again, to block out the bright sun.

"I don't know," he responded quietly. "I tried doing something about it, plenty of times, in fact. The faculty just never did anything; said I needed to learn how to take a friendly Bayside joke. That I was being too sensitive."

I couldn't believe it. "Seriously?"

"In ninth grade, I got pantsed by one of the guys on the football team, another one tripped me after that, and then I got this cooler filled with yellow liquid dumped on me. I'd like to say it was Gatorade, but it didn't smell like it."

"Sheesh."

"I went to the principal about it with my mom and they wrote it off because they couldn't find out who did it. It happened so quick, I didn't see anyone."

I shook my head. "That's insane."

"So I learned to just stay to myself. They don't mess with me as much anymore. You just came in at a bad time."

"I thought you hated me after that. I tried to apologize but you ran off so—"

"Don't worry about it, it wasn't your fault. Plus, I think I'll be all right for a while anyways."

I opened my eyes and looked at him. "Why's that?"

He smirked. "I'm hanging around an ex-con now. No one will dare come close to you. As long as I'm by your side, I'm protected."

I elbowed him with a laugh. "Yeah, whatever, man."


Thomas stood at the end of my driveway awestruck; he'd even taken off his glasses to wipe the lenses as if what he'd been seeing was wrong.

"Dude, your house is massive."

"Aren't they all in Bayside?" I replied.

He shook his head. "Not like this."

"Come on, let's go inside." I walked up the driveway and he followed.

"Nice room," he joked when we walked into my doll-infested bedroom. "Got any weird fetishes I should know about?"

I threw a pillow at his head; he dodged it at the last minute.

"Whoa, check out the view." He marveled at the New York City skyline out the large window. "I've always wanted to go."

"You mean you've lived boat distance from New York City since forever and never went?" I grabbed my laptop out of my backpack and sat on the pillows I'd made a makeshift bed with the night before.

"Correction. It hasn't been forever," he said. "I moved here from New Jersey the summer of my eighth-grade year and no. I've never been." He turned around and faced me. "Have you?"

I cleared my throat. "Nah, I lived in Philly all my life. This is the first time I've been out of the city."

*Hamilton, NY,* I searched on Google.

"Thomas." I signaled him over. "Come here real quick." Thomas walked over to me. "What can you tell me about this place." I asked showing him the first image the search engine pulled up, which was an aged sign with Hamilton's name on it. It looked like it had been painted over millions of times.

"It's the town across the tracks, that's basically all I can tell you. The family I was telling you about yesterday from that house that burnt down forever ago lived there." He sat down beside me.

"That's all I've been able to find out myself other than a few historical details like how it was founded and whatnot." I went back on the search engine and scrolled through the results. "All that keeps coming up is the town's website, which I explored when I could during school, other than restaurant reviews . . . That's new." I clicked on the Harlem Renaissance History webpage. "It says here that Hamilton was also famous for its explosion of art and music during the time of the Harlem Renaissance in New York City." I began to read from the article. "'Reputable figures such as Armstrong and Count Basie visited the town frequently for its hospitality. Many figures such as these and more performed with townspeople in Sunlight Theatre, now turned into a vintage record shop and café owned by Easy MaeCollins.'" I snapped my fingers. "I can't believe I almost forgot."

"Forgot what?" Thomas asked.

"Did you just read what I did?"

Thomas looked confused. "What we covered in US History about the Harlem Renaissance?"

"No. Easy lives in Hamilton."

He lifted an eyebrow. "So?" he said slowly.

"Have you ever heard of him?"

He nodded. "Yeah, my dad used to listen to him."

"Tom, Easy is more than just some old sax player to me. Easy MaeCollins is one of my musical inspirations, next to Ambient Light of course. But that's not the point."

"I didn't know you played music," Thomas responded. I ignored him.

"Dude, you have to show me how to get into Hamilton."

"*What?*"

"Show me the way to get into Hamilton. I want to visit the Sunlight. How far is it away from here?"

"I don't know, thirty minutes or so on foot. But Zach—"

I stood up and headed for my room door. "Great, my dad won't be home for another two hours. Let's go."

"Zach!" Thomas chased me down the stairs, his voice bouncing up and down along with his feet as he we exited down the long, winding staircase. "Zach! You gotta listen to me. I don't think this is safe."

My hand was already on the doorknob. I turned around.

"Why?"

He stopped to catch his breath. "You know how Bayside's an all-white town and they don't take Black people too kindly?" I gave him a blank stare. "Well," he continued, "I heard they don't take white people too well over there."

I smiled and turned the knob to open the door.

"Well, good thing you're with me, huh, Tom?"

# Justin

MY HEART FELT LIKE IT WAS HANGING OUT IN MY THROAT when I reached the front door of her house. The moon barely showed over the clouds that covered the blackened sky. I leaned on my heels, then back on my toes, repeatedly. Something I did when I was nervous. I didn't feel like I had any control over my hand when it reached up to ring the doorbell, until I stopped it before it could. Then that motion repeated itself.

I could smell the food cooking from where I stood, seeping out the open kitchen window on the side of her house. I always enjoyed Mrs. Sails's food, almost as much as Ma's. Tonight the smell made my stomach lurch. My mouth wasn't watering in anticipation at the smell of it, like it used to.

It was cold.

I let out a breath and watched the cold reveal just how much carbon dioxide I'd given to the trees around me. Then I started blowing more breaths out, which caused it to look like I was smoking. Maybe if I could convince myself that I was, I would calm down. I mean, smoking always calmed people down. I kept doing the breath thing which made me look stupid, and when I noticed that, I stopped, even though no one was watching. I lifted my hand to the doorbell again, my fingers tingling. Then I let them fall. I placed my hand back into the warmth of my pockets and closed my eyes, picturing Reverend Sails—tall, thick, balding—standing before me

"Reverend Sails," I mouthed, "I got your daughter pregnant."

# Capri

THE BELL JINGLED OVER THE SHOP, AND I LOOKED UP TO offer a greeting. He walked into the Sunlight with his friend, but all I could focus on was him. The book I was holding slid from my fingers onto the floor.

I noticed everything about him.

When the door shut, he lowered his black hood. His hair was short, cut close and faded like the guys at school. His ears were pierced too. Two small diamonds sat on his earlobes. His face was pale, tinges of red splotched across his cheeks and jaw from the cold, like splashes of paint on a white canvas. His blue eyes explored the shop with childlike wonder as if he'd just arrived at the zoo, not an old record shop with a broken clock and heater. I'd absentmindedly flattened the puff of my ponytail, but it was no use, the coils wanted to be seen and shot back up as soon as my hands tried forcing them down. He looked around, eyeing the pictures that lined the wall of different jazz musicians who had visited the Sunlight and signed photos of themselves. The glass around their pictures began to yellow with age, but he looked at them like they were brand-new.

Ma's voice filled the crevices of my mind; she always said it was wrong to stare at boys. Looking too long at any man, she said, would give him the wrong message. No different than opening my legs to him, inviting him to get me pregnant then leave me. Though shame filled me to the core for staring regardless of Ma's at-home sermons, I couldn't tear my eyes away from the white boy. I felt like I was looking at something dirty, like one of those magazines Justin kept hidden away in a shoebox under his bed that me and Ma found while spring cleaning. She told me it was okay, because boys had needs, but if I ever did it, she'd wear my tail out. She'd have a belt to my butt if she saw me now, gluing my eyes to a strange white boy walking around Hamilton.

They usually never come around here, not unless they have to. Let's take the mayor of Bayside for example: he'll walk through here sometimes during Black History Month or for Juneteenth to take pictures with the reverend and pretend that he cares, even though he's only doing it so that he can post photos on Bayside's social media account about the historical town that moved the enslaved in to become a "united people" all those years ago. When they visit for competitions or sporting events, they walk around with their noses pointed at the sky. They don't say nothing to anybody either, not even "excuse me," when they walk into us, and they treat everything we have here like it has a contagious disease on it.

There's a rumor going around that Bayside Tigers would rather pee in their own water bottles than use our bathrooms and have been doing it for years. The basketball moms even lay napkins down before they sit on our bleachers, like we don't notice. We notice. We notice everything they do and *don't* do, like stick around any longer than they have to. They rush to their cars the moment the buzzer signals the end of a game. That's why it wasn't just the way this stranger was dressed in something besides a polo and khaki shorts that drew me to him; it was the curiosity treading in his ocean-blue eyes. He saw something in this record shop that none of his white counterparts stopped or even wanted to notice, maybe that I never even really paused to notice myself.

I wanted to know more.

"C-can I help you?" I managed to get out.

# Zach

WHEN WE CROSSED THE TRACKS AT THE OLD, ABANDONED
station, I was confident. When we walked down the streets of Hamilton, I was confident. I only put on my hood because Thomas thought it would be smart if I "concealed my identity." It's not like the people walking the opposite way of us couldn't tell I was white, but I did it to make him feel safe. And as I thought, no one bothered me. Sure, I got a few looks, but no one said anything, and their looks of confusion weren't nearly as bad as the daggers I got from my fellow friendly townspeople in Bayside. I was confident the whole way here, but when we reached the large open window to the Sunlight and I spotted her from outside, standing behind that register, my heart stopped and every bit of confidence I had walking over whisked right out of me.

There she was, buried inside an oversized white sweater, carrying this innocence in her face as if she'd been birthed from snow angels. Her curly hair was pulled back, giving full view of her sharp features and the high cheekbones sketched into her caramel face. She read from a novel—pocket-sized. She turned the page but as she read, her coal eyes danced. Her laugh, though I couldn't hear it from the outside, lit up her whole being. As she fell into it, she dipped her head back and let her smile take over, the hugest smile I'd ever seen anyone have come out of straight white teeth and thick, amber-coated lips.

"Here it is," Thomas whispered as if we were thieves on a bank heist. The overcast town felt much colder than the fifty-degree weather we were having. Though the only layers we carried were the hoodies on our backs, I could still see his breath turn to fog when he'd talked. It was as cold in the record shop as it was outside, so I stuffed my hands into my pockets when I walked in. I turned away from her instantly, hoping to play it cool so she wouldn't notice how bad I was staring. Thank God she was reading, distracted, and didn't see the random white boy all googly-eyed over her, staring from the outside window.

It was obvious the Sunlight was once a theatre with the scarlet-colored carpet and the small stage across the room from the glass register counter she sat behind. Photos of all my musical inspirations filled every inch of the high walls that stretched to the ceiling. A chandelier hung from it, giving a warm glow to the store. The mural painted around the ceiling was perfect. It was of the world, each part featuring a person extending out of it, holding one instrument that made one jazz band. France featured a Frenchman with a brown mustache holding a cello; Africa featured a coal-colored man playing on the drums; Israel, a man blowing the sax; America, a trumpet; Asia, singing lead. It was beautiful. I let my eyes take everything in, letting my ears grab ahold of the soft sound of a blues song whispering from the speakers.

*"Don't call me baby,*
*I won't be home come tomorrow,*
*Don't call me baby*
*I won't be home come tomorrow,*
*Don't call me baby, I won't be home tomorrow night*
*I'll be on my way to Chicago, on this cold November night."*

I grazed the pictures on the wall. My inspirations signed these pictures. They all stood exactly where I was standing at one point, but even though all of this was before me, this beautiful place seemingly hidden from the world but tucked away so close to where I lived couldn't measure up to the girl standing behind the counter.

# Justin

*I STUFFED MY HANDS INTO THE BOMBER JACKET ROSE* got me for my birthday two months ago, finding myself still unable to knock on her front door. *Ugh.* How was I supposed to break the news to her father, who trusted me?

Why didn't I get her something like that for hers? Why did I have to *take* that night on her birthday instead of give? It was October first, four months ago. It was the first time we had sex, drowning in the ecstasy of new love, clueless about things taking this turn soon after.

Eighties rap songs bumped on the aged speakers in the only roller-skating rink we had. It was older than the both of us—outdated, from its music and heater that broke in the '90s to the three arcade games that sat on the carpet, which smelled of old cheese pizza. No one cared though; our high school filled it every Friday night, skating, posting pictures, flexing new outfits (even though it was freezing), and hooking up. Not me though. I didn't need nobody; I had all I ever wished for in Rose. That night was extra special because it was her birthday and I wanted it to be perfect. She held on to my hand, her other squeezing the life out of my arm. She clumsily glided across the floor on her inline skates, her knees bent into one another, predicting a fall on its own. I couldn't help but chuckle. The white fluffy hat she wore over her hair was pulled a little too close to her eyelids and her cheeks began to flush with pink. She bit down on her bottom lip in concentration as she tried focusing on each step she made, only to fail.

"You . . . keep . . . laughing," she said in between breaths, "and imma . . . pull . . . you down with . . . me."

I was unable to contain my laughter, until the fifth time, when she'd kept her promise in somehow gaining enough strength to pull me down with her.

"*Ah-ah! Dude on the ice, falling on his behind, never gaining no balance!*" Jay, who somehow glided gracefully to "It's Tricky," rapped when he'd soared by us.

"That doesn't even *rhyme!*" I yelled after him, but he was too far to hear. This time, Rose burst into laughter.

"I think it's time that I give up on this. It's so cold and my butt is starting to feel frozen." She tried getting up but met the ice forcefully again. I stood and extended a hand to her. At first, she didn't take it and tried getting up again; but then she almost fell—again. I caught her before she collided with the floor. I grinned and lifted her to her shaking feet.

"Come on, Rose. Let's get your butt warmed up."

The house provided a warm haven away from the crisp cold in the skating ring and outside. I shut the door behind me, took off my jacket, and kicked off my boots. She did the same.

"I'm sorry," I said, taking off my scarf and gloves. She pointed for me to place them near the heater by the door.

"For what?" she asked, eyebrow lifted.

"I don't know. I just feel like it was a bad idea taking you skating for your birthday. Maybe cooking your dinner would have been a better idea. Now it's what"—I glanced at my wristwatch—"almost seven o'clock? Your day's practically over."

"Nonsense," she said, standing on her tiptoes and grazing my cheek with her lips. "I loved it. I'm not good at it. But I loved it. It was *very* fun."

Rose always had a way of making everything I did that was stupid seem special. I knew not to argue with her.

"Where your parents at?" I asked. The house was completely quiet.

"Church," she replied.

"*Crap!* That's right. I was supposed to have you by the church at seven. Come on, we better get going." I reached down to grab my gloves, but she stopped me.

"Not yet. I want to get warm first. Besides, I'm not sitting in church like this. I got to change first." She walked toward her bedroom. I waited by the door like always. Reverend Sails had one rule: no hanging out in Rose's room.

When she noticed I wasn't coming, she turned around.

"Come on, Justin. They're not here. Plus, it's cold by the front door. You know that heater's half busted." She gestured for me to follow her.

"Your room looks exactly the same," I said once we'd entered it. It had been forever since I'd been in there. The same stuffed animals lined the bookshelves against the pale pink wall, the floors, and her perfectly made bed with the floral comforter. "You still perform in front of them?" I asked, gesturing to all the stuffed animals.

She smiled. "Every morning while I get ready for school. They're the best audience."

I sat on the edge of her bed, which caused her stuffed frog to croak. I lifted it from under my bottom and threw it behind me.

I waited in her room when she'd gone to the bathroom to

change into her sweater dress, riffling through the pages of the pink Bible she had on her pillow to pass time. Minutes later, she emerged from the closed door. The scarlet-colored dress lay just above her knees. Her hair, pulled into a bun. She'd even swiped some crimson lipstick across her thick lips.

I dropped the Bible next to me. "You look stunning, birthday girl."

Rose grinned. "Thanks. I just need to find my tights." She walked to her dresser and began going through her top sock drawer. "If I show up to church without tights, my dad will literally kill me," she said, moving items all around. "*Ah-hah!* Found them." She pulled a pair of white tights from her drawer in victory. I watched as she lifted her dress just above her thighs to slip them on.

"You're drooling, Justin, close your mouth."

My face grew warm. I stood to my feet.

"I'm only messing with you." She walked up to me and wrapped her arms around my neck. "Thanks for everything. I *love* the brace-let." I could feel the cool silver from the charm bracelet I got her on my neck. "I *love* the charm you got me." The heart charm bore a small singe of heat into my back. "And I loved the roller skating date." She kissed the tip of my nose, but I pulled her closer.

"I *love* you, Rose Sails."

Her eyes grew wide with surprise. We both knew how we'd felt about one another, but never said it.

"I . . . I love you too, Justin," she replied. Then, gently at first, her lips met mine.

But then, only seconds after, when I *knew* I should have pulled away, I didn't. Instead, I pulled her closer until I could feel the warmth from her skin behind the fabric of her dress on my leg.

Until we were lying entangled across her bed. Until we kicked the Bible along with all the other stuffed animals onto the floor next to us. Until I heard her wince in pain when I'd knocked on and opened the door she intended to keep closed until her wedding day. Until I snatched away the innocence her father guarded. The girl I'd promised to have at church where she'd grown up, where she belonged. Instead, I dove into deep waters with her, drowning in ecstasy and love while only streets away, her father searched through the crowd from his pulpit to call upon his Rose to sing. When he didn't see her and worry filled his protective heart, he probably looked at his wife, who gave him a reassuring nod that filled him with peace.

They both knew she was in good hands.

"So, you just gonna stand and look at the door?" My heart leapt from my stomach to my mouth, and I swallowed it back down. The memory of October first abruptly stopped and there I was, standing like an idiot outside the Sailses' home.

I calmed when I saw it was just Tyree standing on the other side of Rose's fence. I walked down her porch steps to where he stood.

I sighed. "Just trying to gain enough courage to go in there."

Tyree pulled his beanie over the tips of his ears. The flickering streetlight above us shined against a crooked tree casting shattered lines across his face.

"I saw that y'all had something going on in lunch. Let me guess: you said or did the wrong thing and now she's making you pay for it. Now you're standing outside of her house to try and search for an apology fitting for her forgiveness?"

I let out a faint laugh. "Something like that."

"Well, make sure that you're honest. None of that fake stuff to touch her emotions. Nothing rehearsed, just from the heart. Girls like that, and trust me, they know when you lying. They want to hear something that's real. You'll get that weight off ya shoulders too, when you giving them something honest and you won't regret it in the end either. Nobody regrets telling truth."

I knew Tyree was right even though he didn't know what was going on. I needed to be straight up with Rose's parents. I needed to let them know that I loved their daughter and had every intention of going to college and raising our child. We had a plan.

"How you get so good with apologies?" I asked Tyree.

Tyree chuckled. "I got three sisters, a mama, a long-distance girl, and a lot of forgotten month-by-month anniversaries. Let's just say I had a lot of practice."

I smiled and gave him a nod.

"Don't worry about ball practice later tonight. You don't need it," Tyree said. "It's more for Jay. Actually, all for Jay. I will need you to lead the group run in the morning. I got a meeting with my NYU advisor for classes." Tyree got what I'd been wishing for. He signed his National Letter of Intent for football during the early signing period two months ago, just in time for Christmas. He was already busy preparing for his journey out of Hamilton and across the bay to New York City.

"You really got that scholarship, huh, man?"

Tyree smiled proudly. "Been working my whole life for it. It's crazy that I'm finally leaving all this behind."

I looked around me.

"I can't wait to get out of here, man. See the world, you know?"

Tyree nodded. "Yeah, I know what you mean, man—finally see some stars shining bright for once." If I could get that question answered right for that Snow Fairy and keep playing my butt off, it was only a matter of time before it would be my turn.

My heart rate slowed down a bit. "Thanks, man."

"Don't worry about it. See you at the game tomorrow night." With that, he disappeared down Rose's dark street, the glow from the streetlight igniting against his silhouette. I breathed deeply and turned toward Rose's house.

*Aight, Justin. You can do this.* I walked across the path where I'd walked so many times. I hoped that after this visit, I'd be able to walk down that path again.

# Capri

"I'M THOMAS," SAID THE WHITE BOY'S FRIEND, A SHORT, underdeveloped Black boy with ear-length curly hair, extending his hand for me to shake. I stretched out mine and we did this awkward handshake we both didn't know when to pull away from, so it lasted too long. After our hands finally parted, he stuffed his into his navy hoodie pocket, pulled it back out to scratch his head, then stuffed it back in. I'd never seen this before. He carried a different vibe than the boys in Hamilton did; it was obvious he wasn't from around here either.

"We just came here to browse." He smiled as if he'd been hiding something. That, or he was just as uncomfortable as I was. His blond friend grazed the photographs over the walls with his fingertips—such a delicate touch, as if the photos were relics in a museum he wasn't supposed to touch but ached to. I watched him the entire time.

"Zach, no *Zach*, don't touch those," Thomas hissed at his friend. He turned to face me. "I'm sorry about him."

I shrugged. "I don't mind." *Okay, Capri, great, no stuttering.* "Y'all from around here?" I tried to sound like I didn't care, but I wanted to know more about the mysterious strangers.

Thomas shook his head and opened his mouth to respond, but before he could, his friend appeared in front of the counter.

"New York. We're tourists. We came to see Easy MaeCollins."

His voice was deep, heavy and slick like thick oil. He stared straight into my eyes with such confidence, his own wrapped in long blond lashes that stretched almost to his brows. I swallowed. He was so close I could smell his cologne. New York. Someone from the place that gave Essie her wings was standing in front of me. No wonder why he felt so different; he was from a place where barriers bowed before dreamers, where stages made way for wonderers, where the lights never turned off, even after midnight.

I forced my voice to keep steady, though my heart was racing loud. "Easy stepped out to get a part for the heater. You're welcome to wait here for him if you want to. He might be thirty minutes or so."

Thomas checked his phone. "I actually have to be home by six and *New York City* is a boat ride away, so we should get going." He pulled on Zach's arm, but Zach didn't budge. He just continued staring at me. I swallowed.

"Actually, call your parents," Zach replied. "You can crash at my place tonight. My dad won't be home for another hour or so. We can wait."

He didn't look away as he talked to his friend, but I couldn't look away either. I heard Thomas sigh.

"There's seats over at the bar if you . . . um . . . want to sit there and wait," I suggested.

Thomas stalked off but Zach stayed. He stretched out a hand to me. "Zach."

"Capri." For some reason, my hand wouldn't lift to shake his; it just stayed glued to my side, but he didn't bring his back. It stayed stretched before me.

"Nice to meet you, Capri."

Finally, as if I were lifting a boulder, my hand stretched and connected with his. He squeezed it softly.

"*Ahem,* Zach . . . can I talk to you for a second?" Thomas asked from the barstool at the café.

# Zach

**"WHAT?"** *I HISSED ONCE I'D REACHED THOMAS. HE SPUN* his chair back and forth nervously, over and over again. I grabbed at his shoulders and the spinning stopped. "Calm down."

His eyes grew wide. "Calm down? *Calm down?* We just left the safe confines of Bayside where we both live."

"*Shh,*" I hushed, gesturing back to Capri. If the feud between the towns was as big as Thomas said it was, I didn't want her knowing anything about us being from across the tracks.

"You said we lived in New York City! That is a straight-up lie, Zach," Thomas whispered, then rolled his eyes. "I knew I should have never sat with you at gym."

"Dude, dude, calm down. We're just here to meet Easy. If we leave now, it will be like we came here for nothing."

Thomas sighed. "You like her."

"Who?"

He pointed to Capri. I turned around.

"I don't know her, Tom. How can I like someone I don't know?"

He shrugged. "It's possible. I saw you staring at her on our way into the shop. She's pretty." I smiled and turned around, she was staring our way, but when I looked over, she stuck a record in front of her face to hide her apparent blushing.

I laughed. "Yeah, she really is."

Then I noticed what she was holding.

Was that?

No, it couldn't be.

An original 1996 Ambient Light vinyl.

# Capri

MY FACE GREW WARM WHEN ZACH TURNED TO LOOK AT me. I could hear his footsteps come closer even though my view was blocked by the album cover.

"Is that Ambient Light's debut vinyl in its original packaging?"

I lowered the record to the glass counter below me. His eyes were bright, dancing almost.

"Yeah," I replied. "It is."

"May I?" he asked. I slid the vinyl over toward him and he gently lifted it with such delicacy, he may as well have been handling a priceless vase or a newborn baby.

"I can't believe it," he whispered to himself. Then he looked at me intensely. "How much?"

"I'm sorry," I said. "It's not for sale."

Not only was this record rare, but it was also signed. Easy kept it in the glass case under the register for show. He agreed to let me listen to it anytime I wanted if I played it on the record player in his office and returned it as soon as I was finished. So, I did. On Sunday afternoons, I turned his record player loud, so I could hear it while dancing on the small stage in front of the store. Every Saturday night when the town gathered for open mic night in the front of the store, I sat in his office and listened to it again from the beginning.

"Crap." Zach lowered his eyes, like his entire world crumbled. "It's rare, I know, *and signed*. This is insane. I love these guys."

I smiled. "Me too."

He looked at me, his eyes shining again. "Really? I thought I was the only young one who liked them."

I shook my head. "It's an old band so most people our age don't know who they are." He handed me the record.

"This is the one with 'Dawn' on it, right? I haven't heard the original song in ages. It's only available on this record, right?"

I nodded. "It's on the second album too, but the song's edited and not the same; the verse where he says, 'Light no longer drives its horse here. It only flies above the sky and leaves the dark in its place' was removed."

"Rides," he said, matter-of-fact.

I was confused. "What?"

He smirked. "'Life no longer *rides* his horse here.' Not drives."

"No," I corrected slowly. "'Life no longer drives its horse here.'"

"Rides."

"Drives," I repeated. "I've been listening to this record since I was like three and I listen to it every weekend."

"Me too," he replied.

"But I thought you said you haven't heard it in ages."

He crossed his arms. "I know Ambient Light. It's rides."

"Drives."

"Rides," he replied.

"Drives," I hissed.

"*Drives*."

"Rides!" I yelled. Then I caught what he did. Justin used to get me with that all the time.

He smiled proudly. "Right, rides."

Even though New York City boy was from the city where Ambient Light started their band, he didn't need to be that confident in himself. This girl from little Hamilton was their biggest fan. I would prove that he was wrong.

"Okay, *Zach*. We can solve this. Let's go listen to it." I stood from my stool and crossed to the other side of the register. "Follow me."

"Um, guys, where are you going?" Thomas called out, but we both ignored him. Zach followed me to the back of the store, next to the bathrooms, through the janitor's closet, into Easy's office.

# Zach

**I PRETENDED TO PLAY IT COOL WHEN WE REACHED THE**
door that read *Office* instead of going ballistic that I was actually
entering the private room of one of the dudes I'd looked up to
since I could remember. She pulled a key from her back pocket and
unlocked the door. I still couldn't believe that I was in the Sunlight.
I don't think my brain had a proper chance to take it all in.

"Okay, Mr. Know It All," Capri sang with a smile. "We'll see
who's right about this." She swung the wooden door open and
walked into the office nonchalantly as if walking into the office of
Easy MaeCollins was like walking by a fast-food chain in Philly. It
smelled like an old antique store, like aged wood and apple pie. A
small chandelier similar to the one out in the shop shined its dim,
flickering light against the wooden desk and shelves he had lining
the left wall. Capri walked by Easy's desk, which held a laptop,
saxophone-shaped desk lamp, and a few stacked papers. I tried
ignoring the fact that there was a shelf filled with books by DuBois,
Hughes, Jacobs, Ellison, and so many more of my favorite writers.
I also tried ignoring that the wall behind his desk was lined with
original signed vinyls from every jazz singer I ever listened to.

"Wow," I whispered, turning full circle, unable to express with
one word how amazing this felt. I finally entered the museum my
brain had always dreamt of; it actually existed.

Capri took out her key again to open a closed wardrobe. "Yeah, it's amazing, huh? But listen, don't touch anything, okay? Easy's real particular about his stuff." I quickly pulled my hand away from one of the vinyls I was planning to run my fingers across. She pulled the doors to the wardrobe open to reveal a vintage vinyl player. My jaw dropped.

"This is beautiful. I can't believe he got his hands on one of these. I mean, this is insane."

Capri gently pulled Ambient Light's record from its case and stuck it on the turntable. She lightly placed the needle on the vinyl and its music began to fill the room.

"'Dawn' is the second song on the record," she explained. "So we have to wait for 'Lowlight' to play through before Dawn does."

I didn't mind at all.

*Raindrops fall*
*to find their homes*
*in silver puddles*
*I drop*
*To find*
*My home*
*In you.*

I could hear her humming along to "Lowlight." Each riff Granite took, Capri followed at his heels.

*So, won't you catch me when I fall?*
*Won't you answer when I call?*
*Won't you bring me to your lips*
*As we stand in the lowlight, of these fireflies*
*Seal our love with your kiss.*

"This is heaven. I've never been somewhere like this before. All these guys"—I gestured to the walls around us—"I've grown up on. These guys inspired the music I make. Their music was true music."

She nodded like she understood, then smiled a little. I watched as she walked away from the player to the wall behind Easy's desk. She let her eyes trail over each record.

"My mom used to come here every time she got back from performing to buy a record and we would listen to the entire thing until she went back to perform again. I know what you mean. All this music is really amazing."

I walked up to where she stood and looked at it too. "Jazz music speaks all by itself," I said. "It makes its own wind that lifts you up and lets you ride on its current. Sometimes you're up, and then sometimes you're down; but the ride is amazing. Then there's the blues. It tells a story that sticks with you, it teaches you life lessons. Rock and roll preaches this sermon on rebellion with an out-of-this-world vocalist who doesn't give a crap what the world thinks. And hip-hop, it really gives a voice to the poets many usually don't pay attention to. All this music has a story, and you don't have to pick up a book and read about it to understand it. You just need to listen."

"That's the most beautiful thing I've ever heard," she whispered. When I turned to look over at her, she was staring at me intensely. I cleared my throat. And then I heard applause from behind us. We both turned around; Easy stood leaning on his cane in the doorway right behind us.

"Never heard nobody speak about music like you do, son," he said.

I had no words to respond with. I just stood there, frozen. My heart felt suddenly as if I had just run four miles. He spoke so calmly. Of course he did; he was in *his* record shop. He wasn't the kid that had discovered him online and had been listening to him since he was seven.

"I . . . I . . ."

"This is Zach," Capri introduced. "He's from New York City." Easy's cane drummed its own beat as he used it to walk closer to us. He sat in his desk chair and spun it around to face us, only inches away from where we stood.

"*New York City,*" Easy repeated to himself with a smile that was suddenly reliving every single good memory he'd spent there. "What part you from, Zach?"

"Bronx," I lied before I could think.

Easy frowned. "Really? You with that boy that was hanging around the record shop like a fly on a piece of broccoli?"

Then, I remembered. *Thomas.* I scratched my head. "Yes, sir, I am."

"He just told me he was from Bayside and had to be home before them streetlights came on."

There was my heart again beating so hard, I felt the whole room could hear it. What if Thomas was right? What if they hated white people who lived in Bayside as much as he said they did?

"Yeah, he's from Bayside, but I'm not. We met through a mutual friend and thought we'd take a trip to Hamilton to check out your record shop."

He raised an eyebrow. "But here you are, Zach, in my office."

"I bought him here," Capri cut in. "We was debating about an Ambient Light song, whether a lyric said rides or drives."

Easy let out a deep belly-shaking laugh. "Don't come at Capri with Ambient Light. She knows everything about those guys, even they blood types probably."

Capri hid the blush she carried by putting her head down. A coil escaped from her ponytail into the front of her right eye. I fought back the urge to whisk it back to its home.

Easy cleared his throat; I quickly turned back to look at him.

"So, what's a New Yorker doing in Hamilton when you got all those nice record shops over in your city?"

"Mr. MaeCollins, sir. Yours is different than all the ones they have in New York City." I tried saying "New York City" like I heard the guys in the movies do it, replacing the "or" with an "aw" and all, so he'd believe me. But I probably ended up sounding stupid. I paused, waiting for him to say, *"You fake!"* But he didn't, so I continued. "Sir, not only is this place the most beautiful record shop I've ever been to, but I'm a big fan of your music. When the internet told me you were in Hamilton, I wanted to come and meet you."

"Looks like you just did." Easy stretched out his hand to me and I grabbed ahold of it. "Nice to meet you, Zach."

"You too, Mr. MaeCollins."

"Please, call me Easy. You know, that friend of yours left when I came into the store. He wanted me to tell you he was sorry, but he had to go."

*Sheesh, Thomas.*

"You might be wanting to get home soon too," Easy continued. "You'll have to cross into Bayside to grab their bus to get to the ferry that leaves for New York City, but I'm sure you already know that. That's probably how you got here." I nodded as if he was correct. "You only got about a little less than an hour before the last one leaves for the night. You don't want to be stuck in Hamilton for a night, and you surely don't wanna be stuck in Bayside either. You don't look like Bayside material, and you sure seem like Hamilton material, but you don't got the color for it."

*"Easy,"* Capri said with narrowed eyes.

"No, he's right. My father is expecting me for dinner anyway. It was nice meeting you, Mr. MaeCol–Easy. Really it was."

I brushed by him back into the store. Capri followed.

"I'm sorry about him," she said.

"It's all right." I swallowed the lump of embarrassment that arose in my throat and tried to laugh it off. "He's right. I'm definitely not Bayside material. Heck, I'm not even New York City material. I'm Philly material. That's exactly where I need to be."

I walked to the entrance of the shop.

"Please, let me walk you out of Hamilton," she said, still trailing behind.

"Don't worry about it. You're still on the clock. Besides, it's best you don't walk around alone at night. It's not safe."

I could finally hear her laugh. It fell softly from her lips like flurries of snow.

"It's not safe for *you* to be walking around in Hamilton alone after dark. Come on, I'll walk you to the tracks."

# Capri

THE AIR WAS CRISP; SNOW LAY MELTED ON THE GROUND from the storm we'd had almost a full week ago. It was dark, but the streetlamps shed their spotlight along the street. He walked in long strides; it was a fight to keep up with him.

"I'm sorry about Easy. He's not usually like that. He's probably just mad about the heater being busted." My voice sounded foreign; much higher than it usually did.

"Don't worry about it." I could barely hear him speaking, he was walking so fast. But when we reached a line of shops—the bakery, cleaners, and a produce market, all inside old row homes attached to one another—he stopped. I'd almost bumped into his back but caught my footing at the last minute.

I watched him closely as he stood, hands in his pockets, pale face inching from his black hoodie. The slight slope in his straight nose, his long eyelashes that shined against the dim moonlight, the redness splashing over his lips and cheeks again from the cold. He stared and stared, as if somehow he'd been here before, as if he were glancing at a nostalgia-triggering teddy bear from childhood. Like how I looked when I watched Essie's dancing tapes. A slight smile danced on his lips as he continued looking upon the abandoned homes, now shops, that I myself walked into so many times.

"What are you looking at?" I asked.

"Everything," he said. "It reminds me of home." I dug my

heels into a patch of softened ice holding on for dear life in its fight against the salt that tried to see its demise.

"You're not from New York City, are you?" I finally asked.

"Nah," he whispered. "Philly." He looked at me. "Are you mad that I lied?"

I shrugged. "Not at all. After a while, I figured you weren't from New York City. You don't have the accent."

A laugh made its way from under his breath, sending a bit of fog into the air. He replied, "Standing here takes me back. When I look at this little plot where these stores are, it's like I almost never left."

All three shops held the same red-and-white *Sorry We're Closed* sign on the doors. Dim lights echoed in the windows, you could barely see all the supplies each store had, only their shadows. After minutes of standing there, he started walking again, but slower this time. I was thankful to follow; standing around allowed the cold air to cling to my thin legs and walking placed heat back into them.

"So how long did you live in Philly?" I asked.

"I was born there," he replied. "My dad moved us to Bayside two days ago, into my grandmother's house."

Hearing the word "Bayside" on the lips of anyone was no different from hearing profanity spew from the mouth of a child. It's usually soaked in innocence, but those with a little more experience know the dirtiness that lies between each letter. Only there is no bar of soap on earth powerful enough to cleanse the word. Too much history and blood clings to it. Hearing that Zach was really from Bayside should have caused me to scream for him to leave, to use every reservation I've been raised to have about them as the ammo behind it. But like Adam and Eve staring at that fruit, a forbidden curiosity filled me to the core. This boy didn't bleed Bayside. When he said the name, it was with the same disgust someone in Hamilton would have said it with. So, I didn't put the fruit back by the tree and run home. I didn't want to. I stayed to find out more.

"So, Bayside. You're a Bayside boy."

He sighed. "Not even close."

I laughed. "You know, if anyone here found out you were from Bayside, they wouldn't be too happy."

"What's up with that anyway?" he wondered aloud. "Why do Bayside and Hamilton hate each other so much?"

"Ajah McKulley."

He turned to me, confused. "Who?"

I went into the story I'd heard so many times from so many different people—a story as redundant as a bedtime tale, memorized, second nature, blood-soaked history.

"Her family lived in Hamilton but moved to Bayside in the fifties, but they were still struggling a li'l bit, so she worked for a family in town for extra money. She was their cook, maid, babysitter, anything the family needed, including the father's personal assistant. He raped her and got her pregnant. Of course, they fired her. She didn't lie about who the father was, and her family didn't move even after receiving threats. The day after the baby was born, she went missing. Her family found her ice-cold body hours later, at sunrise, in the bay. People in Bayside say it was suicide, but Hamilton people don't think that's what happened. Her father turned to Hamilton for help and justice, and they tried, but nobody was listening to anybody Black, especially for rape and murder charges against a white man. Nobody can prove it, but everybody thinks it was the husband who murdered her. Her father wouldn't give up though; kept fighting for someone to figure out what happened to his daughter. Weeks after that, his house was burned down and everybody was dead—his wife, son, and his grandbaby. He was the only one who survived. The people who burned it down timed it perfect; he came home from Hamilton to the screams of his children and wife trying to escape from the top window. None of his neighbors came to help. He eventually moved back to Hamilton. Died here. Sad part about it was his daughter was only fifteen."

"Sheesh." He shook his head. "I heard about the house burning down, but I didn't know the family's side."

I laughed. "You'll never really hear that over there."

It was silent as we walked, just the sounds of our footprints crunching against the snow.

"I hate it in Bayside you know." His voice broke through the silence. "It lacks so much of what I'm used to—culture, diversity, the smell of pretzels and food trucks. I've been there only two days and I'm already tired of it. But this place, Hamilton, it reminds me of where I grew up. The record shop, the stores, the homes, heck the smell, it's all so familiar."

"What are you saying?" I teased. "Hamilton smells like the dirty city?"

He smiled slightly, but his face grew almost immediately serious again. "I used to want to get out of Philly because I thought that life outside was so much better but being in Bayside totally opened my eyes."

We neared the abandoned station, the marker to where the towns separated. Bright blue lights lined the old ticket booth. A *Bayside Station* sign, now worn, browning, and missing some letters was plastered to the top with thick nails. I could look a few miles across the tracks, past a small plot of grassland, down a small hill, and see Bayside. I could see the moon that lay above it. I could see the nicely built homes and lights from their large grocery store and diners. I could even see the huge football field, lined with silver bleachers shining off the moonlight like diamonds in the backyard of the high school. But then if I turned around, I could see Hamilton, a mirror reflecting the exact opposite.

The foggy sky that hung above it. There were the shops in the old buildings and the rectangle-shaped homes, sitting on top of each other. Our football field didn't shine throughout the night like theirs; when it was dark, it looked eerie, as if it were abandoned. The grass was cut uneven, and the white lines drawn on the field were crooked. The bleachers were still wooden, not aluminum. Embarrassing, even. But for the first time I wasn't ashamed of it. Zach looked at Hamilton with so much wonder and amazement. The things I grew to despise, he longed for. He was helping me see everything with fresh eyes.

"Look at me, only talking about myself." Truth is, I didn't mind hearing him talk. He was like a mystery book that I wanted to read cover to cover and then over and over again to search for the clues that I missed the first time. I wanted to know him inside and out; so much depth seemed to lie there. I tried not to let it show on my face.

"Don't worry about it. I'm not that interesting," I said.

He scoffed. "I beg to differ. What inspires you? What are your dreams?" He turned around and started balancing on the tracks, back and forth; he wasn't ready to go home yet. Truth was, I wasn't either.

My cheeks grew warm. "I dance a little. I want to be a dancer, but it's complicated."

"Why?" He stopped balancing on the tracks and walked back up to me.

"My family doesn't approve of it. I mean, performing is what put my mom six feet under, so when they see me doing it, they get scared like the same thing will happen to me."

"Your mother was a performer?"

I nodded. "Yeah, a famous performer, actually." I found myself smiling proudly at that. "Her singing and acting were out of this world. But she was the most beautiful dancer I'd ever seen, to this day. She was so graceful. It was like watching a fairy flying or something. She wasn't really ever home, touring and all. But when she was, she'd let me watch her practice, or just dance for fun. Sometimes, if I was lucky, we'd dance together. She'd hold my hand and put my little feet on top of hers. We'd let the music carry us; we'd both become fairies and fly."

"She sounds like she was an amazing woman."

"She was."

Silence.

"What if it does?" he asked suddenly.

"What if it what?"

"What if it kills you. Dancing I mean. What if it kills you like it did your mother?"

I'd thought of this so many times before. Sometimes if I were dancing at the Sunlight and my heart raced too fast, I'd think about how much faster Essie's beat before it stopped entirely, if she felt it. If she knew what was coming and didn't care. If I would stop or if I would keep going like she did. If I'd finish my performance until the end and let what I loved be the thing that killed me.

But I'd never admitted this to anyone, maybe because no one

ever cared to ask, unless it was to strike fear inside of me. Easy, Justin, and Perry were always great. They complimented me, supported me, and offered the most beautiful advice. They pushed me to reach for the stars. But they never asked me how I'd feel if I got out, reached my dreams, and still ended up like Essie. If everything the older people said was right. They acted like it was a myth, like it would never happen. They viewed it as a fear tactic, something the older people say so none of us leave. But it was a reality. I'm Essie's daughter and all. My heart could be unknowingly weak just like hers. Perry, Easy, and Justin leave the reality of death out of the happy ending they imagine for me. That's what we do for people we love; we encourage them with the positive and leave out the negative, so they don't become too afraid to reach.

Not Zach, this stranger wanted to talk about the reality I built walls around. Now they were being knocked down. Somewhere within me, I've wanted this; to be talked to when someone could go home instead, for someone to see me instead of walking through me, to ask me about who I am, and talk about Essie like she really *lived* while she breathed earth's air instead of using her as a lesson on how to die early.

"What if it kills me?" I repeated, finally. "Maybe it will. Maybe it won't. I don't think that matters to me. You read about those actors and singers struggling to get what they want and when they do, you see this glow in their eyes. I don't care if following my dreams kills me. I want that glow in my eyes, because if everybody else can see it on the outside, imagine what it feels like on the inside. Then I remember Ma, my grandmother who raised me, and how she made so many sacrifices. And then I rethink everything."

"I know what you mean," he replied. "I don't get any real support from my family. My dad thinks making music is just a stage and I'll grow out of it."

"What about your mom?"

"My mom," he repeated. "She might as well be dead. She abandoned our family for her job and moved to another country." He ran his fingers through his hair and looked up into the Hamilton sky as if he could see the bright stars that eluded the rest of us. "I was mad about it at first, but right now, I don't know if I really am anymore." He looked at me and grinned, giving a small glimmer of his straight, porcelain smile. "This is the first time I've actually been able to *really* talk to someone since I lost Dee. . . ." His voice trailed to a halt. His lips fell into a frown, but after a moment he regained his footing and smiled. "I just feel like I can really talk to you, Capri."

And then my heart slowed, and my tongue froze, but he kept speaking.

"I mean, *really* talk. I needed this. To think me, a Bayside boy talking to a Hamilton girl. Looks like we're breaking the law." He scooped up some snow and tossed it at me. Some found my face, which made it colder. I grabbed some snow and threw it back, which caused an all-out snowball fight. Before we knew it, we both lay on the floor, on the inside of the abandoned ticket booth, trying to catch our breath, looking up at the sky through the large hole in the roof.

I lay on the side closest to Bayside, giving me full view of the brightest stars.

# Zach

**"SO, YOU MAKE BLUES OR JAZZ SONGS?" SHE ASKED,**
gazing into the sky.

"None," I responded. "Which is funny I guess, huh? Since I got starstruck over Easy at the record shop. I don't think my music really has its own genre. It's kind of everything, I guess. Blues, jazz, rock and roll, hip-hop, soul, gospel, ambient. It doesn't sound as bad as I'm probably making it out to."

She let her head rest on her elbow and faced me. I did the same to her. One of her coils fell from her ponytail over one of her golden-brown eyes. She smiled.

"Actually, Zach, it doesn't sound bad at all."

I stared at her, trying to cement her face on my brain. I wasn't sure if I'd ever see her again, but I didn't want to forget her. I forgot things so easily, like how my mother's laugh sounded, the color of Dee's eyes. But I didn't want to forget Capri—her smile or how she looked with the coil trailing across her forehead to her short, curly lashes. I didn't want to forget the color of the big cardigan that covered her neck, arms, and hips. Or how her legs seemed to stretch for miles in the blue jeans she wore.

Then her eyes widened, and she pulled her phone from her pocket. I wondered what she was doing, when the dim light from her screen lit against the crevices of the room. She threw me one of her wireless earbuds. "Here, put that in your ear," she instructed before placing one in her own. I followed her command, not really knowing *what* was going on, until the music began to play.

"We never got to find out who was right," she said with a grin. "I kept a recording of the song on a voice memo so I could listen to it on the way to school and church and wherever else I was going."

"Wow, you *are* a superfan," I teased. She rolled her eyes and pressed against the button that worked the volume.

"Shut up and listen," she said with a grin.

*"Don't you see?*

*Love no longer flies its course on the ground*

*it is free now.*

*It flies above the sky and leaves the dark in its place."*

"You have *got* to be kidding me," she whispered when the lines we'd argued over filled both our ears. I watched her as the song played from the beginning again, eyes steady waiting at full attention for the lyrics she trusted, but never heard. "I listened to this song every day," she said more to herself than to me. "I never knew he was talking about love."

I was just as confused as she was. I'd remembered hearing this song, but never heard the right lyrics myself.

"So this song, the entire meaning of it changes now," I said. "It's about love not life. That's probably why Granite chose to take the verse out when the album was reproduced."

Capri laughed to herself. She was uncovering an amazing mystery. "Because it gave the meaning away. Ambient Light's songs are all supposed to be a mystery."

"And now we just solved one."

"Only forty-six more mysteries to go."

I pulled the earbud out and sat up.

"Guess you don't know Ambient Light like you thought you did, huh?"

Capri rolled her eyes, trying to hide her grin.

"Please, I just got one lyric wrong. I *know Ambient Light.*"

"Wanna bet?" I challenged, gesturing to her phone. "How many songs do you have in there?"

"All of them," she replied.

I put the earbud back in my ear. "I don't think my dad will notice if I miss dinner."

"Ma's working late tonight, and my pa never notices when I'm gone. I guess I can stay a little longer."

We both smiled at each other and lay back, our hands behind our heads. The stars lit the abandoned room where we spent three hours. Halfway through the first album, she paused the music, and let her voice break through the silence.

"Zach?"

"Hm?"

"I kind of got an opportunity that I'm terrified to take." She laughed to herself. "I can't believe I'm sharing this with you. It's for a dance camp. Camp Sharp. I made it to the second audition in New York City."

I looked over at her in surprise, but she looked as if she were ashamed of it.

"Camp Sharp? Capri, that's amazing." I don't even dance and I heard of that place. I knew the biggest choreographers for hip-hop and R&B artists went there. "When is it?"

"This Saturday." She rested on her elbows and blew out a large breath, visible fog forming out her mouth from the cold.

She used her fingers to write swirls on the dust-covered floor. "I don't know if I'm gonna go through with it."

"Why? What are you afraid of?"

"I don't think I'm *afraid*," she replied. "Just worried. Ma don't want me dancing seriously anyway, and I feel like I should be honoring that. That's the least I can do to repay her."

"I don't think your grandmother would be looking for anything back. I'm sure she'd want you to meet your goals."

Capri laughed. "You haven't met my grandma, Zach. She's made it very clear that she wants me to pursue something that doesn't sprout wonder and false expectations."

"I think you should go. Camp Sharp, for a dancer, is the door to so many possibilities."

"Is it really worth trying? I mean, do you know how good these kids are that I'm auditioning against? They got like years of professional training from real dancers that get paid for it, and me? I dance by myself in Hamilton. I could be just wasting my time."

"And if you are?" I asked. "You could waste your time, you could disappoint your grandmother, or you could be on your way to getting everything you ever wanted. Don't let this opportunity pass you by. If you do, you'll regret it forever."

She stared into my eyes, a little fear whirling through them. "You think so?"

I nodded. "Think about it, Capri. Dancing is your dream and you're holding back because you don't want to disappoint anybody and you don't think you're good enough. But Camp Sharp sees something in you that *is* good enough. That's why you got an audition."

She bit the insides of her cheek, contemplating. "It's still a lot to think about, for now."

"I was planning on sneaking off to the city this weekend. . . ."

She shook her head quickly, tossing away every thought that entered her mind. "I'll let you know if I change my mind. Can we just change the subject for now?"

I sighed. "Sure."

She pressed play on the album, and we listened through to the end. We were almost the same person; we both longed for things that others said were unattainable, but we tried for them anyway. I mean, I bet that's what they said to the guy who looked at the moon and said, *I'm gonna make a way for someone to touch that*. And soon enough, he did.

# Justin

LIGHT FROM THE HOUSE CREPT INTO THE BLANKET OF night covering the yard when she opened the front door. Immediately the smell from the inside—pot roast, cornbread, and pie—came full force into my nostrils, which caused me to feel even more sick. I tried remembering Tyree's words; searching for them to give me strength like a pregame pep talk. I was supposed to be honest—fully honest about the situation, fully honest about the way I felt about Rose, fully honest about everything. I only wished my heart would climb down from my esophagus.

She pulled me close. I wrapped my arms around her.

"Justin," she whispered, "I'm so glad you came." I hoped she didn't notice my uneven breathing.

"Well, if it isn't Mr. Collins!" Rose's dad greeted, grinning. He stood under the archway leading to the dining room. "Come on in, son. We were just about to sit down for dinner. Mrs. Sails cooked up a feast!"

"Oh! Stop it, Keith," I could hear Mrs. Sails saying from the kitchen. "I just cooked a little something, nothing serious."

"Nothing serious," Reverend Sails repeated, lifting a hand to shoo her humble words away. "All your sweet-tasting something-somethings are something serious. Something mighty good." He winked at me and Rose, a glimmer in his eyes. "Come on in, boy, and shut the door behind you. It's almost time to pig out. You better have more than one plate too, Jus. You need the bulking for the remainder of this season."

I always admired the way Reverend and Mrs. Sails interacted. It was obvious they were still in love. The little glances exchanged across the table, the flirty remarks, the blushes that overtook Mrs. Sails when Reverend spoke always filled me with hope. I wanted that to be me and Rose after twenty years of marriage. I wanted to still be in love like the reverend is, I wanted Rose to always have the blush on her face whenever I kissed her cheek or wrapped an arm around her waist. After the conversation I would have tonight, I hoped I'd still be able to.

"Glad to have you here, son," Reverend Sails said to me when they all gathered around the dining room table for dinner. Bowls filled with mac and cheese, yams, collards, stuffing, and a pan of cornbread sat on a white tablecloth. Not just any white tablecloth; the good one with lace at the bottom. One only brought out for holidays or major celebrations, like when they met a church offering goal for their new building fund or charity.

"What's the occasion?" I asked, trying to keep my voice steady, gesturing to the tablecloth. Mrs. Sails walked into the kitchen, holding a pot roast in her oven-mitted hands. She gently placed it in the middle of the table.

"Well, Rose said you had something very important to tell us," Mrs. Sails said joyfully. "We know you've been applying for those scholarships, so I cooked something real special for you." After twisting a few bowls to ensure a perfect table, she slid her phone from her white apron. "All right, Justin and Rose, big smiles, okay?"

I forced a smile on my face—a very tight-lipped, fearful one.

"Come on, Justin, get in a little closer to Rose," she directed.

"Just this once you can get close," Reverend joked from across the table. I wrapped an arm around Rose's seat. I could see small drips of sweat making their way from her hairline to her neck. It felt like we stepped into an oven.

Mrs. Sails placed her phone back into the pocket of her apron. "Okay, let's say our thanks to the Lord, and then dive in." She took her seat next to Reverend Sails across from the table.

"Bowed heads and closed eyes," he directed, and then began to pray. I couldn't even hear the prayer. I could only keep my eyes open, glancing at the well-put-together family I was about to ruin. I looked at Rose, and again, guilt filled my heart. She looked so innocent, her hands placed absentmindedly over her stomach covered with layers of clothing.

"Amen," Reverend Sails finished.

"Amen," I whispered.

I routinely piled food upon my plate as the bowls were passed by direction of Reverend Sails, who kept telling me to scoop more and more, a little more. Proud smiles showed on both her parents' faces as they awaited the news. Probably college news. Any kind of news, as I was still tight-lipped. I chewed slowly, eating with one hand, holding on to Rose's under the table with the other. I swallowed large lumps of food. Yams and mac that tasted sweeter than usual, the roast and greens saltier. Rose didn't rush me; she just gave gentle squeezes at the same moment when my heart rate would spike. I wondered how she knew when it happened.

"So, Justin," Reverend Sails said, mouth full. "Are you going to tell us the good news?"

I swallowed the large lump of food I'd been chewing for minutes and dropped my fork.

Mrs. Sails nudged him with her elbow. "Oh, honey, let the boy finish his food first. He can tell us over sweet potato pie."

I looked at Rose pleadingly. I couldn't eat another bite.

"*I love you,*" she mouthed. "*Very much.*"

Then I found myself standing. "Actually, I think I'll tell you now."

Reverend Sails leaned back in his seat, awaiting the good news. And it could be good news, under different circumstances at a different time, like seven years into the future for instance, with a ring on their daughter's finger.

"Rose is . . . I mean I—"

Reverend Sails grinned. "Come on, boy, spit it out."

I cleared my throat. "We, we're . . . what I mean to say is . . ."

I felt a whisk of air blow next to me when Rose quickly stood up from her seat.

"*Daddy, I'm pregnant.*"

At first, there was silence. Long, dead silence. The faulty heater humming underneath us stopped singing. The buzzing light above stopped its tune, the breathing of each person seemed to quiet completely. No noise, no speaking, no background noise for minutes. Me and Rose stood frozen like God pressed pause on His remote, freezing time. Even Reverend and Mrs. Sails sat eerily still, until Mrs. Sails somehow managed to fall from her chair onto the floor. She began to breathe heavily to the point where I thought I witnessed her drop dead right there in front of me.

"Get your mother some water, quick," Reverend Sails directed to Rose with gritted teeth. He pushed his chair from under him and kneeled by his wife, fanning her with a cloth napkin. Rose was gone for what felt like hours while I sat there scared out of my mind being in the room with her father alone. I waited for him to hop across the table and strangle me. He let out the breath he was holding when Rose sprinted into the dining room with a glass of water. She knelt and placed the cup to her mother's lips. I watched as she took little sips, her breathing still sputtering like a car that wouldn't start.

Reverend Sails glared at me.

"I outta kill you, son," he seethed, slowly standing. I backed farther and farther from the table until I collided with the wall and Reverend Sails stood before me. "I outta take you in that yard and shove my axe into your back." His finger bore a flaming hole into my chest.

"I love Rose," I said, barely above a whisper. I fought to keep my eyes open, starting straight ahead into the fiery eyes of her father. I worked hard to lean into the ounce of boldness that crept up on me. Reverend Sails's face seemed to morph into the embodiment of hate; eyes wide, teeth clenched, red skin. But I stayed still.

"I love Rose," I repeated, my voice coming out steadily, pushing hard against the sentence. "I love Rose."

Still, Mrs. Sails fought for her breath on the floor. "Get . . . him . . . Keith," she whispered, but I continued to repeat the truth, the one truth I knew, more than anything else.

"I love Rose. I love—" I was cut off by an ear-splitting sound I *thought* came from someone slapping their hand against a door. It was so loud. But then pain whiplashed against my cheek, to my neck, and I knew no one had slapped a door. It was the sound of Reverend Sails's fist smashing against my face.

"Daddy, no!" Rose screamed. She ran from where she knelt next to her mother and pulled on her father's arm. But he wouldn't turn around, his eyes so glazed over with anger he wouldn't even look at her. She cried "Daddy" over and over again like a broken record, but he didn't turn to face her.

"You love her?" Reverend Sails asked, ignoring the swelling starting under my eye. "You love her?" he repeated. "Then take her home with you. She ain't living here no more. You knocked her up, she's your responsibility. Pack your bags, Rose, and *get out of my house!*" He screamed the last part, and he walked the opposite way, so he wouldn't have to look at her, the one standing behind him, pulling on his arm.

"Daddy," Rose whispered, tears streaming down her face. "*Daddy, look at me.*"

And finally, he did. He looked at her. The hate that washed his face was gone. He just looked tired. He cradled Rose's face, her tears soaking his palms.

"After all we done for you, Rose? All we taught you? This is how you repay us? This is how you choose to ruin your life?" he whispered. "Your life is over now, Rose. You ruined it."

I winced.

Rose couldn't say anything. She stood still. Everything stood still, even time. He let his hands fall from her tear-stained face.

"I want you out. I don't care where you go, but it ain't gonna be here. I ain't raising no baby. You made your bed? Lie in it." Then he glared at me again. "I want you out of my house or I'm grabbing that axe." He faced his wife, who gained control of her breath, her eyes now filling with tears. "Lila, help her pack her things," he commanded hoarsely.

His room door slammed shut behind him.

Rose told me her mama told her she loved her after they

silently filled up a trash bag with her sweaters, skirts, and under-wear. But Rose wondered what love really was. Mrs. Sails hadn't tried to convince Reverend Sails to let her stay. She still shut the front door when we left, same as he did.

# Capri

*I LET THE STARS THAT I SAW IN THE SKY OVER THE* railroad station carry me all the way home. I couldn't put a finger on how I felt, but I knew I'd never felt it before. My stomach felt as if it had been frozen over with snow, then warmed by a light fire, flickering heat throughout my body. I felt like I was high, even though I've never been high before, but I'm sure if I had, it would have felt like this.

I could just picture Ma sitting in that sofa chair, her hair tied up in her cheetah-print scarf, draped in the beige, grease-stained nightgown she'd been wearing since I was born, waiting to meet me at the door with one of those slippers she used to hit me and Justin with when we acted up. She was gonna ask me where I've been, and I was gonna have to make up a lie. Hopefully, working late would suffice, but it was already close to one in the morning and the record shop closed four hours ago. I prepared to just take the whack on the back with the slipper and hear her yell at me for an hour until she tired herself out. But surprisingly, when I came home, I was wrong. Ma was sitting on the sofa with the headscarf and the nightgown, but she didn't look mad—just real sleepy and a little weak. She held in her hand two mugs filled with lemon tea; I could smell them as soon as I opened the door. She wasn't sitting by herself either; she was sitting next to an equally tired-looking skinny girl dressed in one of Justin's T-shirts and my yellow pajama bottoms. Her hair was disheveled, falling in all different directions, the ponytail on the crown of her head barely maintained. She grabbed the mug gently from Ma and brought it to her lips, not even wincing from the heat, even though I could see the steam from where I stood. I shut the front door behind me.

"Hey, Capri," Rose whispered.

Ma looked up and gave me a nod. "Hey, Pri."

I waved slightly, half relieved that I could jump into bed, bury myself in my covers, and replay my night again and again until I fell asleep and dreamt about it. But the other half of me was confused; I wondered why Rose and Ma looked so tired and sick—why dark circles were engraved beneath their eyes. Why Rose looked like she had been crying. Then I was filled with worry.

"Is Justin all right?" I asked cautiously.

"He all right, he just sleeping," Ma replied. "Come over here. I got something you need to know." I walked slowly over to them; Ma patted the spot next to her and I sat. "Rosey gonna be staying with us from now on."

"Why?" I asked.

"Because I'm pregnant." Rose's voice sounded weak, like an old radio on the fritz.

*What?*

"You're what?"

She sighed, her eyes misting over with tears. "I'm sorry we didn't tell y'all sooner, but Justin felt it was best to wait until we knew what we were gonna do with it."

"She told her parents tonight and they kicked the poor babies out," Ma explained. I sat there, frozen. That was why Justin was acting so weird, avoiding everybody, the little time he spent at home with his head buried in those books.

"How many months?" I asked.

"Almost four," she replied.

I tried to force a smile. "I . . . congratulations." *Right. That's what you say when someone finds out they're having a baby.* Her bottom lip quivered, and a few tears fell from her face. Ma patted me on the knee as if to shush me, like I was some little kid who didn't understand nothing. Then she looked deep into Rose's eyes.

"Have you been to the doctors yet, Rosey?"

She nodded her head. "I . . . we went to Barry's around the time when we first found out. We talked about letting it . . . the baby . . . go. So, we went to Barry's to do it."

Barry was one of the three doctors we had in Hamilton. He delivered babies at people's homes; I had no idea that he offered abortions. Ma's eyes darted from the left and right; she looked confused. Upset that she hadn't known, I guess. Surprised too, as she took it all in.

Rose continued. "He asked me if I wanted to hear the heartbeat before I . . . and I said yes. When I heard it, I felt it. I can't describe it, but I felt it so deep within me, living, breathing and I fell in love with it. I ran out of there before he could even wipe the gel off my stomach. Justin was sitting in the waiting room, and when he looked at me, he knew nothing happened. He grabbed my hand and we just walked out."

"Barry real trustworthy, he didn't share y'all secret with nobody. He kept it to himself. You should be very thankful," Ma whispered.

"I am . . . we are," Rose replied. "But I wish . . . I'm wishing we did. If I knew my mom and dad would hate me for it, I would've done it." Rose was all out crying now, cupping the hot tea mug in her hands. Ma put hers down and held her tight, shushing her sharply.

"This ain't about your parents, Rosey, you said it yourself. You fell in love with that child growing inside of you. Don't let nobody make you regret none of your choices, not yo momma or yo daddy. It's your life . . . you choose how you wanna live it. Don't worry about nobody else but you. We gonna handle this together as a family, 'cause that's what we are." Rose started saying something, but I couldn't quite make out what it was in between her congested crying. I slowly stood from where I was sitting and walked into my room. I gently shut the door, my heart heating, my chest beating faster than it had while dancing.

It rang three times before he picked up.

"Capri?" He sounded as if he'd already been sleep.

"I'm going," I replied, leaning against the door for support. When I said it, my knees grew weak.

"What?"

"I'm going, Zach. You can take me. I'm gonna do it."

Silence filled the space between us. "Are you sure?" he asked. "What about your ma?"

"She just said that nobody should worry about anybody else when it comes to their choices. Not your family, not nobody. I choose to go to this audition in New York. We can meet tomorrow at the tracks."

"No," he said. "I'll meet you in Hamilton. At the Sunlight."

"Are you sure?"

"Hey, I'm not sure what got into you, but I don't want you backing out at the last moment and not showing up. I'll meet you at the record shop tomorrow around eight."

I smiled. "Okay."

"Capri?"

"Yes?"

"This is your first step. I know Essie would be proud of you."

I knew she really would be too.

# Justin

I LAY IN MY BED ONLY HOURS AFTER ROSE HAD GOTTEN kicked out, and already there was more piled onto my list of regrets and wishes. I wanted so desperately to wake up from the nightmare I had been living in. To be *the* Justin Collins again. The one who made good choices, who always thought ahead, who didn't abandon his responsibilities, like the sister he promised to care for. I ached for things to feel normal again; things hadn't felt *normal* for me since Rose told me she was pregnant.

I was worried about how Ma would take the news, but she only hugged us. Told us both we'd be all right. She wanted to talk about some things with Rose and told me to lie down and get some rest before practice in the morning and the big game the next night. I was happy she wasn't mad at me for keeping it a secret so long. She just looked a little disappointed. I preferred that any day over the look I saw on Reverend Sails's face.

*How can you kick out your only child?*

I'd been fighting with insomnia for months, weighed down by everything. Every time I tried drifting to sleep, my heart would bounce inside of my chest and I'd wake up. October first kept replaying in my head. The times we snuck into each other's rooms and had sex after that. The way we gratified our flesh without a second's thought, like we were indestructible. The day the condom broke. The day I got the text. The day I sat in the waiting room at the doctor's office, knee bouncing, silently hoping Rose wouldn't go through with it. I didn't know why I wanted to keep it, but I just didn't wanna let it go.

Hours passed, and I was still lost in my thoughts. I looked at the desk clock on my windowsill: four thirty. Everyone was sleep. I heard Ma walk Rose to the walk-in closet with the washer, dryer, and small cot that doubled as a guest room. The door closed softly, and the soft whimpers that made their way under it subsided after a few hours. I was grateful Rose was getting sleep, breathing steadily as she'd done when we lay in her bed together, my arm around her waist, her head on my chest. I'd watch her chest rise and fall slowly as she dreamed a different reality. I always wondered what she could possibly be dreaming of when a small smile would form on her lips. Maybe life outside of where we were. Perhaps the day we talked about marrying and leaving it all behind. I never went to sleep when we lay next to one another. No dream could top the feeling I got when I was that close to her. Why would I sleep in those moments?

Now I ached to dream, to sleep, to escape.

For the first time in years, I let myself think of Mama. Not just a passing thought when a familiar smell ran through the air, or an image of her face when someone mentioned her name. This time, I really concentrated on her. She was a grandmother now, after all. I wondered how she would have reacted to the news. She was in high school when she had me. I remembered being a young child, lying next to her in her pitch-black room, staring straight up at her ceiling that she'd scattered with glow-in-the-dark star stickers.

I could almost hear her voice around me.

*"Life ain't like no box of chocolates like that movie says. It's*

more like a box of stars. Wanna know why? You supposed to say 'Why, Mama,' when I say deep things like that," she would whisper, then poke the side of my stomach, which always made me laugh.

"Why, Mama?" I would whisper back, trying not to wake Capri, lying in her crib completely in dreamland.

"Well, my son. I'll tell you," she'd reply, and I was sure I could hear her smiling. "Some stars is dimmer than others, just like some life experiences we got is dim. Sometimes the dim things make us feel like giving up, throwing in the towel, and just lying down to stare at that dark sky. But we gotta remember, even though the sky is dark, there's stars still shining, and we gotta be grateful for that too, even if they is dim."

I never understood what Mama meant when she repeated the same thing each and every night, like a bedtime story. I just liked hearing her speak about the things she believed. She could convince anybody to believe in what she did, even as ludicrous as it may have sounded. But maybe now I did believe her. My sky, as of now, seemed pretty dark. The whole town would figure out what I'd done. Things weren't going as planned. Rose was kicked out. She'd be living with me now. I had a baby on the way. Nothing in life would ever be how it once was.

And I was terrified.

But still, through the dark sky, filled with dim stars, I could see a flicker of hope. At least I still had my Rose. I was in love with her, and I knew though things might be rocky from now on, we had each other. Life was hard right now, this season's stars shone dim, but I would still be grateful that a light was still shining.

"You know, it's funny. Sometimes, we stress over the things we can't control instead of letting life take its course and smiling *through it all. We can still wish upon dim stars you know."*

I took a breath. I wasn't sure if I was wishing or praying—maybe both. Whatever would work, I'd take.

*I need everything to fall into place, to be exactly how it's meant to be.*

"It's Saturday morning, people of Hamilton! This is Easy MaeCollins soaring through your radio waves from the Sunlight Record Shop. Come on, guys and gals, let's get you out of bed and into that Saturday routine. For this very special Saturday, I thought I'd start y'all off with a classic nineties grunge piece. Here's Ambient Light's 'Don't Let Me Go.'"

I slapped the snooze button on the seven a.m. alarm, not quite awake from my dreamless sleep. My eyes finally fell closed for more than ten minutes, after the sun shone through the crevices of my blinds, casting its blue light across my room. I wished the night lasted longer than it had; that way I didn't have to face the new day. But then, at the same time, I was hopeful. Mama's memory made me feel like everything might turn out all right. I forced myself awake and hopped out of bed, ready for my morning run.

I just had to work harder. I was gonna make sure that dim star would shine bright. I knew from now on, life wouldn't be the same, but that didn't have to be a bad thing. No, if I had anything to do with it, it would be the exact opposite. Life's sudden change rocked me a bit, but it also gave me a push. I'd get that scholarship, I'd get into a great college, get into the NBA, and make sure that my child and wife would want for nothing. I wasn't worried about it not happening no more. I couldn't be.

Just like Mama said, even dim stars could be wished upon.

# Zach

THE BELL JINGLED OVER THE SHOP DOOR WHEN I WALKED in the morning after Capri and I spent half the night together. I looked forward to seeing her again, anticipating being able to spend an entire day with the girl that managed to, in one night, make me feel as comfortable as I'd felt in Philly—a little more hopeful.

I watched her lips stretch into a wide grin and move into a "you made it," but my earbuds were still in so I couldn't hear her. Before I knew it, she ran from behind the counter and pulled me into a hug, knocking the cords straight from my ears, which surprised me a bit. I wasn't expecting such an excited greeting, but I quickly wrapped my arms around her so she wouldn't view my hesitance as rejection. I took the opportunity to bury my nose in her curls, which hung free, out of her usual ponytail. She smelled like cinnamon.

"I'm so happy you came," she whispered.

"Me too."

"Wow, this more serious than I thought," someone said, causing us to pull away.

There was a girl standing behind the counter, her arms crossed, staring at me as if I were an attraction at a museum. She was way lighter than Capri and taller. Her hair was dyed a bright blond and a bone-straight ponytail hung from the crown of her head down to just around her waist.

"Perry, this is Zach. Zach, Perry," Capri introduced. Perry stuck her hand out for me to shake, even though I was by the door. I quickly walked up to her and shook it.

"Hi, I'm Zach."

She smirked. "I know. Capri just told me."

My face grew warm. "Right. Nice to meet you, Perry."

"You too." Her eyes fell from my face to my feet twice, then she looked at Capri. "You were right, Pri, about *everything*." Her eyes fell on me again. "Don't worry, it's a good thing. A *really* good thing."

"Okay, okay," Capri said, her face tinted crimson. "It's about time we get going." She pulled on my arm to lead me out the door.

"*Capri!*" Easy suddenly called from his office. "*Ca-pri!*" he called again.

She sighed deeply. "One second. I'll be right back. Don't move." She headed to the back of the shop where Easy's office was.

I let my hoodie fall and looked around. I'd lain in bed the night before, fixated on what Easy said. Maybe he was right about my not fitting in in Bayside, but he wasn't right about Hamilton. There was something about this entire town that made the pit of my stomach ignite with feelings I hadn't yet figured out. I felt anxious, but I wasn't afraid—comfortable, though I wasn't welcomed. At home, though I lived in the next town over.

"So, did you have any problems crossing over here?" Perry asked. She made her way from behind the counter and leaned her back against the front.

"Not really. I keep my hoodie on, so no one really pays much attention to me."

She scoffed. "Trust me, hun, people paying attention. I got like sixteen group texts asking if anybody knew who was the white kid walking around here." She crossed her arms. "We just ain't gonna harass or burn your house down like y'all would do to us over in Bayside."

The bell rang over the shop.

"So there *is* some white meat in Hamilton, I had to see it for *myself*, walking in our hood, bringing all his *wealth*."

I turned around to see a really tall, dark-skinned guy walk in with a group of about eight other guys, all dressed in blue-and-gold basketball shorts, sneakers, and white T-shirts.

Perry rolled her eyes. "Jay, your rhymes still suck. Give it up."

He brushed by me to the counter where Perry leaned, trying to squeeze his large frame next to her. "You gonna be mad when I make it big and I ain't asking you to be in any of my videos." He pulled on one of her large hoop earrings; she shrugged him off.

"*Please*, the only videos you gonna be starring in is on social media for all them fouls you be causing, making us lose all them games."

I tried ignoring the other guys he came in with that made a semicircle around me, staring me up and down. I guess I wasn't the only one who noticed. Perry cleared her throat and introduced me.

"This is Zach, he's from—"

"New York," I finished for her.

"Right. New York," she repeated, adding an overexaggerated wink.

The guys gave me a head nod.

Jay, who was leaning next to Perry, suddenly appeared.

"So, you from New York, huh? I went there once, almost got a record deal. I can spit you something if you're interested." He stood so close to me that I could smell the pancake on his breath.

"Nobody wanna hear you spit. I bet he don't even know nothing about rap," one of the guys said.

"Actually, I do," I replied.

"See, he *do*. You spit?" Jay asked, still standing close to my face. I backed up a little.

"Not as much as I used to."

"If you spit, spit something against me, right here. Right now," Jay challenged.

"I haven't done it in a while. It's—"

Jay began to cackle obnoxiously. "White boy scared. See, I told y'all white boys get choked up and almost piss their pants in the presence of anyone Black. Look at him, crossing his legs so he don't spill his white-boy piss on the floor." The boys around him laughed, all except one who walked slowly around the record shop, brushing his hand against the vinyl players across the wall. He seemed to be in an entirely different world, disconnected from everything going on around him.

"Hey, you," Jay said, nudging my shoulder. I refused to allow my body to lift a hand, to rub out the pain his meaty hand caused. "White boy. Why you here anyway? You know this is Hamilton, right? It's a lot different than your New York City culture. This is an *all dark* city. We ain't mixed with no wiglets."

Perry piped in: "Leave him *alone*, Jay. My gosh."

"Actually." I took a breath and let it out, immensely tired of all the crap I was getting from Bayside because I wasn't "white" enough, and now Hamilton because I was *too* white. "I'll spit something."

Jay looked pleased that his teasing made me angry enough to go against him. I was disrespected and judged when I was challenged in Philly as a boy. This wouldn't be any different.

"Aight, drop the beat ho—"

"You better *not* finish that sentence or you gonna wind up beat and left in somebody trash can," Perry practically yelled, her hands on her hips.

"Just play the song, Perry," Jay whined.

"Yeah, you better call me *Perry*, not nothing else. I ain't one of them dumb chicks that pull down their panties because they desperate to be with any basketball player even if he as bad as your triflin' tail." She muttered a few more things but scrolled through her phone and plugged it into a small, egg-shaped speaker on the counter. A simple drumbeat rang out. Jay smiled proudly, bobbing his head to the beat. He even gave the boys surrounding us high fives.

*"Yo, Yo, Yo, we got this white boy who think he nice boy,*
*he ain't bigger than a little piece of rice boy,*
*I bet he sweet like sugar and spice boy.*
*Ohh I taste him in my tummy, yummy, yummy!*
*with his hoodie and his fade, knockoff Jordans*
*looking like crap,*
*when he should be at a hoagie place, making us a wrap!"*

The boys around him all whoo'd as if he were Tupac and just spit this amazing thought-provoking rap, instead of a childish rhyme about food and sneakers. He paused to let me go, standing in front of me with that cocky smile of his. I'd only just met him but was already annoyed with the guy. He reminded me of BradBrock; thinking he was God's gift to the earth. I closed my eyes and listened closely to the beat, allowing it to tell me what it wanted said over it, what message it wanted rang out, what emotion it was spewing.

*"I'm about to blow up on this rhyme like a bomb,*

*Tell me why yesterday*
*I was with this man's mom,*
*but don't get mad,*
*I put a smile on her face.*
*She said you haven't been able to do that since the second grade!*
*Hanging D-pluses on the fridge,*
*remember them days?*
*And when you messin' with Zach, you digging your own grave!*
*Cuz I got that old-school flow runnin' through my veins,*
*And the stuff that I spit,*
*Will make the crowd go insane!"*

The beat stopped the same time I did. The shop was so quiet; I could hear the squawking of the broken heater. Twenty eyes watched me; I couldn't read the emotion in them. I instantly regretted getting carried away with my rhymes and subconsciously clenched my fist as I braced myself for Jay's to hit me in my face. Then suddenly, Perry's laughter sliced through the silence. It was a high-pitched squeal that reminded me of those hyenas from *The Lion King.*

"Yo, *yo*, he said he put a smile on your momma's face!" she cried in between laughs. "And you . . . you haven't been able to do that . . . since what . . . what you say, Zach?"

I cleared my throat. "Uh, the second grade?"

The hyena laughter belted out again.

"I can't *stand* you," she cried, throwing her head back, still in a laughing fit. I tried to hide the smirk grabbing my face. I'm weak around laughter; it's contagious.

"What you think you some kind of poet?" Jay's voice caught me off guard and I jumped.

"I . . . just spoke what was on my mind."

He glared at me, biting on the side of his cheek. "That wasn't that bad. It was mad nerdy, but it wasn't that bad." He stuck out a hand for me to shake. Slowly, I took it.

"So, you never answered my question," Jay said after dropping his hand from mine. "Why you here, man, in this small town nobody ever come to?"

"I came for Capri, to take—"

He lifted an eyebrow. A few guys chuckled into their palms loudly. Before I could finish my sentence, Jay started speaking.

"You mean Capri Collins? The girl that don't say jack to nobody?"

"That's why she never gave *you* the time of day, Jay," one of the guys piped in. "She likes them white."

My face heated.

"First you appear out of nowhere, you white and you got rhymes, you live in New York but you choose to come to Hamilton, now you say you got Capri Collins on lock?"

"I didn't say I had her on *lock*, I just—"

"What did you say your name was again?" Jay inquired.

"Zach," someone answered before I could. The distracted boy from earlier stepped out from the group of guys and stood before me. He was my height, maybe a half inch taller. He, unlike the other guys, had a baby face, no facial hair, and on his head, a short clean cut. What stuck out against everything else the most was the black-and-blue bruise growing out of the skin under his eye. He held in his hand a book—one I'd read a million times.

I gestured to it, trying to lighten the threatening glare he'd given me. "*Souls of Black Folk*. Amazing book."

"How you know my sister?" he asked, not at all impressed that we share the same taste in literature.

"Your sister?" I asked.

"Capri. She's my little sister. How you know her?" he asked pointedly.

"Why you always on her back, Justin?" Perry piped in. "She don't ask you nothing about Rose."

"This ain't about Rose," Justin spat. "It's about this dude from New York nobody know nothing about, talking 'bout he got my little sister on lock." He looked me up and down. "How you know her?"

I cleared my throat. "I never said that I had her on anything. I met her yesterday when I came here to meet Mr. MaeCollins."

"And did you meet him?" asked a Latino boy as he made his way through the circle to stand by Justin.

"Yeah," I replied.

"Then why you here again?" asked another lanky Black boy appearing on the other side of Justin. Suddenly the room grew tense. I fished for words, suffocating.

"I came to take—"

"Fix the heater, since it's busted," Perry quickly said, sharply staring at me. "He came to take it back to *New York* to work on it."

I released a breath. "Yup, just fixing the heater for Mr. Mae-Collins. I know Capri because she works here. She's the one who's supposed to show me where the heater is."

*Thank God for that.*

Her brother stared as if he'd not believed anything Perry said. I stared back innocently. His eyes searched mine, deeply. The only thing that broke the stare was the fact that his eyes needed a blinking break. "Why they ain't get Bernie to fix it? He fixes everything in Hamilton."

"Man," the lanky boy said. "You know Bernie got arthritis."

"He ain't fixing no heater with them meaty knuckles. They gonna roast," the Latino boy joked, which caused the boys to laugh. Justin rolled his eyes.

"Where's Capri at right now?" he asked Perry.

"In Easy's office. He called her back there."

He reached into his backpack and took out a brown-bagged lunch. "Ma wanted me to drop this off to her." It fell against the counter with a liquid squish. "I think the soup spilt in it while I was running. Tell her not to tell Ma."

"Okay. I'll tell her when she get out."

"Thanks," he replied.

Jay walked back up to Perry. "Will I see you at the game tonight? Cheering for the Jay-man?"

Perry gave him the flat hand. "Get your nasty breath out my face. You too close, Jay, and if anything, I'd be cheering for somebody else. You suck." The record shop filled with the loud laughter of the guys, but Jay tried to play it cool.

"Come on, Jay, y'all took a long enough break. We gotta get back to running," Justin instructed, walking toward the door. Everyone stopped what they were doing to follow him out the store. I let out a breath when they exited and started running down the street. Almost immediately, Capri came out the office, followed by Easy. She held in her hands a stack of yellow flyers.

"Well, if it isn't Zach," Easy said. "We heard you say you wanted to fix my heater."

"I uh . . ."

Capri smiled. "Zach, don't listen to him, he's only kidding. Right, Easy?"

He shrugged. "Halfway, halfway. The boys didn't scare you too much, did they?"

"Nah," I lied.

"I think he scared them more than they scared him. You heard his rhyme? Ten times better than anything I heard Jay do," Perry piped in, her lips stretching into a grin. "You sure showed him too. Ha, *put a smile on his momma's face.*"

"I'm afraid we didn't. But I'd like to hear it one day," Easy replied.

Capri narrowed her eyes in his direction. "Easy also has something he wants to tell you."

He sighed heavily before speaking. "I didn't give you the Hamilton welcome you deserved yesterday. I was upset because of the heater not working, so I took it out on you. I must admit, I don't usually act that way."

"You don't?" Perry cut in. She pursed her lips.

"Hey, keep messing around and I'll fire you."

"I. Don't. Work. Here," Perry replied through gritted teeth.

"Well then, I won't pay you," Easy responded back through gritted teeth.

Perry looked surprised. "I'm getting paid?"

"I *was* but now that you wanna be all smart mouth . . ."

Instantly Perry's face brightened. "Good morning, Boss, what can I do for you today?"

"You can start by scrubbing them toilets in the back."

Perry's face melted back into the frown. She grumbled under her breath and walked toward the back of the store.

"Toilet brushes are under the sink!" Easy called back to her with a pleased smile. Capri cleared her throat.

"Right," Easy said, catching his train of thought. "I wanted to apologize, Zach, I didn't mean to offend you, especially since I hear you're such a fan of mine." He stretched out a hand for me to shake and I gladly took it. "So, Capri tells me you're accompanying her into New York?" he asked.

"Yes, sir," I replied.

"Now what does a Philly Bayside boy know about the Big Apple?"

I looked at Capri.

"It's all right," she laughed. "Easy knew you were fibbing anyways."

Easy smiled. "And to pay me back for lying to my face, in *my* record shop, you gotta pass these around on your way out of Hamilton." Capri separated the flyers she held into another pile and handed them to me. My eyes widened when I read what they said.

# Capri

**"YOU'RE DOING A COMEBACK TOUR?" ZACH ASKED, HIS** crystal eyes growing wide with satisfaction and amazement.

Easy smiled, clearly happy he'd seen the second reaction to his announcement a positive one. I was happy for him too, but it took us a while to get there. When Easy called me back to his office after Zach walked in, I was a bit annoyed. I wasn't a fan of leaving Zach to fend for himself in the front of the store. Especially when I heard the boys walk in. But Easy assured me that Zach would be fine because he was from New York and he'd probably dealt with much worse than a few high school boys. He said this with narrowed eyes, stretching out each word, and that's when I knew we were caught.

"He's not from New York City," I admitted. "He's from Bayside."

Easy smiled and shook his head. "I knew that already, Pri. I'm just wondering why you wouldn't tell the old man who's been by your side since the beginning."

I didn't answer at first. It was like asking Justin why he lied to all of us about Rose's pregnancy. Because he was afraid of how everyone in Hamilton would react to him getting the holiest girl around here knocked up. When he finally told the truth, she got kicked out. So why would I feel comfortable enough to just announce to everyone that Zach, who wasn't just a white boy, but a white boy from Bayside, was taking me to New York City to audition for a dance camp?

Lying was my only choice and it wasn't the first one I'd told that morning. Before Ma could wake up and blast gospel music, I was already mopping the kitchen floor. When she asked me why I was awake, I told her I'd be picking up an extra shift at Easy's to buy Justin and Rose a present for the baby. Ma didn't look at me all crazy like I thought she would. Instead, she cried. She expressed how she didn't understand why the reverend kicked Rose out, that Jesus wouldn't have liked that. I knew Jesus wouldn't like my lying either. When I showered after cleaning, I scrubbed at the guilt that seeped from my pores, promising Jesus that I would keep taking extra shifts to get something for my niece or nephew before it was born.

"You know what you doing is dangerous, hanging around that boy," Easy warned.

"And that's why I lied to you," I replied, before realizing it. "Listen, you have been amazing to me since Essie . . ."

He cleared his throat. I sighed.

"Since Mama passed, you've always encouraged me to pursue what my heart wants. Not to care what nobody thinks about it. You said it was okay to take this job working for you, sneaking behind everyone's back to dance. It was all good when I auditioned for Camp Sharp behind Ma's back too, and it was even better when we planned this elaborate trip to New York City together. Now, it's a problem because I'm going with Zach."

That's the moment when we heard a beat playing from the front of the shop make its way to us. I turned my heel to see why the music was playing, but Easy grabbed my arm.

"Capri, do you have feelings for this boy?"

I paused. *Do I have feelings for Zach?* I knew an ember of something began to flame between the two of us, but I didn't count the cost until that moment. Our skin was one thing but living on two separate sides of the tracks was a different matter. It would make whatever was starting to happen complicated, maybe even impossible. Easy continued staring, awaiting a response.

"When Zach first walked in here last night, I was curious. I could tell there was something different about him. Then we got to talking about Ambient Light and that's when I realized how talking to him felt different than talking to anyone else here, and it had only been a short time. He's different—different than everyone else in Bayside and Hamilton too. He doesn't even like it there, Easy. He's really from Philly and he's cultured and kind and . . ."

"He deserves an apology from me," Easy finished. "I judged him too quickly yesterday before I got a chance to know him. If he is the reason why you feel confident enough to follow behind your mama, well I guess there is something about him that I'm missing. You gotta understand where I'm coming from though, Pri: I don't want nothing bad happening to you. White folk will stick by you until it's inconvenient, remember that. I've been through it before. I just want you to be careful. Stick up for yourself. That's the only way to get respect."

I've heard countless stories about Easy's run-ins with the white people that tried taking his songs and passing them as their own while he was coming up. Even keeping him from some of the clubs he had every right to play in. I pulled Easy into a hug; never was there a time I ever felt anything other than safe in his fatherly embrace.

"I promise I will be careful. Listen, Zach isn't the only reason why I'm following in Mama's footsteps. You have shown me what never giving up looks like, what stepping out past fear looks like." I pulled away and looked straight into Easy's eyes. "I'm still terrified about this audition. I'm terrified about taking this trip to New York City, the last place I saw my mom perform, but I don't want fear to keep me away from it. You never let it after all you went through, why should I?"

The corner of Easy's mouth turned up in a smile.

"You got your mama's fire."

After our conversation, Easy told me all about his comeback tour. I was proud of him for returning to the stage. I knew the entire world outside of Hamilton was waiting to hear him play again. He'd come up with the details the night before, contacted his old friends, and even stayed up until the early hours of the morning working on flyers. While he spoke, I was ecstatic. Then just moments later, when I was standing next to Zach while Easy told him all about it, uneasiness replaced my excitement.

"You got it, Zach. I'm returning to the stage again. That's what I was talking to Pri about in the office. My old playmates and producers been asking me for a long while," he said. "I finally decided it was a good idea. I was thinking about Capri and how she's been given an opportunity to follow her dreams. Since she never wanted my help in attaining them and wanted to go at it alone with the auditions and all."

Zach lifted an eyebrow, clearly interested. Easy continued.

"See, I'm gonna do a comeback tour this July to August, twenty states East and West Coast. I'm sure the first few rows of the audience will be filled with the best names in Hollywood. So I figured I'd take a lucky musician from New York along to be my opening act. Figured, I'd put up some flyers here in Hamilton, get y'all to put up some in New York City, and hold some auditions . . ."

"Auditions?" Zach exclaimed.

Easy nodded. "I'll audition the best Black talent in New York. Black kids don't always get the chance you white kids do when it comes to music. No offense now, but there is some real amazing Black talent in New York City that don't get noticed, talent that the white man just ain't gonna turn his ear to. I figured, I got the connections, why not help out my own? Whoever wins will be the new face in the rhythm and blues genre."

"Black talent," Zach whispered. "Only Black talent?" When he said this, I couldn't help but notice his cheeks turn pink. I knew Zach loved making music, and Easy was one of his biggest inspirations. There was no doubt the opportunity to perform his songs in front of Easy was a dream come true.

Easy smiled, glancing up at the ceiling as if it suddenly sprouted a rainbow, butterflies, and a beautiful meadow or something. "Only Black talent."

I could see the wheels turning in Zach's head when he quickly dropped the flyers I'd handed him on the counter. He pulled his phone from his pocket and began scrolling through it.

"Mr. MaeCollins . . ."

"Call me Easy."

"Easy," Zach corrected. "Do you mind if I played something for you?"

"Not at all," Easy replied.

Zach pressed play on his phone.

Suddenly the small space where we stood filled with the melody of an acoustic guitar, then drums, then a piano, and finally strings. Easy bobbed his head to the soulful song we were hearing stream from Zach's phone speaker.

The instruments all seemed to have a voice of their own at first, then they joined together in a choir of their own—a choir that sang what sounded like the blues, then acoustic rock, then soul. A choir that blended so well together, like a perfect spring day. Each once stood on its own, like the birds, and the warm spring breeze, and the light mist of rain that fell during the night. But then, a rainbow showed up. Yes, it got better. A human voice began to sing over the spring choir.

The voice sounded slick, like warm honey. It was high for a guy's voice, but well controlled; it flew high and higher, and then lower, digging within the earth effortlessly, rolling along the rhythm of the music that carried it. I thought Rose was the greatest singer I'd heard, and she was great, but this, this was something entirely different. A genre I couldn't put my finger on. Something I'd never heard.

"Wow," Easy and I whispered at the same time when the song came to an end.

Zach's eyes had been closed as the song rang from his phone. When it ended fully, and the song locked itself back into the safe where it laid, he looked up.

"That was . . ." I tried looking for words to describe what I'd just heard.

"Amazing," Easy breathed out. "I haven't heard anything like that since, ever. Who was that?"

Zach smiled widely. "It was my friend. He makes music. I figured I'd let you hear him so he could be the first to audition for you. So you wouldn't forget him."

"No way I'm forgetting him," Easy said quickly. He leaned on the counter and fished a small notepad from his shirt pocket. He pulled a small pencil from the inside of the silver loops that held it together. "What's this friend's name?"

"Thomas, Thomas Kell," Zach replied. Easy began to write. I noticed Zach nervously chewing on his bottom lip.

Something wasn't right.

"Thomas, was that the young Black boy I met yesterday?"

Zach nodded.

"Uh . . . yes, sir. He sings and makes his own music. I'm his . . . manager?"

His words came out sounding more like a question than an actual response.

"His manager, huh? Well, Zach, you just got your client a second audition. I'll be holding them next Saturday at our open mic. Have him come with that guitar of his, singing just like that." Easy laughed to himself. "If he sounds anything like he did on that song in real life, there won't be any more auditions. I won't have to choose anyone else."

"That might be a problem," Zach whispered.

Easy's smile fell. "Why?"

"Well, his parents are overprotective. His dad doesn't want him making music. He also can't be out here on the weekends or in the dark so . . ."

"Well, have him come by sometime this week. Wednesday would be perfect. Sneak out after school, just like you did yesterday. I look forward to hearing him!" Before Zach could say another word, Easy was humming the song he'd just heard, all the way back to the office.

Zach still held the phone he'd played the song on in his hand. He was squeezing it so hard, his knuckles turned from red to white. When he noticed me staring, he forced a smile.

"Ready to audition?" He walked out the shop before I could reply.

I knocked three times before I turned the knob.

I told Zach I forgot my good luck charm back in my locker in the employee lounge, even though there's no such place and no such charm. I needed to talk to Easy. Even though I wanted Zach to wait in the front of the store away from the windows, he insisted on waiting outside. He said he needed some fresh air.

"Got cold feet?" Easy asked from behind his desk.

"My feet will be ice cold all day, but I'm choosing to ignore it," I replied.

"Then why you standing there like you're thinking about turning back and really working this shift Perry got covered for you?"

"It's not about Perry," I admitted. "That song we just heard . . . the one Zach played, it was beautiful."

Easy smiled widely. "One of the best songs I've heard in a while. I can't wait to hear more from Thomas."

"Yeah . . . but what about Zach? He's a really good performer too and I think . . ."

Easy lifted a hand to silence me. "All right now, Pri, I've apologized to the boy, but I'm not going back on my word. I know you fancy him, and I got my own feelings about that too, but I'm keeping them at bay for your sake because he makes you happy. But the more you hang out with this boy, the more you'll see that he's got it different than our people do. There's a privilege chained to his ankles, and they're ringing to a different tune. Everybody hears it. Our tune don't ring as loud, sometimes it's never heard the way it should be. Don't be so selfish now."

There was that feeling coming out my pores again. *Guilt*. Maybe he was right. Maybe I was being selfish, but I couldn't get Zach's face out of my head after Easy said he was auditioning only Black talent. He idolized Easy. He just needed a chance. I'd help him figure it out.

"Right, I . . . I better get going."

Easy started humming the song Zach played us again before saying, "Good luck, Capri. Remember who you are."

I nodded and walked out, my brown skin reflecting off a mirror hanging on his door. How could I forget?

# Zach

**THE WHOLE TIME, MY FINGERS TINGLED AND MY HEART** raced. I knew that today wasn't about me. It was about getting Capri to that audition and watching her kill it. For some reason, I felt like a seed had gotten planted somewhere in the soil of the universe with my name on it, and it was going to sprout something that would change the world.

She hummed as we walked, but slowly, it got quieter until she made no sound. Nothing was audible except our footsteps. Then, when we'd reached the clearing just before Bayside's main road, she froze completely.

I smiled. "Don't tell me you're getting last-minute nerves. It's too late to turn back now." I looked at my phone's time. "The ferry leaves soon."

She didn't smile back or spew out a sarcastic remark, like I expected. Instead, she crossed her arms over her chest and frowned.

"The last time I was in Bayside was when me and Justin were real young kids. We came here to catch the ferry to New York to see one of Essie's shows. We ain't been here since that day. I was always taught to stay away 'cause we ain't wanted here."

I slowly walked up to her, closer, and closer, my feet crunching against the leftover snow buried in the grass. The tip of her nose was bright red from the cold, her eyes distracted, darting everywhere, from left to right, not focusing on what lay ahead for her.

I placed my hands on her shoulders. "Hey, hey," I repeated softly until she fixed her eyes on mine. "Last night you said you're not gonna let nobody ruin this for you." I gestured to the town in front of us. "That means them included. Capri, you're so close, don't let your fear of whatever happens or doesn't happen keep you from doing what you came here to do."

She nodded, the glassy look in her eyes washing away. *Good, I was getting somewhere.*

"I promised I'd be with you all day. If I can sneak out of my house and come to Hamilton, despite all that was said about it, spit a freestyle from the top of my head while nerves eat at my insides, face your scary brother, and spend my life savings on a ferry ticket to New York City, you can hold my hand and walk through Bayside to that audition in New York City that I *promise* you're going to ace."

She took a breath and let it out, sending fog all around us.

"Life savings, huh?"

"Every little penny. I was saving up for a new soundboard too. Now it's all gone and there are no refunds." I stretched out a hand in front of her.

She reached out her hand, but hesitated. "You'll be with me the entire time?"

"I won't leave for a second, even if I have to pee, I'll just go to the girls' room."

A small smile formed on her lips, then I felt the warmth of her palm in my own. I squeezed her hand and she squeezed mine back, in response. Her hands were soft, her fingers entangled with mine. I could feel her pulse, her life beating against my own.

"Sorry, I'm nervous," she whispered. "My palm is sweating. Gross, huh?"

Suddenly she pulled away; I could feel it no more.

"No, I . . . I mean. It's fine. A promise is a promise. I'm not letting go. Though, maybe for a quick napkin break, for my now very wet hand."

She stuck her tongue out at me and nudged me with her shoulder. I reached out for her hand again.

"You ready?"

She grabbed it tightly. "Come on. I got an audition to ace."

# Justin

*I RAN IN FRONT OF MY TEAM. THEIR FEET SOUNDED LIKE* an army, marching. I wanted it to be a silent run. I told the guys to stay quiet and focus, but they didn't. They kept talking about the victory party they'd be having after we won the game that night. My mind was racing as fast as my feet.

I'd run into Rose in the hallway that morning, after I got out the shower.

"Justin, good morning," she whispered. The house still glowed with a dark blue morning light. Everyone would still be sleeping for another two hours or so. Usually when I got up early to run, I'd text a good morning message to Rose or call her, knowing I'd go straight to voicemail because she forgot to charge her phone overnight, but determined to say something nice that she could wake up to. I'd tell her how much she meant to me. How I longed for the day I could sleep next to her at night and wake her up with kisses.

But this morning, there she was, standing outside the bathroom in my sweatshirt that stretched almost past her thighs, her eyes groggy, red and swollen from crying. Her lips were cracked and her hair disheveled. I always dreamt of seeing her when she'd woken up before her hair was brushed and makeup put on. This was unlike anything I'd imagined on my own. The girl I sat behind in every class, the one I followed and played with as a child, was here with me, emotionally sick, pregnant, and hurting.

But things would change sooner than later. I knew it.

"You're up early," I whispered, planting a kiss on her cheek, then her other, finally placing a light peck on her lips. She smiled, as she'd always done when I greeted her like this.

"Stop," she chuckled softly, hitting my chest with her palm. "I have morning breath."

"You have to try harder than that, my love. Nothing's gonna stop me from kissing the mother of my child." I gave her another light kiss, which she fell into. She rested her arms around my neck and stared into my eyes.

"Someone's in a good mood this morning," she whispered. "Especially after what happened last night."

"Because dim stars still shine," I replied with a grin and that's all I needed to say. Rose was clearly confused.

"I'll explain it later, but don't be sad anymore. Everything is going to be all right. Don't lose heart, not for one second, all right?" She nodded. "I have to go to practice, but listen, we can talk all about everything after the game tonight. I have a plan."

She shook her head, smiling. "All right, love. Tonight. It's a date."

I kissed the tip of her nose. "Get back to sleep before Ma wakes up and makes you clean with her."

She nodded. "All right. I'll see you at the game."

"Jus, man . . . you running . . . like you getting . . . chased by the cops or something . . . slow down," Carlos, who was running beside me, huffed between gulps of air. I kept my pace, focusing only on the streets ahead of me.

*Passed Banneker Street, next Douglass.*

"We been running . . . since seven . . . it's almost eight thirty."

*Passed Douglass, next Angelou.*

"We barely had a break other . . . than the record shop."

*Passed Angelou, next Hughes.*

"What . . . you . . . bringing to the party . . . tonight?"

I stopped running.

"Break!" I heard someone yell, followed by cheers as soon as he stopped. "The maniac stopped running, guys! We can take a break!"

Carlos bent over to catch his breath. I grabbed the water bottle from my backpack and threw it to Carlos, who chugged ferociously, as if he were stranded in the desert, and this was the only water he'd had in days. He threw it back to me. I took a sip.

"I ain't going to the party." I rubbed my mouth with the back of my hand. "I got something to do after the game."

"Like what?" he asked, still trying to catch his breath. "Another run? Reading another one of them books piling in that backpack you never leave home without? I mean, don't that hurt? All them books on your back, giving you all that extra work when you run?"

I ignored his question. "Look, man, I'm not going."

"Not going where?" Deondre asked, appearing next to them.

"The *victory* party I'm throwing tonight," Carlos replied.

Deondre rolled his eyes. "Come on, Jus, you ain't been to no parties this season."

"Last season either," Carlos added. "Not since he started dating Rose."

"*Banging* Rose," Deondre coughed into his hand.

"Hey," I spat. "This ain't about Rose."

"That's what you said to Perry after that Zach kid said something about Capri," Carlos interjected. "It's always about Rose. It's been about Rose since you started dating her. You ain't even got no time for your boys no more."

Deondre placed a hand on my shoulder and looked me in my eyes. "We ain't wanna say it, but we know something's been up with you. You ain't been the same."

I looked behind me to make sure no one was listening. The guys were all crowding around Jay, who was acting out some story, very dramatically, sauntering down the street like some girl. Everyone was laughing.

"Look, y'all," I whispered. "Rose and me . . . we. . ."

Deondre shooed off my confession. "No, you don't have to explain, man. We know what happened with y'all."

My heart grew hot. "You do?"

Deondre nodded. "We was playing on the courts with Tyree and he told us about y'all's fight."

"Don't be mad at him for saying something," Carlos cut in. "We was asking where you was at and he told us you was working things out with Rose at her house."

"Yeah, but I—"

"We know you stressed about that and getting the scholarship," Deondre said. "But you don't have to be, man. You the best player Hamilton High got and those scouts would be insane not to choose you."

"Plus, you the only one here besides Tyree that actually wanna go away to college," Carlos added, which made me laugh. "Yo, I threw this party for you too. You getting too serious for nothing. We're a team, we got ya back. We gonna win this game tonight, my man. And after that, we gonna party. No more worrying about that scholarship or your issues with Rose, whatever they are. You can deal with them later. Right now, you gotta enjoy being a senior. Enjoy being with ya boys before you run off to some A-rate school and forget all about us."

"I ain't gonna forget y'all," I assured them. "But I don't know about that party. Me and Rose was supposed to meet tonight to talk about some things—"

Carlos lifted his hand to stop me from finishing what he thought was a ratty excuse. "If she loves you, she'll understand you switching that talk for another day. Come on, we know we're gonna win, we've been practicing like crazy. You deserve to celebrate before you're whisked away and forced to do all that crazy training at that A-rate school. We only got a few games left and a few months before we graduate." He gave me a challenging look. "One night."

"One night," Deondre repeated.

I thought about it. They were right. I hadn't been to a party in ages. I deserved one night to myself, one night free of thinking about everything. I felt better than I had in weeks. In fact, I felt hopeful, thanks to Mama. I owed myself *some* sort of release. One night.

"Aight."

Deondre's and Carlos's eyes grew wide. "You serious?" they asked in unison.

I nodded. They both pulled me into a hug, lifting me off the ground in the process.

"We gon' party tonight!" Carlos yelled.

I rolled my eyes.

"Come on, y'all, put me down," I said. "We party tonight. We run for now."

Deondre grinned, saluting. "Whatever you say, captain."

I started to run again, the guys following suit. This would be a good night, I believed it with every fiber of my being. The old Justin was going to reign one more time.

# Capri

IT WAS SO BRIGHT IN BAYSIDE THAT ALL THE SNOW
already melted.

"Is it always this bright here?" I asked, using my palm as a visor
to block out the sun.

"I guess so," he replied. "You okay?"

"Fine," I replied. "It's just a lot different than I remember it.
Everything looked so much bigger before, less familiar." It was
weird; the town almost mirrored Hamilton entirely, the way the
shopping district sat right at the entrance and all. Except instead
of row homes, their town stores were a line of brick colonial-style
buildings. Even the streets were the same: the church was in the
same spot we had ours in Hamilton, except their stained-glass windows looked like they'd been repainted every day or polished with
the rays of the sun. The grocery store was situated in the same place
as ours, too, but it was way bigger. The shops kept the same hours
as Hamilton—open at nine. It was only eight thirty.

Thirty more minutes until the town was bustling with people—
white people. White people who separated themselves purposely
from Black people like me. The sun did a good job showing it.

A memory pushed its way forward.

*Essie was quieter here. So was Justin and Ma. We stood real
close to one another, Ma and Essie holding my hands, Justin holding Essie's other hand. At first it was like that, until Ma said I was*

walking too slow and scooped me up. I wondered why they were walking so fast, so close. Why Essie stopped rehearsing her songs for her show out loud once we crossed the train tracks. But I knew if Essie was quiet and not singing, face straight as a nail, it was for a good reason, so I stayed quiet too.

Ma said "thank you" a lot, to everyone, for everything. When the ticket man for the ferry asked us why we was going to New York, Ma said, "To see a show, thank you." When he handed her the change and our tickets, she said a "thank you" for the change and again for the ticket. When he said, "Next," and gestured to the person behind us, she said, "Thank you."

"I want the spot by the window!" I yelled once we got on the ferry. I squeezed out of Ma's arms and ran as fast as my little legs could take me through the crowd gathering on the boat, to the bench in the middle, and scooted way over to the edge closest to the window. I wanted to see the whole boat ride. I waved my hand above my head.

"Over here, everybody! I got us a seat!" When we were all settled and the boat began to fill, a little girl in a puffy white dress approached us. I'll never forget what happened next.

"I wanted that seat!" She stomped her foot on the ground, arms crossed, glaring at me. "It's the best seat on this stupid ferry and she's sitting in it!" She stomped her feet over and over again, and soon her mama and papa approached her. They didn't tell her to knock it off or pinch the fatty spot under her arm like Ma or Essie would have done me. They just smiled—plastic, tight, polite smiles, like the people on those toothpaste commercials.

"Excuse me," her mama said, still smiling tightly, talking through her toothpaste teeth. "Do you all mind moving to the back?

We ride this ferry into New York City every weekend and my little Virgie needs this seat. You see, she gets really sick if she doesn't sit here."

Before Ma could say anything, I spoke up. "But this is my seat. I was here first."

"My seat!" the girl yelled, stomping her foot.

"I imagine you're not from New York City. You're from Hamilton, right?" the little girl's mama asked.

"So, what if we are?" Essie piped in. Ma silenced her by placing a hand on hers.

"It's just, we don't normally service people from Hamilton. They have a ferry of their own," the little girl's mama said.

"That ferry's been shut down for years, y'all know that," Essie replied.

"Oh, yes, we do. But that's up to the Hamilton mayor to petition the State of New York to get it fixed. I mean, it is a state boat. Unlike this teeny, tiny ferry. It's privately owned and only runs for Bayside families and people visiting Bayside from New York City. I'm just saying, I'd hate for that to cause you nice people to run into any problems."

"We'll move. No problem. Thank you." Ma stood up; Essie and Justin did too. But I stayed sitting.

"My seat!" the girl yelled again, glaring.

"Capri, get up and let the little girl have her window seat," Ma instructed sternly.

"My seat!" the girl kept yelling.

"Come on, Capri . . ." Essie leaned over to grab me, but I shrank away.

"Is there a problem?" the man from the ticket booth said, walking up to us.

I looked at Essie, then Ma. They both had pleading eyes. If we didn't take this ferry, I wouldn't be able to get to New York City. None of us would.

I stood up and walked past the family. Essie grabbed my hand.

"No problem here, sir," the girl's papa said after that. "We were just talking to this lovely family from New York City visiting Bayside."

The ticket man gave a toothpaste smile. "Well, I hope you enjoyed your visit."

"We sure did. Thank you," Ma said with a smile, before leading us to the bench in the way back of the ferry. It was a tight fit. Justin had to sit on Ma's lap and me on Essie's. And there was only a white wall, no view out of the window. I looked at the little girl who took my seat; her mama was taking pictures of her in front of the window.

"I hope she fall in," I whispered so low I didn't think nobody could hear me.

"Hey," Essie hissed. "No. We don't talk that way. Listen to me, Capri. They ain't all like that. They ain't all stuck in their old ways like that. With those people, you just gotta be kind to them and maybe that will change them. If it don't change nothin', you still be kind. They wanna be stuck in their prisons of ignorance, that's on them. But I ain't gonna let you be like that. You'll see. You'll go to the city and you'll see that it's different. It's people from everywhere living together in peace, loving one another, appreciating their differences. They ain't all like that, you hear me?"

"Yes, ma'am," I replied.

Essie gave me a kiss on my neck and grabbed my hand.

"You'll see," she repeated. "They ain't all like that."

"Capri? Capri? Are you all right?" Zach waved his hands in

my face. I blinked away my thoughts. "You look like you just saw a ghost."

"I'm fine, just thinking."

New York City looked so close from here; the skyline was beautiful. The ferry's dock was different than I remembered, no longer wooden, but aluminum. A few families stood upon it; some older people sat on the benches. I tried ignoring their stares when Zach walked up to the ticket booth and came back with two tickets.

I narrowed my eyes at him. "I thought you said you bought them already, your whole life's savings and all."

He shrugged. "Tom-at-o, tom-ah-to. I would have said anything to get you here. Are you hungry?"

"A little," I replied, just as my stomach began to growl. "But we can always eat in the city, right?"

"The first boat doesn't leave for another fifteen. Come on, I know a place where we can get some really good takeout."

"Zach . . . ," I protested, but he looked straight into my eyes, which shut my lips right away.

"I'm here. I'm not going anywhere, all right?" he said. I nodded. "We'll get some food to go. We'll eat it here. No one's gonna bother you. I'm right here." I let out a breath. He stretched out his hand and I grabbed it.

He walked us across the street to a diner with bleached white walls, covered with old singers and performers from way before we were born. While he ordered our breakfast, I walked to one of the walls filled with pictures. I recognized a few of them; one in particular stood out to me. She was beautiful.

"Lena Horne," I whispered, letting my fingertips graze across the black-and-white photo.

"Who's that?" Zach asked from behind. I could feel his breath on my neck; I ignored the chills it gave me.

"I thought you knew everything about nineteen forties Hollywood and before," I joked.

Zach poked my side. "*Very funny.*"

"She was a famous African American dancer, a singer, and actress. Triple threat. My inspiration. I used to watch all her movies with my mom and learn all the dances. The "Brazilian Boogie Woogie" was my favorite. I knew the whole thing by heart and danced to it almost every day with my mom." I stared into Lena's eyes. "She was beautiful, huh?"

"She was," he replied. "I'm kind of surprised they got her hanging up in here. I thought they were against anything with color."

"Hey," I said, turning around slightly. He was still close. "Not everyone's like that," I whispered. "I met someone who's different."

He lifted an eyebrow. "Oh, yeah?"

"*Zach?*" We both turned around to see a blond girl wearing a bright yellow dress. She ran up to him and pulled him into a hug. "I didn't know you were a morning person!" Before Zach could say anything, she pulled him along to a booth nearby. "Meet my parents."

While he politely talked to the older couple before him, I watched from the counter.

"Hey! I didn't think I'd see you in Bayside," Thomas called out from behind the counter.

Surprised, I smiled, happy for a familiar face. "Hey, Thomas. How's it going?"

"Good. Spending the day in Bayside with Zach?"

"Actually, no. We're going into the city. I got an audition with

Camp Sharp and Zach and a few others sort of convinced me to go. We're waiting for the ferry."

"Wow, that's awesome." He handed me a white to-go bag. "Do you want coffee with the donuts? It's on the house."

"You got hazelnut?"

He nodded. "Coming right up."

Zach had taken a seat at the booth with the girl, who clung to his arm. He caught my eye and smiled, but I quickly looked away.

"That's Virginia. Her father practically owns all of Bayside," Thomas said, nodding his head in the direction of the family Zach was sitting with. "Hence the beauty of 'old money.' She always brags about her ancestors coming from England and helping to build this town up." Hiking up his voice to a high soprano to mock Virgie's voice, he added: "Bayside wouldn't be as architecturally lovely without the Moore's." He switched his voice back to its normal tone when he continued to explain. "Apparently, every one of the men served on the police force since forever. They feel charged to protect and serve Bayside since they were one of the families that helped build it. Her dad, Officer Moore, replaced that dock outside the ferry, and the boat too. You can thank Virginia for the fact that *every seat's a window seat now.*"

Suddenly, the name, the window seat.

"Virginia? She rides the ferry a lot with her family?"

Thomas nodded and passed me my coffee. "Every Saturday morning, they go into New York City for the weekend. Do you know her?"

"No. Just wondering." She definitely grew into the big head I remembered her having. "She blew right past me, didn't even notice I was here."

"That's her. She's got her eye on the prize. Her silent treatment didn't work on Zach. He could care less. So now she's back to throwing herself on him."

He wasn't lying, she was practically on Zach's lap.

"Thomas?" I asked, turning my stool around to face him. "Do you make music by any chance?"

He cocked his head to the side, looking at me questioningly. "No?"

"Never a day in your life? You've never made music?"

"No," he repeated. "Never a day in my life. I'm about as talented as a deaf mule. Why?"

I pretended to shrug it off as a random question, when I really wanted to verify what I was thinking. Zach was lying. "No reason, just thought you looked like someone who could."

"Ready to go?" Zach asked, appearing before me moments later.

I stood up. "Thanks for the coffee, Thomas."

He waved. "No problem, Capri. Nice seeing you."

We walked back across the street to the ferry, and I half listened as Zach complained about Virginia being the most annoying human on the planet. I figured what Zach showed Easy and me wasn't Thomas's song, but now I knew for sure. How did Zach imagine that he'd get away with passing his song off as someone else's?

"Is there a specific place you want to sit?" Zach asked once we boarded the boat. I looked around and pointed to the middle bench window seat.

"There."

"There it is," he repeated and so there is where we sat. Moments later, we were approached by Virginia. I prepared for the stomping and us having to move our seat, but instead she squeezed in next to Zach's other side.

"Is anyone sitting here?" she asked, though she'd already sat. "So, my dad loves you," she sang, wrapping a hand around his arm again.

"I only said two words to him, Virginia."

"Please, he knows a good guy when he sees one. So, we're going to the city for half the day since my dad has the night shift at work tonight." She yawned. "Why are you going to the city?"

Zach gestured to me. "I'm going with a friend to an audition."

"Really? Who?" she asked, looking around. "Who's the friend you're going with? I hope he won't mind me taking his seat. Or you know what"—she gestured to me and flashed a toothpaste smile—"Hi, would you mind moving to the back so we can make room for his friend?"

"Actually, Virginia, this is Capri," Zach introduced. I waved. "She's the friend I'm going with to New York City."

Her face immediately fell, confusion written all over it. "Your friend. I see. And you are from Bayside, I suppose? Since you're riding this ferry?"

"Actually—" Zach began, but I cut him off.

"New York City. I came to visit Bayside yesterday before my audition. Zach wanted to see me practice so I crashed at his place. Now he's coming with me back into the city."

She still looked confused. "You mean you slept over his home?"

We both nodded.

"Zach," she whispered, "since when did you make *friends* with someone like her? You only just moved here."

"Internet," he replied coolly. "We met online."

"*Ah*," she replied. "Sounds like something you would do just to get reacquainted with the people your dad moved you away from. I think I'll go sit with my parents. Nice meeting you." She stood up as the boat began moving, which caused her to fall backward onto Zach's lap. She cradled her hands around his neck and let out an overexaggerated sigh.

She grinned at me. "Oh look, Zachy saved the day. Thank you, honey." Slowly and seductively, she stood up and walked to the bench where her parents sat.

Zach rolled his eyes and gestured to her. "She's so annoying, see? I told you. My father tried hooking us up. I don't know what they were thinking, but—"

"That wasn't really Thomas's song, was it?"

His jaw tensed. "What are you talking about?"

"The song you showed Easy and me. That wasn't Thomas's song. It was yours," I repeated. "You lied to Easy so you could get into the competition."

"So, what if I did? I'm not the only one lying to get what I want today, am I?"

I crossed my arms over my chest. "Coming from the white boy who came up in Hamilton yesterday saying he lived in New York when he actually lives in Bayside, lied about spending his life savings on ferry tickets, promised to stay by my side in this white-washed town just to ditch me for his girlfriend's parents, had me lie about sleeping over, *and* then got all defensive when I called you out about passing your song off as Thomas's to Easy, my mentor and your idol, which is probably the biggest lie of all. If our lies were grains of sand, mine would barely fill a tiny seashell. Yours would make an entire seashore. So, to answer your defensive question, no, you're not the only one lying to get what you want right now. Yes, I lied to your girlfriend to get onto this boat. I lied to my family to go to this audition. I've been lying to my entire town, hiding the fact that I want to be a dancer, just so they won't talk me out of it, just so I won't break Ma's heart and I shouldn't have to." I looked away from him, out the window, remembering how hard it was getting over here the first time with Essie, how we all had to lie to the man collecting tickets just to go to New York City. "Don't you understand? I'm finally doing what I've wanted my entire life, and I have to sneak around. It shouldn't be this complicated. You didn't have to lie to that girl to be on this ferry. She's practically in love with you. You can waltz up in that diner without having to worry about hiding in the background, in case someone finds out you're from the forsaken town across the tracks and sent right back to where you came from without a way out. I'm sure some of the stakes that brought you here are high. I'm sure you had to make some sacrifices. Zach, we're both desperate at this point to reach our dreams, but it's different for you."

"Look. I'm sorry." He let his palms wash over his face in frustration. "You're right. What I did was uncalled for. I shouldn't have left you at the diner alone, I own that. You don't know Virginia, Capri. She never gives up. If I would have stayed with you, and she noticed you sooner, she would've made sure you didn't get on this boat. And about Easy, he's my idol, Capri. I don't think you've noticed but you have a legend as your mentor and he won't even look at me twice, because I'm white. I understand that he wants to give a Black singer an opportunity, and I'm sure there are many more talented than me. But I want a fair shot. I know my skin comes with privilege; I recognize that it makes things easier for me.

"I thought I was different from these people in Bayside, but I'm realizing maybe not so much. I hope you can forgive me, because I'll try my best to do better from here on out and if I'm not, call me out on it. But you said it yourself last night, Capri. You weren't going to let anyone hold you back from accomplishing your dreams; not your family, not nobody. I'm tired of waiting around. I'm tired of waiting in line for my chance and then having it taken from me the moment my dad decides to move away, or my mom decides to pack up and leave, instead of walking straight up to it and taking it. I saw the opportunity today and I had to."

He spoke so quickly his sentences seemed like one word, but I heard him loud and clear. That was why I was going to New York City. That was why I was keeping today a secret from my family. This might be my only chance at reaching my dreams and seeing them become a reality and if I didn't take it, I would have regretted it forever.

I didn't answer him at first. He lifted an eyebrow, stretching out his pinkie finger. "I pinkie promise that I will try my best to expel the selfish prick inside of me. Exorcism style." I couldn't help the laugh that escaped from my lips. I grabbed his pinkie with my own and we shook. He continued. "What I did was crappy. But I want to make it better. I don't want to ruin this friendship before it even starts." He looked down. "And Capri? Virgie's not my girlfriend. Not even close. Not even a friend. I don't want anything to do with her. I just needed her to be distracted so that we could get out of here, even for a day."

"Fine, thanks for the apology," I replied. "So, what are you gonna do about Thomas?"

He shrugged. "Honestly, as of now, I'm not so sure." He let

out a breath and dropped his head into his hands. "What did I get myself into?"

"You helped me get here. Now I'm on my way to New York City because of you. We'll figure out Easy's competition together," I assured.

He lifted an eyebrow. "Really?"

I nodded.

"Cross my heart."

# Zach

THOUGH THE NEW YORK CITY SKYLINE LOOKED VERY CLOSE to Bayside, the ferry ride took a little over an hour. We'd finished our donuts and split Capri's coffee over twenty-five of those minutes. A short while after that, her head was resting on my shoulder, and she was fast asleep. I could faintly hear Granite Michael's voice through her earbuds. I decided against listening to any music. The ferry ride wasn't quiet; voices loomed over one another, along with the sound of the boat washing against the waves, and the captain was announcing how many minutes we were away from the island almost every fifteen minutes that passed. But Capri, tired of the noise on the boat and in need of sleep, plugged in her earbuds to drown everyone out. For me, public travel, even if it was on a boat cleaner than some of the plates at Philly diners, felt sort of like home. When we reached the island and the ferry came to a safe stop, I figured it wouldn't hurt to wait until everyone was off the boat before I awoke Capri. To be honest, I kind of enjoyed the setup. Every few moments or so, the smell of her hair would ride on the wind from the sea and settle itself around us which I didn't mind. She smelled amazing.

For most of the trip, I watched her closely, sleeping soundly. Just last night, I wasn't sure if I'd ever see this girl again. I tried getting out each word that I wanted to say to her, nervous about the last. Regretting watching her go without saying how I felt because I was too much of a coward to. Afraid to tell her that although she was barely a notch above a stranger, in only a few hours, she grabbed a part of my soul that I didn't even know existed and brought light to it. She reminded me of what I had once been fighting for but stopped after Dee died. I knew I needed to work my hardest at attaining something real: my dreams.

I was more than pleased to know that this wouldn't be the last time I'd see her. From this point on, I'd make sure of it. I'd have her during Halloween, Christmas, spring break, the summer. I'd always have her . . . like this. With me, leaning on me, guard down, trusting me, knowing that everything would be all right as long as I was here.

Of course, not all things go according to plan. For example, I thought it would be best to wait for everyone to leave—especially Virgie—before waking Capri. But only seconds after we'd docked, Virgie sauntered up to Capri and me. The sound of a camera snapping rang out around us.

"I just thought I'd catch a picture of you and your friend," she said with a menacing grin, as she slid her phone into her pocket. "After all, you guys look *so* cute, and I know your dad would want a picture of his son with another—"

"Seriously?" I hissed. But then remembered Capri had her earbuds in, so I spoke loudly. "You're really gonna snitch on me? I don't know if you noticed, but I'm not afraid of my father."

"Whatever. I'm sending it anyway. You will learn, *Zachy*. It might take a while, but you will learn to live life the way you were created to. Other people are not as blessed as we are. They envy us. But one day you'll figure it out instead of lowering yourself. You'll be dating the girls you're supposed to, embracing everything that life naturally hands you, and not being sorry to take it."

I stared past her as if she didn't exist—as if she were just a vapor in the wind I needed to get around. I was beginning to learn that with Virgie, it was best to let her talk and not respond. She stared back for a moment, but when called by her parents to walk off the ferry, she stomped her foot loudly in frustration, then finally walked away, which caused Capri's eyes to flutter open. She lifted her head from my shoulder and took off her earbuds.

"What was that?" she asked.

"That?" I searched for an answer. "Oh, someone dropped a book or something."

She stood up and stretched her hands above her head. When she looked out the window and realized we were now on the other side of the water, Bayside now just a shadow of fog, a huge smile erupted on her face. "I can't believe we're here."

"Me either."

She grabbed my hand and led me off the boat. "Come on!"

The second my feet made contact with the end of the dock, my ears were reawakened to the sound of crowds, horns, and cars whizzing by. My nose—oh my nose!—gladly breathed in the smell of hot dogs, pretzels, pollution, and nicotine. It smelled like home.

I sucked in a noseful of air and lifted my hands and screamed up at the sky, "This is heaven!"

Capri rolled her eyes, though they were glowing with excitement.

"Now that you've had your smell, and experienced heaven, we have to figure out how to get to the theatre." So, we got the address and let my phone be the guide. She wanted to save hers for photos. She snapped almost *everything*—the graffiti on the walls, the fresh baked bread and pretzels sold on the sidewalk, the people, street performers, skyscrapers.

Watching her walk around New York City was like watching a child explore a toy store. She ran, spun, and weaved in and out of the crowds. Though it was hard to keep up with her, I was happy to follow someone so excited. For a moment, I thought I'd lost her in the crowds as I rushed behind her. But instead, in the middle of the crowd bustling around us, she stood completely frozen.

"Why'd we stop?" I asked, turning full circle.

"This is the place," she whispered.

"What place?" I looked down at my phone. "My phone says we're still ten minutes away." She wrapped her hand around my arm and led me down a nearby alleyway. My phone vibrated within my hand, and *rerouting* flashed across it. I was going to make a joke, asking her if she were pulling me into an alley to murder or mug me, but thought best not to. Her face was serious, her expression stiff, she walked us quickly. Right turn here, then left, then right, then straight until . . .

"Zach, meet my mother."

She stopped us at an abandoned theatre. A few people in blankets lay on the ground around it. But Capri showed no fear against the strangers, she only looked ahead at the worn picture stamped from the ground, stretching high above us. The photo was aged, rained on, almost the color of the brick building it was pasted to.

Her face was clear though. It reflected, almost exactly, the girl who stood beside me. She looked just like Capri, her wild hair pulled behind her into a ponytail. Her eyes, transfixed, focused, like she had a task she had to complete. She soared in the air, arms out, legs stretched. She was flying.

"They gave her this to honor her for the amazing job she was doing in all the shows she'd been performing in." Capri walked closer to the building and grazed her fingertips on the wall. "I remember her running us to see this before her show." She turned around and looked at me. "Here." She passed me her phone. "I want you to take a photo of me, okay? I don't want to forget this happened. Even if nothing else works out today, if I don't make it, if I don't get to see New York City ever again, I want to remember that I came. That I was here, that I saw her again." She let out a deep breath. "On the count of three, you take the picture, all right? On three exactly."

I lifted her phone until I could see her entire body on the camera. "Ready on three."

She grinned. "Three!" She yelled and jumped into the air, perfectly mirroring the jump her mother was doing in her picture on the wall. I quickly snapped the photo while she was in midair. She ran up to me after it was taken.

"Did you get it?" she asked.

"I did."

She gently took the phone out of my hand and examined the photograph. "Wow," she said breathlessly. "I spent years trying to remember how she looked in this picture, and now it's almost as if I'm dancing with her." She looked up from the phone. "She *was* beautiful, huh?"

"No, Capri, she *is* beautiful. Look, she may not be *here*, physically, but she's in you. She's watching you, pushing you to accomplish everything she believed you could. She's the reason why you're here, right now in New York City doing this."

Capri's eyes filled to the brim with tears. She blinked, and they danced down her cheeks.

"Do you really believe that?" she whispered. "That she somehow has something to do with this?"

I grazed her cheeks with my thumb, wiping her tears away. "The question is do *you* believe that? Do you believe that you being here isn't an accident? That the same city that called her is calling you? I *know* she has something to do with this."

Capri smiled faintly, her eyes fixed on mine. "I think so too."

*"Excuse me, you're standing on my home."*

We both turned around. An older man with no teeth and a cane stood glaring at us. He gestured to a sleeping bag that we, sure enough, were standing on.

"Sorry, sir," we said quickly, before taking off. Capri made sure to take one last look at her mother before her picture was out of sight.

"This is it. 3133 Broadway."

We stood before a brick theatre, with a bright red door. A sign was taped to it that read *Closed for Camp Sharp auditioning. If auditioning, inquire inside.*

I felt her hand slip into mine and in a shaking voice, she uttered, "I can't believe I'm here."

"You got this, come on," I assured, leading us inside.

"Name?" a bald man with Coke-bottle glasses asked from behind a desk set up in the lobby. He didn't look up; just tapped his pen against the clipboard he held. Capri opened her mouth to answer, but nothing audible came out. "Name?" he asked again impatiently. Finally he looked up at us, his brown eyes searching for an answer. He lifted an eyebrow.

"Capri," I answered for her.

"Last name?" the man asked slowly. Again, she said nothing, which caused the man to huff. "I need the full name of the one auditioning . . ."

"Collins," she finally forced out. "Capri Collins. I'm the one auditioning."

The man sighed as his acorn-colored eyes glided left and right across the list. Finally, "Oh yes, Collins, Capri. Good then." He snapped his fingers, and a young girl behind him quickly walked up to us with a large piece of paper. She handed it to the man, who handed it to Capri. "This is your number," he instructed in a robotic tone. "Whatever you do, do not lose it because here, it's your identity. It's the way the judges know when to eliminate you or allow you to move forward. It's how someone at each station will refer to you. You only get one number, so you lose it, you lose your spot. God knows we've killed so many trees with all of this paper as it is. Any questions?" Capri shook her head. "Good, you'll tape it to your leotard once you put it on. Carter will take you back to the room where you will wait to audition." He narrowed his eyes at me. "Your friend can go left around this corridor and watch from the crowd with the rest of the parents and family. Next."

The young girl who passed us the number introduced herself and led us away from the lobby. She, like him, wore thick glasses and talked a mile a minute. "I'm interning for Camp Sharp and hopefully by the summer I'll be working full-time with them. I just graduated from college last spring—marketing. But it's my dream to work with Camp Sharp." Walking us down an ivory-colored hallway lined with signed pictures of vintage actors, she continued on. "I love the chance they, meaning Camp Sharp, of course, offers you young people and I would love, love, love to use my degree to further their advertisement, you know? So more kids can hear about it and audition, maybe even from out of the country, am I right? I mean, how many country-renowned dance camps actually give four scholarships away? I can understand one, two, three, *but four?* That's generous."

The lights were dimmed so low it was a bit hard to walk without stumbling over my own feet. We walked by the box office and she led us to a burgundy double door. Capri held tight to my hand.

Carter gestured to the door. "Okay, this is the entrance to the audience where you can watch Capri perform. Capri, you can get changed in any of the bathrooms, though I would suggest the one closest to the hallway before the box office. The hand dryers in that are motion-detected." She winked at Capri.

"Changed?" Capri asked.

"Unzip, please," she directed.

Capri unzipped her jacket. Underneath was a pair of black leggings, a black T-shirt, leg warmers, and worn gladiator boots.

"You're not dancing in *that*, are you?" Carter asked. "And how did you suppose you would dance in those boots?"

"Barefoot?"

I could tell Capri was even more nervous at this point. She forced a smile. "Look, the acceptance packet didn't say anything about a specific wardrobe requirement other than professional dance attire. I assumed this would be okay."

"Listen, your concentration *is* lyrical, so I suppose for your solo performance it is all right to dance barefoot, but you must wear a leotard and tights to perform in the group audition. That was stated in the packet. We included a small card attached to the acceptance letter with very specific wardrobe requirements. Did you read that?"

Capri dropped her head. "I didn't. I must have not noticed it, I'm so sorry."

Carter sighed. "You seem like a very kind girl, but I'm afraid if you don't have these things . . ."

"Is there any place we can pick up everything you just said she needed?" I quickly asked. There was no way we were going home.

"There is a thrift store two blocks away, but her audition is in less than thirty minutes . . ."

I looked at Capri. "I will be *right* back, all right?"

"But Zach . . ."

"Trust me. I got you."

She sighed but nodded. I left before Carter could protest.

*Leotard, leotard, leotard. Ugh, I didn't even ask what size she wore. Probably a small, medium?*

*Medium, medium, medium.*

*Aha! Here.*

*This is a leotard?*

*It's so small . . . so tight.*

Someone cleared their throat from behind me. I turned around to see a girl who had more piercings on her face than a pin cushion. Her hair was bleached light green. She stood with her arms crossed, staring. Her name tag read Flo.

"Can I help you?" Her New York City accent was heavy, her voice as flat as the ground below me. She narrowed her eyes at the bright pink leotard I held in my hand.

"Hi, Flo. I'm looking for a leotard and tights for a girl about five-nine. She's skinny, but I don't think she can fit into any of these."

She rolled her eyes. "That's because you're in the infant and toddler section." She stretched out the words "infant" and "toddler" and pointed above her to a sign hanging on the ceiling, that of course, stated that fact. "You're in the wrong section. Leotards for her size are over there." She pointed across the store.

I tossed the leotard I was holding and she caught it.

"Oh, right. Look, Flo, Capri's audition is in like fifteen minutes, and I promised I would be there for her. Could you help me?"

She sighed. "There's nothing else to do. Come on." I followed her to the right section.

"Thirty-two eighty-seven," Flo said from behind the register about ten minutes later. The only thing that wasn't a size zero or made for someone who starved themselves was a dark red leotard. The tights, however, they only had packaged, which was fine. I wasn't sure I'd want to be dancing in someone's sweaty used tights. I handed the girl the credit card my father gave me *in case of emergencies*. She swiped it and gave me the receipt to sign.

"Thanks for your help." I signed and put in a three followed by two zeros on the empty space left for a tip.

"Whoa, dude, you mean to leave that much?"

"You were a big help." It's not like my dad would miss the money from his inheritance anyway.

She smiled. "Tell your girlfriend, 'Good luck.'"

I ran out of the store, through the crowds, back to the theatre as fast as I could.

I stood outside of the stage door where Capri texted me to meet her. Seconds after I told her I'd arrived, she opened the door. I handed her the bag and looked at my phone's clock.

"Almost three minutes to spare," I said, managing to sound calm and collected, though my heart was racing inside my chest. "I ran DO NOT WALK signs this entire way." She responded by pulling me into a hug.

"Thank you, Zach."

# Capri

THE INSIDE OF THE THEATRE WAS ONE OF THE MOST
beautiful things I'd ever seen. Burgundy seats, looking more comfortable than the creaky beds in my house, spun in a circle around
a stage that sat in the center. Artwork from Shakespearean plays
like *Hamlet, Pericles, Macbeth, Othello*, and *Romeo and Juliet* were
painted on the ceiling. When the lights dimmed, the artwork lit up
with glowing stars and a large moon painted onto the sky. Families
filled almost every empty seat on the entire first floor of the theatre,
proudly awaiting the auditions they came here to support. Me and
the other performers stood behind the curtains on the side of the
stage located in the middle of the theatre. I scanned the audience
and saw Zach sitting in one of the seats closest to where the judges
would be. I'd never seen a stage in the middle of the audience
before; the chairs seemed to wrap around for miles. I hoped the
choreographer would go easy on us, with performing on a stage like
this. The other performers were equally caught by surprise because
of the stage setup. They whispered among each other nervously,
wondering how hard this might be. I silently prayed.

Seconds later, the back doors flew open. Three judges walked
down the aisles to the front row, followed by Carter. After they took
their seats, I followed the other six girls and four guys performing
to the center of the stage. I stood out among all their black leotards and couldn't help but smile at that; Essie always told me the

importance of standing out. Zach did a perfect job; under the spot-light, the crimson-colored leotard cast a glimmer of gold against my skin, just like the lights always did with Essie's. Under the lights, she glowed. Now I was glowing too. I stood upright with my shoulders back.

"Good morning, performers," one of the judge's voices rang through the speakers around the theatre. "I am William Knight, the head of the scholarship division at Camp Sharp. This is Wynona Peters, the chair of our jazz and lyrical program," he said, gesturing to a woman whose hair was completely shaven sitting next to him. "Phyllis Welling, choreographer for many Tony Award–winning shows." A dark-skinned woman with long locs piled on top of her head lifted her hand. "And finally, Ivan Hartsfield." A younger man, probably in his twenties, stood at his introduction and the audi-ence and performers applauded. "I'm sure you know Ivan from the countless ballets he has starred in."

I recognized them all without him having to say their names. Reverend Sails always talked about the joy we'd experience getting to meet Bible characters in heaven, finally conversing with the people who helped guide our lives through the pages we feasted on. In that moment, I couldn't imagine any feeling comparing to what I felt standing before the judges who I followed on social media, whose videos I devoured, whose routines I studied and memorized, the ones I envied for the lives they lived. Maybe I was just the number taped to my stomach and that's all they'd know me as, but they were going to watch me dance and that alone filled me with something I couldn't get from meeting King David or Queen Esther.

"These special guests, along with myself, will decide who will reach the last and final audition for our eight-week intensive dance camp," William Knight continued. "As you all know, this camp is often used as a forerunner for our alumni, offering them many opportunities in Broadway shows, world-renowned ballet and dance companies, and scholarships for dance colleges that I'm sure you all hope to attend. Unless you get picked up before then." He winked and all the audience members laughed. He continued: "Based off your performances, we will only pick four of you. If your number is called and you're asked to leave the stage, we ask that you do not go home, but instead, take a seat in the audience and wait until the auditions are over. We do not want you to go home without a reason for why you did not make it. Today, we would like to see an audition that is completely improv, instead of what was planned." He paused at this.

I could hear the performers beside me gasp. At least they could breathe. No air could escape my lungs because William Knight's words knocked it right out of me. *Improv?* Before some of the best performers in the world? I couldn't help but notice a menacing smile come over the judges' faces when they surveyed our responses. I began ferociously gnawing on my thumbnail.

He continued.

"We here at Camp Sharp want to know that our students are just as great off guard as they are when they rehearse. You must be prepared for everything. We know that this came as a surprise, but we decided not to audition as we've done before with repeating a dance that a choreographer teaches. We want to know if, under pressure, your dance moves are still just as calm, clean, and collected. You will dance to the music that *we* provide just in case you still came prepared with a routine. Do not be worried, we have selected music based on your dance concentration. We will begin with number one: a jazz and musical theatre concentration." He snapped and the other performers immediately scattered offstage. I followed closely behind. A teenage boy was left alone on stage, the first to endure the impending torture of having to come up with a routine on the spot. The rest of us watched him from behind the curtain on side stage. I felt nervous for him. William Knight lifted his hand. "Whenever you're ready, number one."

The boy took a deep breath, and an up-tempo jazz song rang out. First, he began snapping to the beat. As the song's drum became steadier, he rocked his hips left and right. He lifted his hands above his head; his fingers, extended and stiff, began to flutter. He went into a jump the same moment the tempo slowed, which surprised him and caused him to fall. He tried to save it, by rolling on his side. He lifted a leg above his head. *Good save.* The music took its original speed and he began to dance to the beat, performing pretty well for someone who had no idea about his song. As the music came to an end, he twirled on the balls of his feet, and jumped across the stage just as the final drum sounded.

He walked off the stage with a smile, even adding a wink to the clapping audience. The next three auditions were equally amazing. Nobody would believe the songs hadn't been rehearsed. Well, except this one girl who fell while trying to complete a triple tour en l'air and ran off the stage in tears.

This was my first audition before a panel of judges, the first time I'd perform before a crowd of strangers. I found myself gazing at the forbidden fruit again; standing on what the tracks held me from my entire life. Standing where Essie lost her breath, more alive than I'd ever felt before. I wasn't hiding in the back of a record shop, dancing behind a locked door and *Closed* sign, praying no one would walk in and catch me. I didn't have to worry about hiding an acceptance letter in record cover sleeves. Everyone seated knew why I was here and in just moments, they'd look at me, not through me, and I could show them that I, Capri Collins, just like my mama, am a dancer.

William Knight's voice echoed through the stadium. "Number six, lyrical concentration. Please take the stage." Carter, who stood side stage, gently pushed me forward.

"Capri, that's you."

# Zach

WHEN CAPRI WALKED ON THE STAGE, NERVES SHOT through me.

*Please do well. Please do well.*

Her eyes met mine and I mouthed, "You got this." She nodded before closing her eyes.

Before the music began, she breathed in, then out. Her face relaxed. She didn't look upset, angry, or uncomfortable. Suddenly she looked calmer than I'd ever seen her. The music soon filled the auditorium. She stretched a hand before her. She lifted her arms over her head and let the music carry her. She rested on it as it changed, following it closely on a journey and didn't stray away. Instead, she went with it. She followed it through its quick tempo moments, and slow moments, high and low moments, breaking into splits, spins, jumps, turns. Wherever it wanted to go, she rode along.

# Capri

*I BREATHED IN THE SILENCE AROUND ME. THE JUDGES* were stone-faced, gripping pens in their palms, ready to keep score. There was Zach, sitting in the audience with a wide smile, lifting a thumbs-up. I could see the families of the other performers; surely they were hoping I would break a leg so their sons or daughters, cousins, or friends would get the spot we all wanted. All of them waiting, watching to see what I'd create.

I focused on my feet, planted firmly on the cool stage. The bright lights hanging above me warmed my shoulders like the afternoon sun and the orchestra seated before me acted as a gulf, creating a separation between the crowd and myself, between the opinions that would rise but never reach me. Because for the first time I wouldn't let them.

I was finally miles away from the tracks that always kept fear raging within me. Fear wouldn't follow me here. Not Ma, not Hamilton, not the history that kept us all chained to it. I wasn't in Hamilton anymore. I was finally standing in the home Essie bragged about, the place where we skipped rocks to, the place where she's painted on buildings, where she's given awards, where she may be gone but never forgotten, where her spirit still soars above.

Before the music could start, I stretched my hand before me, asking her to dance. If I were in her kingdom, I wanted her to show me the steps I should take. It's like the sky opened above me because I could feel her more than I'd ever been given permission to. I didn't have to search for Essie in memories or in the dark, eyes closed tight, waiting on my dreams to present her to me. That silence I took into my lungs before the music began released out of me and the Essie imprisoned in my memories released too.

When the conductor tapped his stand, and the music began, I let my whole body fall into her and we danced together, through the pages of my life, beginning with the past and ending with the present. I stretched my arms above my head and swayed, allowing Essie to cradle me into her arms like she'd done when I was a baby. I closed my eyes as we rode upon the changing tempo like fallen leaves in the wind, just as we'd done when I was a toddler, and the fall came. We followed the music together. Wherever it wanted to go, we rode along, like we'd done when she'd play the cast albums to all her shows, and we'd dance to the changing music freely on the Sunlight's stage. Essie was with me. She'd always been with me.

# Zach

A PAUSE BROKE INTO THE MUSIC, LEAVING ONLY THE LOW fluttering of the piano. Capri rested on the ground, as if she were sleeping. She lifted a hand as if to grab at something that kept flying away. She grabbed at it, but kept losing it, it fell from her hands, over and over. But then a key change took place, and with one fingertip, she grazed what she'd been reaching for. With another hand she grabbed ahold, and it picked her up and spun her. Whatever it was joined her, danced with her. She began to sway her hands outstretched in front of her, as if she were dancing with someone physically. The invisible force spun her, lifted her. She was astonishing. Everything in that moment stopped for me. That was when it all changed. Not like it wasn't on the verge of changing already, but the seed that we'd planted sprouted in my heart. It bloomed the most beautiful tree with roots that would stretch and anchor forever. My eyes followed her; I didn't even stop to blink. My body wouldn't let me. I couldn't take my eyes off her.

# Capri

THE PIANO PULSED SOFTLY—IN AND OUT, LIKE ESSIE'S heart before it lost its beating. I rested on the ground, as she'd done in that casket I last saw her in on that day separation from my Essie paralyzed me. I fought so long after that to reach her again, but only found her in what little bit I could remember. I lifted my hand to grab at the memories that faded further away with every passing day. I grabbed at them: the way she looked when she laughed, how her fingertips felt against my scalp when she braided my hair, the way her embrace hid me, kept me secure. I thought she could never go away. But those memories of her kept fading, flying above me, disappearing like the seasons. I raised my hands outward to grab them, but they always fell from my hands, over and over. I needed to keep them close, but I knew one day, I'd forget them, maybe lose them forever.

Then, there was a key change. Like the key change in my life. The acceptance letter, fear almost making me miss this chance, Zach coming into my life, encouraging me to come here, seeing my Essie here flying on that wall. Suddenly, the few memories I held on to fell like scales from my eyes. I could see. I could that Essie wasn't just my past, she was with me, in the present, in every experience, every moment, if I simply paused and noticed.

With one fingertip, I could graze what I'd always been reaching for. Essie was back. With another hand I grabbed ahold of her. She picked me up into her embrace and spun me. Mama joined me again, and I danced with her. I swayed; my hands outstretched in front of me. Mama's spirit spun me, lifted me so that I could fly with her. I knew when it came and knew when it left.

Mama was here, with me, showing me her world. Before I knew it, the music ended. Polite claps echoed through the theatre. Above all the claps, I heard him. Zach screamed as loud as he could and I couldn't help but laugh because the truth was, I wanted to scream too. A shimmer of gold shined from my peripheral, and I swear in the corner, hidden behind the curtains, I saw my mama, clapping for me too.

# Zach

**"YEAH CAPRI!" I YELLED. THE JUDGES ALL TURNED AROUND** and stared me down. Capri cupped her hand over her mouth to hide her laughter, but her eyes were glowing. I slowly took my seat but continued to clap. I knew she was amazed that she'd done this. I couldn't imagine the emotions flowing through every part of her being. I was so proud of her.

# Justin

*I FELT THE WAY I ALWAYS DID DURING EVERY GAME. AS IF* I'd been stranded on a desert for forty days without food or drink—hungry—and got my hands on a buffet of fruits, veggies, cakes and pies, meats of every kind—things I would devour. Adrenaline soared through my veins. When life didn't make sense, when books didn't give me the answers I looked for, playing ball gave me an escape for just two hours. And for two hours, I ate until I was full.

"Justin, ball, ball!" Jay yelled from his spot close to the sidelines, a few feet in front of me. He was surrounded by three guys from Harvest Creek. Even though Jay stood more than a few inches above them, I knew it would be a horrible idea to pass the ball to him. *If* he could even catch it, it would still get scooped up in one second. The score was 124 to 123, Hamilton High trailing only one point behind Harvest Creek. They weren't as easy to beat as we thought, especially with Goliath on their team. But Hamilton gave Harvest Creek an equal workout. Heat and sweat poured in currents, from my forehead down to my heels. My heart beat double time with the ball I dribbled as I made my way through Harvest Creek's defense, like I was skating.

I could hear Hamilton's crowd on the bleachers yelling but couldn't make out what they were saying over the roar. It was mostly a bunch of dads who once played on the team, trying to coach us. I usually hated when it was loud like this, but today, I needed it. I needed to know that others believed I could do something amazing. Because I *was* about to do something amazing, and I wanted everyone paying attention.

When I reached the three-point line, there stood Goliath himself. His arms were outstretched, a menacing smile on his face as if I, six-one, was just some puny child in front of a bear. I wasn't scared though. I had something to work for now and I wasn't giving up.

I paused and bounced the ball while my team members held Harvest Creek's back. I studied Goliath as I always did a player way too confident on the court. His legs were clumsy. He had no real control over his height. He relied on his jumps to block shots. They stuck him by the court every time. He'd give a menacing glare to scare whoever held the ball out of running the basket in, because he was slow. When a fear-filled shot went up, no matter how skilled, Goliath would block it. That wasn't happening, not with me. Not with four seconds left on the clock. Everyone in the stands, including Jay with his annoying voice, yelled for me to shoot. I bounced the ball. Stared at Goliath.

"Yeah, *shoot*," he teased, in an unbelievably high voice for his height. "Shoot the ball, number three."

"I will." With one more bounce, I faked Goliath out on his right side, and spun to his left, which caused the clumsy giant to trip over his own size sixteen feet, landing on his butt. I paused and gave him a cocky smile before shooting a layup that fell right into the basket milliseconds before the buzzer went off, signaling the end of the game. The boys on the sidelines and the ones on the court ran up to me, roaring with excitement. I couldn't help it. I let out a gut-busting laugh because I knew without a shadow of a doubt, even with a kid, all things were possible. I was the best player in Hamilton. I would get that scholarship.

"This is gonna be the party of the century, man. I'm tellin' you, yo!" Carlos yelled into my ear over the applause of the crowd and the music the cheerleaders were dancing to.

"I ain't gonna miss it!" I replied. After all, I did have a lot to celebrate.

The air was heavy, boiling with tangible heat from so many bodies squeezing into the small, rectangular, one-level home. The odor of liquor mixed with the smell of melting cheese pizza filled the crevices of the house, bouncing off the walls back into the oxygen we had to breathe in. I never knew how much I missed it.

The crowd, as small as the space was, parted for me when I walked through the door. I grabbed at the hands extended to me, high-fiving them, shaking them, pounding them. They yelled my name. I soaked it up.

"Aye! There's the victory guy! With only four seconds on the clock, he fakes, he lefts, he shoots, and he scores! And the crowd goes wild!" Tyree yelled over the music. He stretched out a hand for me to pound and I did.

"How was the scholarship thing this morning?" I asked. Tyree gave me a thumbs-up.

"I'm in, I'm in," he repeated, as if he didn't believe it himself. "You next, man, we gonna be college guys."

"I know, man," I replied. "It's unreal."

"You got the scholarship in the bag," Tyree said. "You ain't got nothing to worry about!"

"I know. I only wish you were gonna be pursuing sports

instead of medicine. We might have crossed paths in the pros!"

Tyree smiled and shook his head. "Nah, man, medicine is where I belong. People need me out there. Kids need us to do these things so they can know they can come out of a place like this and turn into a pro like you or be a doctor like me."

"Oh, come on! Tell me y'all ain't talking about college at a time like this!" Carlos said, approaching us with two beer bottles. We both grabbed one and took a sip.

"What else is there to talk about?" Tyree asked, a grin forming on his face.

"I don't know," Carlos slurred, clearly drunk. "Dancing and drinking? Dancing with girls who are drunk?" Before we could reply, Carlos waved over two girls who were standing against the wall. They walked up to us in their jean shorts and skintight crop tops.

"This is Ambelle and Lonnie. They seniors at Harvest Creek. They wanted to come to the winning party and they also wanna dance with the winners."

Both girls were hot, there was no denying that. Tyree lifted an eyebrow at me. I shrugged. What was one dance?

"That's my college boys!" Carlos cheered. He gave a signal for the music to be cranked up and it was. One of the girls took Tyree's hand and led him on the dance floor, the other grabbed me by the shoulders and pressed her body against me, moving to the thumping rhythm of the song. Two hours and five beers later, I wasn't sure if I would be able to hear again.

"Some victory party, huh?" I asked Tyree. He smacked my shoulder.

"All because *you* won! You brought the victory to Hamilton.

When that Village scout comes to Monday night's game . . ."

"Here's another beer, boys," said Ambelle, who Tyree had been dancing with, fresh off a drink run. We'd been sitting on one of the couches pushed against the wall. Finally the music slowed to more mellow tunes; a few people stood by the wall drinking; others sat on the couches talking while couples kissed and slow danced on the makeshift dance floor.

"Nah, I'm done for the night," Tyree said, grabbing the beer from her and placing it on a lamp table. "I've had five too many."

Lonnie cackled, completely drunk. "You are too funny, Tyrone. *Five too many!* You sound just like my grandpa! Just hold on to it in case you get thirsty." Tyree grabbed it from the table but didn't drink any of it. Ambelle lifted a beer to me.

"I might as well. This *is* my last party." I took a long chug, until my throat burned.

Tyree stood and stretched.

"I think I'm gonna head home."

"You out this quick?" I asked.

"I heard they bringing out bud, man. You know I quit like three years ago. I don't need to get into no trouble." I stood up and we smacked hands, my head swimming.

"You need somebody to drop you home?"

Tyree shook his head. "I'm only a few blocks away. Imma walk. I need some air. Hopefully, it'll wash this drunkenness off."

I chuckled. "Aight, be safe."

"Will do. Congrats on the win again. I'm telling you, man, that scholarship is in the bag next week. If you keep your eyes on the sky, you know you ain't got no limit."

I watched Tyree walk through the people on the dance floor

singing, completely off key, "Fly Like an Eagle." I couldn't help but laugh as I took his seat. Ambelle and Lonnie sat on either side of me, rubbing my arms and chest with their long fingernails.

"You know, you are just *so* cute," Ambelle whispered.

"As a button," Lonnie added. "You got a girlfriend?"

"*Yes, he does.*"

I snapped my neck up. Rose. She was taller in her red sweater dress. Looked thinner than she had in a while. Maybe it was because I couldn't see straight. Her hands were on her hips, hair piled into a messy bun on top of her head.

"What are you doing?" she asked.

"Chill, we're just hanging out with the winning shooter," Ambelle interjected, with an attitude. Rose's glare made her stand up and walk off. Lonnie followed suit.

"What are you doing," she repeated, "with these two girls all over you?"

"We just hanging out," I heard myself say. "Hanging out, Rose. Calm down."

"You're drunk."

"We're celebrating," I corrected. I stretched out a beer to her. "Have some."

"*Seriously?*" she asked.

"Hey, Rosey!" Carlos greeted, walking up to us, Deondre on his heels. "Coming to celebrate the victorious win with your boyfriend?"

"I'm coming to take him home. We were supposed to talk about something important."

"He told us," Deondre said. "But that can wait."

Rose cocked her head back. "Excuse me?"

"It can wait," Deondre repeated. "We thought that he needed some R and R. Especially since he hasn't been to a party in ages. Whatever you guys have to talk about, you can do it later."

"It *can't* wait." Rose reached down to grab my arm, but I pulled her onto my lap.

"Rose, come on," I whined. "We both need some stress relief."

"No, Justin. We need to talk about our future. We need a plan."

"We can discuss that later," I slurred. "Who needs a plan anyway? It's time to be *freeeee!*" I leaned in to kiss Rose, but she backed away.

"Justin."

"Rose," I sang with a grin. "Rosey, Rosey, Rosey. My love."

"I thought you had a plan," she whispered desperately.

"He does!" Carlos yelled. "He's gonna make it pro." Everyone around us cheered. I grinned proudly.

"*That's* your plan?" she asked. "You making it pro? That's how you're gonna take care of us?"

"That's how he's gonna take care of *us!*" Deondre yelled, causing everyone to burst out in cheers again.

"Justin." Rose placed a hand on mine, looking deeply into my eyes, blocking out everyone around us. "What happens if you don't? We need a plan B."

"What are you talking about?" I replied, snatching my hand away from her grip. "A plan *B*? What happened to all that talk about letting me chase my dreams first?"

"That was before I got kicked out. Before I found out my parents weren't gonna help us. You need a job now. We both do."

"No, no. We need to go to college. Remember? You said we'd find an apartment; you'd work while I chased my dreams, even without their help," I reminded her.

"I wasn't thinking straight. Things are different now. I talked to your ma. We'll go to college. Hamilton Community College is a great college. You can go online someplace else if you want. You can also get a trade at the tech school."

No. No. Ma wasn't going to fit me in her little bubble like she did with Capri. The room felt like it was closing in.

"No!" I yelled, standing up. "I won't be like them. I won't be here for the rest of my life. I won't die in Hamilton."

"Do you really think your ma is gonna let us live with her forever?" she replied, standing to face me. "There's barely any room for me now. We're gonna need to save for an apartment, Justin. When the baby comes . . ."

I quickly lifted a hand to cover her mouth.

"*Shhh!* Nobody knows about that," I slurred. Rose spit on my palm. I quickly wiped it against my jeans. "You're disgusting!"

"Really? *I'm* disgusting? Me? You're the one not acting like you'll be a father in five months!"

When Rose yelled that, the music stopped. Everything, everybody did.

She shook her head. "I can't believe you, Justin."

"Rose . . ."

"No. No, I can't believe you. What happens if the scholarship doesn't come through? Then what?" She waited for an answer, and I tried to think of one, but my brain was drowning in beer. I wanted to snap out of it. Deep down inside, I wanted to tell her I'd fight for her, that I'd think of something. But then, I looked around me. I looked at my friends standing around with their mouths wide open.

How could she hang out all our dirty, wet laundry in front of everyone?

I wasn't ready for them to know yet.

I gritted my teeth, seething with anger, pain, embarrassment. "Look, Rose, if you and Ma don't believe in my dreams, that's just fine. Whatever—I can't care less. You don't have to. Just like you don't have to be there when they come true. You don't have to be at my games, you don't have to be a part of my life. I'm gonna get that scholarship. I'm gonna go pro, and I'm gonna make millions. Right, everybody?" I looked around for my friends to cheer me on, but they remained silent. "Right?" I screamed. A few people clapped. I looked back at Rose. "Who says that baby is even mine, huh? It can be anybody's."

Rose's eyes quickly filled with tears. They fell down her cheeks, under her chin. "Are . . . you . . . serious?" she barely breathed out. She let a bout of silence soar between us, giving me a moment to snap out of it, but I couldn't. I wouldn't. "I understand. You never wanted this child, you never wanted me the way you said you did. I'm tired of fighting for you, Justin. I'm tired of always having to tell you that everything will be all right. I'm tired of your moodiness; I'm tired of being tired. I'm tired of being the only adult who understands that she may have to put her life on hold for one *moment* to think of someone other than herself for *once!*" She closed her eyes and let out a breath, the next words only audible for me to hear. "We're done, Justin. I'll clear my clothes out your ma's."

"Where you gonna go?" I slurred. "You got *kicked* out."

"I don't know, but I'll figure it out." She exited through the crowd. I should've chased after her, but I didn't. I stood still, watching her walk away, unsure if she would ever be back.

"Turn on the music!" I shouted, and almost instantly, the floor thumped around me. I grabbed the closest girl I could see and began to dance with her.

The light of the only dim star in my dark sky immediately burned out.

# Capri

AFTER THE CAMP SHARP AUDITION, ZACH AND I DECIDED
to celebrate over New York–style pizza, I'd always wanted to try it,
see if the hype was real. I could hardly focus on the gooey cheese
and tart tomato sauce, when all I could think about was how it felt
to dance my heart out, with the one person that kept me believing in dreams to begin with . It was almost as if I were climbing a
mountain, breathless from the journey, but when I reached the top
and looked over the horizon into the setting sun, I became a part of
the mountain I'd just climbed. I wasn't the same person. I'd been
reborn. I was divine. The music, everything, my body, it all merged.
It's almost as if the music let me in on all its secrets; it entrusted my
body and invited my Essie along too. I felt her.

It was wild.

Essie was right. Dancing alone was one thing, but on a stage,
under the lights? That was a completely different experience.

"And then, it ended. I wasn't even there, Zach; I don't know
how to describe it. I was in a completely different world. In a completely different realm. The music, it took me to its core and so I
danced with it." Zach begged for me to describe to him what I felt
while I *defied gravity*. I tried my hardest to put it into words even
though that was one of the hardest things anybody could ask me
to do. "I felt it everywhere and just let it take my body wherever
it wanted."

He nodded like he understood, and for some reason I believed him.

"No one else did what you did, Capri, no one danced alone as if they were actually dancing with *someone*. I mean, it was brilliant. It was . . . I can't describe it in words. I just, I felt everything." He lifted a cheese fry to his mouth, but let it fall back into the basket in front of him. "You know," he said thoughtfully, "I never knew dancing could have such an effect on me."

"Neither did I," I said with a laugh. "I mean, I performed at the Sunlight, picturing a crowd in front of me and all. But I never danced—*really* danced like I did there on that stage. I never thought I actually would do that great, especially completely improv."

The cheese fry made its journey back from the basket.

"Well, at least there aren't any more surprises," Zach said. "Your next dance is a routine choreographed by you and you have until May to figure it out." The cheese fry stopped at the entrance of his mouth. "That's not a lot of time."

We'd waited an entire hour in the audience while the judges made their decision. I was burning with nerves while Zach tried to distract me with funny reaction videos on his phone, to no avail. What felt like an eternity later, my name and two others were called for the final audition, and I lost all ability to breathe. Finally, after what seemed like *two* eternities, I calmed down enough to listen to the judges' closing instructions. The judges told us that our last audition had to be a full-on dance routine, like you see in a stage production. They wanted us to have costumes, an original story, and a routine based on an event that changed our lives. "Inspire us," they'd said. They were only choosing *one* of us. The two other people that danced, they were good—like, *really good*. Honestly, I was nervous out of my mind. But I had an idea that I thought would help make my routine truly inspiring.

I bit the corner of my lip. "Actually, I thought I'd ask you something." Zach lifted an eyebrow. "I want you to help me with my last audition. I want to dance to one of your songs."

He froze, chewing slowly on the fry that he'd finally taken a bite out of.

"You what?" he asked slowly.

"I want you to perform live while I dance. I mean, I don't have it all together just yet, as far as what I wanna portray and everything. But I know I want to do this with you. You were here for me today and you being in that audience and convincing me to come to New York City to audition for a dance camp, onstage, in front of everyone? I really appreciate that, and you are so talented, Zach, I ain't never heard nothing like your music before. It's real."

He jumped from his seat and did a very sloppy ballet spin. With a full-on grin, he added, "I'd be honored."

# Zach

**"I'M NOT READY TO GO HOME YET," SHE WHISPERED.**
We walked back from the record shop we'd just explored to the ferry so we could wait for the boat to take us back to our respective sides of town. We'd stayed at the pizza parlor eating our giant slices, munching on cheese fries, and drinking soda for two hours. Then we walked around the city a bit more, visiting parks, exploring the record shops and thrift stores. Now, it was almost seven o'clock, which was the time when the streetlights would come on in Bayside and all my neighbors would settle in for dinner. Like always, I'd just warm up one of those microwavable dinners and work on a song or something until Dad came home from work and forced me to come downstairs and listen to how his day was. About how much simpler things were in Bayside, how happy he was that he'd moved us here. But as of right now, I wasn't in Bayside; I was back in the city, and honestly . . .

"I don't wanna leave quite yet either," I said. "You know, this must have been how Jesus felt."

Capri laughed. "What do you mean?"

"You know, when he left heaven to come to earth? That's how it feels leaving New York City to go back to Bayside."

"This is heaven for you?" she asked.

I nodded. "Something like it. I mean, look around. Listen to the sounds of everything around us. It's so freeing."

A man sitting against a storefront belted a sad tune on his saxophone.

"I hear it," she responded. "It's like everything is able to make as much noise as it wants. Even the lights."

They were bright, despite the fact the sun had already set. New York City has its own suns.

I stopped in my tracks and let the bustling crowd walk by me.

"You know, we don't have to go back just yet," I said.

She shook her head. "No, we have to. We already stayed longer than we should've and my phone's dead. So, if anybody tried to call me, they got a voicemail, which means when they finish the open mic at Easy's and come looking for me, I'm doomed. When I'm doomed, I get my butt worn out, and trust me, Ma don't care *how* old I am, she will—"

"Capri," I interrupted. "As much as I enjoy hearing you talk, I think you should look up."

I watched her eyes wid. Her jaw dropped.

"No. Freaking. Way."

Right, above us, words lit up by a sun of its own read:

CLUB HORIZON PRESENTS AMBIENT LIGHT TONIGHT

Under the sign, a crowd of people were already lined up down the sidewalk and around the corner.

"We have to, Capri. This is seriously not a coincidence. This is life smacking us right in the face and telling us to do this."

She looked away from the sign.

"And I would totally agree with you, if it wasn't sold out." She was right. A big red-lettered *Sold Out* flashed below the concert announcement. But I wasn't going to let that change anything.

# Capri

"SO?" ZACH SAID AS IF HE WERE SOME OVERHYPED character in a movie. I couldn't help but chuckle at his silliness, but still "so" wasn't a powerful enough word to convince me that he had a foolproof plan to get us into that concert without getting caught. He could read the hesitance on my face. "Listen," he said in his normal voice again. "I've done this before at home, all right? We can get into this sold-out concert. It'll just take a little bit of work."

I crossed my arms. "I'm not mugging nobody for tickets."

He rolled his eyes. "We're not gonna *mug* anyone. We just walk in with a big crowd." He waited for me to agree, but I wasn't going to so quickly. Not with the huge men I saw near the entrance with the word *Security* in all-white letters on the back of their black shirts. I could see myself now, handcuffed and sitting on a curb next to Zach, who for some reason doesn't have handcuffs on, successfully talking his way out of jail time, while I sit there knowing nothing I say will get me out of it.

"I'm not *like* you, Zach. Remember? If you get caught breaking into a concert, the cops will write it off as some little rebellious teenage mistake. Something they did when they were younger. It'll be cute to them and a story you'll tell your kids every time you hear an Ambient Light song playing on the radio. Me? It will be the exact opposite. The cops will think I'm a criminal and the only story I'll be telling my kids will be from behind bars, because even if they ever decide to let me out, I won't *want* to leave because Ma will kill me."

Zach reached over, uncrossed my arms, and gave me his signature ocean-blue stare. The one that shot little daggers right into the deepest parts of me.

"Before you make a final decision, I want you to think about today, everything that happened for you. After you do, then whatever decision you make about this concert is what we'll do. Deal?"

I closed my eyes and thought about this morning. Lying to Ma. Sneaking into Bayside. Feeling like I was going to throw up. Sneaking onto the ferry, still feeling like I was gonna throw up. Almost fighting with Zach, only for us to make up almost immediately. Finally getting my window seat but falling asleep the entire way to this city. Exploring this city with a really cute guy. Almost getting bumped from my audition; said really cute guy coming through last minute. When I thought about this, my lips turned upward, butterflies filled my stomach. I kept thinking.

Seeing my mother soaring high again outside of Hamilton, still erect in the city that she loved so much. The city that never forgot her. She met me here, on that stage. and helped me ace that audition. Maybe, just maybe, Essie wasn't done showing me what it felt like to embrace freedom, even when fear was close by. Maybe she was showing me tonight that it didn't matter that I was forgettable to Hamilton, because tonight, I'd have a night I'd never forget. Ambient Light! They were here before my eyes, and Zach, this really cute guy, had a plan. Maybe this once, I could finish the night continuing to be the Capri I'd always dreamt of being. The fearless one.

I opened my eyes to see Zach smiling wide.

I grabbed ahold of his hand and walked us toward the middle of the line. "Come on before I change my mind."

"Thanks for holding our spot, Dad," Zach said to a random old guy with a long beard, covered in tattoos, whose earbuds were blasting so loud, I could hear the eighties electric guitar ringing out of them. He couldn't hear us but gave Zach a nod. We squeezed into a tight space behind him. Surprisingly, the people behind us made room. My heart thumped so hard, I thought I was going to collapse. Even though I was taking a chance, I needed Zach's plan to work.

"Okay," he whispered into my ear as the line moved closer to the entrance. "Follow my lead, if you feel like they're going to grab you run away as fast as you can, leave me if you have to. The security guards are really overweight and don't look fast enough to grab us both. Got it?"

I nodded.

Slowly, step by step we made our way closer to the door.

"Look, Capri, I've done this more times than I can count, but it takes focus. When we reach the front of the door and the guards are scanning in tickets, we walk in between the people they're scanning for, got it?"

I nodded, droplets of sweat drizzled down my neck.

"Okay," he whispered when the group in front of us got their tickets checked, "this is us. Go, go, go." He pushed me forward into the building, and effortlessly, we were in. The comfortable heat from the inside calmed my heart rate down.

*Yes!* It was happening! I would be seeing Ambient Ligh—

"Your bag, miss," said a woman standing next to a metal detector. Her voice made me jump. I handed my purse to her and she began to check it. "Walk through the detector please," she instructed dryly. I walked through and was handed my bag back.

"Walk through," I heard her direct Zach, but before he could, a security guard grabbed his arm.

# Zach

*I FELT A MEATY HAND GRIP MY ARM. MY HEART STOPPED* pumping, but I worked to remain calm. "Heyo, officer," I said with a smirk. The man didn't smile back. The blue and black lights from the club's ceiling shined against his bald head.

"I don't think I collected your ticket, kid." His voice was hoarse, and his breath smelled like stale cigarettes and garbage. I lifted the back of my hand to my nose to block out the rancid scent.

"Of course you did. You scanned it in and everything," I answered from behind my hand. I looked over at Capri; she looked like a frightened child at summer camp after hearing a scary story.

"Oh yeah?" the man asked. "Then where is it?"

"Come on, man! You're holding up the line!" someone yelled from behind us. The security guard gripped my arm even tighter and began to lead me out of the club, until someone spoke up.

*"Son!"*

We both stopped in our tracks to see the man with the beard that Capri and I used to cut in line. He ran up to us and pulled out a ticket.

"Here it is, son, I told you about giving me your tickets and stuff. You almost made us late for the show!" He gave me a small smack on the back of the head, then looked at the security guard. "Kids these days, huh? I always told his mother that we should have sent him to military school, maybe then he would learn to be a little less careless, am I right?"

I felt free again when the security guard released his grip from my arm. I rubbed the rawness his meaty hand left from it.

"If that's his ticket, where's your ticket?" he asked my "dad." The man with the beard pulled out an identical ticket. The security guard licked his teeth and looked at us both. He stared in between us. The man with the beard kept a cool smile on his face, I worked to do the same. The security guard huffed, turned around, and walked back to the door. I walked in the metal detector and caught up with Capri, who stood completely frozen.

The man with the beard handed the extra ticket to some guy who stood near us. "Thanks for letting me borrow this, man." The guy shrugged, and walked into the doors leading to the stage. "Sneaking into concerts, huh, kids?" he asked us, placing his hands on his hips.

"We would've bought the tickets ourselves, but they were sold out!" Capri blurted.

"How much do I owe you for that save?" I pulled out my wallet, but he lifted a hand.

"Nothing. Only thing you owe me is working hard to be a bit better at sneaking in. Both y'all's eyes were as wide as a ferret's." He opened his eyes wide, to reflect ours, then laughed. "I used to do this all the time when I was your age. I'm just happy to have been able to take part in getting another one over on The Man." He lifted a fist; Capri and I slowly did the same. The guy grinned and nodded. "Yeah, see y'all kids understand it, down with The Man," he said before walking away.

"You okay?" Capri asked.

I let out the breath I was holding for the whole exchange but kept my voice steady. "Told you it would work. I do it all the time."

She smiled. "Sure you do."

I grabbed her hand and walked through the doors leading to the stage.

It smelled strongly of booze and cigarette smoke that clung to the clothes of those who smoked outside. The floor was sticky, and the lights were so dim I could hardly see what was in front of me. Hah, it was just as beautiful as I remembered concerts being. I held tight to Capri as we weaved through the crowd toward the front of the stage.

"We're fine right here, I can see," I heard her say in a voice ridden with fear. We were close enough to the stage to see, but still a few people were in front of us; it wasn't close enough. This was Ambient Light we were talking about.

"Maybe," I said over the crowd just as Dee said to me during the first concert we'd snuck into. "But I want us so close that our eardrums will be ringing till the morning." I continued to lead her through the crowd until we were the closest we could be.

"I can't believe we're here. I can't believe we're this close." She reached her hand out in front of her through the small separation gate and touched the stage with her fingertips. She looked at me. "I was terrified, you know, to come here, to New York City, to this concert, but this is turning out to be the best night of my life." She walked up to me slowly, but as more people filed in, the crowd pushed us closer together. "Thank you, Zach," she whispered.

Suddenly I forgot where I was.

I only focused on her eyes, wide with excitement. I lifted my arm and wrapped it around her waist. I pulled her in as close as she could possibly be, until I could feel her heartbeat on my chest. Her lips parted slightly, just enough for mine to fit into their crease and embrace them. I was falling so fast, so hard, that the waters were approaching closer and closer to the shore and I was about to dive headfirst into them.

"You don't have to thank me," I whispered. "Capri, being here with you, it's taught me so much about taking chances. But, most importantly, it's shown me that I lo—"

Screams filled the venue around us, until it pierced my ears. Ambient Light walked onstage and we pulled apart. Granite Michael took his place behind the microphone, his cherrywood electric guitar strapped around his black muscle tee. The other guys took their place behind their mics, another behind his drum set.

"Hello, New York City!" Granite yelled, his raspy voice filling the air around us, echoing ten times over. Capri clapped and screamed along with everyone else. "We're happy to be back here, to see some beautiful younger faces in the crowd." He looked straight at her, and she smiled wide. "New York City is a place filled with culture, diversity, and everything else great. It watered so many artists and blossomed them into some pretty rad crops. We want to thank you all for reaping from us and letting us give you a taste of our craft." Everyone clapped. "Most importantly, we want to show our appreciation for one thing: you guys. Our family is made up of so many colors, diverse in its very essence, willing to lay down everything to dwell together and enjoy our music. Because that's what we're here for!" With that, he began to play the chords for the beginning of "The Lost Embrace" off their second album, and it was so much better live than anything I'd heard through my earbuds, no matter how loud they were.

I watched Capri sing along to the songs, arms raised above her head. She was having the time of her life. And being next to her, so was I.

# Capri

**"WE WANT TO SING 'THE LIGHT IN OUR FEARS,'" GRANITE**
said an hour later, while a blood-red grand piano was pushed out on
wheels to the middle of the stage. "This is the song I wrote after my
mother died of cancer when I was seventeen. I didn't understand
what was going on, I was angry, upset, and felt lost. But I knew, that
through my fears, tears, and worries, there was a light. There was
a light that shone through the darkness I was facing, walking me
straight to hope. No matter how dark life gets for you, remember
the light never glows too far away, it's waiting to lead you to hope."
A few people clapped and he took his place behind his piano and
began to sing:

> *"Light shine, steady*
> *Pulse, slows down*
> *She won't awaken tomorrow,*
> *The darkness swells around.*
> *The laugh that will never sound,*
> *From her cold lips.*
> *This darkness is here and now,*
> *And I'm crashing through this fear,*
> *Like glass, Like glass.*
> *Don't leave me alone.*
> *Light fall down*
> *Light shine down*

*And lead,*

*Lead me on."*

Zach grabbed my hand and squeezed it. Ambient Light harmonized together in a hum that sounded like heaven had opened up and angels joined the song. It was beautiful and moving at first, but then, suddenly, a sharp pain thundered through my head—strong enough to make me cry. The darkness Granite was singing about— the weight of it—hovered heavy around me, pulling me toward it.

I knew nothing would ever be simple or normal again. I also knew that the way I'd felt, today, when I felt free, when I fell in love, would soon come to an end. This city was a capsule away from my reality, a dream Zach and I would both have to wake up from soon enough. Essie's spirit felt so alive here, but it would crawl back inside its casket and bury itself again. Back in Hamilton, I'd have to reach hard for her again; I'd have to dance until my body pulsed with pain before I felt even an inch of her presence. When the curtains closed over Ambient Light and the concert came to an end, Zach and I would have to return to our respective cells across the tracks from one another—two separate worlds. Ma would find out. I couldn't lie to her for long. She'd tear my tail up for sneaking away or worse, she'd break down. I'd have to get her the soft tissues from the corner store like Pa did for months after Essie's homegoing, because she'd really believe I'd be next if I left. I'd skip the Camp Sharp audition because guilt would rip me up or I'd be under house arrest until I got my nursing degree, and my chances of being like Essie would vanish, just like tonight. It would only be a memory, her painting, the stage, dancing under the warm lights, the music filling the air around me—the boy who held me close.

This is what was hurting me. I cried harder, the music, thankfully, masking the sound as I hid myself in Zach's jean jacket, resting my forehead against his chest. I wanted to remember how this felt, how he smelled, like pine. His arms felt like the embers of a fire sparking heat, comfort as a snowstorm rages outside. They warmed me and made me feel safe. I knew I would never feel them again, not like this. Who was I kidding even coming here? Giving in to his fantasy, putting on his rose-colored glasses? I could feel the dark skies of Hamilton stalking me like prey, crouching in wait to pull me back into her dungeon. Ambient Light hummed, and Granite belted out this song, I felt the darkness catch hold of my body, and my grip on Zach faded away.

> *"Where is the light?*
> *Is it dawning?*
> *Do I feel it surrender?*
> *Or is death, taking another?*
> *Leaving her breathless*
> *Leaving me breathless*
> *Leaving us cold."*

# Justin

*I WALKED BACK INTO THE HOUSE I'D JUST LEFT.* RED plastic cups, once filled with liquor and punch, trash, and cigarette butts lay all over the ground. Just moments ago, my hand was wrapped around the butt of some girl from calculus class. She was a horrible kisser, but I was drunk, so I didn't care. I just wanted to forget my argument with Rose. My phone kept buzzing in my pocket, but I ignored it. I guessed it was probably Rose calling to make up, but I was still seething. I wanted her to feel the weight of embarrassing me in front of all my friends.

I could feel calculus girl's phone buzzing from her back pocket, too. And then, when a song on the speaker ended and a moment of silence filled the room, I could hear a bunch of phones buzzing at once all around the party. That made me pull out mine. Surprisingly, it was Ma. I had no missed calls from Rose, only Ma and Pa.

I quickly dialed Ma back; she picked up before the first ring could sound fully.

"Hello?"

"*Justin? Oh Justin, thank God! It isn't you!*" she wailed.

"Ma? What's wrong?"

"Someone was shot down at the abandoned railroad tracks. They didn't tell us who it was yet, all we know is that it was someone from your school. I'm heading to the hospital now with your pa. We thought it was you, Justin."

"No, no, I'm at Carlos's house. I'm fine." I tried gathering my thoughts, but they were racing a mile a minute. "Do you know where Capri is?" I asked, sounding way more frantic than I intended.

"She's working overtime at Easy's. Will you go by and bring her home until we get back?"

"Of course, yeah. I'll leave right now."

I slid the end button on my phone and gestured to the crowd.

"Hey! Turn the music off!" I yelled, once, twice, then three times. Finally the rap music blaring from the speakers came to a halt. "Hey, everybody, go home. Your parents are looking for all y'all. Somebody in our class got shot by the tracks or something."

Everyone was eerily silent.

Carlos made his way through the crowd. "Everyone in our class is here. Right?"

Deondre stood next to him, looked around the room, and nodded. "Yeah, everyone's here."

Suddenly my heart stopped.

"*No,*" I whispered. "*No. No. No. No.*"

"What?" Carlos asked.

Deondre walked up to me. "Justin, man, what's up?"

There were only two people that left the party early. My mind was racing.

"Rose," I whispered. Rose left the party angrily, and if it was her, then the baby . . . I pulled out my phone and called her. After three rings, she answered.

"I said I'm done, Jus—"

I hung up the phone. I'd worry about her later. I only wanted to know she was safe and alive. The other person that left . . . I tried ignoring the sick feeling developing in my stomach. I rang his phone again and again, to no avail.

"Tyree . . . I think . . ." My thoughts were crashing into one another. The tears fell from my eyes before I could finish my sentence.

Deondre's eyes searched mine. "How do you know?" he whispered.

"I gotta find my sister, man. I gotta bring her home." I ran out of the party before I could hear anyone say anything. Ran down the street faster than I ever had, past the crowds gathering outside, straight to Easy's record shop. When I approached it, all the lights were off. I banged on the door.

"Easy!" I yelled. "Open the door, nigga!"

Finally the door opened. But it wasn't Easy who opened it; it was Perry. She held a broom in her hand. I ran past her through the store to Easy's office; Capri wasn't in there, so I ran into the bathroom, but she wasn't there either.

"Where's Capri?" I asked.

Her best friend crossed her arms. "Why are you always on her back? Calm down."

"Tyree was just shot."

"*What?*"

"I need to know where Capri is. I need to have her home until I know things are safe."

Perry used the broom to keep herself steady.

"*What?*"

"You gotta tell me where she is," I pleaded.

"I don't know, Justin. Who shot Tyree? What's going on?"

"What do you mean you don't know?" I asked, ignoring her questions. "You were here with her all day."

Perry sighed. "She's in New York City."

"*What?*"

Perry closed her eyes tight and shook her head. "She's in New York City. She got an audition with Camp Sharp and left this morning to go."

I tried remaining calm, but I heard my yell echo through the record shop. "You. Let. Her. Go. To. New. York. Alone?!"

Perry shook her head frantically. "No, no I didn't! She went with Zach."

"Zach Williams?" I asked. "He was at the party I just left."

Perry bit her lip and looked down.

"No, I . . . she went with Zach. The guy you met earlier."

"The heater guy?"

"No. Yes. Well, he's not really the heater guy. He's from Bayside."

"*What?*" I screamed, which caused Perry to jump. I couldn't believe it. Why was Capri with someone from across the tracks? How did she even know him? A thousand questions swirled around in my mind. "When is she coming back?"

"She was supposed to be back hours ago, Justin. I don't know where she is. She's not answering any of my calls."

My heart sped. The ferry in Hamilton had been down for years. She would have to pass the tracks to get back home. That could be Capri on those tracks.

"Check your house," Perry suggested. "She might have just gone straight home and went to sleep or something."

I ran toward the door.

"Justin, wait!" Perry called when I'd been almost down the block. "Is he dead?" she asked.

I shrugged, a lump forming in the back of my throat. "I don't know."

She fell to her knees and hid her face into her hands. I just needed to get home.

# Capri

"WHAT HAPPENED HERE?" ZACH ASKED. I WONDERED THE same thing. We'd *just* made it onto the last ferry ride of the night, thank God. It was nearly a quarter past eleven, so we'd rushed out of Bayside toward the tracks leading back to Hamilton, but we could see from a few miles away, near the clearing, flashing police lights.

"There was probably another fire or something," I said, peering, trying to catch a hint of what was going on.

"Yeah, maybe. But I don't see any fire trucks," Zach replied. "How are you gonna get back home? It looks like they blocked off the entrance to the tracks with, like, ten police cars."

He was right; it seemed like police cars were encircling the entire station, but I couldn't see much of what was going on from where we stood. I turned to face him in the dark; his pale face lit up with the blue and red flashing lights. He looked distracted by what was going on down there, worried. But I didn't want to focus on that; I wanted to focus on what was going on up here, above the lights, with Zach, because it wouldn't last much longer.

"I had the most amazing day of my life. I almost don't want it to end. I mean, I totally don't want it to end."

He looked down at me. "Me either."

"I still can't believe I snuck into a rock concert."

He smiled. "You were great." But he looked behind me again, his eyes still painted with distraction.

"Zach."

"How are we gonna get you back home?" he asked again. I smiled, playfully punching his shoulder.

"I'm already in huge trouble as it is; I'll just have to take the long way around."

"Do you want me to go with you?"

"No, it's fine. I'll walk by myself."

He shook his head. "I don't think that's safe."

"This is Hamilton and Bayside we're talking about. Nothing crazy ever happens here. Look, I'll be fine, all right?" He kept shaking his head, glancing down at the tracks, then back up at me, over and over again like he was conjuring a story, some horrible reason for why those lights were flashing.

I laughed. "Zach." But he didn't respond. "Zach." I tapped his shoulder. "Zach," I said again, more serious. "Look at me." Finally he did. "This isn't Philly, and it's not New York City. It's Hamilton, a town passed over by Bayside all those years ago. Some kid probably was lighting up cigarettes again and accidentally caught something on fire. I'll be fine, okay?"

He sighed. "Okay. Fine."

He said he wanted to watch me walk to Hamilton until he couldn't see me anymore, so the entire time, until we took the long way far from the station to the other side of the train tracks, I could see his silhouette on the hill, hovering above me like a ghost. I don't know why I didn't want him walking me to the entrance of Hamilton that night. I guess deep down, I knew something wasn't right. He already looked worried, but I didn't want him to worry even more. Because truth was, deep down, I was just as worried. Nothing ever happened in Bayside or Hamilton, and that was what scared me. Sure, there were little things here and there, but nothing to this extent. I'd never seen so many cop cars in my life. What Zach didn't notice was that there were both Hamilton *and* Bayside police parked in the same place: at the train tracks, the barrier resting between both of our towns. This meant whatever was happening there had to do with both of us. Whenever something *did* happen that was between both of us, it involved blood and lots of it.

The end of Ajah McKulley's story popped in my mind. The part we never talk about. After her father saw his family burning alive, he tried to take out with his bare hands the man that raped Ajah. The people of Bayside wrapped a noose around his neck, hell-bent on hanging him for it. It was the cops that led the mob to the abandoned train tracks where they were planning to lynch him; their intention was to let his body serve as a warning for the people of Hamilton to stay away. When the angry mob reached the tracks, Hamilton police along with everyone in town were there, ready to do whatever they needed to save Mr. McKulley. Bayside didn't want a war; they loved their town too much to see it destroyed, so they threw Mr. McKulley over the tracks, and Hamilton caught him. They realized they didn't have as much power over Hamilton as they thought. Whatever brought our towns together for the first time since Mr. McKulley wasn't a little fire. It was so much more.

Hamilton was lit up, and the streets were filled as if it were the autumn festival or New Year's Eve. The streetlights seemed to be brighter, or maybe it was the fact that the sky was much darker than it usually was. They stood on the sidewalks, in the streets, some of the stores were even still open and people were piled inside. It seemed like no one was home that night. Small crowds were scattered everywhere. Some were talking in hushed tones, others were crying. The screams were echoing off one another, and the tears fell in torrents from their faces.

"*Oh, Jesus! Help me Lord!*" a woman screamed at the sky. She brushed by my shoulder and ran to her teenage son, whom she cradled in her arms, swaying back and forth. "I thought it was you!" I heard her yell, as the boy began to cry.

"Capri! Capri!" I heard my name being called through all the bustle. I turned around and saw Perry running through the crowd toward me. "Capri!" She couldn't catch her breath; her face was stained with tears. I could hardly make out what she was saying.

"Capri. *Huugh. Huuugh.* He's gone. *Huugh. Huuugh.* He's gone."

My heart stopped beating. "Who? Who's gone?" But she only shook her head and began to cry again.

"Who is gone?" I yelled, but she didn't respond.

*Justin.*

I ran as fast as I could through the crowds and to my house. All the lights were turned off. I ran onto the porch. I felt like I was swimming underwater for hours and just now came up for air. My lungs were aching. I banged on the door.

"Open the door! Hello! Anybody, please! Open the door!" Tears fell from my eyes, down my face, off my chin. "Justin! Justin!" I banged and banged, and then finally turned the knob. It was open. I walked into my small house slowly. "Ma? Pa? Justin?"

"Capri?" someone called through the darkness. I reached for the switch on the wall and clicked it up. The small desk lamp next to Ma's love seat lit up the room. Justin stood at the entrance to the hallway. I ran up to him and he wrapped his arms tightly around me.

"Where have you been?" he asked.

"I . . . I . . ."

He pulled away and looked straight into my eyes; his were glassy, his cheeks washed with tears.

"I tried calling you half the night, Capri. We all did. Ma sent me to the record shop to come get you, but Easy shut it down early for the night."

"I . . ."

"I ran around this whole town looking for you like a chicken with its head cut off. When we heard the news, we thought it was you." He shook his head, tears trailing down his face. "Until I talked to Perry. She told me you were in New York City auditioning for that camp. She told me who you were with, Capri."

I winced. "Does Ma know?"

"No, I didn't tell her." He banged his fist against the side of the wall in frustration. "I didn't want to stress her out even more, when . . . when everyone's . . . when . . . we found out . . ." He started to fall silent, like Perry did on the street.

"What happened, Justin? Why were all those police cars out on the tracks?"

Justin fell to his knees, cupping his head into his hands.

"They killed him." His voice was hoarse.

"Who? Who killed who?" He didn't answer me, just shook his head, screaming into his palms. I leaned down until I was level with him, prying his wet hands from his face.

"Justin, I need you to tell me what happened."

He stared at me, his eyes bloodshot. I'll never forget that stare; it was free of any sanity, washed with hatred, my brother completely absent.

"Tyree. He was shot at the tracks by a Bayside cop."

And then I felt it. It was more intense than at the concert. I felt it all around us. The darkness closed in. I felt as if I was dreaming. Like everything around me was synthetic. The air I was breathing, the floor I stood on.

Justin's phone rang out around us. He cleared his throat.

"Hello?"

I could barely hear who it was on the other side of the phone, but his voice was deep.

"I'm good, man. I know, my ma's at the hospital right now. She just told me that he didn't . . . that Tyree . . . he didn't make it." He paused, and both sides of the phone were silent. "Yeah, I'll be right there." He hung up the phone and stood up to walk toward the door.

I followed. "I'm coming with you."

He turned around sharply. "No, you're not. You're staying here."

"What? No. I'm going wherever you go."

He pushed me away from the door so hard, I landed on the couch.

"You're drunk," I accused in sudden realization.

He lifted his hands. "You're just now realizing that? Look, it doesn't matter. You're staying here."

I stood up. "No I'm not."

"Look," he spat, "I don't know what the heck you thought you were doing today, or why you kept this audition thing a secret from us. But that was real dumb, Capri. Going to the city with some dude you just met, what, a day ago? Anything could have happened. He could have sold you into a prostitution ring or something.

"First," he continued, "I don't want you seeing that guy anymore, not now, not ever. Second, I don't want you *leaving* this house tonight until I got this crap figured out, understood?"

"Just . . ."

"I want you here, okay? I want you here when Ma comes back with Pa from the hospital. You hear me?"

Against my will to rebel, I took my seat back on the couch and a few seconds later, the front door slammed shut.

When Ma came in about an hour later, I felt it was best to pretend that I'd fallen asleep on the couch. That way, I wouldn't get sent to my room like I was some little girl while she and Pa discussed what they knew about what went down. But Ma didn't say much; she just kept repeating, "He was only a baby." Finally I couldn't take it anymore and ran from my spot on the couch, into my room, and slammed the door.

"Just let her be," I heard Pa say.

As soon as I fell under my covers, I pulled out my phone and dialed Zach. . . .

*"Hey, it's Zach. Not here right now, so uh, hang up."*

Once . . .

*"Hey, it's Zach. Not here right now, so uh, hang up."*

Twice . . .

*"Hey, it's Zach. Not here right now, so uh, hang up."*

Three times . . .

*"Hey, it's Zach. Not here right now, so uh, hang up."*

Then four . . .

But got no answer.

# Justin

**FIFTEEN MINUTES LATER I WAS BACK AT THE HOUSE** where we'd just gotten drunk and celebrated a victory. Now we all felt this heavy sense that we'd lost so much more than we could have ever won. Both Hamilton's basketball and football teams were sitting on the couches and floor; Deondre and Carlos were standing. When I came into the room, a fullback on the football team, Hananya, spoke. His cheeks were stained with tears, and his bloodshot eyes shined bright red against his coal-colored skin. He bit down on his jaw, trying to keep his voice steady as the tears continued to trail down.

"Aight, y'all, this is what I know. Tyree was killed tonight by a Bayside cop on the tracks."

"Do they know why?" another boy asked.

"No," Hananya replied. "They don't. They just know he was walking on the tracks, closer to Bayside's side. My ma called me from the hospital."

Silence filled the room.

Carlos stood and threw his hands up in the air.

"Man, why this gotta happen to us, here?"

Jay punched the cushion on the couch he was sitting on. "No, why this gotta happen at all?" He hid his face in his hands. "I can't believe he's *dead*, man. We just saw him, man. We just saw him."

"What we gonna do?" Deondre asked what everyone else was

thinking. They all looked to me for the answer. The pain I felt cut deeper than anything I'd ever experienced. I didn't know which was making it worse—the liquor, the crap between Capri and the kid from Bayside going down right under my nose, or the argument I had with Rose—but each of these things piled on top of Tyree had me seething. About everything. No matter how hard I worked, it seemed everything that meant something to me was pulling in the opposite direction. I couldn't right it. But more, I couldn't stand feeling so . . . helpless. I looked around at the guys all around me; even Jay was quiet and completely focused on what I'd say.

"We're gonna do something," I said finally. "We're gonna fight back."

I was tired of staying quiet. If life wanted to throw a punch, I'd sock it straight in the face.

# Zach

DAD WASN'T HOME WHEN I'D GOTTEN IN THE NIGHT
after watching Capri's silhouette disappear into the Hamilton fog
and I didn't think anything of it. I just figured he was working late,
like always. I tried my best to believe that the sirens and lights
weren't serious, as Capri had insisted, but still, I collapsed into
a deep sleep feeling like something didn't seem right. When I'd
awakened the next morning, even the air was different. Everything
was. First, my phone, which had been charging from being completely dead the night before, had four missed calls from Capri and
five from Virgie when it came back to life. I tried calling her back—
Capri, not Virgie—three times, but it went straight to voicemail. I
texted her twice. During that time Thomas called me.

"Dude! Dude!" he was yelling from the other end of the phone.

"Whoa, calm down," I said with a laugh. "I'll tell you everything
that happened in New York, just calm down."

"No, man, turn on the news! Turn on the news right now! This
is crazy!" Thomas exclaimed, then he began to hyperventilate.

I reached for my remote control and clicked to one of the early-
morning news channels. The one I chose was based out of New
York City. The blond woman on screen was seated next to a stiff-
faced Black ex-football player.

"New this morning, a deadly shooting in Bayside, a town on the
outskirts of New York City. We have the full story brought to you by
Tina Landry. Tina?"

The camera shot to the train tracks that separated Hamilton from Bayside; bright yellow cautionary signs surrounded it. A brunette woman with a microphone hashed out the details.

"A mystery in the making. This is the spot where seventeen-year-old Tyree Thompson was shot and killed by a Bayside police officer in the tenth hour of last night. Immediately after the shooting, the officer called for medical assistance but when a response team showed up on sight, it was too late. As of now, the officer has not been brought into custody and many in Hamilton, where the young boy was from, wonder just why this is the case."

The camera shot to the entrance of Hamilton where all the stores lined the streets. In front of one of the stores, Tina Landry held a mic up to an older woman. A boy about the age of twelve rubbed her back, consoling the woman as she was crying, and I could barely make out what she was saying through her tears.

"That was my baby! *My baby!*" she kept repeating. "I don't know why this man that took my baby's life isn't in prison already. I don't care if he no cop or not. He took my baby's life. My baby . . . my baby . . . my baby."

I squeezed the phone in my hand, unable to swallow.

The camera switched to a man in a suit. His name flashed across the screen, but for some reason it was blurry; I couldn't focus on it—Reverend something.

"Tyree Thompson was a straight-A student, he served well in our church. He was a good boy, excited about his scholarship to attend NYU next fall. We just want to know what happened, what really went down on those tracks to cause this child's life to end so quickly. We just want answers."

The newswoman stood in front of the tracks again, mic in hand.

"Though Hamilton remains clueless on the matter, Bayside has a testimonial from this surviving officer of what really went on." The camera switched to the entrance of Bayside, almost identical to Hamilton. The sergeant of police, an older man with white hair, dressed in uniform, stood before the camera; many other police officers stood behind him, staring straight ahead.

"We know that the officer was only acting in self-defense. The drunk Hamilton boy charged at him, and the officer did what any one of us are trained to do: fire. We will be investigating the incident further to prove that the officer was acting in self-defense. For now, our prayers are indeed with this pillar of our community and his family. We hope to see him healed and this unfortunate situation behind him as soon as possible. Thank you."

Again, the scene cut to Tyree's mom.

"Are you going to pursue a case against the Bayside officer who murdered your son?" the anchor asked. Tyree's mother nodded through her tears. She looked straight at the camera, her eyes bloodshot from sadness, anger, crying, lack of sleep.

"We gonna get the answers we asking for, we gonna get the truth. My son ain't no threat, he's a good boy. He ain't never do no wrong to no one, he ain't ever carry around no weapons. We gonna get the truth, I swear it. We gonna put my son to rest. But we ain't putting this to rest until we see that officer in prison and until we know what really happened on the other side of them tracks."

The reporter nodded furiously, then brought the mic back up to her own mouth.

"As for the citizens of Hamilton, the untimely murder of yet another unarmed black male won't be put to rest until the matter is solved. This is Tina Landry with Wolf 29 News."

"Hello?" Thomas kept saying through the receiver.

I dropped my phone on the ground and ran down the stairs. I needed to see Capri.

Sunday morning was usually Dad's off day, but when I reached the bottom of the stairs, there he was. It looked as if he'd brought his entire office into our kitchen. Papers were strewn about everywhere, his laptop was out, and he was typing away, something serious. He banged his fingers against the keyboard, as if somehow making lots of clicking noises echo around the kitchen made the words come faster. He didn't notice me until I was almost at the entrance of the kitchen. He looked at me, above his glasses, and stopped typing.

"Oh, good. I'm glad you're up."

He was still in the button-down and blue tie that I saw him leave in for work the morning before, except the once crisp white button-down was stained with coffee and the blue tie was crumpled and drooping down his chest. He crossed his arms and gave me the tired lawyer interrogation look. His eyebrows were so creased together, they almost became a unibrow.

"Where were you last night?" he asked.

I mirrored his expression. "I could ask you the same thing."

"I was working on a case. This morning I came home and decided to finish the case work here, at home. I was tired of looking at those ragged walls in that law office; they need a new paint job. I mean, being here all night? It's hard." His face turned red, and he began to seethe with anger. "Especially when you call the house to check on your son, and he is nowhere to be found."

"I was with Thomas—"

He banged his fist against the table. "Don't you dare lie to me, Zachary. I want the truth, now!"

"I went to New York City."

He shook his head. "Don't you act like you made a little inno-cent day trip. I know what you did. Bad enough I had to get a pic-ture sent to me from Virgie . . ."

"And I'm supposed to be afraid of you finding out that I went to support a friend on her audition in New York?"

He scoffed, then pulled out his phone. He slid it across the table. On the screen was a picture of me on the ferry, wide-eyed from Virgie's flash photography. Capri lay asleep on my shoulder.

"You expect me to believe you went to support a friend? Who is that?" he asked.

"None of your bus—"

"Tell. Me. Now. Or I'll ensure you'll never step a foot out of this house as long as you're a senior at Bayside High. Tell me!" he demanded.

I let out a breath. "Her name is Capri. She's a friend."

"The heck she is," he spat. "And where did you meet her? The internet? Because I've never seen her in that rat pack you used to hang out with in Philly."

"She's from Hamilton, and what do you care?"

"What do I care? What do I care? What are you doing hanging out in Hamilton?"

"Having my own life, Dad. How about making my own choices instead of being holed up in this godforsaken town filled with char-acters from *Leave It to Beaver!*'"

"Do you know what happened on those tracks last night?" he whispered.

"Yeah. No. I mean, no one knows. I just saw the news story."

"That trash? Those anchors are biased on this Black Lives

Matter crap already. The only reason why they're reporting this story is so they can get more people tuned in on their channels. That's all they'll be talking about for months until this case settles." He wrinkled his entire face. "Do you know those people in Hamilton already pressed charges?"

"Good. The news said he was unarmed."

"The news only knows as much as they can guess, all that fake news crap. Anyway, Officer Malore is all right—thanks for asking."

"Officer Malore? Virgie's father?"

"Yes, Officer Malore. The man whose family helped build the town that you call home, the man who served years and years protecting this town from outsiders and harm, is being accused of murder."

My mind was swimming in ten different directions. Virgie's father killed someone?

"Wait," I said, trying to piece everything together. "You talked to him?"

Dad looked at me as if I were the one talking crazy. "I'm representing his case."

"You're doing *what*?"

He lifted a hand to shut me up. "Officer Malore is a good man. He deserves a great lawyer to represent him. This has emotionally affected him just as those people in Hamilton are—"

"You know what happened, don't you? What *really* happened to Tyree?"

"It's my case. Of course I know."

"Then why aren't you letting Tyree's mother, of all people, know what happened to her son?"

"Because it's evidence. We don't give our evidence or case notes to the opposite party."

I pulled out my phone. "I gotta call Capri."

Dad stood quickly. "The heck you won't." I looked up at him. His face turned red.

"If anything, you should be calling Virgie. You should have seen her last night. She is devastated."

"And the boy's family isn't? Has anyone from Bayside even checked on anyone from Hamilton?"

"We haven't done a lot of anything yet. We aren't omnipresent. My gosh, Zachary. We are citizens of *Bayside*, that means we must stand with Officer Malore and the rest of this town. A town flooded with reporters right now when the shooting only happened twelve hours ago. You need to join me in doing what's right."

"What are you saying?"

"I'm saying that I don't want you anywhere near Hamilton." He stretched out his hand. "Until then, I'm going to need your cell-phone."

I squeezed my phone. "No way."

"Zachary."

"No!" I exclaimed. "You're not taking my phone. You're not taking my ability to speak with Capri. You can't have it."

He pulled out his own phone and took a seat in his chair.

"I knew this girl was more than someone you went to an audition with. You like her, don't you?" I looked away from him. "Well, that's not gonna fly here, and I don't think it's gonna fly with Hamilton. You know the history of these towns. Ever since that Ajah girl lied about your great-uncle, it's been a problem."

I lost my breath.

"What? That was a *Whitman*? Our family killed that poor girl?"

My father shook his head. "And she's already brainwashing you with that Hamilton history. Your uncle did what he had to do to shut those people up and stop them from destroying this town. Now look at us, they're giving us problems again. We're back exactly where we started." He sighed; a tired smile spread across his face. "I'm only doing what I must to protect you, Zachary. I don't think it's a good idea during this backlash for you to be going to Hamilton or talking to that girl."

I bit down on my jaw. "You can't stop me."

"You don't think they'll want revenge? That if they see you, a white boy from Bayside walking around that town, they won't put a bullet in your head?"

"You mean like Officer Malore did to that boy?"

"Fine." He began to dial. "I will be canceling your phone plan until further notice. No calls."

I rushed to my room and slammed the door as hard as I could.

Thoughts raced through my head a mile a minute. I wanted to know what happened, what *didn't* happen. Most of all, I needed to check on Capri. I'd missed so many calls from her, I needed to know if she was all right. But I needed to play things smart. I knew my father. In order to get what I wanted, I had to do what *he* wanted. He'd canceled my phone before; it took ten minutes after he'd called the phone people for it to cut off fully. I used the time to call Capri. Thankfully, she picked up after the third call.

"Zach?" she whispered. I could barely hear her above all the noise in the background.

"Capri? I'm so happy to hear you're all right. Where are you?"

"I'm at the church right now."

"The one down the street from the Sunlight?"

"Yes, but—"

"Listen, I'll be there in thirty."

"Zach, wait—"

"I'm gonna get answers for Tyree's mom. I'm gonna find out what happened."

"Zach . . ."

The bell sounded, signaling my father's canceling success, and the phone shut off. But I had a plan, I'd get them their answers. Bayside wouldn't get away with another murder. I wasn't going to let another Whitman win. If one Whitman was supporting it, I would make sure another would stop it.

"Going out?" Dad asked just as I wrapped my hand around the front doorknob. I slowly turned around to face him. He leaned against the hallway arch, next to the alarm system. I forced a smile on my face.

"I thought about what you said, and you're right. I have to fight for what's right and stick with the ones who deserve my loyalty. I'm going to talk to Virgie now and see how's she doing."

Dad stared me down for a moment, like he did to his victims before a cross-examination. I stared back, working to keep my face from giving away the truth. I'd lied so many times before to him in Philly about study groups that were really late-night parties and it was easy, but this was different. One wrong blink and I'd be sent right back up to my room, never to see Capri again.

"You want me to let you out the door under the assumption that you're going to the Malores' home? How do I know you won't just keep walking until you get to Hamilton?"

I sighed, trying to look disappointed.

"Listen," I carefully explained, trying to keep my voice steady.

"While I was upstairs, I got to thinking. You've been through so much since I was born. You lived in a city you hated and represented cases you didn't believe in and you *still* stayed around. Then your wife and my mom left us. You moved us out of the city to this beautiful town in this beautiful house and I was too stupid to realize it. Here you've been the entire time, patiently waiting for me to come around and I think, after our fight, I'm starting to come around, I mean."

Dad lifted an eyebrow, but I continued.

"I may not be fully there yet, but I want to try and see things your way. I think talking to Virginia and seeing how she's doing might be the first step in understanding why you want to help this family. You finally have a case you believe in. I think it's time I try believing in it too."

I held my breath, waiting for his response. He nodded, a proud smile blooming over his wrinkly, exhausted face.

"I'm proud that you're finally realizing the family you belong to. I see you're even letting that hair of yours grow out."

*Because there are no real barbers here,* I thought to myself.

He walked up to me and ran his thick fingers through my buzz-cut that started to grow out a bit. "A real *Whitman*."

I have to remember to change that crappy last name when I turn eighteen. I twisted the doorknob and ran across the street; he watched me the entire way, to make sure I wasn't making any sudden turns in the other direction. I let out a breath before knocking on the door. I had to do this for those who deserved justice. I had an opportunity none of them would ever have. If I kept that top of mind, I could get through this.

"Zach?" Virgie's house was dark; she squeezed out of the door that she held half open and stepped outside. Her usually perfect hair was disheveled, and her makeup dried on its journey down her cheeks, staining them with dark blue and red shadows. She also stood shorter without those heels she always wore, her bare feet were tiny, like a child's. In fact, Virgie looked very much like a kid without all the makeup, heels, and clothing. She swapped her usual short skirt and tight top for an oversized sweatshirt and ripped jeans. She looked tired, even more tired than my father. Her eyes were swollen and pink. "I would invite you in, but my father was just able to drift off to sleep." She tucked her hair behind her ears. "Mother and I don't want to wake him."

"I understand," I replied. Then an awkward silence floated between us. I rested my weight on my heels then toes, back and forth.

She gestured to a rocking swing under hanging flowers on their porch. I wondered how they could look so vibrant in the winter. I stuffed my hands into the pocket of my hoodie and sat beside her. The cushion from the seat was chilled by the morning air.

"My father told me what happened this morning. I'm sorry," I offered. *That's it, Zach. Slow and steady.*

She sighed. "Yeah, we had a rough night last night. All of us." She looked down and played with her fingernails. Some were clicked off, underneath where the faux nails once lay were ones bitten to the core. "My dad, he's so afraid."

*He should be. He killed someone.*

"He shouldn't be. My father said there's a good case here. He's working really hard for your dad, so he won't face any of the charges he deser— . . . the people in Hamilton are saying he deserves."

Virgie looked up, her weak eyes dancing with a glimmer of hope.

"Really? You think there's a chance my father won't go to prison?"

I shrugged.

She wiped a stray tear. "I'm so afraid, Zach. I don't want to lose my father. He's so afraid too; you should have seen him last night. He kept saying, 'I killed a child. I killed a child.' His hands were shaking, and he kept staring at them as if they were covered in blood."

Chills ran through my body.

"Did he happen to tell you what happened?"

She looked at me for a moment, searching for something it seemed. But then she blinked away whatever was there.

"He told us after he came home. Your father was here taking notes. I tried calling you, over and over. But you didn't answer."

"Why didn't you call your friends?"

She bit the corner of her lip. "I don't know. I felt like you wouldn't be after some story you could pass off to someone else as soon as you found out what happened." I swallowed. "And here you are, on my porch, checking up on me." She smiled and gave a glimpse of the old Virgie. That made me realize that what I was doing was wrong. Playing on someone's emotions, no matter how bad they were, wasn't okay. She looked so lost.

"Look, you don't have to tell me—"

"No," she said, placing a hand on my arm. "You know. Half of me knows that you're gonna tell your girlfriend in Hamilton everything that I'm about to tell you." She let out a breath and let her hand fall from my arm. She played with her nails again and continued to look down. "My brother was killed in Iraq three years ago in special operations."

"I . . ."

She lifted a hand to shush me. "They told us that he suffered a bullet to the brain and that was it, he was gone. They said he probably didn't even feel it. Mom and Dad accepted it, but . . . but I know it wasn't true. He would call to video chat with us every Sunday night, while we had dinner. But before he died, he hadn't done it in months. I knew he was missing. I knew the enemy had taken him. But they told us that he was transferred to a place where there was no video chatting."

She looked at me. "What kind of *crap* was that? When we viewed the body the day before we buried him, he had a deep scar, right across here." She used her pointer finger to stretch a straight line across her throat. "He wasn't shot by a bullet. Something else happened to him and they didn't even tell us what. I know I would've been able to let him go if I would've just *known*. If they would have just told us the truth. But they didn't." She used both hands to catch the tears that fell from her eyes. "So, I'm gonna tell you what I know, because that boy's mother needs to know what happened to her son. What *really* happened. Even though they're gonna lose this case, and wish they never messed with my daddy, they need to know before they put that boy in the ground, so they can bury that story with him."

"Are you sure?" I asked.

She nodded.

# Capri

"CAPRI, BABY, YOU ALL RIGHT?" MA RUBBED MY SHOULDERS
and kissed my cheek. I nodded, though I wasn't. "Come on, baby,"
she said, grabbing my hand. "Let's go back in the sanctuary."
There were so many people in the church that morning, that some
was standing between the aisles and around the back and front.
They even squeezed people into the choir seating and overflow we
hadn't used since 1958. Each time somebody stood up or moved
above us, it sounded like the whole thing was gonna collapse. I
saw two news reporters followed by people with cameras standing
up there recording—the reporters writing stuff down with these
weird smiles, like Tyree's death was just another big story for them
to tell.

The basketball team canceled practice. So did the cheerleading squad. Everyone from my school was there. Nobody made no
excuses to their parents as to why they had to miss out on church,
like usual. Even Rose was there, pregnant and all, sitting in a fold-
out chair by a fan her mama made somebody get out the back closet
without her noticing. I caught her staring at Rose during the beginning of service like she'd disappear in midair if she took her eyes off
her more than three seconds at a time.

The choir sang "Pass Me Not," and Tyree's mama and sisters sat
in the front of the church next to the church mothers who dressed
in white. The clergy cried the whole time they sang it. Tyree's mama

wept loud to the point where it put heat all through *my* body. If this was how it was now, and there wasn't even no homegoing yet, I didn't want to even experience it. A big picture of Tyree in his football uniform was blown up on the church projector, sitting on the side near the cross we used for the Easter play.

It was the same picture of him on a poster board when we walked in the building. He knelt with one hand on his left knee, and his other holding a football. He smiled widely, the smile I'd always see in the halls. It was so familiar, so hard to forget. I overheard people tsking when they walked by the photo this morning. They kept saying, "His mama will never see that smile again." I was just worried about seeing Zach. Half of me was happy he finally returned my call, happy to hear his voice in all this chaos. But scared for him to come down here. Things was too crazy to have somebody from Bayside here in Hamilton. Especially with the sermon Reverend Sails was yelling.

"Church!" he slurred. "This ain't no day of celebration! It's a day of weeping, a day of mourning, a day of crying for our brother Tyree Thompson."

"Yessa!" someone yelled, followed by a bunch of claps.

"'Gone too soon' is an understatement. He was snatched— snatched from his mama, his sisters, grandmamma, his daddy, his pa, his little brother Tevin, and his girlfriend Kennedy. Somebody say, 'Snatched!'" Everyone yelled, "Snatched." I could hear Justin yell it the loudest. He stood in the back of the church with the men that gave their seats up for the women. He had this look in his eyes, this faraway look. It didn't seem like he was even there no more.

Ma made breakfast, and Justin just stared at his plate. She

told him to eat, but he said if Tyree was never eating again, neither would he. So, she took his plate away and put it in the fridge. Before we left, I saw him stick his sausage in a napkin and stuff it in his pocket. He got home about four in the morning. I know because I couldn't sleep myself. I kept feeling like I was hearing Tyree's screams from the tracks. I couldn't sleep knowing his blood stained the same ground me and Zach had laid on as we discussed our futures just two nights before. Ma said to give Justin some time, he'd come around. But being in that church, I didn't know if anybody was going to.

"He was pulled straight from this earth by the devil himself! Why can't we stick together? I say why can't we stick together?"

*Why, Pastor?*

"Division. Division between these two towns, Bayside and Hamilton. Them white people ain't gonna look out for us! We gotta look out for ourselves! That cop could've paused, saw Tyree and took him home. No, he pulled the trigger on all he views as another nigga, just like that town been wanting to do since the murder of that poor girl Ajah!"

*Amen!*

"Since they ain't sticking with us, we gotta stand against them. With our arms outstretched, we have to push against them! We have to wrap our arms around each other and stand! Like the Bible says, we wrestle not against flesh and blood but the power of darkness! We have to stand and after all we've done, stand some more! Who is that power of darkness?"

"Them Bayside people!" congregants yelled.

"Them Bayside people, and whoever stands with them! Like Jesus said, if you ain't for me, you against me!"

*Yessa, Pastor!*

"So we gonna stand with one another. With Mrs. Thompson and Tyree's family. We gonna stand for the death of Ajah and her family, that never got justice. We gonna stand against the dark powers of this air, we gonna stand against Bayside and every other white person who stands with them. We will march until we see that cop buried deep within the trenches of prison. Right where he belong! 'Cause he took a son!"

*Son!*

"'Cause he took a child!"

*Child!*

"'Cause he took a boy!"

*Boy!*

"And we gonna fight back! We will have a reckoning and Tyree and Ajah's death will be accounted for! We will fight back! We will stand strong! We will see that murderer *tried*! *Defied*! And *un-victimized*! Even if we need to be *undignified*!"

The church grew in an applause and a roar. Justin's yells soared over everyone else's. When the congregation calmed down and the reporters got everything on tape, the reverend spoke again.

"Now, the burial for this great child will take place at the Hamilton cemetery behind this here church on Tuesday. We ask that this be a time for immediate family and friends only. We know you loved this boy and his family, but we ask that you show support by *being* a shoulder for this family to cry on. Please, reporters, we ask that you withhold any surprise appearances. There will be a public memorial at Hamilton High tomorrow for Tyree's fellow team and classmates to celebrate his life. Another memorial will be held next Thursday along with a candlelight vigil tonight and every night at this church, until we see fit to stop.

There are refreshments in the hall downstairs. I know that many of you have lost your appetite, but Sister Billings grieved in the only way she knew how and from the time she got that call about Tyree, she been slaving in the kitchen to cook us all something. Amen?"

*Amen.*

"Let us close in prayer." The congregation bowed their heads, though I know a few were thrown off by the fact that Rose was not asked to sing a closing song as she'd been every week since I was four, and she five. I'm sure everyone heard the news of her pregnancy, but no one cared or said anything because of what happened with Tyree. That worked in Rose's favor.

I wasn't hungry and stayed outside while everyone gathered in the basement and hallways to eat the fried chicken dinner platters Sister Billings made. Their table talk was just gonna consist of what they guessed might have happened; nobody knew nothing except the officer and Tyree, but only one was alive and he was keeping it hidden. Tyree's mama tried contacting the officer all night last night into this morning, but he still ain't spoken up. I'm not guessing he will no time soon, not until the court date.

"Hey. Why you out here all by yourself?" Perry asked. She sat next to me on the church steps. I wanted to tell her it was because I was on the lookout for Zach—who was psycho enough to come see me—and head him off before anyone saw him, but instead, I shrugged.

"It's loud in there." It was cold out; my breath disappeared into the air around us.

She sighed. "I can't believe Tyree's dead."

A cricket chirped nearby. I stretched out my leg to squash it, but it jumped away.

"He's never coming back, you know?" Perry asked, even though she wasn't looking for an answer. "We're never gonna see him again walking the halls of Hamilton High. He's just gonna be buried behind this church forever. I heard they giving him the spot next to Ajah."

"I like how everyone is so devastated over him and only a quarter of everybody actually said more than five words to him. You talked to him what, once?"

Perry's mouth sat ajar. "I can't believe you said that, Capri. It ain't about if we knew him personally or not. It's about sticking together as a community."

"To do what? We can't bring him back."

"I don't know. To stop this from happening to someone else? It's been, I don't know how many people this year that was shot by cops for no reason? Now it's one of ours, like really one of ours. It happened here, Capri. Not in Carolina or Florida or Cali, but in one of the smallest towns in the world. It happened in Hamilton. It's time for this stuff to stop."

"And what are we gonna do about it, Perry? Change the world?"

"Whatever we can to make sure this cop is in prison. To show other cops an example of what they better not do again. Why you so bitter about this? You of all people should be upset. He was one of Justin's best friends."

"One of Justin's, you right. Not mine and not yours."

She stared at me, and I noticed it was out of her own natural eyes, no contacts. Her hair wasn't in a weave or an added ponytail like usual. Just out in kinky curls dyed blond to just above her ears.

"What?" I asked.

"What's wrong with you?" she asked, searching my eyes for an answer. I looked away before she got it. Before she saw that I was just as afraid as everyone else. Afraid that what I'd been hearing all my life was true—that stepping inches from Hamilton was a death sentence. And the reality of dying wasn't something I was ready for, no matter how much I tried convincing myself I was. Leaving was impossible, especially now. There was no way Ma would even talk about me getting out of here, even for summer camp. Not after Tyree's death. On top of all that, everyone expected my devotion to be for Hamilton and Hamilton alone.

If I chose Hamilton, it meant I couldn't choose New York City. It meant I would stay here and protect this town and convince every child after me to hold a grudge against the outside. I hated the way things were going—hated that everything changed overnight just at the cusp of my new beginning. I hated the fact that I was terrified that what happened to Tyree was so close to home. That it could happen to someone else, maybe even to Justin. I wanted someone to sit here and tell me that everything was going to be all right. That I could offer my allegiance to Hamilton and still leave it. But I knew it wouldn't be that easy. There was no place I'd rather be than New York City, with Zach, back in that capsule, away from everything. In a place where I could feel Essie alive again, instead of the town where her corpse lay. I wanted to escape to where I didn't have to feel pressure to abandon a budding relationship with Zach because of a murder he didn't commit.

I cradled my face into my hands and sighed, my thoughts and fears whirling like a tornado. "Perry, I just don't like what all of this is doing to everybody."

"What, causing us to stick together?"

*No, keeping us imprisoned here.* I shook my head. "You don't understand."

"I want to, Capri. I want to understand. But you have to communicate what's going on up there." She pointed to my brain. "Things is crazy for all of us right now. Capri, what's gotten into you? Why are you being like this?" Perry fanned her hands over my face to get my attention, but then she dropped her hand when she looked past me. "I get it now."

I turned to see Zach. He was running toward me so quickly that his hoodie fell off his head, puddling around his shoulders.

"Seriously?" Perry asked.

I stood up. "Please, don't say anything to anyone. All right?"

She sighed. "Capri, you heard what Reverend Sails said. We have to stick with each other. Zach is from Bayside, you're from Hamilton."

"Just yesterday you were helping us sneak away together."

"That was *before* Tyree was killed by one of them."

"You serious right now, Perry? *One of them?*"

"Capri! This is serious! Your ma and Justin wouldn't want you hanging out with—"

"He gave me the greatest night of my life last night, something that inspired me to keep chasing my dreams. Now this happens and it seems like everything is about to get stopped up! He, *one of them*, is the only reminder of what I felt last night, and I don't want to throw that away because of some murder neither of us had anything to do with! If you gave him an inch of a chance and thought for yourself instead of letting this town brainwash you, you'd realize that he is nothing like the people in Bayside. He's trying to be different than everyone else, Perry. I know I've only just met him and spent my whole life here, but I've never felt more freedom than I have with him. He's really different, Per, he's really different." At that word, Zach appeared next to me. "Cover for me," I said quickly, but Perry shook her head.

"No."

"No?"

She popped out her hip. "I've got an inch to give. I'm coming with you guys."

I looked at Zach, who shrugged. "She can come. The more the merrier. I was hoping we could get your brother to come too."

*Justin?*

I thought about how he'd been handling everything, and how he was during the service. Was this a good idea? No way.

"I don't think tonight's a good night for him."

He shrugged. "Doesn't hurt to ask. So where to?" he asked me, but Perry replied first.

"I know the perfect place."

# Zach

HAMILTON WAS DESERTED. NO ONE FILLED THE SIDEWALKS
with talking or rushing in and out of shops like I'd seen when I'd
come to here before. The bats and balls I saw kids playing with
in the streets were pushed to the side near the gutters and the
shops were all closed. I assumed Perry was leading us to Easy's,
but she walked past it, head straight, hands in her pockets, and
eyes forward, with the two of us on her heels. She hadn't even
spoken directly to me since I met up with Capri; just told us to
follow her.

"Is she all right?" I whispered to Capri, hoping Perry couldn't
hear us.

"I don't think anybody in this town is," she whispered. "You
should have heard Reverend Sails this morning. He was so . . ."
Capri searched for a word, waving her arms in front of her ". . .
so different. He usually preached on love and unity, but today he
sounded like Malcolm X or something."

"I don't blame him. Officer Malore killed somebody's unarmed
kid who never raised a fist at him."

Capri looked up at me, eyes widened. "So, he wasn't charging
at him?"

I paused at first, remembering the details that Virgie gave to
me, and I swallowed the lump that arose in my throat. I shook my
head. "No, he wasn't."

Something flashed in Capri's eyes that favored fear and she reached out to grab my hand. I didn't say anything—just let mine intertwine with hers. When we touched, life froze. For just a moment, I felt that flash of normalcy I'd felt the day before. I was thankful for that.

We walked that way, in the empty town, holding hands until we reached a torn-down park. There was a field that was half the size of one used in high school football games. It looked like half of it had been covered over with asphalt and used for basketball. There weren't any nets, just a metal rim attached to a decaying square board. Next to it stood a playground. Against the glare of the sun, there was large metal slide very different from the one in Bayside. There were no twists and turns coaxing children to scream in excitement and pleasure as they slid downward, just a straight steep drop. The swings weren't painted, and the seats were missing from two. Just one swing hung in the middle of two unattached pairs of metal cords stretched almost to the ground. The playground looked morbid. I looked away.

"So, the park? That's the perfect place?" Capri asked Perry, who rolled her eyes.

"Yes, the *park*," Perry replied. "I figured this would be the last place anybody would go since the whole town's gonna be at the church and then the Thompsons' house, which is on the other side of the town. And this spot is closer to Bayside. So, if on the slim chance anybody comes, Zach can make a quick escape."

I lifted an eyebrow. "Should I be more fearful than usual about being in Hamilton?"

They both nodded, but Perry spoke, her words dripping with annoyance. "You should be. As a matter of fact, I'm being gracious taking you both here so you can talk to Capri or announce your love to her or whatever you're here for. I'm betraying my town right now, so make it quick." She spoke sharply and quickly and gestured to the aluminum bleachers. Capri and I walked toward them, but Perry cleared her throat. "No," she said. "We're going underneath. Not on top. It's safer for y'all, especially if you gonna be touching and all that."

My cheeks filled with heat, and I let go of Capri's hand.

A few seconds later, we were sharing the ground under the bleachers with candy wrappers, empty beer bottles, cigarette butts—even an old television set.

Perry crossed her arms and looked straight at me.

"So, what do you want to tell Capri?"

I cleared my throat and tried to look at Capri, which was hard because Perry sat herself between us. So, I stood and faced them both. Capri sat with her hands in her pockets, her back hunched over, her eyes tired and far away. I wanted to know why her demeanor was dark, and her face stormy. I needed to talk to her alone, I needed to tell her that she'd be all right, that we'd be all right—that we'd get through it together and how this wouldn't change whatever we'd started.

But I knew that would have to wait and that hurt me more than anything.

I sighed. "First, I want to get something straight. Coming here for me wasn't easy." Perry rolled her eyes and heaved a huge sigh, but I continued to speak. "I found out this morning what happened to Tyree Thompson and I want to say I'm sorry. I can't imagine the pain you all are going through, your school, your friends, your family, your community. I'm sorry that it had to happen so close to home." When I said that, the anger fell from Perry's face, enough so that I could see traces of the sweet girl I'd met the day before. "I came here because I know what happened to Tyree Thompson. My father is representing the case of the officer who killed him, and I used that to my advantage to get an account of what really happened. I think Tyree's mother deserves to know."

"Zach, no." Capri stood to her feet. "That's court information. This could put you in danger."

Perry stood up. "You hardly know us to wanna help like this."

"I know," I replied. "This is probably the craziest thing I've ever said, but I feel like it's my duty to tell you guys. Hamilton almost feels like *my home*. Life is so familiar here in Hamilton. You guys remind me of the people I grew up around and it makes me feel like I know you guys deeper than my own family, you know?" A hint of a smile creeped across Capri's face and I couldn't help but feel as if we were in New York City again, away from everything. "Now, you can do whatever you want with this information I give you, because I promised not to tell anyone outside of Capri. Capri, I felt something yesterday that I haven't felt in so long. I want to talk deeper about that soon, because I know time is limited. My dad cut off my phone, so I won't be able to communicate like I want to, but I want this to continue, all right? Whatever it is, I don't want it to stop because of this. I'm here because I don't want it to end."

Slowly she walked closer toward me. "I don't either," she whispered.

"Okay, y'all, this is cute and all, but it's cold out here and I don't got nobody to help warm things up like y'all do. This third wheel wanna get back inside," Perry said, interrupting us from behind.

"Perry's right," I said, working to regain my focus. "You ready?"

They both nodded. I took a breath and started to tell them everything I knew.

# Justin

*I WATCHED HER TAKE SMALL SIPS FROM THE PLASTIC CUP* filled with watermelon punch. She nibbled on her chicken, but wasn't eating the mac and cheese, string beans, and yams that Sister Billings piled on her plate. She sat alone, in the corner on a foldout chair; the same fan that gave her air in church was moved down to the basement by one of the deacons. I couldn't help but notice that she looked paler than usual. I wanted to see if she was all right but stayed where I was.

Now that I was sober with a massive hangover, I wanted to apologize. Truth was, regret filled me to the core. I couldn't even scarf down the lemon pound cake Sister Billings made for dessert, which was usually my favorite. I had no room for my dinner plate either; it just sat in front of me getting cold and spat on by Carlos, who talked a mile a minute, his mouth filled with chewed-on chicken and mac and cheese.

I was surprised Carlos could even swallow his food with how tight he pulled the tie he wore. His neck turned from red during the service to a pale white. He tried so hard with his three-piece suit and tie to look like he was a regular at church when he hadn't been since Vacation Bible School in first grade.

"So, what I think we should do is cross them tracks, go to Bayside, and rock their town off its perfect soil, until we get some answers about what happened to Tyree," Carlos said, wagging his half-eaten fried chicken leg the whole while he talked, pieces of food still flying from his mouth onto all our plates.

"You think that's a good idea though, man?" asked Deondre, who was sitting next to me. "Shouldn't we be more discreet about everything? We don't wanna end up dead since apparently waving around a gun and shooting at whoever you want is accepted over there."

I looked again toward the corner of the room. Rose's friend Keonna was showing her something from her phone. Rose stared intensely, rubbing her little stomach bump while Keonna talked.

Carlos shook his head. "No, I think we should do what I say. I was talking to the guys until four this morning. We can't go about this peacefully or they gonna think we're soft. We need some spray paint. We need to break some windows with bats. We gonna have to shut down some shops. We need to turn their vanilla tails red with fear."

I tapped my foot against the concrete floor.

Deondre, unsure, sighed. "Nah, man, I just think we should stay over here and chill out. It's only been a few hours since everything happened. Maybe the news will give us the real story. The reporters told us they're trying their best."

Carlos smacked his chicken leg on the table, which caused my eyes to turn from Rose. "Tyree ain't deserve to die like that, all alone and bleeding out. I ain't gonna stand here and witness that cop go free when he got all that blood on his hands. I talked to the guys from the team; we're fighting back. Right, Justin? That's what you said, we gotta fight back." His eyes bore into mine.

Don't get me wrong, I was just as angry and confused as everyone else in Hamilton, but I was drunk the night before and the liquor helped fuel my hateful words. It also was the reason why I'd argued with Rose. I liked what Reverend Sails said in service about sticking together and fighting, but he wasn't specific about *how* we'd fight. Not like I could ask; he didn't even glance in my direction the entire time he was preaching.

I cleared my throat. "I think we should fight back." Carlos gave a nod; Deondre rolled his eyes. "But," I continued, "we gotta be smart with it. We play Bayside tomorrow night, right?"

"You think we still gonna play that game after what happened?" Deondre asked.

Jay, who walked up to the table with his third dinner plate, sat down. "I heard Coach say he wasn't gonna put the game off. He said we still have to maintain a sense of"—he made air quotes with his hands—"'sportsmanship, despite conflict.' Plus, it gives the TV networks more of a reason to stay here and help broadcast this thing to the world. What, we decide we're gonna slash their bus tires or something?"

I shook my head. "No, we're gonna beat the crap out of them on that court by winning the game. That's how we gonna fight back." I looked at Carlos. "We'll show them that we're no softies." Then to Deondre: "But we're still gonna give a good fight."

"Sounds like a good idea," Jay piped in, mouth filled with food. "But"—he squeezed a forkful of yams in his mouth—"that's the day that Snow Fairy is coming to look for someone to give that college scholarship away to. You still gonna accept that and try to go pro? Or stay in Hamilton and get a job to take care of that baby of yours?" I waited for Carlos or Deondre to tell Jay it was none of his business, but they all looked at me for an answer.

Carlos laughed to himself after I didn't respond. "Now I understand. You know what, Justin? I feel a hint of selfishness coming out of you."

"Selfishness?" I asked. "How?"

"I feel like you just wanna win because you know them scouts is gonna be there. I don't think this got nothing to do with Tyree. It got more to do with you getting that scholarship."

Suddenly Deondre's smile fell. He looked torn, confused.

"I think," Carlos continued, boring his eyes into mine, "that's probably all you been thinking about. You don't care nothing about what happened to Tyree. All you care about is going pro."

"That's not true, Carlos. I just agree with Deondre. We should be smart about this."

"Smart?" Carlos laughed. "Ah, that's just a cop-out from you. You know what I'm saying is right. You're only worried about look-ing good in that game tomorrow so you can get out of this hole you was raised in. But you here now, and we just lost one of our best friends. So, where your loyalty at? Y'all sitting here like some punks instead of doing something about it. What if it was you, what would you want us to do for you?" My eyes fell to my shoes, so Carlos looked at Deondre, then Jay. But they all remained silent. He stood, glared at us, then walked off.

"I . . . I think he right," Deondre whispered.

I turned to Rose, who I caught staring at me. The moment our eyes met, she darted hers away, back to her friend's phone. I pulled my seat back, my heart growing heavy in my chest.

"Just focus on winning that game against Bayside. This one is gonna be for Tyree." I didn't wait for Deondre or Jay to say anything else before I found myself walking across the room to Rose.

Keonna rolled her neck when she saw me, her features growing dark. "What do *you* want?" she asked rudely. I ignored her.

"Rose, can we talk outside?"

"She don't wanna talk to you," Keonna interrupted. She put her phone on the table and crossed her arms in front of her chest. "So, you can just *step back*."

I squatted until I was level with Rose, but she looked at her shoes.

"Please, look at me. I can't take you looking anywhere but here." I pointed to my eyes. "Rose," I whispered, "we have so much to talk about." I saw her almost look up, until Keonna jumped in.

"*Please!* You wanna talk to Rosey? You need to act like a man and talk like a man would instead of rolling up here with those puppy dog eyes, like you the most important thing in the world or something, your trifling tail . . ." She continued to trail on in her squeakily annoying voice, but instead of giving in to my desire to tell that girl where she could go, I reached out slowly for Rose's hand.

"Please," I whispered, gently pulling her hand into mine. "Let's talk, outside, just us two. If at any moment you don't wanna talk, just say so. Until then, please, please hear me out. I'm sober, I'm willing. I'm willing to talk things out. Please."

Finally she looked up. The sight of her bloodshot eyes made me jump. Bags lay on top of her swollen flesh.

"Are you feeling all right?" I asked her, but of course Keonna answered for her.

"Do you *think* she's feeling all right? She spent all last night crying over you when she should have been resting. Ain't get no sleep because a yo tail." I could see it. Rose looked so tired. I hadn't gotten any sleep the night before either. I knew with everything that happened, Rose would have trouble sleeping, just like everyone else in the town, but I knew now that she had a sleepless night because of me. She needed all the rest she could get. I slowly guided her to her feet, still holding on to her hands. They always reminded me of flower petals: soft, delicate, beautiful. She looked at Keonna one more time before walking out of the basement with me.

"I'll be right back, Keonna," she whispered.

She nodded, but clearly disapproved.

"Wanna go for a walk?" I asked when we'd reached the end of the church steps. "I need to get away from the crowds." I held on to her hand, and we began to make our way through town to the direction of the courts.

Finally, after what seemed like half of our walk, Rose spoke. "You said you wanted to talk. So, talk." Her voice sounded weak; it didn't carry as much force as it had the night before. I let my words pour out like a waterfall.

"I'm sorry for everything I said last night. I was so stupid, for everything. For getting drunk, for dancing with those girls, for kissing someone."

Rose's eyes grew wide, and she snatched her hand from mine. We stood at the end of a crosswalk.

"You kissed someone?" she asked, her lip quivering.

"After we argued, I was so upset that I just . . . I just wanted to forget. Plus, you'd broken up with me."

"For *two* minutes, Justin!"

"Look," I said slowly, "I came here to explain myself, so please listen."

Rose grew quiet.

"It should have been me. Everything that happened to Tyree, it should have happened to me. I was so wasted. I was with him when he got wasted. I let him walk home alone wasted and now I feel like I'm responsible. I'm so confused right now. Capri and I aren't talking. My friends are confused and that's hurting me too. But what hurts me most of all is that I hurt you. I didn't mean anything I said yesterday." I slapped my hand on my forehead. "I'm so stupid. And now my mind is wandering in a thousand different directions."

"Mine too," she said. "What happened to Tyree is not your fault and I don't know about your friends being confused, but what I do know is that I don't know about us, Justin. You really screwed up." She focused on the swinging traffic light hanging on the wire next to us; it flashed from yellow to red. "I still don't know if I can be with you. You embarrassed me yesterday, in front of everyone. You told everyone this wasn't your child."

"I know. I know. But I was drunk."

"And what happens next time you're drunk, Justin? Do I have to be afraid of you hitting me or something?"

"No!" I exclaimed. "No, no. That's not me. That's not my character, you know that. I was just so stressed out about everything, about the baby, our future, your parents kicking you out. I just had a lot on my mind."

Silence.

"You're not alone," Rose whispered. "That's what you need to realize. None of us are doing this alone, not me or you. We supposed to be a team."

"I know. And I promise we *are* a team. I'll never do anything like that again. I promise."

I meant what I said, but I knew I needed to show action to prove it, and I planned to. From that point on, I promised I'd show Rose how much she meant to me, no matter what.

She let out a large breath. "Keonna was showing me some stuff about adoption online."

My eyes grew wide. "That's what she was showing you on that phone?"

Rose nodded. "And I'm contemplating it."

"No way. We decided we'd keep it."

"We did. Before our relationship ended and I had to think about what it would be like to live as a single mother. I'm not ready for that, especially with no support from my family. But no support from you either? Our child doesn't deserve that. He deserves so much better. He deserves a family who will be able to support him the way he deserves."

"He?"

Rose grew quiet. "I was having some pains after I left the party last night, so I went to Dr. Barry. He had to check on the baby and told me it was a boy."

I couldn't help but smile. I was having a boy! That feeling quickly went dark. I couldn't lose my son. Gently I lifted my hands to Rose's cheeks and grazed them softly with my thumbs.

"I promise," I vowed, looking into her eyes, not turning to the right or left. "I promise that I will be so good from now on. Whatever you want, I'll do. Just please don't give our little boy up."

She looked into my eyes, contemplating, questioning for what felt like years. I held my gaze. Finally, with a sigh, she agreed.

"You have to step it up."

I kissed the tip of her nose, a wide grin filling my face.

"I can't believe I'm having a son!" I yelled to no one in particular, just the air around me, the buildings surrounding us, the street no one drove on because the entire town was at the church. We walked across the street toward the bleachers where I'd first found out about the pregnancy. "You know, when I make it pro, I'm gonna give him the entire world. Both of you." I squeezed her hand. "I'm talking private schools, vacations, the best designer sneakers, I don't even care if he grows out of them and can only wear them once."

Rose let go of my hand again. "You're *still* talking about going pro?"

"The scout is coming to the game against Bayside tomorrow. That's the day. That's the day when I find out I get the scholarship. He emailed me, he said he had his eye on me."

"And what if you don't get it, Justin?" Rose asked, her voice rising. "Then what?"

I shook my head. "I'm going to get it."

"And if you don't?"

"Please don't do this again," I pleaded. "I'm gonna get the scholarship."

"And until then, where are me and your son fitting into this?"

"You fit in! I looked it up online. Village U has a childcare program. With your grades, we can both get a full ride. You can do online classes and take care of our son while he's a newborn. I'll still work after school; we can stay in the dorm for families. I figured all of this out. We can do this."

Rose cradled her forehead in her palm. "What happens if that falls through? What if you don't get that scholarship? Then what? Where does that leave us?"

"I will *get* that scholarship," I said, gesturing around us. "I want to get out of here, Rose. I know you do too, and what happened to Tyree and what isn't happening to the cop proves that something's gotta give. This isn't where I wanna raise my son. Look, Keonna was right, it's time I step up, so that's why I'm gonna make that happen at the game tomorrow. Don't doubt me. That's how we gonna fight back. That's how I'm gonna show those people in Bayside that they can't push us around. That's how I'm gonna show everyone in Hamilton I'm still the same Justin Collins that is responsible and dependable. That's how I'm gonna show the world that I can rise out of a place like Hamilton and *be* something. I'm doing it for Tyree."

She raised an eyebrow. "And how does winning a basketball game and playing college ball avenge Tyree's death?"

"Look, you don't understand. It's us fighting back. It's us taking away their pride."

Before she could protest again, that's when I heard it: the softened talking of three voices under the bleachers we stood near. I recognized one, the voice I'd heard every day since it entered the world. I lifted a finger to Rose's lips, to shush her, and walked toward the sound of the voices.

"Justin!" Rose called, but I continued to walk, lifting a hand to silence her.

"*Shush!*"

She followed close at my heels. The voices became louder; I could hear a male's low-toned voice floating around too. Quickly, before any of them could notice, I walked under the bleachers and couldn't believe what I saw. Standing there was Capri, Perry, and that white kid from Bayside who dragged my sister to New York with him.

When they saw they were caught, they backed away as if they could hide in plain sight. I didn't care about Capri or Perry;

I'd handle them later. It was the boy that filled me with rage. His hoodie was pulled over his head to hide the pale skin that stood out like a sore thumb under the shadow where he hid. His joggers were baggy and sneakers clean. If his back was facing me, I would have easily mistaken him for one of us. He dressed no different than Carlos, Tyree, Deondre, and me.

But he wasn't one of us. There was a night and day difference.

I recognized people like him, read about them, popping up in and out of history repeatedly. White thieves snatching countless inventions and songs from us, then claiming it as their own for their benefit. It was just packaged differently now. Now the white boys put on their "Black boy costumes," until they were ready to grow up and work for their dad's accounting firm or something. Tacked on hype shoes, loud rap music, hashtags, and joined social causes to be rebellious or just relevant and turned mute when the hype was over.

When he needed to use his privilege again, he'd toss his costume straight into the garbage and become a white societal clone, just like the rest of them. Opinionated, racist, act like he never even batted an eyelash to our women or our culture. He'd teach his kids to hate us, fear us, lock their car doors when we walked by them, *as if we couldn't hear it when they did.* He'd take them to games where they'd cheer for us to make a basket or touchdown, but when we knelt, he'd say we're disrespecting his flag. He'd turn off the news when faces like Tyree's flashed by, nonchalantly say he deserved it because of some warrant he had or some detention they brought up from high school. He'd tell his son Black girls are ugly and ghetto and for him to stay away. But when he'd bed his wife at night, he'd be thinking about all the Black girls he screwed with the lights off.

Let me, Carlos, and Deondre try stapling a costume on our

bodies, put on some clean suit, shave all our hair off, and cover up tattoos. Let us go to college and get a good degree, become some doctor like Tyree wanted to. If we walk on the wrong side of the tracks, we'll still get a bullet to the back. The kid in front of me, his skin is his privilege and grace, ours is our curse and damnation.

Just one look at him and clearly, I knew what it was *he* wanted, why he stepped his Jordan 23s over to our land. He wouldn't get her. Not under my watch. I was her brother and if I let anybody, especially a white boy, fulfill his pornographic fantasies with my sister to say he did it with a Black girl once, I was the real enemy. He couldn't just point and say "mine" here. His white privilege wouldn't work with me. Maybe everywhere else in the world, but not here. Not in Hamilton. I might never have no control anywhere else in the world, but I had control here. Over my family, over my sister, over my land, and I'd personally see him out.

"How you just gonna show yourself here?" I asked through gritted teeth. "After what y'all did to Tyree?"

The boy lifted his hands in mock surrender, feigning innocence. "I was only talking to Capri and Perry about—"

"You took my little sister to New York City with you to do only God knows what. Now you're with her again after what you did to Tyree?"

"*I* didn't do nothing to Tyree," the boy interjected. "Relax, Justin."

When he said my name, I wanted to lay him out. "Don't say my name like we friends, 'cause we're not. We're enemies." I wanted to make that clear.

"Justin, he's only trying to help," Capri interrupted.

"I'm only here to help," the boy repeated, but I wasn't hearing it. I lifted a hand to shush my sister.

"And you think we need your help? You think we're some type of charity case that need you to come over here and help us? Like y'all came to Africa to 'help' us, but brought us over to be tortured for four hundred years? It's never pure motives with y'all. Y'all Bayside white trash dumped my ancestors in this ghetto, gave us nothing but scraps since, killed an innocent girl and her family, then turned around and murdered my best friend. Trust me, you helped enough." I clenched my fist, prepared to pick him up and throw him back where he came from if I had to.

"Look," the boy said, his voice falling to almost a hush. "I'm sorry about what happened to Tyree. He didn't deserve to die like that. But, if you would just hear me out, okay? This is different than the Whitman case against Ajah all those years ago; you guys can actually get justice this time. My father, Dick Whitman, is representing Officer Malore, the man that murdered him."

"Your dad is *sticking up* for the officer that shot my boy?" This was unbelievable. I couldn't believe Capri had entangled herself up with this dude. Full-on rage dripped all over me. I needed her to see what was going on. "Capri, he just said he's a *Whitman*. His family murdered Ajah! Are you really associated with this trash?"

"You should hear him out," Perry pleaded. "He knows what . . ."

He succeeded in brainwashing Perry and Capri, but not me. For all I knew, he could have been trying to gather information from us for his dad's case. I thought back to the sermon this morning. Reverend Sails was right. We had to stay loyal to our own; no one else could be trusted. Especially not from Bayside.

"Go!" I yelled before he wormed his way deeper into the space between my sister and me. "Go back to Bayside, I don't wanna see you here no more in Hamilton. Next time you cross them tracks, it's ya head. You hear me? If I see you anywhere near my sister, you're done."

The boy tried speaking again. "Justin—"

"Go before I do something you'll regret," I threatened.

"Just go, Zach," Capri whispered. Zach looked back at her and opened his mouth to say something else to me, to pull me into his tricks. He realized I was immovable. He walked by me toward Hamilton's exit.

I looked at my sister, my heart still racing. Her arms were crossed over her body, tears staining her cheeks. I couldn't believe how far apart we'd gotten. She wouldn't have kept Zach a secret months ago. She wouldn't have kept New York a secret either. Control was seeping out my fingertips and I needed to find a way to get it back.

"Go home, Capri, or I'll tell Ma everything."

"Justin . . ."

"*Go!*"

Perry wrapped an arm around Capri and led her away.

"I can't believe you," Rose said. "You wouldn't even hear him out."

I turned to face her, undone. "What? You on his side now?"

"No, I'm not on anyone's *side*. I'm just saying, what he could have said might have helped."

"We don't *need* his help. He's probably just working with his dad to see what's going on here. We can figure this all out on our own. Trust me, I know white guys like that. He probably only wants to screw Capri."

"What's *happened* to you? It's like you're not even the same person."

"I'm awake!" I yelled. My voice cracked. I wiped my hands over my eyes to claw away the tears. "I'm awake, Rose. Everything— everybody's always looking to me. My ma, Capri, my friends, you! This whole town has been looking *at* me as some perfect example since the day I buried my mama. I couldn't even grieve her at her funeral. Then I spent years trying to prove to everyone that I could be everything they wanted me to be and got you pregnant. Now they don't see me as nothing but a failure. A statistic. That's how everyone is gonna see me now and it's haunting me day and night. All my mistakes are playing like a record in my mind, and it won't shut off no matter how hard I try. Now I'm here trying to figure out how to get us out of here so we ain't raising our son where he can get shot if he playin' too close to Bayside." My voice fell into a whisper. "My sister is sneaking to the city with a stranger, and Ma and Pop, they're trying to hold themselves together. They been trying to hold themselves together since we were kids and orphaned."

Rose used her flower petal fingers to wipe the tears from my cheeks. "See, that's your problem, Justin," she whispered. "You always try to do stuff alone. It's time we do this together, all of us. The whole city, we need to stand together just like my daddy said."

"And what about them? Your parents?"

"I'm sure they'll come around, and if they don't, we gonna be okay. Look at me." She pointed to her eyes and mine followed. "I can't take you looking anywhere else but here. No matter what happens, I'm here."

# Capri

*I PULLED MY BEANIE OVER MY EARS AND STUFFED MY ICE-*
cold hands into my hoodie pocket. The entire high school got
pulled from their classes to gather on the football field. We were all
scattered around the grass. The freshman and sophomores got to sit
on the bleachers, the juniors and seniors had to stand. That meant
I was standing. I kicked at the soft soil under the frosted, yellowing
grass. It took a lot to even remember that it was Valentine's Day.
No one passed out cards or roses and the paper heart decorations
hung limp from the ceiling, as if they were mourning too. A few feet
ahead of me, three girls clung to one another. They all held candles.
I could hear them weeping from where I stood.

Justin erupted on us before Zach could even get the entire
story about Tyree's murder out to Perry and me. We only heard
what the news already kept saying: Tyree was leaving a party drunk
and walked to the abandoned tracks instead of home. That's where
it stopped. It wasn't like hearing the whole thing would've helped
much anyway. Why would anybody believe two girls from Hamilton
who weren't even there the night Tyree's murder happened?

I saw his picture everywhere; all over the lockers, the walls,
scattered on all the lunchroom tables. Now it was blown up and
plastered on the only projector screen our school could afford. The
same picture that filled my mind with its image each time I tried
to drift to sleep. He smiled widely in the photo; now his lips were

glued shut, his smile taken from the world, just as Essie's had been.

"Hamilton High, we're gathered here to celebrate the life of Tyree Thompson, a son, an honor student, and a heck of a football player. We're here to remember Tyree for his kindness and his humble spirit. Most importantly, we're here to honor Tyree's short life and bid him farewell as he travels to heaven to rest in the arms of a Holy God." Principal Mann, a man not yet in his forties, tried to keep his voice steady; it kept going in and out like an old radio.

He was thinking the same thing as everyone else: it could have been him. I think that's half the reason he cried when he spoke and why *he* kept talking about how much he loved his own family. It seemed like the whole student body got up to speak about Tyree, and everyone said good things about him—how he always smiled, always encouraged people, volunteered as a big brother in the community, and served as a youth leader at the church. And the reporters were pointing their cameras at the action, eating it all up.

The protests started the night before, after Justin basically chased Perry and me from the bleachers. She went back to the church to eat, but I decided to go home. I climbed into my bed and covered my head with my comforter, but then I uncovered it. For some reason, I kept feeling like that was disrespectful. Only the dead got their faces covered. I closed my eyes and tried focusing on the quiet; I thought maybe it would help me rest, and it did, until the chants began.

I couldn't sleep. Everything was so loud. From the time the sun just began to set, to the early hours of the morning, I heard the same sentences chanted over and over again:

*"Black Lives Matter!"*

*"No Justice! No Peace!"*

*"The land of the chained! A home to the enslaved! America America stop digging us our graves!"*

That night in bed, I plugged my earbuds into my ears and turned up the music, but I could still hear them, even with my window closed. They marched down the street all around Hamilton, as if they were the children in Israel, marching around the city of Jericho, trying to get some walls to come down. I climbed through the little window over my bed and onto the roof and wrapped my hands around my knees. Below me were news reporters with bright lights, filming everything. Hamilton had been forgotten and now it was the center of attention.

I looked up into the sky.

There's something about the moon, the way it just floats so high, it only comes out when things are really dark; it's like it almost wants us to know that in every dark situation there's still light. I wanted to believe that. Hamilton seemed to have lost all its light. Even when the streetlamps clicked on after six, even with all the candles everyone held. The fire that flickered on the wicks seemed to tease; even they were snuffed out with one blow.

*"Black Lives Matter!"*

*"No Justice! No Peace!"*

*"The land of the chained. Home to the enslaved! America, America, stop throwing us in graves."*

They walked arm in arm like chain links on a bracelet and chanted the same sentences, their united voices mirroring the voice of God, loud and thundering. Even when the reporters left hours later and there was no one else around to listen, they sang their song anyway. They sang their ballad to the sky, to the fireflies, and to the moon and stars above them. I don't think they cared who listened; they just wanted to sing it.

It's like the guy that sings on the street corner near Al's Soul Food and Laundromat—all the old blues songs that no one listens to anymore. He sings about how hard life is and how no one cares about his broken refrigerator. He doesn't care if anyone stops to listen, he just wants his song flowing through the air; maybe he hopes someone will catch on one day and sing along.

*"Hands up! Don't shoot!"* they yelled and I winced, watching as a group of kids from my school set fire to the only statue we had erect in Hamilton. It was of William Bay, Bayside's founder. His silhouette erupted in flames, and many danced around it, cursing his body to hell and all of Bayside too.

I tried concentrating on the stars.

I've felt isolated since the beginning. Since the sirens wailed through the city the night he died. When the protests began to happen the next day, when the women started carrying all that food to Tyree's house. On our way to school Ma made me carry a sweet potato pie over with Justin, except when we knocked, they didn't answer the door. I noticed there was no car in the driveway.

"Maybe we should wait until they come back," Justin suggested. When he talked, I could see his breath. It was freezing. I shook my head.

"They probably won't be back anytime soon. We should just leave it here." I looked down at the pie Ma made; she spent all day trying to perfect the recipe. She said her pies were like medicine to the soul. I'd wondered if she really believed that after she'd thrown out her third because it was a little too brown at the top.

"You tryna leave it on the doorstep, Capri? Really? So all the ants can get to it? I'll wait. You can wait with me if you want." He sat down on the creaky patio. Before I could even answer, I sat next to him. I kept trying to bring up things to talk about—prom, TV, music—but Justin didn't indulge. He just sat there looking at all the flowers and pictures that were spread out around the small patio. I kept trying not to look at them, I felt like I wasn't supposed to be here. I wasn't ever part of this community or the school like Justin was.

I never really talked to anyone. I went to school, work, and home every day, the same routine. How did I have the right to mourn, to join in the protest by and for people and a town I never cared about to begin with, if all I've wanted to do is get out? Justin was always part of everything, he was popular. It seemed like he always knew the right things to say. I wouldn't know what to say other than "I'm sorry." I didn't even know if I truly was.

I left a few minutes later.

Justin was thirty minutes late for school.

# Zach

THEY CALLED AN EARLY-MORNING ASSEMBLY IN THE GYM
for juniors and seniors during first and second period. I couldn't
say I was upset about it. I hadn't studied for the biology or Spanish
test we were to have that day. Thomas met me at my locker and we
walked to the gym together. Things were silent as we walked, which
was unusual. Thomas always talked a mile a minute, but this morning, he was silent. I was too. It seemed as if the overcast in Hamilton
finally made its way to Bayside and it was downright dreary.

There were chairs set up in a large circle all around the sidelines, and a microphone stand set up in the middle. The wire from
the mic stretched underneath one of the chairs next to three projectors set up, though there wasn't anything on any of the screens. The
lunch lady sat behind a banquet table loaded with donuts, bagels,
fruit, and coffee. That was the first thing everyone ran to.

"You hungry?" I asked Thomas, gesturing to the table.

He shook his head. "Nah."

"You sure you don't want any food? The donuts have icing
on them." I playfully punched his shoulder, trying to lighten the
invisible load filling the air around us. He rubbed his shoulder.

"I'm gonna get us a seat; you can grab whatever you want."
With that he walked away, through the crowd of students to a seat
next to one of the projectors. He lifted a leg on the seat next to him,
not caring that some girl was about to grab a seat there. I don't even

think he noticed her; his eyes were droopy, almost zombielike.

Virgie stood in line a few feet ahead of me with her friends, Lila and Ginger from the diner. She hadn't looked at all the way she did just yesterday morning. Now she looked normal again, in a sweater dress and tights, her hair pulled into a tight bun and makeup precisely applied—so much different from the dried trails that made their way across her cheeks the last time we'd talked. Brock and Brad piled their plates with donuts.

"So they give us free breakfast every time a cop shoots somebody?" one of them said, then faced Virgie. "Your dad should kill people more often."

I expected a flash of something to cross Virgie's face—some sort of emotion. But it remained blank. She smiled and playfully smacked his shoulder.

"Oh, Brock, you're too much, really."

"Seriously," Ginger spat, no hint of laughter or playfulness. "Too much."

Finally, an emotion. Ginger offered Virgie a bagel, but she swatted it off and mentioned something about calories. When her friends went on to talk about something else, Virgie's eyes fell to the floor as she chased a stray tear with her hand without anyone noticing. She glanced behind her, just to be sure, and that's when our eyes met. I gave a small wave; she did the same. After piling my plate with food, I took my seat next to Thomas, just as Principal Walsh took his spot behind the podium.

"Students of Bayside High, good morning." Principal Walsh's voice echoed around the auditorium.

Students in unison responded with, "Good morning, Mr. Walsh."

"Today we have called together this assembly to discuss the events that transpired over the weekend between a Bayside officer and someone from Hamilton."

"Someone from Hamilton had a name," I heard Thomas say to himself from beside me. I chewed slowly on my bagel. I suddenly noticed all the cameras held by reporters filming all around the gym. One man walked his straight up to the center, right in front of Principal Walsh. Suddenly the berry-flavored cream cheese I was eating felt too thick to swallow.

"As you all know, Bayside has now become the center for reporters from all over to come and stick their noses into the business of finding out what happened between Officer Malore and that boy. They have flooded our grocery store, homes, and even churches with questions and cameras, digging to develop accusations against the innocent Officer Malore, who only fought to protect himself. Our very own Virgie Malore has been attacked by news reporters to answer questions about a story her own father has not revealed to his family yet. Especially with all of the turmoil he is going through." The bagel I tried swallowing got caught in my throat, which caused me to cough loudly. Everyone, including Principal Walsh, looked my way. I reached for the juice of the kid next to me and chased the problem bagel down. I cleared my throat, and he carried on.

"We send our deepest sympathies to your family, Virginia." A few people around her offered sympathetic glances; Lila patted her hand gently. Virgie responded with her well-put smile. "Well, today, while you are safe within the four walls of this establishment for education, we will instruct you on how to answer the reporters when they come your way and that is with two words, *no comment*. Come on, children, say it."

In unison, everyone sang, *"No comment."*

"Good, good," Principal Walsh praised. He clicked the small button he held in his hand and the projectors were covered with the words *No comment*. "Now, as you see, we have invited those reporters here to the school to provide a final answer to the chaos they have put upon us. We will answer it in our own way. You all have heard of the Black Lives Matter movement. This has led to the African American race upholding themselves as superior to every other race.

"This same movement has led to uprisings, looting, more innocent lives being lost during protests, fire starting, and danger-ous protests, similar to what I heard coming from Hamilton last night—a late-night protest in which they caused damage to a center figure of property we provided them with the first year the town was established. The statue of our great founder, William Bay, now lies in ashes in Hamilton's town center. God knows what else these people are planning on destroying that we've gifted them with. Their homes? Their school? This BLM movement has allowed many ignorant people to ride the tide of hashtags and social media blackouts. But as you all know, in Bayside, we pride ourselves in treating every race as it deserves to be treated. We pride ourselves in upholding the Bayside ritual that whatever another race needs, we will give. Hence, the history of our town."

With another click of a button, the projectors were filled with an old black-and-white picture of two white-suited men with large mustaches standing next to a dark-suited Black man. The statue that was burned down stood proudly in the back. They shook hands with large smiles on all their faces. "This was taken with the free New York City citizen Micah Hamilton after we split up Bayside to give a part of our town to the newly freed enslaved. As you can see, with proof, we are firm believers that their lives mattered. That is why we gave them this town. In addition to this, we provided lumber and anything else they needed to have a well-kept and normal town. To this day, we have given Hamilton many things, like a ferry system."

"That's broken," I said, coughing—loud enough for Principal Walsh to hear me. But he pretended he didn't.

"We've given football uniforms, clothes during our Thanksgiving clothing drive, and even offered in the nineteen eighties and nineties free AIDS testing here on our soil. But we have been met with betrayal. When Officer Malore was forced to shoot that Hamilton boy, who was both drunk and violent, the people of Hamilton didn't want to hear the story our chief of police had given. They listened to the media and sought to press charges against Officer Malore. Sure, the state of New York would have interrogated this officer, but Hamilton could have told them that we were friends, a friendly state, and just buried that boy. Officer Malore and his family wouldn't have to live under this stress or receive death threats. But, instead, here we are. Now our town is riddled with media fabricating this story that this boy was innocent.

"This boy wasn't innocent," he continued. "This boy was a criminal. He was an underage drunk, for the sake of humanity! Officer Malore was only doing what he thought best to protect our women who took late-night runs, and our children, who played and stargazed under the streetlamps at night!" he yelled into the microphone with authority. Handclaps scattered around the auditorium. Thomas shifted in his seat. When the claps died down, a cordless microphone was handed to a student who was seated a few people away from Thomas and me.

"Now, juniors and seniors, we have decided to do something different in proxy of our usual Black History Month assembly, as it is February, on the date we would usually showcase the history of how Bayside moved the Blacks of Hamilton further in society. But seeing as our neighbors have decided to yell their chants all night, we have decided to dedicate this day to honor and show love to all races. This will be an *All Lives Matter* celebration." Claps began to echo again.

*What?*

"We will begin with one student at a time. You will share your negative experiences that you, as a person, have faced. Whether it be sexism, racism, or prejudice of any kind. We ask that after this is through, you say *all lives matter*. We will begin with Mercedes." He gestured to the girl who held the microphone. She cleared her throat before speaking.

"Have you all ever heard of the typical white girl? I'm so tired of how on social media everyone thinks because I'm white and blond that I'm a ditsy and love pumpkin-spiced coffee, oversized sweaters, leggings, and boots. *All lives matter!*" Claps echoed around us and it continued. The students ran down complaints about how hard their lives were because they were judged by people assuming they liked rock and country music or were rich, or whatever, when there was a bigger issue. When on the other side of the tracks, a kid our age was being embalmed. When the microphone got passed to Thomas, Principal Walsh spoke to the cameras.

"Here is Thomas, a great student. Thomas will now share his experience being an African American student at Bayside High and how he has never been racially profiled. He will give testament to the love he has been shown here. Thomas?" The camera faced him, and his hands shook. His lips were quivering.

"I . . . I . . ."

"It's okay, man, you got this," I whispered.

He let out a breath. "I've been called a nigger by my classmates. People have drawn pictures of me with big red lips and have called me Watermelon Thomas. I've been accused of wanting to have sex with every girl I ask a question. I've had food dumped on me and been bullied merely because I exist. And the Hamilton boy, the one you keep referring to as *boy*, his name is Tyree Thompson, and he was innocent."

The mic screeched when it dropped to the floor and Thomas ran out the side door. The cameramen looked to each other and smiled. Principal Walsh stood frozen.

# Justin

*I HAD ONLY ONE THING ON MY MIND, AND THAT WAS* playing my tail off.

We banged our fists against our lockers and screamed out our war cries. Even the football team piled into the locker room in support. We were ready to dominate in our game against Bayside.

"Listen up!" Coach Hill yelled. "For some of y'all, this is the last game you'll ever play for this school. Seniors, you served well!"

"*Aroo!*" we thundered.

"I could give a speech that will send these walls shaking, but I think the best person to give this pregame pep talk is Justin Collins, the captain of this basketball team and one of Thompson's best friends." He gestured for me to stand; the boys thundered with their wolf wails but quieted when I faced them.

"Today is the day we show them people in Bayside how to fight back!"

"*Aroo!*"

"Today is the day we show them people in Bayside who the best is!"

"*Aroo!*"

"But most importantly, today is the day we honor Tyree for everything he was for us. A friend. A confidant. A teammate. We ain't just winning this game just to win. We winning this game to show Bayside who they messing with. That we strong, that we capable, that we matter. They killed our brother! They killed our friend! And we gonna honor him in this game and show Bayside that Hamilton wins!"

"*Aroo!*"

"Who we doing this for!" I yelled.

"*Tyree!*" the boys thundered, stomping their feet and banging their hands against the wall.

"Who we doing this for!" I yelled again.

"*Tyree!*" the boys yelled louder. They stood to their feet.

"Who we doing this for!" I yelled.

"Yourself!" Carlos stood before me, his muscles tensed in anger. "Yourself!" he chanted. "Yourself! Yourself! Yourself!" He chanted this over and over until the room was completely quiet. Carlos's voice thundered with passion louder than all of the voices that had just chanted around him.

"Y'all tell me, how is Tyree being avenged through us shooting some balls inside of a net? That ain't doing nothing for him. That ain't showing Bayside nothing except that we got skills playing basketball, which they probably already expect from y'all niggas. We ain't showing them nothing. Like Coach Hill said, this is the last game some of us is gonna ever play. But that was our choice." His voice caught. "How about Tyree's last game he played in December? That wasn't supposed to be his last. No, they made it his last."

A few guys started to nod. I backed away and Carlos took my place, facing the crowd.

"Like y'all said, they took something from us. And they ain't tryna give us no answers about what really happened neither. They don't care about us. Y'all seen that news story today? That 'All Lives

Matter Day' they had? Look, I might not know much, but I do know one thing, and that's that this game we playing"—he turned to me, shooting his pointer finger straight into my chest—"it's for him." I opened my mouth to say something, but Carlos kept talking. "We gonna play this game tonight and we gonna win because there ain't nothing I'd rather see than some white boys getting whipped on the court. But in the end? To be real, this ain't doing nothing for Tyree." Carlos began to nod his head up and down furiously, over and over, each nod knocking the sanity right out of him. "But that's okay, because in the end, I got something planned for all them people in Bayside." He laughed. "Now y'all can join me in really avenging our brother's blood." He glared at me. "For real."

Coach Hill walked up to Carlos, but Carlos lifted a hand to stop him. "Coach, no. Life for life. Life for life. Life. For. Life. That's what I say." He walked up to Deondre, who held the banner with Tyree's picture in his hands. Slowly they unwrapped it together and walked out the locker room, holding the banner in front of them. The rest of the team followed in silence. I kept my head up as everyone walked out but when they left, I couldn't hold it up any longer. I looked at my hands, the ones that always held everything together. Everything was slipping out of them right before my eyes. Even my own team didn't trust me anymore. I tried shaking everything Carlos said out my mind, but was he right? Was I *really* being a traitor because I was willing to do anything just to get out of Hamilton?

Coach Hill placed a hand on my chest, stopping me before I walked out.

"Hey, you play your butt off in that game. Don't let nobody make you feel like you ain't doing nothing for Thompson. We all mourn in our ways, but you can't afford to do nothing stupid. You got a kid to worry about."

I nodded, shaking away the guilt-ridden feeling Carlos's speech left me with, and walked through the locker room doors.

# Zach

SO THE NIGHT THAT ONLY CAME TWICE A YEAR ARRIVED. The night that brought two towns together to compete in a rivalry that stretched through generations. To some, the basketball game, more important than the seventh game in the NBA finals. Tonight's win was deeper than proving which team was better than the other. It was about proving which town was superior, which town would have the real power—especially since the media was covering the whole story, hobbling behind us in their news van. Yes, three school buses drove Bayside High's most devoted fans, followed by a line of luxury cars and minivans, to Hamilton High, where the basketball game would be held. On my bus, they chanted the school's song over and over, yelling the words *"fight"* and *"Bayside."* I couldn't take it anymore and plugged in my earbuds to drown them out.

A song from Ambient Light immediately played, and suddenly, she broke through every crevice of my mind. I could see her as if she were already before me. Her brown skin, almond eyes, thick lips. The way her hair smelled, how she danced on that stage during her audition, how we swayed together at the concert, her face buried in my jacket. Capri was the only reason I squeezed myself into the last spot on the basketball team's bus, between Brock and Brad, squished like an anchovy between their sweaty bodies. She made it worth it to convince my father that I approved of the assembly and Principal Walsh's words so much that I wanted to support Bayside in everything against Hamilton, including this basketball game. Capri was the reason I begged the coach to let me ride with the team because the other buses were filled to the brim. The chance of seeing her that night was the only reason why I agreed to wear my father's old Bayside High sweatshirt he'd dug out of the basement, smelling like mothballs.

I needed to see her. She looked so broken and afraid the day before. I wanted to let her know that I was there and wasn't going anywhere, that I'd keep my promise of standing by her no matter what happened.

The bus bounced as it drove over the train tracks leading to Hamilton.

"I can't believe they did that. It looks like some sort of shrine. Sickening," Brock announced in disgust. Everyone on the bus looked to their left, where Tyree's memorial was set up. When the bus driver slowed down to catch a glimpse of it, Brad almost smashed me trying to get a look, almost trapping me underneath his sweaty pregame armpits before I managed to squeeze out from the seat. Carefully I stood and walked to the back of the bus where I could get a better view.

Tyree's picture stood on a gigantic poster board; around it were two more poster boards loaded with photographs of him with family and friends. Below it was what must have been hundreds of stuffed animals and flickering candles.

"They're gonna start another freaking fire with all of that," someone complained.

Trophies shined against the asphalt for all the achievements he made during his life. His football helmet caught the glow of the evening sun, casting a bright halo around it. When the view of his memorial was out of sight, everyone took their seats and scrolled through their phones, talking about the normal things they'd discussed in the halls, prom, senior trip, celebrities, and social media. Still, just as Thomas had said in the assembly, Tyree wasn't even a name to them—just another fly they wanted to shoo away.

I hadn't seen Thomas since he stormed out of the auditorium. By the time I ran out of the place to catch up with him, he was gone. He hadn't been in any of the classes we shared for the remainder of the school day either. Some people were whispering that he'd gone crazy and probably ran away to live in Hamilton or something, as if nothing he'd said on television was true.

I stepped off the bus into the damp air, happy that I'd gotten to breathe in something besides Brad's and Brock's pits. Per usual, the sky over Hamilton was starless, though the moon floating above Bayside provided some light. A slight drizzle pelted against the huge umbrellas the girls from school opened when they came off the bus.

"*Ugh*, I hate coming here," Virgie complained as she walked beside me toward the entrance. Her friends Lila and Ginger followed closely behind her, all of them taking short baby steps to stay underneath the umbrella. "I have to bring my own toilet seat covers and the toilet water is burnt yellow."

"I don't even know how you can *use* the toilets here. I'd rather go in the grass. Who knows what weirdos are hanging out in those restrooms?" Ginger added.

"Is that all you guys do when you come to Hamilton?" I asked. "Tear it down?"

They all stopped in their tracks and looked at me as if I were crazy.

"Oh, would you look who's talking: the weirdo from Philly," Lila remarked.

Ginger, halfway out the umbrella, shot a piercing glare. "Why did you even come? To finish what your weird friend started earlier on the news?" she spat.

"No," Virgie cut in. "He came to see his Hamilton girlfriend." She was the only one who wasn't glaring and for a moment, I saw the same uncomfortable-looking girl I'd just spoken with the morning before. "Come on, let's try and get a good seat. I'm only here so the news cameras can show my dad's not a coldhearted murderer." I watched them disappear into the school and then there was the smell again. Fresh pregame sweat. Brock and Brad stood on either side of me, pulling me close into their lumberjack chests. Then the noogies began, boring small knots all around my head. I worked to break free from their grasp, but to no avail.

"Virgie told us you had a girlfriend who went here," Brock whispered. "So, you're into Black chicks, man?"

Before I could say something sarcastic, Brad chimed in.

"I heard they're freaky, like real freaky, and they ain't half bad looking either. They got that shape, you know?" He used his hands to mark the silhouette of a very shapely woman, making sure to emphasize her behind and chest.

"So, you gonna introduce us?" Brock asked me. "Maybe we can snatch some up and see what they look like naked after we win tonight's game." Apparently, this was some type of clever statement because Brad smacked hands with him. I used this time to walk away while they talked about scoring more than baskets that night.

The school building looked as if it could have been an abandoned prison: one large, highly aged rectangle stretching to the darkening sky, surrounded by an aluminum fence. It was different from Bayside High, which wasn't fenced in and was made up of multiple buildings. The original building structured a lot like Hamilton served as the art and musical theatre wing, but even that building, as old as it was, didn't look as broken down as this school.

Seeing it from far away on the few trips I made to Hamilton didn't give full effect to how torn down it was. Each window, though it was cold, was cracked open for air circulation and the few that were closed, air still found its way into because they were broken and stuffed with cardboard. Bricks that lay on the exterior of the school varied from natural brown to whatever color someone decided to spray-paint them, including blue, yellow, and orange. The sign that read *Hamilton High School* was the only thing that wasn't torn; instead, it looked brand-new, with its gold lettering being the only thing that caught onto the moon's silver light and royal blue backdrop. It was apparent that the people here maintained that sign because they were happy to belong to Hamilton High School.

"Just like I remember," someone said from beside me.

"Dude! Where have you been?" I exclaimed, pulling Thomas into a hug. A few people walking by scoffed at the display of affection, and on a normal day, I would scoff at my own sappy display, but I ignored them. I was so happy to see him and still so proud of him for what he'd done in the gym. He gave me one half-hearted pat on the back.

"You're . . . squeezing . . . my . . . kidneys," he managed to breathe out.

"Sorry, man." I pulled away. "How did you get here? I didn't see you get on any of the buses."

He pointed to a Black man checking the locks on his car in the lot beside the school. "I got a ride from my dad. I figured I wouldn't be greeted with a large celebratory welcoming party after what I said, while the whole country tuned in."

"What you did was awesome and I'm sure that everyone watching from Hamilton was really proud of you."

He shrugged. "Yeah, but I didn't do it for that reason. I was just so sick and tired of everything, you know? I guess what happened to Tyree Thompson gave me courage to . . ."

"Stick it to The Man?" I finished for him.

He grinned. "Yeah, something like that."

"So, you came to support Bayside High? Or Hamilton High?" I opened the red door, which had paint chipping to the green underneath. "Because I really didn't expect to see you here."

He held up a camera that I suddenly realized dangled from his neck. "Yearbook, actually. I'm surprised they didn't kick me out of the club."

"You didn't give them a chance to yet," I joked.

"Hey, at least I'll have photographs of Bayside getting their butts whipped."

Immediately we bumped into the backs of the people that stood in front of us, and those that came in behind us bumped into us. As a matter of fact, there was barely any room to move in the hallway of the school. Something was holding the Bayside group up and it stood dead center in the middle of the hallway.

"Whoa," said Thomas, staring wide-eyed at the sight before us.

My jaw fell to the ground.

They surrounded a statue of Micah Hamilton, their town's founder, dressed up as a cop in white face. Below it stood about twenty guys who circled it. I could only see their eyes, filled with malice, shooting straight in our direction. What the boy in the center wore was enough to bother anyone, Black or white. The satin red pillowcase he'd worn on his head matched the baggy potato sack–fitting blanket he'd cut armholes in to mirror what the KKK wore. Next to him, the bunch of boys stood straight ahead, frozen. They wore black hoodies, but their faces weren't visible, because on them were masks of familiar faces that I'd seen over the years on the news—faces of the boys, men, and women killed in racist attacks. Each one held a poster above their heads that read the name, birth, and death date of the person's face they wore. In red writing before the names, they wrote, *I Am.* The boy in the middle, dressed like a KKK member, held a poster board with a photograph of Tyree. Written in what looked like blood, was one word: *Uncomfortable?*

They all stared straight ahead; when they blinked, it gave life to the masks they'd stamped to their faces. About five or six different stations surrounded them, the reporters sticking microphones in their faces, asking them questions, snapping photos. But they didn't respond. Just stood dead still with their hands raised, holding the posters.

"Come on, children, to the gym. All basketball players, straight down the hall to your respective locker room! We have a game to win!" Principal Walsh yelled from somewhere in the crowd, though his voice shook with apparent fear. The hallway began to open up as people followed his direction and moved closer to the auditorium.

"What was that?" Thomas asked.

"A war cry, I guess," I replied. We followed the crowd toward the gym, everyone muttering about what they'd just seen. "Gosh, Capri was serious when she said things had gotten serious."

"You talked to her?" Thomas asked. "I thought you said your dad turned off your phone."

"He did." We walked through the gym doors. "I snuck over here yesterday."

"What?" Thomas yelled. He stopped walking.

I sighed. "She needed to know what happened."

"Whoa, whoa, whoa, I'm confused. What are you talking about?"

I gestured for Thomas to follow me to the end of the bleachers and lowered my voice.

"Virgie told me what really happened on the tracks that night."

"What?!" Thomas exclaimed. I shushed him.

"Dude, you have to be quiet."

"Sorry, sorry," he apologized. Then, in a whisper, he exclaimed, "*What?*"

"After my dad told me he was heading Officer Malore's case, I went over to Virgie's house and she told me what really happened. Listen, my father told me the case was in their favor because only two people knew what happened that night and one of them is dead. Sure, the dashcam on the cop car showed what happened up to the chase, but as soon as Officer Malore got out of his car and followed Tyree to that dead end, nothing could be seen. The people over here have something right, man. Tyree was innocent, unarmed, and never put up a fight."

"But they have no proof," Thomas said to himself.

I nodded. "Exactly. My dad's been talking for him, dancing around the truth." I stopped talking when a few people from Bayside walked between us to grab seats. "So," I continued when they were out of sight, "I snuck here yesterday to tell Capri."

"And did you?" Thomas asked.

"I started to, but never finished. Her brother interrupted us and kicked me out of town."

"So, is that why you came here today? To find a way to tell the entire town?" Thomas asked.

Now it was my turn. "What?"

"You're one of the only people who knows what happened to Tyree. You can't keep it a secret."

"I won't. I'll find Capri and tell her the rest of the story."

"That's not enough," Thomas replied. "Listen, we have to find a way to tell the town."

"Zachary Whitman!" a familiar voice called from behind. A thick sandpaper hand wrapped itself around the back of my neck. "Wow, it's only been a few days since I saw you last, and your hair's almost longer than my dog's."

Easy MaeCollins stood next to me with the same smirk he wore every time he shot a joke at someone on a talk show or interview. I went to give Thomas a look to keep everything quiet.

"Should you be talking to me?" I asked Easy. "Is it safe?"

"Safe?" He lifted an eyebrow. "Safe, right. You're talking about what you saw in the hallway? That's just the drama team's silent protest. I thought it was pretty thought-provoking myself." He looked at Thomas and smiled. "So introduce me to your friend, Zach."

"This is Thomas," I said. Thomas waved, his hand shaking

slightly from nerves, but he managed to keep his expression leveled.

"Tom, Tommy, Tom the bomb." Easy grinned widely. He extended his hand and shook Thomas's so tight, he winced. "Zach's told me all about your talent. Looks like singing's not all you do; you take pictures too, huh?"

Thomas, confused, stuttered his response. "S . . . s . . . sing?"

Easy nodded. "I heard one of your songs and I'd like to hear you sing live."

Before Thomas could say or stutter anything else, I spoke.

"I'm not sure this is a good time, Easy." The grip he held on the back of my neck tightened.

"What? There is no better time than right now, my friend! With everyone at the game, I don't think that Thomas's disapproving father and mother will even guess that their son could be singing at the Sunlight in Hamilton. This is a once-in-a-lifetime chance, my friend, for your dreams to come true." He looked at Thomas when he said this, because he obviously thought he was auditioning the next best Black artist in music. But I took it for me and he was right. I never knew when I would have another chance like this.

"I'll be there!" I spit out. "I mean, he'll be there. We will both be there, together. As a team. Together."

"There we go!" Easy proclaimed. "Capri's at the store right now, so she will let you in. I gotta make my runs and say a few hellos to some friends, but I'll be at the Sunlight in twenty. You know where it's at, right, Zach? You've been here a few times." He patted me on the back, gave Thomas another hearty handshake, and disappeared.

Thomas stood, staring at me, his eyes wide as if he were someone from Bayside coming into Philly and witnessed a drug exchange right in front of him.

"What was that about?" he asked.

"I'll explain on the way," I replied, then headed toward the exit. "But we have to go, now."

# Capri

*I CAUGHT MY BREATH, JUST AS THE SONG CAME TO AN* end. My feet burned from the intensity of the routine I'd just put them through. I danced the same routine, over and over and over since I'd come into the store. We were given the option to leave school early today after the memorial. It was hard to take tests or focus on lectures when somebody would suddenly burst into tears from looking at Tyree's empty seat or card-covered locker, or a teacher would start talking about the mystery behind his murder. Not a lot of people left, but I did. I needed to get away from it all. I was fine with the extra hours Easy had given me. I knew that we wouldn't have any customers since everyone was either at the Thompsons', the basketball game, or setting up one of the few hundred memorials for Tyree scattered around town. Some stores were still "closed for mourning," and others open for discussion about what they guessed had happened.

Everyone had their own version of the story from someone who heard it from someone who heard it from someone who made it up, because they were all way off. The magazines and newspapers that rolled in at the grocery store said different things. Some said that Tyree was wrongfully killed. Some agreed with what the people in Bayside believed: Tyree charged at Officer Malore, who shot in self-defense.

Some news stories even said Tyree had a gun. Other's told half-truths about Tyree, stating that he was a good student, but had a heavy drinking problem and violent past. He had no prior criminal history, but his detention slips and trips to the principal's office were reported in the articles and news stories like he'd killed someone. I was amazed at just how much could be put together in just a few days. Around noon, before I called Easy and practically begged for him to let me work, my whole family sat in front of the television. The news would be premiering what they'd recorded at Bayside High's emergency assembly that morning.

It was like the Super Bowl; everyone was gathered close around the television like their favorite team was taking the field. Except there wasn't any screaming from Justin, Deondre, and Carlos, and Ma wasn't frying chicken and yelling at Pa for picking at the golden-brown pieces dripping oil on the white paper towels she sat them on. Still, Justin and his friends all surrounded the television screen watching intensely, even the stories that had nothing to do with anything that was happening over here. Carlos watched most intensely. He didn't get up to stretch his legs during the commercials; his eyes were glued to the screen as if turning away for one minute would ensure he'd miss the entire program.

I was pretending to study science on the couch under the dim light in the family room, so no one would try to include me in the conversation. Honestly, I only watched to catch a glimpse of Zach. I was hoping that he was all right after Justin had threatened him. Ma tsked, shaking her head disappointedly when she walked into the room. She even left work early; this was a lot for everyone.

"I can't believe that man got them kids complaining about they pumpkin coffee and hair color. It's more important things to be discussing." She was in the bedroom with Rose, who'd been complaining of a splitting headache since they'd gotten home from school.

"No disrespect, Mrs. Justin's Grandma, but you're wrong," Carlos replied. "That principal can't force them to do nothing they don't want to do. Privileged kids like that got a choice. They like the spotlight on them. They all the same." It was the first thing I heard him say all afternoon.

"Just look at them," Pa said, mouth full with the hot dogs and beans he heated up on the stove. "That All Lives Matter stuff." He pointed his spoon at the screen as a boy complained about people thinking since he was white, all he did was smoke weed and listen to white rappers. "They need to focus on Tyree right now, they need to be getting to the bottom of this stuff. This ain't no news."

Justin shushed Pa when a Black boy with big curly hair was shown on the small television screen. He looked familiar. When he began to speak, I recognized him as Thomas. The word "nigger" was bleeped out when he announced he'd been called that name at Bayside; the camera turned off after he ran out the auditorium, and the story cut back to a reporter rehashing the tension in the room.

"Now that's news!" Pa said with a laugh. Everyone else joined him except Carlos, whose eyes were still glued to the screen, his face completely straight. I couldn't stop staring at him. He wasn't playful Carlos who always bounced around the house with a huge grin; he looked like he was in another dimension.

After the news story ended and the boys began to discuss with Pa what they thought happened, I knew I needed to get out.

Easy only agreed to let me work after I promised to shelve the new inventory, but I'd been at the Sunlight for almost five hours and didn't touch the box filled with old records. I knew if I sat cleaning and shelving those records, the quiet would make me fixate on how everything was changing—how hatred toward Bayside was skyrocketing, how my chances of getting out of Hamilton grew slimmer. Ma had told me she registered me to start an online psychology course that would keep me busy all summer before my senior year, grant me some college credits, and jump-start my freshman year in Hamilton's nursing school.

I didn't want to think about any of this, so I did the only thing I knew how to do to keep me from having to think. I danced. I danced. And I danced a lot more. When I did, everything else washed away—stress, the fear that tried to make me believe my dreams were impossible, the worry that I'd never see Zach again. It all vanished. I danced so hard, my feet and legs began to heat with pain so intense that I had to wrap them with bandages and place warm cloths on them. While I did, I scrolled through social media, but almost every post was commentary on Tyree, his eyes staring back at me.

I turned my phone off just as the bell over the shop rang; in ran Zach, followed by Thomas. To say I was surprised to see them was an understatement. I hobbled over to the door.

"Are you all right?" he asked, staring at my swollen feet.

I nodded. "I'm fine, I was just dancing. Did you sneak out here?"

He shook his head. "No, kind of. I guess." He bit on his bottom lip. "Easy sent us here. But don't get me wrong, I wanted to see you."

I smiled at that. "I wanted to see you too. I actually thought I would never see you again."

Zach scoffed playfully. "You think one threat from your overprotective brother can keep me away from you?"

I grinned, but Thomas cut in before I could offer a flirty line back.

"I don't mean to interrupt, but can anyone please explain to me while I'm not running down the street like a crazy person why I'm here, and why Easy MaeCollins thinks I'm auditioning for him when I can't even sing the notes to 'Row Your Boat' correctly?"

"He's auditioning tonight?" I asked. I would have thought Easy wouldn't want anything to do with Bayside after what happened to Tyree. But then I remembered, this was his comeback tour; Easy was invested in making it great. I think he believed even more that putting on this tour would bring a sense of healing back to the world.

"Yes, and don't worry," Zach stated. "I have a plan."

Moments later, Thomas stood onstage with Zach, getting coached on how to forge piano chords at the old keyboard we'd set up and Easy's nearsighted prescription glasses were hidden away in the cash register drawer. We didn't need his eyes to get the audition for Zach, just his ears. I felt weird at first, going along with everything. But then I remembered his support in New York City, the way he looked at Essie, how he talked me out of stage fright, brought my leotard, and how he screamed at the top of his lungs after I finished dancing. Over the past few days, Zach had been a constant. He helped me escape my present. I don't know if I could have done any of it without him. Easy was like a father to me, but he was stubborn. If I tried convincing him to give Zach a chance, he would have said no immediately. He needed to hear it all for himself. This was Zach's only chance and I was willing to help him get it, just like he did for me. When Thomas found out what was going on, he reluctantly agreed and I could see one thousand worries fall from Zach's face.

"That's what friends are for. Just promise me you'll pass all those cute groupie girls to me when you're famous," Thomas said with a grin. But I saw something else in his eyes that told me girls wouldn't be all he wanted in return for this favor. Still, we didn't have time to worry about that.

When Easy walked into the Sunlight, he took his seat where he'd always sat every open mic night. The "Golden Seat" was what he called it, where he said the acoustics bounced off the walls and catered to him. The Golden Seat also happened to be located at the perfect spot where Thomas's playing and lip-syncing wouldn't be noticeable with Easy's horrible eyesight.

"All right!" he yelled after he sent me to find his glasses, and I'd reported that they were nowhere in sight. "I'm blind, Tommy, but I can still hear. Show me what you got."

And then it started. Zach stood in the back of the stage, tucked behind a curtain right across from me. He gave me a thumbs-up and he began to play the little keyboard we set up behind the stage. He sang into the mic attached to the keyboard. It wasn't the song he'd played for Easy and me days ago; it was something else equally beautiful—a ballad, completely stripped, save for the piano. The melody wasn't simple by any means, classical with pop elements, but jazzy at the same time. His voice riffed and rolled in falsetto the entire beginning of the song but gained its strength toward the end. He sang with such passion, talking to the listener, giving us a story of love that flew into his hands, but was something he was on the verge of losing.

*"The first time our eyes met,*
*She stared straight through me*
*To a part of my heart, she made her way into me.*

*Could this be love that I'm feeling inside?*
*Could I hold her like I want to?*
*Could she rest in these arms?*
*And say you're strong enough?*
*But am I enough?"*

His eyes were closed, he hummed the melody. Then it sped up and he banged against the keys, each syllable matching its intensity.

*"But. It. Doesn't. Work. That. Way.*

*This ain't a fairy tale*
*'Cause I know that one day,*
*She will fly away!*
*'Cause she got these things*
*These wings*
*Stretching wide,*
*She's flying high!*
*And here I am,*
*Under the ground,*
*I'm buried six feet under,*
*I feel I'm six feet under,*
*While she's flying far away.*
*Please stay.*

Then his eyes opened and met mine—his whole being moved with the lyrics he sang. His voice gained such strength, like I'd never heard. It became so wide, so powerful, fire shot up my spine, because he sang the next lyrics straight to me.

*"Could this be love that I'm feeling inside?*
*Could I hold her like I want to?*
*Could she rest in these arms?*
*And say you're strong enough?*

*Am I strong enough?"*

Then the music stopped; he sang acapella softly.

*"And here I am,*

*underground*

*Watching her fly away."*

When the song came to an end, Thomas accidentally pressed an actual chord on the piano. It sounded horrible, but Easy clapped his butt off and gave a standing ovation. I stared straight at Zach, at a loss for words. He stared back with equal intensity and didn't even focus on the fact that one of his greatest inspirations was loving his song. He just looked right through me, to a part I didn't even know dwelled inside. It felt like my heart completely ceased beating— like it didn't know what to do anymore.

## Justin

HE SAT IN THE VISITORS' BLEACHERS, SECOND ROW, THREE seats to the right in a gray suit. His gold pinkie ring kept shining against the lights above, causing a glimmer to reflect every time he lifted the pencil he held. I couldn't help but notice that it didn't have an eraser, which meant there was no room for mistakes.

So, I played carefully.

I ignored the crowd and concentrated on the net across from where the ball was always thrown to me. I sprinted down the court, quicker than I ever had. Every jump was higher than it ever was, every dip stealthier, every pass more careful. I'd already scored sixty points for the team, putting them us two ahead of Bayside. I couldn't lie and say that the game I was playing against Bayside was easy; in fact, it was the hardest game I'd ever competed in. But I was gonna win it. I had to win to get that scholarship. The stakes were high. Everyone had reasons for wanting to win the championship game, both Bayside and Hamilton. Mine wasn't for the reason I'd been shooting at everyone who asked. It wasn't for Tyree, entirely, though I still thought of him the whole time I played. Tyree was the main reason I played ball to begin with. Winning wasn't for Rose or our son either. Deep down, this game was about proving something to myself. Proving that I was more than capable to start something, finish it well, and make a name for myself while I was at it. To gain control over the one thing I still had in my grasp: my future.

The score was 132 to 134; the end of game buzzer was about to sound but I wasn't nervous. I was excited for the man with the glimmering pinkie ring to promise me a scholarship.

"All right, boys, you're four points ahead and we're at ten seconds left," Coach proclaimed to our huddle. We smiled proudly. "No, no, no, no smiles until that bell rings and they announce that we won. Play hard, y'all. Thompson's picture is right there hanging under that scoreboard looking straight at us, waiting for us to accomplish something for him. Just like Collins said, we doing this for him."

I ignored the tug in my belly that told me it wasn't entirely true. On the count of three, we yelled *"Tyree!"* and took our places on the court.

I stretched my legs and rolled my neck from side to side. We were playing offense and I knew the deal: the boys on Bayside would try and run out the clock, then go for a three to win the game, but I wasn't going to let that happen. Both sides played the game so far without talking to each other. The looks we gave Bayside were threatening enough, and though they played their best, they couldn't get what they'd seen in the hallway out of their heads. I saw the fear it put in them, the way they all kept looking toward the spot on the bleachers where the drama team set up shop, staring with those masks, implicating them in Tyree's death.

When the buzzer sounded, we followed the ball with our eyes as it was thrown from person to person to run out the clock. My eyes were fixed on number seventeen. He was a large one, standing at least a half head taller than me. He held the rock in his hands, bouncing it up and down, running down the court; every attempt we made to steal failed because of the heavy guarding given by his teammates. They didn't notice me make my way behind him until we were face-to-face.

"Hey number seventeen," I said, grinning. I could taste the sweat falling from my lips "You gonna hand me the ball like a good boy or do I gotta snatch it from you?"

"I'm not afraid of you guys," the boy replied, face leveled to a calm that was almost psychotic. "Just because you're a big Black guy whose drama team dresses like the Black KKK to scare people doesn't mean I'm gonna cower down . . ."

And just like that, his mind was elsewhere. My planned distraction worked, and I stole the ball right out of his hands. I ran across the court, at two seconds. Just as the clock struck one, the ball was shot from the three-point line; one clean shot right into the net. The crowd roared.

"Who we doing this for?" I yelled in the face of whatever Bayside Tiger stood near me.

"Tyree!" my teammates roared.

I never felt so alive, like everything I'd fought for was about to be handed right to me. I played my whole middle school and high school career for this one moment. I'd brought my team to our last game, and we won. Adrenaline rushed through my being, and I rested in its high. As everyone made their way from the stands to the court to congratulate Hamilton High on our win, I ran to the familiar face I spotted in the crowd. She grabbed the side of my face and kissed me, sweaty and all.

"I am so proud of you," she said between the many kisses she gave. I hugged her, hiding my chin in the crevices of her neck.

"I told you, I told you, I told you I would get us out of here." I squeezed her so tight.

"I know," Rose whispered. "I didn't believe it before. Now I know. You did it, Justin."

*"Justin Collins?"*

We pulled apart and there he was, the Snow Fairy with the golden ticket. He shook my hand.

"Good game, son!" the man said. "I enjoyed watching you. You played your butt off tonight."

"Thank you, sir," I replied. "I'm happy you came out to come see us."

The man nodded. "No, thank you. Well, as you know, I came on behalf of Village University to award someone with a scholarship tonight."

"Yes, sir."

He grinned at me, and gestured to number seventeen from Bayside, who I had just stolen the ball from. The man introduced the Bayside boy.

"This is Clark Kingston. He plays for Bayside High and the face-off you guys just had was one for the books." I stared Clark down, biting hard on my jaw.

"Good game, man," I offered.

The boy licked his teeth. "Yeah, you played your butt off, *boy*. Really wanted this scout to notice you, huh?"

I clenched my fist.

"Whoa, whoa, boys, leave it on the court. Justin, I brought Clark over here because as you know, we only come with one scholarship for both sides of your town. Clark here is the best player in Bayside and you in Hamilton. This decision has nothing to do with your ability to play the game, because you're equally amazing. It has only to do with who we think will act as a greater asset for our university's team."

We nodded, glaring at one another.

"With much careful consideration, Village University would like to give the scholarship to Clark Kingston."

My breath caught.

"*What?*"

Clark shook the hand of the college scout, a huge grin filling his skinny face.

"I can't believe it, sir. A full ride? I . . . I don't know what to say."

"You can say you accept!" the scout said with a laugh. Clark stated that he accepted, but I hardly heard him. In fact, every form of noise vanished from my surroundings.

The scout extended his hand for me to shake. "You are a talented boy; if I had two scholarships to give, you know that you would have had it."

I left the scout's hand hanging in the air.

"You're kidding. This kid doesn't even need a scholarship. His parents have probably put away money since he was a kid to send him to college. And what about the questionnaire you sent us to help with your decision? It isn't even due till the end of the month. I didn't have a chance to hand it in yet..."

The scout creased his brow. "Please understand that you didn't think you'd get the scholarship with the negative publicity surrounding this town. Village U has a name to uphold."

"So, you give a scholarship away to a boy from a town who murdered an innocent boy?" Rose butt in. This was the first time the scout noticed her; he took one look at her stomach and rolled his eyes.

"Mr. Collins, I assume that you have a second choice for schools."

I shook my head. "No, I don't."

Clark grinned wider. "Looks like you can be skilled in everything and still be a loser." He lifted a hand above his head, his pointer finger straight out, other fingers tucked in, and thumb erect. "Better shot next time, I guess, huh, Tyree?" He pulled the trigger on his finger. "I mean, Justin."

He turned to walk away, but before he took one step, I lunged at him, knocking the scout into the man next to him. My legs were on either side of Clark's head, my fists punching the sides of his face over and over, until my knuckles were stained with his blood. I wanted to break every bone in his face. Rose's scream was the only thing that caused the celebrating crowd to notice what I was doing in the middle of the floor. *The* Justin Collins, the one that they expected so much from, finally let everything he'd been holding in out. A Bayside boy standing nearby threw such a blow to my temple that I thought I was thrown into another reality. I fell off Clark onto the floor next to me. Carlos yelled a one-word instruction to our teammates. They lunged at whatever Bayside boy was closest to them. Soon, the gym floor where a healthy war of sportsmanship was fought in Tyree's honor turned bloody, violent. Boys rolled on the gym floor, beating the lights out of one another until the Hamilton police were called to separate us.

We ran until our hearts burned. Deondre, Carlos, me, and Jay breathed heavily, trying to regain the oxygen we lost running down the hill away from Hamilton High to Carlos's house, which stood almost at the end of the town.

"Whoa, Jus, I didn't know you had it in you," Carlos said with a grin after spitting out blood that had pooled in his mouth. We all stood there, broken and bleeding. Carlos's front tooth had gotten punched out. Deondre's forehead had a huge gash and blood poured down the left side of his cheek. Jay's nose looked as if it had been broken; my nose felt like it.

We threw ourselves across the couches in Carlos's house, still a wreck from the house party. Carlos threw us frozen vegetable packs to put on our wounds. I had never been so thankful for peas, my least favorite vegetable; they felt so good on the bridge of my nose.

"Dude, when your parents come back, they're gonna be crazy mad," Deondre said from the couch across from me. He tried to keep his voice steady, but I could hear how much pain he was in.

"I know. Mom and Dad called me from the boonies; they heard about what happened to Tyree on the news. Can you believe they're playing that story all over the nation?"

"I didn't mean that, you idiot. I meant from your house."

The boys forced laughter.

"Nah, I'll have it clean by then," Carlos replied. "I have like four more days until they get back."

I couldn't help but notice how different Carlos's voice sounded. He had a slight lisp now, probably because of his missing tooth. We didn't say nothing about it; we didn't want to dwell on how serious the fight was. Didn't want to really dwell on the sickening but triumphant feeling we had after beating our anger and confusion into others— that sickening but triumphant feeling I had after beating the crap out of Clark. He might have won my scholarship, but every time he looked at his face in the mirror, he was gonna remember I was there.

We all lay on the couches and watched cartoons until we fell asleep, steering clear of the news story we knew we'd be featured on. A knock at the door close to two in the morning woke us up.

I stood slowly to answer, my heart racing, forgetting the wet peas were still on my face. They fell to the ground with a squishy thump.

"Dude, look before you answer. It could be the cops," Carlos warned. Deondre hid behind the blanket he was covered in. Jay and his big self rolled over the other end of the couch and hid behind it.

I looked through the peephole of the door.

"It's just Rose," I announced before opening it. She stood before me, still in the large jersey and jeans she wore to the game. "Hey," I greeted, shutting the door behind me and stepping onto the porch. The air outside smelled damp, but fresh. It reminded me of the times I would walk her home from our dates. "What are you doing here so late?" I asked her. Then I noticed the SUV.

"I was looking everywhere for you. This was the last stop he let me check," she replied, gesturing to the truck behind her.

"He?" I asked.

"My dad," Rose replied quietly. Her eyes were focused on the dying plants hanging on Carlos's porch.

"You're talking to your dad again?" I tried lowering my head so she'd have to catch my eye, but she wouldn't. She nodded.

"He promised me that he'd help me support Noah."

I smiled and gave a friendly wave to the car behind them.

"Noah! You named him Noah? Noah Collins," I said, trying the name out aloud. "I love it." She smiled slightly. "So . . . your dad, you guys are talking again?"

"Yeah. He came up to me after the game and apologized. He told me he and mom wanted me in their lives and they wanted Noah. They want what's best for us."

"I'm glad. I mean, that's great. We'll need all the help we can get with . . ."

"I came to say goodbye."

These were words I thought I'd never have to hear from my first love. And that's when she looked into my eyes, hers glazed with tears.

"What?" I asked, breathless.

"There was a condition to the agreement with my mom and dad. I'm moving to this program in Connecticut."

I searched for words. "Connecticut? What about Noah?"

"He'll be fine. We'll both be fine. The program is for single mothers. It'll provide a home for me and Noah until I finish high school and then I'll have help with college."

"Rose," I said, my head beginning to ache again. "You're not single."

She looked away again. "My dad says that's what's best for Noah and me. And I agree with him."

"What?"

"We're not good for one another, Justin, you know that."

I shook my head. "Rose, don't say that. Don't say that."

"And I'm not strong enough to resist you," she continued almost robotically. "You're not responsible and you follow after your emotions too much. The fight tonight, for example, was out of hand. You don't have any plans outside of basketball and Noah and I need a solid life."

"This isn't you," I whispered. "This isn't you talking, Rose. I know this isn't you." Heat rose in my chest. "It's your father! He's taking you from me!" I screamed to the car. "It's you, you basket case! You're crazy if you think you're taking my son and my girl away from me! That's my son! You can't do this!" I lunged toward the car to scream at Reverend Sails, but Rose held me back.

"See! That's what I mean! That's why he can't trust you with me! Because of this!" Tears rolled down her cheeks. Her voice fell into a whisper. "That's why, Justin. Don't you see? Don't you see?"

The horn beeped, signaling her time was up.

"They can't do this, Rose," I pleaded. "We can fight this; we can run away." She shook her head.

"This is what's best for Noah, what's best for the both of us."

"So what, they gonna take my son away? They can't do this." I let out a breath, and immediately everything spilled out; every ounce of strength I'd collected since the day I found out about Noah poured from me until I fell to my knees. I couldn't stand. "Rose," I pleaded, hands raised above my head. "Don't go. Don't take my son."

The horn beeped again, and Rose turned to leave, but I wrapped my hands around her legs.

"Please. That's not you talking. I know it's not, Rosey. I know it's not what you want."

She stood still, turned, and squatted until she was leveled to me.

"You're right. It's not what I want. But this isn't about what *I* want anymore, Justin. It's about what Noah needs. . . . He needs structure. He needs to be taken care of."

"I can take care of him, Rose," I exclaimed through tears. "I can get a job after school. I'll go to the community college. I'm gonna do it right, just like you said. Bump the scholarship, bump my dreams of going pro. I don't care about it anymore. I just want you. I just want Noah."

Tears fell in stripes from Rose's eyes, which caused me to weep more. I was pleading for her to stay, pleading for her over everything else. Even though tears were still streaming down her cheeks, she managed to smile, softly and gently.

"We always said we wanted to get out of Hamilton." She wiped her eyes and stood to her feet. "Goodbye, Justin."

I watched her climb into the back seat of her father's car and fixed my eyes on the vehicle until it drove away and I couldn't see it anymore.

I screamed so loud at the sky. I didn't care that I woke up families, or that the dogs complained. I needed heaven to hear me, for God to step in. The weight of loneliness drowned me. I was hit with the reality that even the heavens weren't listening to my wishes anymore. Nothing was.

And it wasn't because of anything I did. I tried stepping up after Mama died. I tried being the perfect grandson, brother, and neighbor. I always screamed where no one could hear me. Kept out of drama and trouble. Always said I was okay when I wasn't. Always studied hard for the 4.0 GPA I had. Missed parties, went to church, volunteered on the weekends, tutored, I freaking busted my butt for years on the court. I even applied to college, and *still* lost the scholarship. It wasn't because of any of that. The Snow Fairy said I was qualified. It was because of who I was. My cursed skin. If I got the scholarship, me and Rose would be together. I would have been able to see Noah grow up.

My chances of that were gone, which meant my chances at leaving Hamilton were gone. Which meant now I had nothing left to lose. I wiped my eyes, stood to my feet, and walked back inside Carlos's house. The guys were all at the window, watching the entire ordeal, but when I opened the door, they ran to their respective couches, as if they'd been resting the entire time. I was fully aware of what they'd done but didn't care enough to worry about who was in my business. Any business I had just vanished. I only wanted one thing: revenge. I looked straight at Carlos.

"Blood for blood, huh? How we going about that?"

"I'm glad you asked, ma man." Carlos grinned widely, unashamed of his missing teeth. "Y'all all in?" he asked Jay and Deondre. They nodded, which gave Carlos the drive to share his plan. "So this is what I'm thinking, but it has to be tomorrow or nothing."

"But that's Tyree's homegoing," Jay cut in.

"I was supposed to help carry his casket in," Deondre added, but Carlos shushed them.

"Trust me, guys, this is the only time the town will be distracted enough not to notice us going over to Bayside. . . ."

# Zach

"WELL, MR. MANAGER . . . ," EASY SAID, APPEARING
before me, blocking my view of Capri, who stood on the opposite
end of the stage behind the curtain. I wanted to do a great job singing, piling everything great I'd ever learned from every inspiring
and talented artist I'd ever heard, but it didn't matter once the song
started. Because nothing mattered more while I was singing than
to use the words to tell Capri how I felt about her. Easy waved his
hand in front of my face. "Hello? Mr. Manager."

"What?" I blinked and looked at Easy.

Easy broke out into a smile. "I guess we have some discussing to do. How about a week or two from now when things begin
to die down around here? I'll keep in touch." He patted Thomas's
head. "Looks like you're going to see the entire country outside
of here, my boy. You know, I used to be just like you. My parents
didn't approve of my playing. They wanted me to be a doctor, but
guess what? I did what you did, I made it happen throughout every
setback. You are a strong Black boy and you're gonna change everything for our people."

Thomas smiled. "Thanks, Easy."

"You know, I can tell we have a lot in common. The way you
wrote that song, all that need shining through, the blues and jazz
influence coming out of that. I couldn't see it, but I darn well heard
it. I heard it loud and clear."

Thomas nodded like he understood. I wanted to tell Easy that the song did come out of need—my need to fly with Capri, despite that society enforced constraints designed to keep me from becoming a part of her narrative.

Easy tried releasing his hand from Thomas's hair, but it got caught in one of his curls.

"We just gotta do something about that hair," he said before exiting.

When Easy was out of sight, Thomas stuck out his hand for me to shake. I pulled him into a hug. Easy liked my song, he liked my *voice*, he wanted me on tour with him! This was unbelievable.

"Dude, I can't believe this is happening." I pulled away. "I mean we do have a long way before us, but I'm going on tour with Easy MaeCollins! *The* Easy MaeCollins."

"Yeah, but how are we gonna pull this off?"

"We'll think of something," I replied, not at all knowing how this was going to work out. "Let's just relish in this."

Thomas laughed. "Okay, okay, hotshot. We can relish as soon as we figure out how we're gonna tell everyone in Hamilton what really happened."

"We? I told you at the game, I promised Virgie I wouldn't tell anyone else besides Capri. After I tell her the whole thing, she can do what she wants with it."

Thomas shook his head, still smiling, his eyes lighting up to blinding brightness. "No, that won't do, they won't take her word for it. But they will take yours, the son of the lawyer who is representing Officer Malore. Bayside will finally realize that not everything works in their favor."

I knew Thomas was right, but it wasn't that easy.

"Look, man, I tried telling Justin. It doesn't really look like the town is so bent on hearing anything that anyone from Bayside has to say. Plus, you heard Easy: we need things to calm down quickly so I could talk about the tour with him. Heck, maybe I could even tell him the truth about my singing after the feud comes to a halt."

"Do you really think that's going to happen? That he's going to accept you?" Thomas asked. "He's just as blind as the rest of the people here. He's only willing to use your music if he thinks it's me singing it. The feud ending quicker isn't going to make him want you; he'll just move on to the next act."

"No!" I exclaimed. "You're wrong. Me rehashing what happened with Tyree would definitely not make anything calm down any quicker. Dad would probably disown me and have me on the first plane to Africa. I can't leave here now when everything is going so great."

Thomas threw his hands in the air. "Because you sneaking around is everything going great!"

"I promised Virginia I wouldn't tell anyone but—"

"And since when are we keeping promises to *Virginia Malore*?" Thomas asked, disgusted. "This is a life-or-death situation. But you don't even care, do you? Because this isn't even about *Virgie* or *Hamilton*. You're so bent on getting this tour with Easy that you'll lie your way through that and make me do the same. But when it has nothing to do with you directly, then you wanna act all honest and upright."

"Thomas . . ."

"No, Zach. I'm going to talk for once and you're going to do the listening." His tongue was like a dagger. "I let you drag me here and did your dumb audition, but I'm done. You're on your own. You talk about caring for Capri, but you don't even really care, do you? If you did, you'd love her people too. You'd love them enough to give them the truth, no matter what it costs you. That's what doing the *right thing* is about, right, man? Whether you lose your chance at stardom or not."

"Thomas . . ."

He shook his head. "But you just care about getting famous. Tyree's already dead, right? What's the point? Right? You didn't know him personally, right? You know, maybe I don't know what the point is, other than the fact that his mom and dad and siblings deserve to know what happened to him, and Tyree deserves justice! You're holding it back because you're afraid of the truth coming out and you exposing your sneaky *I'm on your side* act with your father and Virgie Malore's trust? Sorry excuse, Zach."

The stage door flew open and Capri ran into my arms.

"That was the most beautiful thing I have ever heard," she said into my sweatshirt as she squeezed me tightly. But I couldn't rest in the victory any longer.

"He's right," I whispered.

Capri pulled away and stared at me.

"What are you talking about?"

"Thomas, he's right. I'm being selfish. I have to find Tyree's parents. I have to tell them what happened to their son." My thoughts poured from my mouth so fast, I didn't have time to catch them. "I'll do it at the homegoing. That way I can tell the town what happened. I can tell…"

Capri shook her head. "No, no, please don't say that." Her eyes searched mine. "If you betray your father like that, he'll take you away from me." Her fingertips grazed my jawline as she spoke desperately. "Please," she whispered. "I can't have him take you from me. I haven't even told you that . . ."

I touched her hands with my own.

"What? You haven't told me what?"

"No! This needs to stop!" Thomas yelled, causing Capri to jump. "This Romeo and Juliet stuff, it needs to stop! This is real life and it's not about y'all." He shook his head. "You know, I really thought you were both different, but you're no different than Officer Malore, Zach's father, Virgie, Easy, or anyone else. You're only out for yourself." Seconds later, the door slammed shut, and he was gone.

# Capri

ZACH FACED ME, HIS EYES FAR AWAY, JUST AS JUSTIN'S were, just as Carlos's were. His hands rubbed either side of my shoulders.

"Hold on to whatever you were about to say just now, all right?"

"Zach . . ."

"No, hold on to it. I'll see you tomorrow, at the homegoing."

"Zach, do you think they'll believe you? How can you prove you're not just spreading another rumor?"

"I don't know. But I have to figure it out."

"Please."

He shushed me softly. "No matter what, I'll find a way to see you. Even if he moves me to another planet." He kissed my forehead gently. "Hold on to it," he whispered before rushing out of the door.

"You look like hell," Justin said when he walked into the record shop the next morning. He was holding a cardboard box. I rolled my eyes and leaned on the register counter. Between the protestors and Zach running out after Thomas, leaving me in the Sunlight all alone crying all night, I didn't get much sleep. But what else was new?

"I can say the same thing about you," I replied, gesturing to his purpling nose and swollen ear. He shrugged, giving me a smug smile.

"You should have seen the other guy. Besides, you should be *thanking* me. The fight got school canceled today."

"Ma's looking for you. She was worried. You kept her up half the night."

He looked away from me, embarrassed, but the look went away as soon as it came.

"We had to run before the cops came. I crashed at Carlos's place last night. I texted her that."

"Yeah," I replied. "After like three in the morning."

He looked away. "She shouldn't be worried about me."

"We all are, Justin. We heard from your coach how the fight started. I'm sorry you didn't get the scholarship."

"Yeah," he sniffed. "Me too."

"Rose didn't come home last night either. Was she with you?" I asked.

Justin snapped his fingers to shut me up. "Why the interview?" he spat.

"I was just asking . . ."

"Yeah, just like I was asking all those questions about who that Zach guy is to you."

My mouth glued shut. At that point, I wasn't even sure. He'd run after Thomas before he told me that he'd see me at Tyree's homegoing service, which was later this afternoon. I knew they needed to know what happened, especially since Bayside was becoming more secretive as the days went on and Hamilton grew more anxious about the lack of accountability in the case. Especially since there was no evidence countering Officer Malore's claim that he shot Tyree in self-defense and not because he was being quick-triggered. What made it even worse was news that Tyree had gone to anger management courses at age twelve; that was broadcast all over the news that morning. I knew they needed Zach, but I needed Zach, too, and I knew his father wouldn't let him ever see me again if he did this.

"What's this?" I gestured to the box Justin held, changing the subject. Justin pulled out a pin and handed one to me.

"These things Carlos and I made last night for the homegoing."

I examined it. There was that picture of Tyree again, the one I'd seen everywhere. *Black Lives Matter* was posted across his chest. I sighed.

"You know, you should wear one too," he said, pointing to the one he'd pinned onto his shirt.

I smiled at him.

"In honor of your hard work, I'll be happy to wear one." I pinned Tyree's face on my jacket and tried to ignore the memory of his body haunting my dreams.

"So, you coming tonight?" he asked. He quickly quieted, though, when the bell over the door rang and an old man with an Afro walked in.

"The homegoing?"

He shook his head no.

"What's tonight?" I asked. Justin looked behind him as if someone were listening to our conversation and then back at my only Afro'd costumer, who was flipping through the indie records.

"A group of us are going to Bayside to where that cop that killed Tyree lives, and we're going to leave him a little present." He winked.

"Justin. What are you talking about?"

"Exactly what I said, Capri. Deondre found out where that cop lives and we're going to his house."

"To do what?" I asked warily.

"Whatever we decide to do. If I want to burn down the whole city, we will. They deserve it. All those white people do."

"Burn it down? Justin, you could get arrested."

He shook his head at me like he was disappointed. "Arrested? Tyree got killed. That cop murdered an innocent eighteen-year-old boy for nothing. He deserves everything that's coming to him tonight."

"But this isn't about Tyree, is it?" I searched his eyes with my own; whatever strength he tried wearing on his bruised-up face fell.

"It's about a compilation of things, Pri. They win all the time. We can be better qualified for something, better fit, worked harder for it, but it don't mean nothing as long as we got this cursed skin."

"Justin, being Black is not a curse."

"Oh yeah? Well maybe it's not, but it is to them, Pri. Do you wanna know what being Black has given us so far? Hamilton and early death. Do you see how those reporters have turned against Tyree on the news? Now all of a sudden he's a drunk criminal. I lost my scholarship because of the color of my skin and nothing more."

"I know," I said. "I know, Justin. But how about we just let the judge handle it? There's still a case here."

"How about we handle it? The law is against us. All of us. We'll be lucky if that cop gets punished at all. Tyree will never be able to go to college. He'll never be a doctor. What's that gonna do for your nephew? You think his end will be any different?" A tear fell from his eye. "Do you really think those people are gonna give you that scholarship? I imagine you weren't the only person that applied for Camp Sharp."

The white faces from the audition showed back in my memory.

"Exactly. This skin," he said. He lifted my arm and let it fall. "This is all people see when they look at you, including that white boy Zach. He'll leave as soon as he gets to see if Black girls are as easy as the television shows makes them out to be."

I looked away from him, trying my best not to cry.

"Did you actually think he really liked you? Did you really think he sees past your skin complexion? That he wants to settle down with you? What we're doing tonight might not change the way they see us, but they'll respect us. Do you understand that we need to change things?"

"Yes!" I cried. "I understand! But this isn't the right way to go about this. We don't need another murder, Justin."

"Take off the pin," he said dryly.

"What?"

He crossed his arms. "You heard me. Take it off. If you're not with this city, you're against it." I sighed and removed the pin from my jacket.

"You know, I really think you should support this more than you have. We're only trying to make a difference. To change things for us."

"Maybe you're right. Maybe I should be out there marching with you guys, or standing up in church, maybe I should want to set fire to Officer Malore's house, I'm just—"

"You're just what, Capri? Ashamed? You know you're Black too."

"Justin, I *know* I'm Black. I'm just trying to say—"

He lifted a hand to silence me. "You've said enough, Capri. Those people across the tracks, those *white* people in Bayside haven't crossed over to help us in Hamilton since they gave us this town all those years ago. They was happy to kick us out of Bayside and keep us niggers across the tracks and out of their hair. They was happy to separate our towns with those tracks. You see them donating those good schoolbooks they got to make our schools better? You see them helping us clean up after Willie's shop burned down? You see them coming over here to apologize after Tyree was killed? No. They stay over there just like they always done. It's been war since I could remember. It's still war. I don't care. Tyree was killed because he was a Black man walking on the wrong side of the tracks and my dreams was killed because the white kid was a better fit for the all-white college in the eyes of the white college scout. We going to visit that cop on his side whether you like it or not. And you know what? We going for blood." He angrily grabbed his box off the register and turned to leave.

"Justin! Wait!" I ran from behind the register to stop him, but the bell jingled over the store and he was gone.

# Zach

THOUGH I HATED TO SAY IT, THOMAS WAS RIGHT. I couldn't expect anyone else to tell the story about what really happened to Tyree. If Capri or Perry told the media, it wouldn't carry as much weight as it would if someone from Bayside did. I was Dick Whitman's son; he was the lawyer who represented Officer Malore. His daughter was in love with me. No one could help this situation as much as me.

"Time to kiss everything I dreamed of goodbye," I said to myself as I walked up to the Malores' door. "I'll be finishing out my senior year in the Sahara somewhere, far far away from Capri Collins." I knocked.

# Capri

HE WAS LATE, WHICH MADE ME HAPPY. I HOPED HE WASN'T
coming at all. Which made me upset at the same time, because if
he wasn't going through with it, that meant I wouldn't have had
to come to the service to convince him not to go through with it.
I hated homegoings. Truth was, I hadn't been to one since Essie.
Every time there was a service in Hamilton, I would skip it or if I
knew the person, would volunteer in the kitchen and justify it as a
form of paying my respects.

Today, I was all there, meaning in the actual church and not
the kitchen with the women who cooked for the repass. They'd shut
the doors tight to the exit. The church was so crowded that people
were standing in the aisles. Looked like no one respected Reverend
Sails's directions, and he was nowhere to be found. His assistant
pastor preached the service. The entire time I kept my head down.
I tried coming in a little late but was placed by an usher in the fifth
row next to close friends. After I signed only my last name in the
guestbook, someone from the town homegoing home informed the
usher that I was close friends with Tyree and would be helping to
carry the flowers out of the service to the burial yard. They mistook
me for my brother, I guess.

I kept my head down the entire time since his mother insisted
it be open casket. On the left side of the church, across the family
and friends seating, they sat the middle school and younger high

school students, per request of the mayor. He wanted them to know what happened when they were careless with their lives, drank and strayed too close to where they didn't belong, which to me was cruel. The young boys looked straight ahead, stiff as corpses the entire service. But so did their mamas, papas, and siblings. They weren't whooping and hollering like they were on the news and at Sunday's service. They seemed more put together this time. That is until one of the boys from the basketball team presented a movie he put together from his fondest moments with Tyree. I looked up for that. My eyes burned with tears.

It started off with Tyree talking to the camera. He told the camera that he was gonna be a star one day—everyone was gonna know his name, he said. Then he said he was gonna find the cure for cancer. The boys behind the camera shrugged him off and joked with him, telling him he wasn't smart enough for that. But he shook his head and said, "No, man, you just wait and see." This caused his mother to wail out his name. The girl sitting next to me, dressed in all black, tapped her leg quickly and wiped at her eyes.

"Psst!" an usher kept hissing. "Psst!" I turned to the side of me. She shoved a tissue box my way. "Pass this to that poor girl, she crying!"

*I can see that.*

I tried handing the whole box to the girl next to me, but her eyes were glued to the screen. I pulled a tissue out the box and handed it to her.

"Here you go."

She noticed it and grabbed it from me, except she didn't use it. She just balled it in her fist.

"I'm sorry, I'm probably being so obnoxious," she whispered.

"No, I don't mind," I replied. "I know it's hard for this entire town, so I get it."

"Tyree is my boyfriend," she whispered, catching short breaths in between her words. "I can't believe he's gone."

I didn't know what else to do but pat her back, which caused her to rest her head on my shoulder. She slobbered on my white blouse, but I didn't push her away.

"And now for the final viewing," the pastor announced. It started from the front; I almost stood to make a quick escape, but Tyree's girlfriend pulled my arm.

"Can you go up there with me?" she asked. "This is the last time I'm gonna see him. I don't think I can do this alone."

I wanted to say, "No." I *really* wanted to say, "No." But then I remembered how I felt when Essie passed. The reality of it being the last time I was ever going to see her scared me; half of me didn't even want to look at her. I just wanted to remember her as she was when lifeblood rushed in her veins. But the other half of me didn't want to walk away, because that half of me wanted to kiss her goodbye and tell her I'd love her forever.

So before I knew it, I was walking slowly toward the casket. And then, there we were, standing right before him.

And he was smiling.

I can't describe it. It obviously wasn't the openmouthed smile he always gave the world, but it was a different kind. His face didn't look lifeless, his eyes sunken in, or his mouth pulled down into a frown. He looked only as if he were sleeping, enjoying a great dream filled with never-ending sunlight and happiness. And in a way, he was.

"He looks good," she whispered, grazing his cheek gently with the back of her hand. Then she rubbed at the small scar on his forehead where the bullet gave a clean shot, almost covered fully with makeup. "I love you, Ty. I'll never forget you." She leaned down and kissed the scar. Then she breathed out and looked at me. "Are you gonna say anything to Ty?" she asked. "You were good friends, right?"

I shook my head, and against my own will began to cry.

"I didn't know him all that well, but he was so nice."

"So, tell him that," she said with a gentle smile. I couldn't help but laugh a little.

"Thanks for being so nice." And then they came. The tears fell and they wouldn't stop. A few people nearby pulled me into a hug. How could I have been so selfish? Tyree had siblings, parents, grandparents, cousins, friends, and a girlfriend who all cared about him so much and they'd never see him again. His life was taken from him. His dreams were cut short, his voice would never be heard, his kids never born, his life never lived to its fullest. I wondered why I hadn't thought of all that before. I cared so much about living my own dreams, I ignored his. I cried for what felt like hours, and then I was pulled away by familiar arms. And I smelled him. Zach held me close and told me it would be all right. But that was just it, it wouldn't until he did what he came to do.

"I'm happy you're here," I whispered.

"Me too," he replied. He pulled me away from him so he could see my face. He looked deeply in my eyes. "Okay?" he asked, still searching them.

I nodded. "Do what you came here to do."

"Okay, stay right here . . . okay?" I watched him lift his hand to the back of the church. A few people holding news cameras walked down the aisle, which caused the crowd to rustle.

"I said no news!" Tyree's mama yelled. She was distracted enough not to notice Zach climb onto the stage and grab a microphone.

"Excuse me!" His voice rang around the church and it grew quiet; the news cameras continued rolling. "Many of you do not know me, some of you have seen me walking around Hamilton wondering who I was. I'm from Bayside, my name is Zach Whitman."

This caused a few hateful whispers to ring out about Hamilton's history with the famous Whitmans. But what happened next quieted them. "I brought someone with me here who really wants to make things right." He waved someone from the back of the church up the aisle. The man walked slowly, holding his daughter's hand on one side and his wife's on the other. His shoes were polished black, shirt tucked in, pants finely pressed. He held his officer's hat by his side.

In the beginning no one recognized him. His head was down. Before he reached the casket, he swung around to face the crowd.

"My name is Tim Malore." His voice echoed through the sanctuary. Suddenly the crowd rocked like an earthquake. It seemed as though every man in the building tried pushing their way out of the aisles to get a piece of him. The reporters, who brought police with them, created a blockade around him. "Please!" he cried. His voice was strained. "I'm tired of the fighting. I just want to talk." He tried his best to talk over the crowd and their threats. "When Zach Whitman knocked on my door this morning and asked me to come here, I thought he was crazy. But then someone reminded me of the pain I experienced when I lost my own son, who was just about Tyree's age when he died."

"You know how it feels and still murdered Tyree!" someone

screamed through the crowd. Others yelled in agreement, but I couldn't tell where the voices came from. My eyes were glued on the officer and his family. Virgie squeezed her father's hand. He took in a breath before continuing. He kept his voice steady and booming over the crowd's constant murmurs. "My entire family wanted truth about what happened to him, but we never got it. I still lose sleep, wondering what he said in his last moments." Tears fell from his face, though it remained stiff. "I was told to stay silent, to wait for my lawyer and a jury. I grew so worried about sustaining my own life but staying silent has killed me on the inside. It's killing my family." He turned to Tyree's mama. "Please, with your permission, Mrs. Thompson, I'd like to tell the truth right now, in front of all the reporters streaming this live on their respective channels, in front of this town, in front of your family. Because you deserve to know what we never got a chance to."

Though the voices continued to reign around her, demanding she kick him out, he had her full attention. After a beat, she called over an usher who stood next to her pew with a wave. The usher followed the instruction Tyree's mama whispered into her ear and handed a microphone to Officer Malore. His wife and daughter didn't shy away when the usher walked up to them, he didn't grab the mic like it was diseased. He instead looked genuinely grateful for having a chance to explain all he knew. He waited before he spoke, continuing to stare at Tyree's mama. She nodded for him to start.

And just like that, the true story rang out among the church.

"I was driving my car around the railroad tracks closer to midnight on the night Mr. Thompson died, just like I do every shift. It was then that I noticed a tall figure walking along them. It was dark out, but the streetlight illuminated his silhouette. That's when I noticed he was Black. Now as you know, there aren't many Black people in Bayside, so I wanted to see where he came from."

At the word "Black" a thunderous rage struck around the church, louder than before. The rafters quaked under the pressure of those sitting above us who stretched over the balcony hungry to express what has bubbled within Hamilton since its foundation, aching to scream what our ancestors never got a chance to. Together, the congregation shot verbal bullets from their gnashed teeth, directed straight at the Malore family. If the security wasn't guarding them, I was confident that we'd be having four funerals today.

It was hard to make out what anyone was saying; their voices clashed against one another, swirling tension around the room. Still, I could hear Officer Malore's voice loud and clear through the speakers in the church, floating above the vocal eruption bobbing below.

"I wanted to help him get back home," Officer Malore explained over the voices. "He was wobbling. So, I pulled my car up next to him and I cracked my window down a bit, to keep my distance, just in case he was armed. I asked him where he was going and where he came from, but he didn't answer me back. He just kept walking, humming a song to himself. I could see he wasn't wearing earbuds but I repeated myself a few more times, louder, and still got nothing in return. He just kept wobbling around. I asked him if he'd been drinking. It was the first time he'd responded to me."

"What did he say back?" someone asked.

That's when I noticed things started getting a bit quieter, some people in the crowd even started to shush each other.

"He said, 'I ain't been drinking.' Except, I knew that wasn't true. I could smell the alcohol on him," Officer Malore replied. "He'd been drinking a lot, so I grabbed the walkie connected to my car radio. I said that I had an African American man about six feet tall, maybe two hundred pounds or so walking down the tracks of South Bayside at the abandoned station. I announced that my intention was to give him a Breathalyzer test. I kept driving beside him as I said this because I didn't want to lose him. So, I asked him politely if he'd stop walking and sit on the curb, but he kept walking. So, I asked him again, this time with a bit more force. When he turned to look at me, I could tell he was both angry and annoyed. I remember his eyes were bloodshot and wide. His voice came out as a growl. He looked me dead in the eyes and said, 'I said I'm not drunk, Officer.' I'm not going to lie, this scared me. The young man was huge and he was drunk."

"Didn't mean he was a threat!" someone else yelled. A few people murmured in agreement. I even found myself nodding along. We were hanging on every word Officer Malore was saying. I caught a glimpse of Tyree's family. They gripped their snotty tissues in their palms, listening.

"I tried staying calm and asked him if he could stop and take the test so we could both carry on with the rest of our night. He kept walking. So I did the only thing I knew to do. I pulled around in front of him and stopped my car to block him in. When I stepped out of the car and demanded he stop walking, he ran in the direction closer to the center of Bayside. He didn't get far. I chased him on foot to a fence right outside the station that made a dead end. That's what the dashcam didn't get." He paused. The entire church was so silent, the reporters sat on the edge of their seats. We were hearing what the body before us couldn't say. Officer Malore sighed shakily. "He turned around and lifted something in the air. I didn't know what it was. He was so far off that I couldn't see it real clearly. It looked like it may have been a gun."

He paused for a moment. The microphone vibrated in his shaky hand. His wife touched his shoulder to calm him.

"Breathe, Daddy," Virgie, who stood close to her father, whispered. I could barely hear her mousy voice through the speaker.

"I . . . I thought about my daughter and my wife. I thought about dying right there, on duty just like my son. I thought I might have a heart attack. So, I did the only thing I knew to do. I immediately pulled out my gun for self-defense. I'd shoot him before he got to me, before my wife lost me for good and my daughter had no father. I wasn't thinking too clearly. I screamed for him to drop the gun, to put his hands up. He lifted both hands. The gun hung in his hands that were raised above his head. 'Drop the gun!' I commanded. He didn't drop it quick enough. I knew . . . I thought he wanted to kill me. So, I shot, I didn't think, I just shot and he fell to the ground." Officer Malore's expression finally broke and he wept. We could barely hear the words he choked out. "When I ran over to the body . . . Tyree . . . the . . . beer bottle . . . he was holding sat by his feet. He was completely unarmed. The boy was completely innocent, and I killed him." The microphone dropped with a thump on the ground when he fell to his knees. No words, screams, or threats cloaked the choking cries that escaped from his throat. His wife and Virgie wrapped their arms around him, cradling and comforting him. When those from Bayside came to Hamilton, they always stood erect, noses high, shoulders back. Now, there they were bowed low to the ground, huddled in a circle, their backs shaking under the pressure of how a public confession broke their foundation, preparing for what it might collapse next.

Minutes stretched like hours before anyone moved. A creaky pew sang out through the silence, and we all turned our heads to where it came from. Tyree's family was standing. First his papa who grabbed the hand of his mama. Then his three sisters, and finally his little brother. We watched in silence as they all walked up to Tyree's casket and, together, gently closed it.

# Zach

THE CAMERAS STOPPED RECORDING AND EVEN THE reporters were at a loss for words. Officer Malore was led away in handcuffs. Some glared at him, others looked on, confused. Virgie and her mother walked behind him, silent. They were surrounded by the people they judged their entire lives—people who brought no harm to the cop who murdered their son, brother, friend, and neighbor when he appeared before them. They had a lot of contemplating to do.

When I hopped off the stage, Tyree's mother pulled me into a hug.

"Thank you for releasing my son, thank you for bringing him justice."

"Thank you for giving me a chance," I replied.

The family asked if I could join them for the repass after the burial, and I agreed. I figured I might as well eat some good food before being grounded for the rest of my life or sent to Africa forever, stuck eating my mother's horrible vegan concoctions. When the hearse pulled away from the church parking lot followed by a few cars, everyone gathered in the basement to be seated. The smell of the collard greens, yams, and chicken made my mouth water; I couldn't wait to have soul food again.

"I am so proud of you," Capri said again and again, but I wasn't tired of hearing it. I just loved being next to her, hearing her voice.

I wouldn't ever get tired of it. We sat at the table, her hand wrapped in mine. People kept coming up to greet me, meet me, and thank me. I loved seeing their smiling faces; it made me happy and the consequences worth it. Right now, I was happier than I'd been in a long while.

"So how long have you been seeing our grandbaby?" asked a Black woman standing next to a lanky tall man. He wore a fisherman's hat with his black suit. They were frowning.

"I . . ."

"Ma, Pa, this is Zach," Capri introduced. "We met only a short while ago . . ."

"And you should have told us the moment you started seeing each other," her ma replied.

"I know, but I was scared," Capri admitted.

"You know we ain't like that. Maybe some other people in this town like that, but we ain't need no convincing of someone as selfless as this child." Ma stuck out her hand for me to shake, her face softening into a welcoming smile. I shook it.

"It's great meeting you both." Her ma and pop both nodded approvingly before walking off to greet some other people.

"They're nice," I said to Capri with a smile.

She laughed. "Yeah, they're great."

"*Capri! Capri! Capri!*"

"Someone's calling you," I told her.

"I know, it's Perry." Capri looked around for her friend who ran up to the table, next to the boy I rapped against at the record shop the day I took her to New York. They were both sweating all over as if they'd just run a mile. The boy was too breathless to say anything, but Perry managed to speak in between gulps of air.

"Jay, Perry, what's wrong?" Capri asked. But she looked at me, directly at me, tears falling from her face.

"I . . . I'm so sorry . . . I almost . . . we . . . almost . . ."

"You almost what?" I asked.

"We almost burned down their house," Jay spoke hoarsely. "Capri . . . you gotta help us stop them."

And then, just like that, we were all piling in my father's truck that I'd stolen to get here, so that we could quickly get over to the other side of the tracks.

# Capri

WHEN ZACH DROVE US TO THE STREET OFFICER MALORE
lived on, it looked empty, other than the very apparent group of
about seven guys and girls standing in front of his house. They stood
in a huddle; among them I could see Justin and Carlos and what
Justin held. He stood in front of the group facing Officer Malore's
house with a tub of gasoline in his hand.

"No . . . no . . . no. Zach, you stay here," I warned before opening the car door.

He unbuckled his seat belt. "But Capri, I think I can—"

"No," I spat, pointing a finger into his chest. "Zach, you've done
so much already for this town, and we are all so grateful. But this is
my brother; I need to do this part. Okay? Stay here. Please."

I was grateful for everything Zach did back in Hamilton, the
way he gave closure to Tyree's family and the rest of the world. But
it wasn't over yet. I'd stayed silent for so long, selfish for so long and
it was my turn to make things right. I needed to save my brother
before he made the worst mistake of his life. He needed to know he
was above all of this. That if he walked away now, everything would
be all right. I needed Justin back.

Even though it was obvious he didn't want to, Zach leaned back
in his seat and nodded solemnly. "Okay, I'll stay in the car."

I grazed his cheek with the back of my hand; he held on to it
with his. "Okay." I forced a smile. "I'll be a minute." I dropped my
hand. Zach's eyes were misting over with tears.

"Be safe, Capri. We still have to have that talk, okay. The one I hinted at last night at Easy's. I have a lot to tell you."

I nodded before jumping out the car.

"Justin!" I screamed, running up to him. He turned toward me.

"What are you doing here?" Then he looked past me and saw Jay and Perry behind.

"You snitches!" he yelled. Deondre, who'd been standing next to Justin, ran up to Jay and Perry.

"What took you all so long?" he asked.

"You traitor!" Justin yelled at Deondre. But Carlos lifted his hands and literally brought Justin's focus back to the house in front of him.

"Don't worry about them," Carlos directed, pulling a matchbox out his pocket "We came for one thing. We all came to avenge Tyree. They're burying him right now, Justin. Just like that kid from Bayside caused your dreams to be buried. We already covered every lawn on this street with gas." He handed the matchbox to Justin. All we do is light the match, we climb into the van, and we run. Just like we planned."

"No! No, Justin, stop," I yelled. "Think about what you're doing right now."

"I did think about it," he replied. "I thought about it all night, Pri. Where is your alliance anyway? To the town you were born in? Or to the white boy you've just met? Why am I even asking you this? You never cared to begin with, have you? You've always been quiet around here, reserved. You've never gave anyone from this town a chance. Never gave yourself a chance to even be connected to it. This is all I got. This who I am."

"Maybe you're right. Maybe I never gave myself a chance to

love Hamilton, but that doesn't mean I don't love you. It doesn't mean I don't care about what happened to Tyree. What happened to him was a huge injustice, but it doesn't have to end with another one. Maybe I don't understand a lot about this place, maybe I grew to hate the fact that it kept us prisoned in fear. But I understand one thing, Justin. This isn't you." I walked closer to him and grabbed the matchbox. His grip on it was strong.

"Who did you tell I was down here?" he asked, ignoring everything I just said.

"No one, we just came, just us."

"Just y'all?" he asked. I nodded.

"Dude, they took away everything. We're doing this for Tyree, for your scholarship," Carlos said, speaking directly to Justin. "All we gotta do is light. They won't know what hit them. It'll be just like what those Whitmans did to Ajah and her family. We can avenge her family, we can avenge Tyree." The group around them applauded.

"What about your son?" I asked. "Remember him? If you do this, you might not ever see him."

Then Justin looked at me, his eyes bloodshot. His nose was clearly broken, and his face covered in bruises that had grown deeper than what I'd seen just that morning. And there was the button he'd made, still on his shirt.

"This isn't what Tyree would have wanted," I said.

"And how do you know?!" Carlos spat. He was missing a front tooth. "You weren't even friends with Tyree. He was our best friend. He was my boy. He saved me from bullies when I was young, he took me under his wing. He treated me like a brother! How do you know what he would have wanted?"

# Zach

I WATCHED THE EXCHANGE FROM THE CAR WINDOW. I SAW Capri pleading with Justin, but he remained stone-faced. There was no way she was getting through to him. My knee was shaking up and down furiously. It would only take two seconds for them to light the entire neighborhood on fire, to kill everyone inside their homes. I needed to do something. All I had to do was tell them that it was over, that there was no need to do what they'd planned. That the white boy from Bayside that Justin didn't think was good enough for Capri saved the day. That they could go back home and say their final goodbyes to Tyree before he was buried. My fingers tingled when I opened the door to the car and slowly made my way over to where they stood. I could barely hear one of the guys accusing Capri of not understanding who Tyree was to them.

"How do you know what he would have wanted?" he asked, spit flying from his mouth.

I spoke before Capri could.

"Because we just left the homegoing, and I sacrificed my life to convince Officer Malore and his family to tell everything that happened on live television and Tyree's entire family is at peace now." I walked up to them slowly, my arm stretched out. Justin threw Carlos the matchbox, and I thought he'd calmed down. But I was wrong.

"What the . . . ," he yelled. "You brought that murderer to his homegoing? Didn't I tell you to stay away from Hamilton and my sister?"

I held up my hands in surrender. "Look, Justin, it's over! You can still make it to the burial. All of you can if we leave right now."

"See? They have no respect for you!" Carlos yelled.

"I told you to stay inside the car," Capri whispered, tears rolling down her face. I made my way over to her and cupped her face in my hands.

"I know. I know you did, Capri, I just . . . I needed to . . ." Immediately I felt a heavy grip pull on my arm and spin me around.

"You just what? Thought saving the day would get you in her pants faster?" Justin seethed. "I told you to stay away from my sister, you idiot!" And then, he was gone, every drip of sanity that clouded his eyes vanished immediately. "But you white people don't listen! You think you can do whatever the heck you want! You think you can bone our sisters and then leave them pregnant! You think you can take our scholarships!"

"Justin, listen to me," I pleaded. "Tyree was innocent. They know."

"Of course he was innocent!" Justin yelled. "I wouldn't be here if he wasn't!"

I could feel things escalating quickly; I knew in that moment there was nothing any of us could say to deescalate the situation. "Guys, go get somebody! Start knocking on doors and call the cops!" I yelled to Jay, Perry, and Deondre. They started running around the development.

Carlos began to fuel Justin's fire. "I can't believe he thinks he can come down here and get our friends to turn us in to the cops.

Show him, show him what happens when they kill one of ours."

A fire struck my temple when Justin socked me in the face. I fell headfirst onto the asphalt before I could catch my footing. Boulders in the form of fists and boots rained down on me.

"I warned you, Zach," I heard Justin yell. "I warned you that I'd teach you a lesson to stay away from our women." I blocked my head with my hands, but there was no use. Boots rapidly collided with my skull. My eyes searched for Capri. I could barely see her hands clawing to get in the middle of the circle surrounding me.

"Justin, stop! Stop it right now!" she screamed.

Then suddenly, everything happened so fast. I saw some of the girls standing by grab Capri and force her to look at me. She tried to escape, but one held her head up.

"Zach!" she screamed. "Zach, try and get up!"

I inched forward, but another boot stomped down on my ribs. The shattering of bones sent an unimaginable pain through my abdomen. Then I saw it, silver metal reflecting off something tucked within Carlos's waistband. Immediately I turned to Capri.

She stood there frozen, her eyes and mouth wide.

The other guys backed up, leaving only Carlos. He aimed his gun straight at my face.

"The fight is over," I worked hard to whisper, my eyes swollen shut. "Please."

"Fire with fire!" Carlos cried before a spark popped from the barrel of the gun.

I could barely see Capri's blurry figure falling to the ground, but I heard her bloodcurdling scream and tires screeching around me. I struggled to register what just happened. I struggled against the high pitch echoing around my skull and the noise I heard around me. A curtain of crimson red clouded my vision.

Red. All I could see was red.

There was no pain, not at first. Just a lot of noise. Just a lot of red.

I felt her two delicate hands on my forehead, forcing down pressure with her palms.

*Hang on, Zach . . . ambulance . . .*

*. . . police . . . please . . . not like this . . .*

*I can't . . . another . . . no . . . no . . . no . . .*

*Why, God . . . Why me . . . why now? . . . Mama . . . not like . . .*

Her voice faded in and out, as I struggled against the exhaustion taking over my body. From the tips of my toes to the ringing in my head, my body grew hot.

Then for a moment, I could hear her clearly. "Hang on to my voice, Zach." Sirens started to wail around me. I could hear her talking, could feel her pressing even harder on my forehead. I tried opening my mouth to speak, but it was filled with blood. I coughed a few times, but nothing came out. The blood I tried spitting out filled every open place in my body, my eyes, my ears, my mouth. I could feel it pooling underneath my head.

"Hang on," she instructed strictly. "Reach for my voice, okay? Just . . . please . . . reach out."

Suddenly the crimson red curtain over my eyes lifted, and a spotlight took its place. I could see myself lying back on the stage where Capri auditioned, except there was no one in the theatre, just me. Alone, lying under the spotlight, where she lay just days before. I thought about my father, and my mother. I thought about Capri and my desire to love her forever. I thought about Hamilton and Bayside and Philadelphia and New York City. Every memory, every song I performed with Dee, every desire for my future flew above me. I extended my arms as she'd done when she lay down, reaching out for all that flew above me. My fingers only grazed it, it kept slipping away. I lay in my weakness, hungry for life, craving breath working hard to resist death.

"I . . . don't . . . want . . . die . . . but . . . it's . . . s . . . sl . . . i . . . slipp . . ." My words bubbled out of me.

"Please, don't speak, just hang on." I couldn't see her, but I heard Capri's voice echo around the theatre. I could still feel her palms on my eyes.

I watched as I reached out again from the stage, but it all kept slipping out from my grasp. I fought against the death that weighed me down. Then I reached out again, and my finger grazed a memory. Me singing to Capri the night before, about flying. Flying and leaving behind everything that kept her down. I realized that I couldn't be afraid to take the path life extended toward me, even if it was a disappointing path, because eventually life had a way of leading exactly where we needed to be. Maybe going to Bayside, meeting Capri, telling the truth about Tyree was where life needed to take me. Maybe for once, I needed to stop putting things in my own hands. I needed to realize that all of everything that happened is so much bigger than I am. Maybe I needed to stop forcing everything, fighting against life, and just let . . . go.

I stopped reaching. All of the memories above me flew higher and higher until I could see them no more. They flew away with all the anger I held against my father for never seeing things my way, against my mother and Dee for leaving me, and against myself for never believing I was good enough as I was, for never giving myself a chance to be Zach instead of searching for another identity. Then the spotlight covered the stage in glory. All the darkness went away, and a golden light took its place. The burning sensation in my body cooled and with a release of breath, everything stilled, and I finally felt . . . free.

# Capri

I TOOK IN A DEEP BREATH AND HELD IT, EYES CLOSED, remembering the look in my brother's eyes when he sat before me at the defendant's bench, ears attuned to my witness statement. I didn't want to, but I knew I had to. The weight of being the traitor who sung every word she should have kept secret is one that I'll inherit from the town that bore me. Perry, Jay, and Deondre will too, but they are forgiven; they don't share his blood. I do. I remember the way tears of regret stained his cheeks out of eyes no longer blinded by lies and anger. His mind is now clear with a million "I should haves" and thoughts of what could haves that are sure to haunt him from his cell for years to come.

Justin Jacob Collins Jr.

His blood runs through my veins, but we share more than that. We are both slaves to the unknown future that tugs us along without our consent, ignoring our cries for spoilers and secrets. We desire control over what we can't see. Like an unavenged death, a competition we'll never win, or a body we can't bring to life again. But we aren't slaves to the present. We can control that; we have a billion seconds to do so and maybe, if we really thought about our present and how it could possibly change the direction of our futures, we'd make selfless decisions. That's why I testified. I testified because I didn't want to be afraid of speaking. I testified the truth that who my brother was isn't who he is—that he deserved another try at changing his future. I testified to lessen his sentence. I testified to cry out to change and ask her to lend me her ear. When my brother was sentenced and led away in handcuffs, he looked back at me, and I didn't see anger; I saw someone that needed change.

I released the breath I took and I opened my eyes. Dozens of camera flashes clicked around me. Voices wrestled against one another so their questions would be heard, but I wasn't there to answer them. No, I was there to address the present. I tapped on my mic before I spoke, so they'd hear every word that came from my lips.

"We say we want change. That's what I grew up hearing. We want to be looked at for what's on the inside of *us*, but we steady judging everyone else for what they can't help. When we was born, we ain't ask God to be Black or white, or a man or woman; he did what he wanted when he painted us and made us who we are. What would our lives, the world, Hamilton, or Bayside look like if we finally laid down this idea of hate based upon race? You see what it's done from the foundations of our nation until now.

"Zach and Tyree taught us the problem with the world, the problem that grows in each of us. Our discomfort with our neighbor, the people we walk by and judge every day. The Black boy who is painted as a criminal because of the stereotypes we choose to believe and paint on everyone whose skin is darker than ours. Or the white boy who finds comfort in rap culture, in Black history, who dreams different and talks different than what we think he supposed to. *Who do we think we are?* We're not God. We can't choose how someone has to behave. We can't destroy the lives of the people that make us uncomfortable. We can't let our preconceived notions and judgments about other people control the way we treat them, and even see ourselves. None of us are better than the person beside us because of our education level, personality, or the color of our skin. Because the truth is, we all broken. This whole world right now is broken. Look around. We need to pick up these pieces *together* and make it whole again."

They called me after the speech I gave outside Justin's trial went viral, asking for appearances on talk shows, interviews. Even movie directors wanted to share my story—the story of the girl in Hamilton caught in between her brother and her boyfriend, separated by train tracks that lead nowhere but everywhere, that brought change and distrust to a world meant to be far apart from one another, but made them one all the same. But I didn't. I didn't want it to be just another story that went and faded as soon as a celebrity came out with a recipe or another tour—I wanted change. I had to keep my story a mystery so people wouldn't stop feeling sorry about what happened to Tyree and Zach.

He promised me that he'd always be there, that I had to finish what we started, so I finished it. I performed the audition for Camp Sharp with the song he'd written for me and I got in. We got in. I told Easy the truth about Zach, and he opened up auditions for his tour to anyone with talent. Rose had Noah came to visit Justin in prison, so he could see him once. She told him that he'd lost the chance to ever see him again and by the looks of it, with Carlos still MIA, it didn't look like Justin was getting out any time soon.

Hamilton and Bayside tore down the station blocking the two towns and set up a forever memorial for Tyree and Zach inside of the old station. These two towns were meant to stay far from one another, but the beauty of everything that stretches apart is that it always comes back together. People from all over come hear Zach's songs, watch the video they'd shown at Tyree's funeral, and see his memorabilia. He even got inducted into the NFL Hall of Fame as the greatest player with wings. Zach had wings now too; he was able to use them to fly straight to heaven and here I was, now looking up to him.

After ten years passed, the phones stopped ringing. People forget and move on. But I never did. I followed in Mama's footsteps. I'm dancing on Broadway and choreographing theatre shows. I even met someone. He's a gentleman, a director. But there's nothing like my first love. I know it's silly, but sometimes I write to him when I'm alone. I write letters and keep them in a box under my bed. I tell him about everything that's happening for me, every step of the way.

I remind him of his promise to never leave me alone. I ask him how Mama's doing. I have a feeling she's still running around joyful; dancing just like me. I can feel that he's proud of me. I know he's happy where he's at because he doesn't have to worry about fitting in too much. Being too white for the Black people and too Black for the white. He can be free.

Because he's living in a place I grew up hearing Reverend Sails talking about every Sunday. I was never sure if I believed in it, but I started to after I lost Zach. It gives me hope. What's wrong with someone having hope in a place where skin color doesn't matter? Only singing and dancing and doing whatever makes us happy because of The One who gives us light in our world of darkness. The One who painted shades of black, brown, white, and everything in between on the skin that covers all our bones. Who made a palette out of us more beautiful than anything in nature we could ever gaze upon.

Because we are the walking masterpiece. We are the true paint that gives beauty to the canvas of this earth. The confidence we have for the skin we're in, the confidence that bubbles out of us like a waterfall, are the jewels that adorn our ears and necks. That somewhere in heaven seated on a throne made of jewels is someone who died an unjust death, completely innocent. Just like Zach, just like Tyree, just like everyone whose names media buries after a while. And how through His death he justified every person in the world, from death to life. That He's planning on coming back to earth soon, to gather everyone who ever struggled and went through hate because of their race. That everyone who believes in Him will have love, comfort, and justice.

And it will last an eternity.

# Zach

THERE'S THIS PLACE THAT WE CAN GO, YOU KNOW, WHEN we wanna look down to see how everyone's doing. I never go there very often, unless I'm really missing them. The first time I went as soon as I got here was to see how my mom was doing . . . and my father. They're back together, and Dad, he's different. He started this memorial place people can go to listen to the music I made. Thomas still goes to this day too, always tells the people that come how great of a friend I was. Even when the crowds slowed down a few years later, he still sits there, and he listens to the song he pretended to sing for me. He always smiles the whole time he listens.

I do too.

I grow restless sometimes because I can't wait to see her, to hold her, and tell her what I never got a chance to tell her before:

That I love her.

# Acknowledgments
## TK

# AUTHOR BIO:
## TK